To Daddy:

Christmas 1924. —

~~[illegible] Eleanore,~~

~~[illegible] and Jean~~

He was a coward . . . an outcast, an object of contempt. He
had shown the yellow streak!

THE WOLF OF PURPLE CANYON

A ROMANCE OF THE SOUTHWEST

BY
CHARLES KENMORE ULRICH

ILLUSTRATED

GROSSET & DUNLAP
PUBLISHERS   NEW YORK

CONTENTS

ILLUSTRATIONS

THE WOLF OF PURPLE CANYON

CHAPTER I

THE WOLF AWAKES

IT had been a day of enervating heat. Not until the declining sun, an enormous disc of molten copper, was gilding the tops of the scraggly buttes that guarded the western boundaries of the shimmering desert did the town of Purple Canyon begin to display spasmodic signs of life. From several of the three score or more of frame structures that lined both sides of the dusty roadway—which some one with an unappreciated sense of humor had christened "Broadway" —there emerged at intervals nondescript types of men. Many of them were of the desert rat variety. All were evidently seeking recreation and liquor in the only two-story skyscraper the town afforded— Faro Jenn's Red Eye saloon, dance and gambling hall.

Purple Canyon lay, or rather sprawled, like a huge spider on the fringe of the cactus-studded desert which extended eastward some forty miles and as many southward. Here it met an unnamed range of mountains whose snow-covered summits were visible only when some stray gale of wind had sufficiently clarified the super-heated atmosphere of its low hanging clouds of choking dust.

1

The discovery of sundry pockets of gold in Buffalo Wallow, a gully six miles to the northeast, had been responsible for a mad rush and the consequent construction of Purple Canyon, which now, after seven months of vicarious prosperity, had developed into a rendezvous of cheap gamblers, rustlers, gun men, miners, saloon-keepers, women of the slums, and an itinerant back-sliding parson—all the usual riffraff encountered on the outposts of civilization.

Farther westward, along the banks of the Red Sandy, which trailed its muddy length in the beautiful valley between the purple buttes, to be lost at length in the Rio Grande, several ranchers had established themselves. This, despite the lawless efforts of rustlers and occasional Mexican raiders to drive off their cattle that roamed the fruitful valley, and rush them to their secret haunts in the hills across the line.

To protect their interests, the ranchmen had organized an association which with the aid of Bill Thorne, the Sheriff of Big Sandy county, known as "Peach" for short, because of the ruddiness of his huge bulbous nose, had reduced rustling to a minimum. This desired result had not been accomplished, however, without several more or less fatal shooting scrapes, a lynching or two, and consequent threats on the part of the rustlers to have their inning at some not distant day.

Ingress into the valley was by way of a branch line from one of the transcontinental railroads to Butler; thence by a creaky stage that made a leisurely trip each day to Purple Canyon. The stage was now due to arrive within an hour, and the male residents of the town began to cluster about the ramshackle post office which stood next the Red Eye saloon, anxious for a sight of such travelers as were foolish enough to include Purple Canyon in their itinerary.

Although it was still daylight, the deep crimson light that gave the Red Eye its name was already blazing, while from the dance hall within there issued at intervals the murmur of voices, the sound of shuffling feet, and the occasional discordant notes of a violin being tuned up for the evening's entertainment.

Undisturbed by the increasing clamor without, a man lay asleep in a dingy room above Bert Mason's general merchandise store a hundred feet west of the Red Eye. He was about twenty-eight, six feet tall, swarthy, and of robust physique. His sinewy arms and legs indicated that he was an athlete of no insignificant merit. The sleeves of his blue shirt rolled back, revealed forearms of enormous muscular strength. He had doffed neither boots nor trousers on retiring, and an automatic, still resting in its holster attached to his belt, indicated that, asleep or awake, he was prepared for any emergency that might arise.

The room was scantily and poorly furnished. Through the uncurtained open window there streamed the golden rays of the setting sun. The beams, striking the sleeper's face, suddenly affected him, for he moved uneasily, covered his face with his hands, and turned to the wall to resume his fitful slumber.

Near the window was a rough table on which stood a bottle half full of liquor, and two glasses.

The floor was uncarpeted and displayed manifold signs of neglect. On the walls were tacked various photographs and several colored supplements of leading Chicago and New York Sunday newspapers. The photographs showed prize fighters in ring costume, cowpunchers in resplendent regalia, and an actress or two. Oddly consorting with these was Theodore Roosevelt addressing an audience from a platform, one hand resting on a draped American flag, the other raised to emphasize the points of his argument.

On a small shelf near the bed a cheap alarm clock ticked noisily, and beside it lay a pack of cards, the ace of diamonds showing on top. At one end was a cloth bound, well worn volume of Shakespeare, Milton's "Paradise Lost," a pamphlet on the art of ancient Japanese pottery, notably bekkoware, Dumas' "Three Guardsmen," and "Les Misérables," bound in buckram. Several newspapers and a magazine or two were scattered about in a corner. On a chair beside the bed lay a rough coat and a gray sombrero, both much the worse for the wear. A curtain of blue fabric, fastened to the wall at the foot of the bed was partly thrown back, disclosing a man's coat, vest, trousers and shirts which he wore on state occasions.

The clatter of hoofs beneath the window and the shouting of some newly arrived punchers from Big Sandy Valley roused the sleeper. Sitting up, he ran his hands through his tousled black hair and yawned. He glanced about the room like a man who awakes to find himself in a new and unfamiliar environment. He clasped the red handkerchief that encircled his muscular throat, and untying the knot with trembling fingers wiped the perspiration from his face. Jumping from the bed, he staggered to the table, took up the bottle, filled a glass and drank. With steadied nerves he returned to the bed, drew from beneath the pillow a heavy gold watch, and glanced at the dial.

"Five o'clock!" he muttered. "I've slept eleven hours. But believe me, it was some sleep!" He chuckled, then grew suddenly sober. "Wonder how long I can stand the gaff?" he reflected. "What would the governor say if he saw me now? Turn from me in disgust, I suppose. And mother—poor mother!"

His glance turned to a photograph beside the clock on the shelf. He studied it intently for some seconds. It was the face of a beautiful woman in her prime, crowned with dark hair, the features delicately chiseled, the eyes large and luminous, the nose small, the smiling lips slightly parted.

"Mother!" he sighed. "Can I ever hope to win your forgiveness? I may have much to answer for, but, thank God, I have not thus far disgraced you!"

He eyed the photograph longingly. It seemed to him that the sad wistful eyes sought to convey a message, filled with prayerful appeal to him, and that the lips seemed about to speak. He closed his eyes, sighed, kissed the picture and placed it tenderly back upon the shelf.

"I know what you would say to me, mother," he ruminated. "You would tell me that you pray for me every night—that asleep or awake, your thoughts are of me, and that your faith in me will never die. And I swear to you, little mother mine, that your confidence in me is not misplaced."

Then with a sudden change of mood, he crossed the room to the table, took up the bottle, filled a glass to the brim with liquor and held it at arm's length. "After all," he said grimly, "there's nothing like good whisky to drive away the blues—and occasion them, too, by the way. Governor, your recreant son salutes you."

He gulped the fiery liquid, with a dexterous twist of the wrist. Then he tossed the empty glass negligently upon the table whence it rolled to the floor to be shattered into fragments. He laughed, and hummed the refrain of a popular song with cacophonous effect. Vocal exercise, especially when he was drinking, was not his forte.

Picking up his sombrero and coat, he flecked off some of the alkali dust that ingrained their texture, and after adjusting a well filled bandoleer across his chest, donned them both. He examined his revolver expertly, testing the mechanism with a deftness of touch that betokened long comradeship with a weapon that spat sudden death or inflicted grievous wounds as occasion might warrant.

Satisfied with his inspection, he restored it to the holster, opened the door and closed it behind him, and descending the rickety steps that led to a dark area-way between two frame buildings, reached the street.

"Thar comes the stage," said a lounger, pointing towards the post office, where the vehicle was to discharge its passengers, and where a curious crowd had gathered. The young man turned, undecided whether to witness the arrival. His temples throbbed and his head had begun to ache acutely. Unmindful of the salutations of several men who observed him, he returned to the areaway and walked to a stable in the rear. As he approached the door of the rough structure, the shrill whinny of a mustang greeted him.

"Pinto!" he exclaimed, opening the door. "Good old chap! We'll be off for a lope of an hour or so, and maybe the ride will rid me of this headache. After that—we'll see what we'll see."

He saddled the prancing animal, led him out of the stable, vaulted into the seat with the agility of an acrobat, and rode away into the gathering gloom. Within five minutes he had left the feeble lights of Purple Canyon far behind and was cantering along the road that led to Red Sandy Valley.

Unseen by him, some two hundred yards behind, rode a Mexican on a broncho, his hand clutching a revolver.

He had ridden perhaps three miles when Pinto shied suddenly, almost unseating him. Lining the road at this point were several clusters of giant cacti, and among them, despite the gloom, he observed the outlines of several men, one of whom was lighting a cigarette. He caught a momentary glimpse of the man's face, the sinister features of which were clearly revealed in the glare.

"Valdez!" he exclaimed, amazed. "That Mexican bandit and his gang here!"

His brow contracted. What the devil was Valdez doing here, and at night, too? Valdez, indeed! This must be looked into.

Confident that while he might have been heard, he could not possibly have been recognized, he trotted to the right a distance of four rods. Screened by a giant cactus, he leapt from the saddle and permitting the bridle to trail in the sand crept forward several yards, revolver in hand, to reconnoiter. Pinto stood where his rider had left him, calmly nibbling the mesquite grass that grew sparsely here and there.

"*Quien es?*" hailed a Mexican, as a rider galloped out of the darkness a few feet beyond. As the cowboy watched, he realized for the first time that he had been trailed from Purple Canyon.

"Pedro," was the reply. The rider dismounted, his form barely distinguishable in the darkness. The watcher silently crept forward several yards.

"Who was the man who rode by a moment ago?" inquired Valdez of the newcomer.

"The Wolf," was the guttural response.

"*Santisimo!*" growled Valdez angrily. "Why didn't you pot him when you had the chance, *picaro?*"

"He outran me all the way, Valdez," answered Pedro, shrinking from his chief. "I never had a chance, but I'll get him yet!"

The Wolf laughed quietly at the threat. "Small chance! I'll never turn my back to you, *hombre.*"

"He must be bound for Red Sandy," remarked

Valdez, with an oath. "Has he knowledge of our plan? If I thought you would betray me, Pedro, I'd cut your heart out—"

"No fear of that, Valdez," responded Pedro, surlily. "I have sworn to kill the Wolf and I shall keep my oath, unless he should kill me first."

"Which I fear I shall have to do to save my own skin, Pedro," sighed the Wolf lightly.

"Then after him, *esclavo!*" shouted Valdez. "Meet us at the shack at midnight, for we have work to do."

"*Pronto!*" growled Pedro, vaulting into the saddle and applying his quirt. "At midnight I shall be there."

He galloped away to the westward and after a brief conference, of which the white man could catch only a word or two at random, the four Mexicans mounted their horses and cantered after Pedro. The Wolf lay in the sand debating with himself what course he should pursue. That Valdez had crossed the border with his cutthroats appeared to him exceptionally significant, for it portended another raid. That more of the rascally band were in hiding somewhere in the buttes to the westward, prepared to engage in some unlawful enterprise which involved robbery and possibly murder, he did not doubt. Should he warn Sheriff Bill Thorne, who he was aware was in Purple Canyon?

"I think my duty to society demands that I should tip him off," he mused, as he returned to the spot where Pinto was grazing. He whistled softly and with a low whinny Pinto trotted towards him. "I have little love for 'Peach' Thorne, and besides, I'm not on his pay roll. But sometimes a man must do his duty even though it goes against the grain, as in this instance."

He leaped into the saddle and Pinto, sensing the homeward ride, settled down to a steady canter towards Purple Canyon, the lights of which soon became visible far beyond. As he rode, bareheaded, his temples cooled by the deliciously soft evening breeze, the Wolf reflected deeply. He was aware that there was a reward of two thousand dollars for the capture of Valdez, dead or alive, preferably the latter. Somehow, he said to himself, he had little inclination for the job his sense of duty sought to impose upon him against his will.

"I despise this murderous bandit," he thought, "but why should I butt into 'Peach's' game? Hasn't he hinted several times that my record since the raid at Eureka three months ago proved some mysterious connection of mine with this greaser and his crowd? If I tell him that Valdez has crossed the border, he'll think I'm a fool, or a squealer whose word isn't to be trusted. Damn him! Let him find Valdez himself. As for Pedro"—he laughed bitterly— "I am reluctantly convinced that I must go gunning for him as speedily as possible, in sheer self-defense."

He reached the outskirts of Purple Canyon, and as he rode towards the stable where he quartered Pinto during his periodical trips to the town, the strains of the orchestra in the Red Eye, softened by the influence of distance, reached him. The old irresistible craving for stimulant and for external excitement which obsessed him invariably when he was in a state of mental perturbation, seized him suddenly. He led Pinto into the stable, provided him with corn and a bedding of hay, locked the door, then sauntered down "Broadway" towards the notorious dive.

In the modest ten by twelve structure adjoining the post office, Sheriff Thorne sat in his office playing pinochle with Jack Jones, his chief deputy. The door was open, for the night was warm. The Wolf halted and looked in. The Sheriff had just melded a hundred aces when, on lifting his head, he beheld the Wolf standing at the threshold. He grunted a rough salutation and invited him to enter.

"No, thanks, 'Peach,'" responded the Wolf carelessly. "I've got an engagement at the Red Eye."

"Goin' to pluck another bird, Wolf?" asked the Sheriff, chuckling stridently at his conceit. "I heard about your work last night—"

"Rather fine, wasn't it, 'Peach,'" interrupted the Wolf pleasantly. "He was a card sharper from Tucson, but he had bad luck, you know. They all do sometime or other."

"I reckon you were slicker than he wus," replied the official with a significant smirk. "Just a case of a wolf gettin' the best of a coyote, I reckon."

"You always were a devilishly astute philosopher, 'Peach,'" said the Wolf affably. His hatred for the authority personified in the Sheriff was asserting itself, yet he felt inclined to do the official a good turn by telling him that Valdez had crossed the border. He was framing the revelation in his mind when Thorne addressed him coldly.

"Look here, Wolf," he said, "I ain't on to philosophy overmuch, but I'm durned well on to you, and I'm goin' to give you twenty-four hours to get out of Purple Canyon. Savvy, eh?"

"I savvy, *hombre*."

"You've got a bad reputation as gun man in this section, Wolf," went on the Sheriff, "but I didn't know you were a tin horn gambler as well. I'm warnin' you that your room is better than your company in this camp and the sooner you vamoose the better. So I'm givin' you due notice to quit instanter. Get me, son?"

"Surest thing you know, 'Peach,' " the Wolf responded, a scowl of defiance on his swarthy face. "But let me tell you something."

"Spit it out, kid."

Holloway stepped into the office and faced the Sheriff menacingly, a bitter smile on his lips, his hand resting lightly on the butt of his revolver. "It is this," he drawled. "Go to hell!"

The Sheriff recoiled in amazement at this bold and unexpected defiance of law and authority vested in himself. He turned to Jones, who relighted his pipe coolly and glanced wistfully at the drawer of the table at which he sat and in which his gun lay ready for instant use. The Wolf instantly conjectured his design but the knowledge did not ruffle him.

"There's no need for that gun, Jones," he remarked with a chuckle. "There's going to be no gun play on my part. I'm merely calling your bluff, 'Peach.' You know you haven't the slightest legal authority to order me out of Purple Canyon and no man dare face me and say I ever committed a dishonorable act in my life. True, I did kill a man or two, but it was in self-defense, as every one knows."

"I ain't so sure, Wolf," said Thorne doubtingly. "You ain't ever yet told any one your name or where you come from and—"

"That's my business!" interrupted the Wolf. "When I get ready to spring my identity and biography on the residents of Purple Canyon, I'll put you next. For the present, Thorne, I want you to know that I'm thinking of writing the story of my stormy career and that if I decide to do so, I shall do it here in this sun-baked ante-room of Hell, known as Purple Canyon. Good night."

He left the sheriff and his deputy staring in astonishment after him, and passed out into the street.

Walking leisurely towards the Red Eye, he stood for an instant in the ruddy glare of the illumination cast by the lamp above the entrance. Then, inspired by a new idea, he returned to his room, lit his lamp, threw off his hat and coat, tossed them on his rumpled bed, and dropped into a chair at the table.

"He ordered me out of town, damn him!" he muttered, filling a glass to the brim. "I'll go when I'm ready and not before. Here's how, Mr. Sheriff Thorne!"

The Wolf drank, but the draught all but strangled him. He shuddered and threw the glass into a corner angrily. Then he trimmed the lamp, and picking up "Les Misérables," began to read. Between the lines he saw the grim image of Sheriff Thorne, and he tossed the book aside in disgust.

"Fools!" he ejaculated. "They failed to understand you, Jean Valjean, as they misunderstand me. It's the way of the world, I suppose. But nevertheless, it's hard on a well-meaning ne'er-do-well like me."

He grasped the bottle, and was about to drink the remainder of the whiskey it contained, when his eyes fell on the photograph of his mother on the shelf above him. It seemed to be imploring him. Almost he could hear her words of gentle supplication.

A vertigo seized him. He rose, and staggering to the open window dropped to his knees, his arms outstretched across the sill, his eyes searching the glorious depths of the star-studded sky. Venus flamed like a beacon above the western horizon, her heavenly beauty summoning him as though it were his mother's face. Emotions he long since had believed dead within him stirred every fiber of his being. He was as if transfigured.

"Forgive me, mother!" he moaned, clasping his

hands, as though she were indeed before him. "Give me another chance, and I will prove to you that I am still worthy of you!"

His voice broke. Resting his head on his arms, he yielded to the emotion that welled within him, and wept as only a strong man, touched in his holiest emotions, may weep—without humiliation or the consciousness of shame.

CHAPTER II

A CARD GAME AND A PROPOSAL

WITH three score or more persons of both sexes throDng the place, the Red Eye saloon was doing a rushing business. The long bar behind which two bartenders in spotless white were busily engaged in dispensing liquids to the men who argued vociferously with each other over their drinks, occupied one side of the room while in the open space in front of it, roulette, craps, faro and poker were progressing languidly. The gamblers glanced up expectantly at each newcomer, but did not urge them to play. The one rule that obtained was to patronize the bar or vamoose as speedily as possible.

On a raised platform at one corner in the rear of the hall, an orchestra of three pieces, consisting of a piano, violin and cornet, was in violent operation to the strains of which several couples were waltzing erratically. Seven feet from the floor on either side was a narrow gallery made of rough pine boards, reached by a crude stairway. Half a dozen plainly furnished sleeping rooms opened from it. To the left of the stairway there was a door bearing the inscription in large white letters, "OFFICE, KEEP OUT! THIS MEANS YOU!" It was in this room that Faro Jenn transacted her business and where, in a small safe, she kept her books, money, jewelry, and other valuables.

The office itself was handsomely furnished, with several oil paintings of greater or less value hanging to the maroon colored walls. The mysterious history

of Faro Jenn long had been a subject of comment on
the part of the frequenters of the Red Eye. It was
said that she once had been married to "a gent of high
degree" before her arrival at Purple Canyon, and
that when her husband had cruelly beaten her because of her vehement protests against his attentions
to other women, she had obtained a divorce. It was
whispered, also, that she had a daughter in a board-
ing school in St. Louis. But on this important point
there was intangible rumor rather than concrete evidence.

That Jenn was extremely loath to have her private
affairs discussed by her patrons was evidenced one
night when a half intoxicated woman dancer known
as "Cutie" ventured the opinion to "Three-Jacks
Bill," a gambler from up Flagstaff way, that inasmuch as Jenn hadn't displayed her marriage certifi-
cate "so's anybody could see it," there might be some
reasonable doubt as to the credibility of Jenn's testimony as a witness in her own behalf. When this
gossip, in considerably exaggerated form, was called
to Jenn's attention, she girded up her loins and proceeded to do things to "Cutie" with such savage
effectiveness, according to the stories of eyewitnesses,
that the faded beauty "Cutie" had once possessed
vanished utterly, and the poor woman was incontinently thrown out of the Red Eye as a truckman
might toss a sack of meal from a wagon. "Cutie,"
however, recovered within a month and, without de-
manding an apology from her athletic assailant, hied
herself to Tucson.

Jenn was thirty years old, a decided brunette, and,
according to the standards of her class, pretty. She
was of more than average height and weighed fully
two hundred pounds. Her arms, usually bare to the
elbow, were of proportions that a ring fighter might

envy. She invariably appeared flashily dressed and begemmed during business hours, meaning that nocturnal period between dusk and sunrise, during which she reigned supreme in her restricted sphere. Her ample bosom, modestly encased in a V-shaped waist of black silk extravagantly beaded, displayed diamond jewelry valued at several thousand dollars. She wore a bracelet studded wth diamonds on either wrist. Each of the fingers of her hands was resplendent with jewels of varied hues. That she made a handsome show all admitted. But then, as the envious dance hall girls declared, a woman who made such a vulgar display of herself was bound to come to a bitter end sometime or other.

If the herculean bulk known as Jenn could contain within its texture the essence of love for any man, none suspected it until the Wolf appeared on the scene one night. One of Jenn's proudest possessions was a Pomeranian dog, which she guarded with jealous care. It chanced that a drunken cowpuncher from the Texas Panhandle had picked up the animal against Jenn's protestations and sought to pour some whiskey down its throat. The Wolf was just entering the Red Eye when the puncher began his cruel performance in the presence of a conglomerate audience. Sensing the man's design, the Wolf leaped forward and dealt him a blow on the chin that sent him to the floor as if he had been poleaxed.

"You beast!" snarled the Wolf, who was restrained with difficulty from giving his adversary further punishment, "I'll teach you to play scurvy tricks on a dog!"

He fondled the little animal, which tried to show its gratitude by licking his face. As Jenn approached, he placed it in her hands.

"There's your pet, Jenn," he said genially.

"Thank you, Wolf," she said, hugging her pet to her bosom, "I'll never forget this—I'm your friend from now on."

"Thanks."

The Wolf gave a doubting grunt. Then he turned to the bar and sardonically drank the health of the puncher he had felled so unceremoniously. The latter, having been partly revived, was dragged to a room above for repairs.

Jenn, without further words, went into her office, but it was evident that she was extremely agitated. She could not deny to herself the feeling aroused in her by this man, of whose antecedents and real name she was entirely ignorant. Yes, she shyly admitted, he might even aspire to her hand, and she would not refuse him. But when she returned to the hall, drawn by an irresistible desire to encounter him again, the Wolf had gone.

It was several weeks before she saw him again. Then the unexpected happened. Jenn was seated in her office one night, when the Wolf entered. Her face flushed crimson, but ignoring her outstretched hands he tossed a heavy gold watch on her desk. "How much will you advance me on that?" he inquired brusquely.

"A hundred dollars," she replied, after inspecting the timepiece.

"I'll take it, for I want it for a stake."

She opened her safe and taking the money from a well filled drawer, handed it to him smilingly. "Good luck, Wolf," she said encouragingly. "If you need more, let me know."

"I don't think I'll need any more, thank you," he replied and left her.

Five minutes later he was matching wits in a game of poker with Gene Hanson, a professional gambler from the Klondyke, who was known to have fleeced numerous patrons of the Red Eye by his justly questionable manipulation of the cards. The Wolf knew the caliber of the man he was pitted against, and being himself skilled in the art of deceiving one's opponent in a big jackpot, he was resolved to teach this sure thing gambler the costliest lesson of his career.

"Everything goes, eh, Gene?" he asked as he shuffled the cards. A curious crowd gathered about the players instantly, eager to see what might befall.

"Surest thing you know," smiled Gene, placing a thousand dollars in bills on the table. "What's your limit?"

"The sky," replied the Wolf, tossing his bundle upon the cloth in front of him. "There's more where that came from," he added, observing the contempt expressed on Gene's lips at sight of the money, the amount of which he shrewdly guessed.

"Well," he drawled, "I guess you'll have to draw on it soon, if a measly hundred is the size of your pile."

"I'm not so sure."

That the Wolf should have been the apt pupil of one of the keenest card players that had ever stood in shoe leather, was of immense value to him in this contest, for Gene Hanson, he was obliged to admit, was a master at his game.

But luck and a keen vision which detected and foiled his opponent's tricks favored the Wolf, who chuckled audibly as Gene's pile began to melt away. After having three aces beaten by a two card draw to a flush, Gene lost his urbanity and swore beneath his breath. He dug down in his pockets and drew out another roll.

"Five thousand here," he grunted, a baleful light in his deep-sunken eyes.

"A thousand here," replied the Wolf, coolly lighting a cigar.

Fifteen minutes later, the Wolf's pile had grown to three thousand dollars, while Gene could display less than twenty-five hundred. Gene now resolved to make a desperate attempt to reduce the Wolf's winnings to a minimum in the next pot, even though he risked detection in the operation. He had not suspected until now that the Wolf, like himself, was doing sharp work with the pasteboards. He fancied at times that his opponent's movements as he dealt were peculiar, but there was nothing tangible upon which to base his suspicions. Until he had positive proof he was compelled to watch and wait, alert and deadly resentful.

Gene dealt, and he knew that the Wolf was in possession of three kings while he himself held three aces. The case ace was at the bottom of the pack and after he had raised and re-raised the Wolf to the extent of his pile and given the fourth king to the Wolf, he dealt himself the fourth ace adroitly, but not without being seen by the other, who thrust his hand under his shirt as he half rose, and leaned upon the table.

"You're sure you got the right card, Gene?" he asked coldly.

"Whatcha mean?" answered the gambler, placing his hand over his cards. "You ain't insinuating—"

"I mean that you dealt the case ace from the bottom of the deck and that it lies on top of your cards right under your hand," replied the Wolf softly. "I'll prove it to the entire satisfaction of all present."

With a sudden movement, he drew a hunting knife from its holster under his arm, and before Gene could divine his purpose, or the fascinated spectators interfere, he had pinned the gambler's left hand to the table as neatly as a chef might skewer a squab. Gene, pale as death, his face twitching with pain, sought to draw his revolver, but the Wolf's automatic was thrust against his forehead even before his fingers had closed upon the butt.

"Up with that hand!" said the Wolf quietly. "I've heard of you before and I mean to teach you a lesson. If that ace isn't the top card directly under your hand, you win and I'll apologize for my rudeness."

"Damn your apology!" snarled Gene.

The Wolf jerked the knife upward, and as the gambler wincing with pain nursed his released hand, one of the onlookers, Jake Simpson, picked up the bloodstained cards. At that instant, Jenn, attracted by the unusual quiet that prevailed in the place, forced her way through the crowd to the table. She was in a bellicose mood, but when she perceived the Wolf, knife in hand, guarding the money which still lay heaped upon the table until the question of ownership should be decided, her eyes softened.

"What's the matter here?" she asked, nonplussed. She glanced at Gene, who had wrapped a handkerchief about his hand. The sight of the blood alarmed her. "You didn't stab him, did you, Wolf?" she queried anxiously.

"It's nothing, Jenn," replied the Wolf coldly. "I just potted a thief, that's all. Turn the cards over, Jake."

Jake exposed the top card. It was the ace of diamonds!

"You win, Wolf," said Jake. "Gene's convicted hisself of cheatin'."

"Throw him out," exclaimed a puncher angrily.

"Beat him up!"

"Kill him."

"Stop!" shouted the Wolf commandingly. The

crowd shrunk back as he advanced a step towards them. "You should see the whole hand before making up your minds what to do. There are four aces in that hand and the cards were stacked against me. Show all the cards."

In quick succession Jake exposed the ace of hearts, of spades, the jack of diamonds and the ace of clubs. As each card was turned over the anger of the onlookers grew and when the evidence of Gene's guilt was fully disclosed, there was a rush for the cringing wretch which boded him ill.

"Lynch him!" shouted a burly miner, his swarthy face beaming with the lust to kill. "He robbed me of three hundred dollars night before last!"

"And me of a hundred and twenty," exclaimed a young man who was much under the influence of liquor. "I wus goin' to send the money to my mother and would ha' done it but for him!"

"Poor devil!"

The crowd, including the hardened women frequenters of the resort, was growing demonstrative, turbulent and vengeful. Gene, wounded, without a weapon and helpless, palpably grew frightened. The Wolf, glimpsing the terror his mute gaze conveyed, felt a momentary pang of remorse, and as the mob moved forward to visit summary justice upon the wretch, he decided to protect and aid him to escape.

"Stop!" he commanded, one hand clutching his revolver, the other uplifted. "The man has been punished enough—"

"No, no!" roared a miner. "We did things differently on the Klondyke! I'm for a rope and limb—"

"But he shall make restitution in another way," interrupted the Wolf, pointing to the scattered bills and cards upon the table. "There's more than seven thousand dollars here. All who have been robbed by Gene will raise their hands."

A dozen men responded and with characteristic eagerness. What did the Wolf purpose to do? The crowd became instantly silent.

"You lost three hundred, you say?" went on the Wolf, addressing the miner whose insistence upon lynching as a due punishment for Gene had all but provoked tragedy. "Well, here's your money." He picked up three one hundred dollar bills and handed them to the man who, chuckling stupidly, tucked them safely into his bedraggled overalls. "Come along, kid," said the Wolf, handing the drunken youth several bills. "Here is the hundred and twenty which you should have sent to your mother, with an extra hundred added."

"Thanks, Wolf," said the young man. "I'll never forget this."

"Remember, son," chuckled the Wolf, "if you fail to show me a money order made out in favor of your mother before noon to-morrow, I'll sure make dog's meat of you."

In quick succession, the Wolf distributed among Gene's victims sums covering the amounts of their losings, but while he suspected that in several instances the alleged losses were grossly exaggerated, he was sure that a majority of the claims were truthful. Less than two hundred dollars remained on the table when restitution had been made, and observing the stare of wonderment with which Jenn regarded his every move, he picked up the bills and thrust them into her cupped hands.

"There's the money I borrowed from you, Jenn, with interest," he said smilingly. "Now you know what I wanted it for."

"You're either a fool or a prince," she murmured admiringly. "Come and see me before you go. I've something important to say to you."

"All right, Jenn."

She ordered the musicians to play a jazz tune, and in a few minutes the crowd had dispersed, the dancers were resuming their gyrations, the gambling games proceeded with characteristic energy, and the convivially inclined were massed about the bar talking matters over. Gene sprawled in his chair, dazed and apparently helpless. He glanced at the Wolf balefully, nourishing thoughts of revenge upon the man who had not only publicly humiliated him, but what was far more exasperating, deprived him of his stake without which he faced starvation.

"You're safe as far as these people are concerned, Gene," said the Wolf, thrusting his revolver into its holster. "But I advise you to get out of the Purple Canyon, for there's no telling what might happen, now that your system has been exposed."

"I've got you to thank for this," the man replied vindictively. "The boot may be on the other leg some day and it will be my turn to laugh."

"One never can tell," assented the Wolf pleasantly. "But in your case, I'm afraid the boot won't fit. Moreover, don't cackle until you are out of the woods. Good night."

Gene slunk out of the hall, but paused at the door to shake his fist.

"Damn you!" he muttered savagely. "I'll have your life for this some day!"

Within the dance hall, supremely indifferent to the possible results to him of the night's adventure, the Wolf, after drinking again and again with his admiring fellows, walked unsteadily to the office, at the door of which Jenn was awaiting him. The clamor, increased by the shouts of a crowd of punchers from Red Sandy, rendered conversation between them in the open impossible. Seizing the Wolf's arm, Jenn urged him into her office and closed the door, deadening the sounds of revelry to a dull murmur.

"Sit down, Wolf," she said, drawing an easy chair forward into which he dropped tipsily. He wondered what she had to say to him. Her friendship might be well worth cultivating.

"I want to have a talk with you," she remarked, breaking in upon his half drunken reverie. "You did a noble thing to-night, and I want to reward you."

"Reward me?" he echoed in surprise.

"Not in a monetary way," she hastened to add conciliatingly. "What I want is a manager to take charge of things for me here. You know what I mean—"

"Impossible!" he answered. "I'm not designed by nature to manage anything, much less the Red Eye."

"But you are, Wolf! You're just the man for the place. Name your own terms—"

"You're foolish, Jenn! Do you know who and what I am? A wastrel of the frontier, a ne'er-do-well, a man disowned by his family, an adventurer with a reputation as gun man, against whom the hands of all respectable men are raised in horror."

"Leave it to me to capitalize that reputation—"

He sprang to his feet, his manner so threatening that she shrank from him in fear. "I have sunk low enough without that!" he said coldly. "Please return my watch."

Jenn took it from the safe and handed it to him. She was thoroughly aware of his resentment, yet she was determined to reveal to him the sentiment he had awakened in her heart.

"I love you, Wolf," she murmured softly, placing her hands on his shoulders, her face close to his. "I have money for both of us. Marry me and I will share all I have with you."

The Wolf glanced down at her in amazement. "You love me!" he repeated wonderingly. "Why, you haven't known me a month—you don't even know my name."

"I don't want to know it!" she replied passionately. "I know a man when I see one, and you are a man among men! You may be down and out according to report, but when I am your wife, we shall quit this place and I'll help you to win out against yourself and your enemies, whoever they may be. I want you, Wolf, I want you!"

"It is impossible, Jenn!" he said, after a pause. "You deserve a better man than I can ever hope to be. Besides, our roads lead to ends as far apart as the poles. Forget it, Jenn. Good night!"

She sought to restrain him, but he thrust her aside and opening the door walked through the crowd to the bar. Here he drank repeatedly, as if to drown some bitter recollection Jenn's unexpected avowal had revived in his soul.

She herself stood at the door watching him. "His worst enemy is drink," she thought with pity. "If that is once mastered, the rest will be easy. But how, how may that be accomplished?"

It was nearly daylight when the Wolf, "stewed to the gills," as one of the loungers expressed it, was taken from the Red Eye by two men secretly assigned to that duty by Jenn, and put to bed in his room. Under her instructions, for she had an uneasy fear of danger to the man she loved, they guarded his door until Purple Canyon was up and stirring.

Had they known it, sudden death hovered behind

them. Pedro, the rascally Mexican whom we have seen following the Wolf, had been watching his intended victim furtively for hours. The greaser cursed bitterly when he realized that, for the time being, it was impossible to accomplish his purpose.

"*Carramba!*" he muttered as he slouched in the shadow, "I get de Wolf yet, sometime, mebbe!"

Unconscious of all this, the Wolf slept like a log throughout the day which was, perhaps, destined to prove the most memorable of his career.

CHAPTER III

THE YELLOW STREAK

HOW long the Wolf communed with himself as he sprawled across the window of his room, he had little, if any knowledge. But feeling a sudden chill, he rose, lowered the sash, and put on his coat. He took up the bottle standing on the table, but remembering a secret promise, pushed it from him angrily.

"What is this devil that possesses me?" He ripped out a Spanish oath. "Why do I hate liquor and long for it at the same time? Why struggle against the inevitable!"

He paced the room gloomily, shivering, and still craving the stimulant. He wondered what his next move was to be. The Sheriff had given him notice to quit Purple Canyon within twenty-four hours. He knew that official well enough to believe that he would enforce his mandate with all the law's machinery.

"Perhaps it would be best for me to quit this place, after all," he mused. "The Sheriff's against me, and Faro Jenn loves me!" He laughed quietly, remembering the events of the previous night. "I'm not so sure I'm not passing up a good thing by not accepting Jenn. Good Lord! what would the governor say if I should marry the charming Jenn, and he walk in on us some fine day?"

He looked at his watch; it was nine o'clock. From the street below there floated to his ears the manifold sounds of busy life. Washing his face and hands,

27

he left the room and proceeded to the Red Eye, which he had passed two hours ago. He was resolved to make another glorious night of it, and shake the dust of Purple Canyon from his feet forever. Then he would make a final effort to conciliate his father. That failing, he would go to Mexico or any other country where he was unknown and work out the destiny mapped out for him by the gods.

As he approached the post office, he perceived in its shadow a young man and woman engaged in earnest conversation. He recognized the man instantly, but he caught no glimpse of the woman's face.

"Haines!" he muttered, in mingled surprise and resentment. "What's he doing here at this hour?"

The couple entered the post office. He repressed a desire to watch them further, and went on to the Red Eye. The superheated room, packed with its motley crew of bizarre men and women, all but stifled him. His achievement of the night before had been noised abroad, and his arrival was the signal for a cheer in which all joined heartily.

"Bully boy!" shouted several men, grasping him by the arms and dragging him forward. "Have a drink! The place is yours!"

"That'll do, boys," he said, shaking his admirers loose and leaning against the bar. "Set 'em up for the house, and bar nobody!"

The barkeepers worked with alacrity, but it required ten minutes to fill the Wolf's order, for the response to his generous invitation was enthusiastically unanimous. The drinks were nearly ready for consumption and the Wolf was lifting his glass as if he was about to propose a toast, when a man entered. The Wolf flushed, and slowly and deliberately lowered his glass. Sensing interesting developments, the crowd watched and waited.

"Haines!" said the Wolf coolly. "The very man I wanted to meet! How's Ralph Haines, Esquire? You're just in time."

The man addressed halted and facing the Wolf surveyed him with a glance conveying cold contempt. The Wolf returned the stare defiantly.

The onlookers, recognizing that the seeds of tragedy might well lie in this chance meeting, eyed the men with intent interest.

"In time for what?" asked Haines, advancing toward the Wolf.

"A drink with me."

Haines shrugged. Tall as the Wolf, of athletic frame, bronzed and spirited from his life in the open, handsome, sinewy and nimble as a panther, he was a splendid figure of a man. Beneath his coat a bandoleer was visible; at his belt swung an automatic revolver, such as the army men on border duty carry. That he was physically a match for the Wolf in any encounter which the latter might provoke was evident to all who contrasted them as they faced each other, grimly alert.

"I never drink, Wolf, and you know it," responded Haines coldly.

"Have some soda, then?"

"No!"

The Wolf recalled a disagreeable incident of the past which rankled in his memory, a trivial occurrence, but which reflected little glory upon himself. The knowledge rendered him resentful and reckless, and the presence of this man, whose dislike and contempt he felt, roused his fighting blood to action with explosive energy.

"Do you purpose to insult me?" he demanded, a sinister glitter in his deep-sunken dark eyes.

"I have no desire to insult you. I simply decline

to drink with you or any other man. That's my final answer.''

With a motion swift as lightning, the Wolf drew his revolver. But quick as he had been, Haines' automatic was pressed against his body just above the belt. Each had the other covered, and standing face to face, tense and watchful, each awaited that almost imperceptible flicker of an eyelash which would signal the opening of hostilities.

Sensing the shedding of blood, the women who had forced their way through the crowd to the front, now began to edge back again, their fingers in their ears, their painted faces convulsed with fear. The gamblers and miners, avidly eager to witness every detail of the drama that was unfolding before them, surveyed the two men with breathless eagerness, in a silence that was broken only by the ticking of the big clock above the bar.

''I repeat, Wolf,'' said Haines coolly. ''I refuse to drink with you.''

The Wolf gulped painfully. He sought to make a reply, but only a meaningless gurgle of sound escaped his white lips. The hand which held the revolver against Haines' diaphragm trembled slightly, but none save Haines, perhaps, observed this manifestation of the sickening weakness that held his trigger finger in leash.

''Your gun doesn't frighten me, Wolf. Why don't you shoot? If you have the nerve they say you have, shoot!''

Pale as ashes, the Wolf ventured no reply. His eyes wandered for an instant and rested upon Jenn, who stood on the edge of the mob palpably terrified, her arms extended to him in supplication. He failed to recognize her; the lineaments of her face were lost in those of another—a far dearer countenance—that of his mother, who seemed to hover about him as a guardian angel in times of peril.

His hesitation was momentary. But before he could recover himself, Haines had thrust his revolver back into its holster, a smile of contempt on his lips.

"You're a brave man only when you have the drop, Wolf," said he witheringly. "When you sober up and express a desire to apologize, I'll be glad to talk to you. Good night!"

Turning suddenly, Haines vanished through the doorway. The Wolf stood like a man in a dream, staring vacantly after him, his revolver pointing downward. At length, with a long sigh he thrust the weapon into the holster, wiped the sweat from his forehead with a gesture indicative of painful weariness, and swayed as if he were about to fall.

The crowd slowly dispersed to discuss the incident in suppressed whispers. The Wolf was a quitter; the greatly feared man-killer had shown the yellow streak!

Meantime, the man they discussed had pulled himself together. Turning, he took up his glass, tossed the liquor it contained down his throat, and still with his air of galling defeat, pushed it silently across the bar for another drink. When the bartender, in whose eyes the Wolf's stock had greatly depreciated within the last few minutes, hesitated to comply, the Wolf hurled the empty glass at his head with an oath. He missed the man, but smashed a pile of other glasses stacked up in a pyramid in front of the mirror.

Jenn, who had been watching, approached to plead with him, but he thrust her aside roughly. When the bartender at length placed a bottle of whiskey before him, he grasped it and all but drained its contents. He would have swallowed every drop had not Jenn, who clung to his arm, begged him to desist.

"You will kill yourself, Wolf!" she pleaded. "Pull yourself together and be a man!"

He stared at her stupidly for a moment, then nodded assent. "You're right, Jenn. I will be a man! Give me a pencil and paper, somebody, *pronto!*"

The bartender provided these requisites and the Wolf began to write a message in letters an inch high. His task finished, he removed a pin from the lapel of his coat and fastened the paper to the top of the bar. Standing a few feet away he surveyed the notice approvingly.

"Let Haines put that in his pipe and smoke it," he muttered. "My hat's in the ring for fair this time. Whoopee!"

He lurched out into the street, just as the band began to tune up. The crowd, eager to see what he had written, moved forward. Before Jenn could intervene, a burly gambler had possessed himself of the document and read it aloud above the racket:

"TO WHOM IT MAY CONCERN: GREETING—

I hereby give notice that I will kill Ralph Haines on sight. So let him beware.

JIM HOLLOWAY.
(The Wolf)."

The notice was greeted with roars of derisive laughter by the very men who, an hour ago, would have treated the Wolf with the greatest consideration. Even the beneficiaries of his munificence the night before joined in the boos and catcalls that greeted the reading of the death threat.

"It's a bluff!" shouted a gambler whom the Wolf had beaten almost to a pulp a week previously for cheating a drunken cowboy out of his month's wages. "*He* ain't got no nerve! Didn't he have his chance just now to perforate his man and pass it up!"

Jenn slapped the speaker's face with a force that sent him reeling.

"Mind your own business!" she shouted. "Get out of here and if you ever come in again, I'll have you horsewhipped!"

The man slunk away crestfallen, and Jenn returned to her office. "Jim Holloway!" she repeated. "J. H." were the initials on his watch. It was a clue. She was determined to follow it and win the man she loved.

Meanwhile, the thrilling incident of the evening was being discussed quietly at the poker tables. Jack Smith, a veteran gambler, had the floor.

"I'm wondering if the Wolf is the same Jim Holloway I met in Californy two years ago," he said musingly. "They're alike as two peas."

"Tell us about it."

"Wall," drawled the gambler reminiscently, "this Jim Holloway dropped into the Pink Tea saloon at Stony Ridge, with about as much booze in his cylinder as any man can carry and keep his feet. Thar wus a Digger Injun in thar with a mongrel pup and he wus kickin' him good and plenty when Jim jumps him and throws him across the joint as easy as you would toss a blue chip across the table. Thar wus a all-fired row about it and the Injun left swearin' he would hev Jim's scalp if it took all summer."

"This here Jim would fight all creation fur a dog—"

"A few days arter this," resumed Smith, ignoring the speaker, "the Injun wus found dead in a gully and Jim wus picked up unconscious in a shack nearby. He had a bullet in his lung, and he 'fessed that he had killed the Injun arter he had been shot fust. The jury found he had acted in self-defense, but there wus some talk, and Jim soon arter disappeared, for the

which the Sheriff and other town officials breathed
consid'able easier.''

"What grudge has he agin Haines?'' asked a by-
stander curiously.

"Accordin' to report,'' replied the gambler, as he
dealt the cards, "Haines wouldn't give the Wolf a
job on his ranch last spring. The Wolf was drunk
as a b'iled owl and Haines had him throwed off the
place. That's about all we hev heerd of the matter.''

"That don't justify the notice he has wrote stat-
ing his intention to kill Haines on sight,'' suggested
one of the players.

"It's pure booze, that's what it is! He ain't no
more responsible for what he wrote than a baby.
When he gits over his spree, it's dollars to doughnuts he won't remember the threat at all.''

"But if Haines gets word of the notice, he'll be justified in blowing the Wolf's head off instanter.''

The gambler shrugged.

"Haines has too much sense to pay any attention
to the doings of a drink-crazed man. It's your ante,
Bill.''

The man addressed anted, and the discussion
ceased. In the excitement of the play that ensued,
the circumstance that had wrecked the Wolf's reputation beyond recall was soon forgotten.

Along the fringe of the great southwestern desert,
with its reports of Mexican revolutions, embargoes
on the shipment of arms across the border, Mexican
raids and American patrols, mere gun plays without
specific action ending in sudden deaths and speedy
funerals excite only passing attention, and the memory of them is as ephemeral as a passing fog on the
Labrador coast.

CHAPTER IV

THE ENCOUNTER

WHEN the Wolf, or rather, Jim Holloway, as he had signed himself, reached the street, the cool night air refreshed him instantly. He paused, hat in hand, and leaned against a post of the awning in front of the post office, dazed and breathing heavily. He felt ill. But the nausea that suddenly seized him was nothing in comparison with the sense of humiliation that filled him when he realized that he had not lived up to his reputation in his encounter with Haines. He detested himself for the pitiful spectacle he had presented. He was forced to confess the bitter truth—

He was yellow!

He asked himself over and over again with monotonous iteration, why he had not resented Haines' contemptuous gibe by pulling trigger, even though he knew that by doing so he would have signed his own death warrant? Death was infinitely preferable to the fate that was his now that he had publicly displayed cowardice. Within twenty-four hours his shame would be heralded in every haunt where he was known. He would be the butt of ridicule, a creature so low that even the desert curs would disdain to sniff at his shoes.

"It was the drink," he told himself, anxious to find a plausible excuse for his weakness. "That's what made me lose my nerve. Guess it's time I reformed."

35

There was something pathetically humorous to him in the idea of his reformation, and he chuckled tipsily. Although the breeze that swept from the western buttes was cool, his forehead was bathed in sweat. He removed the bandana from his throat and wiped his face wearily. He knew he was drunk; on that point his perception was clear. Yet, queerly enough, he had for the time quite forgotten the latest abnormality he had manifested—his unprovoked and idiotic declaration to kill Haines at sight!

A bit of newspaper, eddying before him in a sudden gust of wind, recalled his fading memory of the event with the suddenness of a dagger thrust. He groaned, swore, then upbraided himself for his stupidity, as he considered the pros and cons of his foolish act and its possible consequences to him.

He vainly sought to fathom the depths of the impulse that had prompted him to write the threat. His hatred for Haines, if it might be so called, was not sufficiently vindictive to justify his conduct. He had no reason to hate Haines. Was his dislike due to the fact that Haines had refused some months previously to employ him as a range rider because he was drunk? He could not conceive why he had resorted to such an extremity in revenge for a slight put upon him by a hasty-tempered man in a moment of anger. Was it because Haines had refused to drink with him? No, he had yielded to an ungovernable impulse while under the influence of liquor, and inasmuch as he hadn't the slightest intention of killing Haines, he had been guilty of a folly that was likely to cost him dear.

He yearned for solitude so that he might determine upon some plan of action in the premises. He staggered along the board sidewalk with bowed head, ashamed to be seen and recognized. He, the Wolf, a title he had instinctively detested, but which by reason of his record had clung to him until he rather relished the distinction it conveyed, was a coward, despised by all, an outcast, an object of contempt to all who knew him!

He had shown the yellow streak!

The truth amazed as much as it startled him. For the first time in his turbulent career he had weakened in the presence of a stronger and more courageous man. He had not thought this possible, and yet it was true. He groaned in bitterness of spirit at the thought that from some roystering ancestor he had inherited not only an almost irresistible craving for alcohol, but a tinge of yellow which had asserted its supremacy over him in the most crucial hour of his life. He realized that his soul was undergoing a transformation, not understood even by himself, and he wondered what had set the machinery in motion, only to overwhelm and plunge him in a pit of misery and humiliation from which nothing, so far as he could see, would ever rescue him.

Although he had never sought to win the reputation as a fighter that was his, he had, none the less, when drunk, cherished with pride the fame that had so come to him. He had concealed his real name, and when one day, in a spirit of bravado, he had termed himself, "the Wolf," the title clung. All along the border, wherever he was known, he was universally regarded as a man among men, whose grit and iron nerve would sustain him in whatever emergency might arise.

But now, as he was forced to admit to himself with increasing shame and rage, an intangible something which he could not comprehend had blasted his reputation beyond hope of repair. Swayed by a momentary impulse of fear, his trigger finger had been paralyzed. In the presence of a bravery superior to that which he had vaingloriously arrogated to himself, he had failed wofully. Haines, cool and grimly serene, smiling in the face of almost certain death, had defied him to shoot.

And he had not accepted the challenge!

What had caused his unaccountable indecision? Was it terror born of the knowledge that to kill Haines meant his own death, swift and sure? He groped blindly, seeking to solve the problem of a psychological phenomenon unknown to his experience. But the solution, to his clouded perception, was as remote as the stars that scintillated dazzlingly over his head.

He was debating whether to flee to Mexico and hide his shame in some locality where he was unknown, or to meet unflinchingly the humiliation and scorn he knew would be his lot as long as he remained in the vicinity of Purple Canyon, when a young woman, advancing towards him, riveted his attention. He paused within the shadow of the post office awning, removed his hat, drew himself erect, and respectfully stepped to one side to give her the road.

She approached without seeming to see him. He fancied he had seen her before; then he recognized her as the woman he had observed in conversation with Haines at the post office just before he had marched to his Waterloo in the Red Eye. Who was she? What was she to Haines? She was tall and finely proportioned, and wore with an air of distinction a light colored riding suit of knee length and a soft, wide-brimmed white hat that lent a charming piquancy to the poise of her head. Under the crimson glare of the Red Eye, Holloway perceived that she was young—twenty perhaps, and beautiful. And that subtle magnetism with which woman through the ages has been endowed thrilled him with the irresistible call of mate to mate.

Owing to the fresh air with which he had filled his lungs, and, perhaps, to the stimulus to observation and thought occasioned by the appearance of the girl —for he and women of refinement had had little in common during the tempestuous days he had spent in the Southwest, Holloway was by now almost entirely free from the effects of the liquor he had swallowed. Yet, as happened so often with the Wolf, he yielded to an impulse which in saner moments he would be the first to condemn, and followed the girl, without apparently realizing that in doing so he was guilty of an intolerable act which she with propriety would resent.

She was approaching the door of the Red Eye when a crowd of men thronged through the passage into the street, halting her progress. One of their number tacked a piece of paper to the building at a height which rendered its perusal by passersby an easy matter. The crowd greeted the operation with bursts of derisive laughter.

"That's some defi," said the leader of the mob. "It's the Wolf's ultimatum. I'd like to see Haines when he reads it in the morning."

"He'll go gunning for wolves, most likely," shouted another of the crew amid laughter.

"But the Wolf hain't here no more, I reckon." The speaker was one of those to whom Holloway had restored a tidy sum taken from his winnings from Gene the evening previously. "Havin' no sand, 'tain't likely he'll execoot his threat to kill."

Holloway halted, his face ashen. He began to see red and his hand clutched his revolver with deadly purpose. But his momentary desire to kill died away almost as quickly as it was born, and he gritted his teeth in silence although his wrath all but choked him. He had eyes only for the girl who had stepped forward to read the placard. Neither she nor the men who surrounded her observed him as he crept towards them.

"What does this mean?" she inquired, after she had read the scrawl. "Who is the man who threatens to kill Mr. Haines at sight?" Her voice was a rich contralto.

The man she addressed, conscious that he had a lady to deal with, politely doffed his hat.

"It's the Wolf, Miss," he said deferentially.

"Why does he want to kill Mr. Haines?"

"They had a quarrel in the Red Eye, Miss. You see, the Wolf, it seems like, has a grudge agin him fur somethin' or other, and when Haines came into the Red Eye a while ago, the Wolf up and asks him to drink with him. Wall, Haines refused to drink, whereupon the Wolf out with his gun to fo'ce him instanter. But Haines, bein' as how he ain't no slouch himself with a gat, had his gun out as quick as the Wolf and thar they stood, each with sudden death in his mit pressed agin the other's bread basket, an' each lookin' fur a sign to open fire."

"And then," she asked breathlessly, "what happened then?"

"The Wolf's nerve left him. Seein' which, Haines laughed, put up his gun, turned his back on him and left the saloon. Then the Wolf proceeded to load up with gin and writ that thar." He pointed to the placard.

"D'ye know Haines, Miss?" asked one of the men.

"Know him! He is my brother!"

"Holy cats!" exclaimed the speaker. "Then you are Marian Haines from Red Sandy?"

"Yes."

Holloway heard like a man in a nightmare. This

beautiful girl the sister of Ralph Haines, the man whom he had threatened to kill at sight! He could feel her scorn, her hatred, when once she would learn the truth. He longed to get away, from her presence, but his laggard limbs seemed incapable of motion, and he was perforce compelled to remain and learn what judgment would fall upon his guilty head.

"I cannot comprehend this at all," said Marian quietly. "You say my brother threatened the Wolf with his revolver?"

"He sure did, Miss."

"And after my brother left the Red Eye, the Wolf wrote that notice?"

"Yessum."

"But even though what you say about my brother drawing his gun on the Wolf were true, it would not justify deliberate murder." She stood awhile, in deep thought. "I think perhaps I can persuade the Wolf to revoke his threat," she said at length. "Do any of you know where he is to be found. Can one of you gentlemen take me to him?"

Halloway gasped. How could he possibly face the girl? He turned to seek refuge in flight, when a burly man grasped his arm.

"You've got to face the music, Wolf," he whispered. "You can't get away, see?" Turning to Marian, he pointed to Holloway, standing beside him rigid as a statue. "Here is the Wolf, Miss Haines," he said. "Talk to him and we'll back you up to the limit! Don't be afraid."

Marian approached Holloway, who stood, torn between his desire to retreat in shame and the compelling fascination of her beauty. In the crimson light that flamed above their heads, it was difficult for her to discern the emotions which struggled behind his dark frown. When an arm's length away, she paused and regarded him with a glance eloquent of mingled entreaty and reproach.

"You are the Wolf?" she asked.

Her voice, strong yet tender of tone, and sweet as music, electrified him. But he dared not venture a reply, and his only response to her query was a slight inclination of his head.

"You wrote that notice?" She pointed to the placard pinned beside the door. His eyes fell, and had he desired to admit the truth he could not have done so. His parched tongue refused its office.

"Please tell these men and me that this is only a jest, a horrible jest," she went on earnestly. "Tell them that you—that you were not yourself; that you fancied you had some grievance against my brother; that you did not realize what you were doing. Won't you, please?"

She paused, but receiving no reply, resumed with increasing agitation: "Surely my brother, who is the best man in the world, has not done you any harm. If he has, please let me speak in his behalf and I will see that justice is done. Please answer me!"

A lump rose in Holloway's throat choking utterance, if indeed he meditated a reply. Marian wondered why he persisted in maintaining silence, and the fear suddenly chilled her that perhaps this man, hardened by crime and filled with the desire for sanguinary vengeance, had steeled his heart against her pleas. Tears welled up in her eyes and trickled slowly down her colorless cheeks. Her grief distressed Holloway beyond measure. He yearned to take her to his heart like a frightened child and assure her that her fears were groundless—that to spare her a single sigh he would willingly sacrifice his own worthless life.

Marian made one last effort. Choking back her

sobs, she stood with hands clasped, gazing bravely at the silent man. "You have a sister, perhaps—a mother? I beg of you in their names! If you kill my brother you leave me alone—unprotected. And you yourself—what of you? A fugitive with the brand of Cain on your brow! Think what that means —hunted, a price on your head, living always in terror and in the shadow of death!"

Her passionate plea thrilled Holloway as it did the hardened men who listened to her in mute sympathy. He longed to dispel her fears on her brother's account by making the avowal that his safety was assured. But under the sway of her emotion as he was, he could only give utterance to inarticulate sounds, the meaning of which she could not divine. His noncompliance with her request seemed to her to be the manifestation of vicious obstinacy, and relinquishing her task as hopeless, she hid her face in her gloved hands and sobbed aloud.

With an effort, Holloway pulled himself together. For no reason of which he was conscious he drew his automatic from its holster. The crowd, seeing the action, fell back in confusion. Lifting her head, Marian saw the weapon in his hand, and instantly she seized it.

"What are you going to do?" She took the revolver from his unresisting grasp.

"Blow out my brains!"

"No!"

"I deserve to die," he responded in a voice so low that she alone could hear it. "In no other way can I atone for the sorrow I have caused you." He turned from her with a gesture of despair.

Her face fell. She tried to answer him, but speech failed her. Her fingers grew limp and the revolver dropped at his feet. Then, turning, she walked quickly through the crowd and disappeared beyond the arc of illumination shed by the Red Eye.

Holloway watched her until she was out of his sight. Then, shoving his way through the group, that fell back silently, he strode to the door, removed the fatal notice, and tore it to atoms.

"The end of the Wolf," he said, with a grim smile. "Now it's to be James Holloway—and decency!"

He walked along the now nearly deserted street to his room, and lighting his lamp, surveyed his surroundings moodily. Conscious of a weight in his coat pocket, he thrust in his hand and brought forth a pint flask of whiskey. He gazed at it with moody interest, while there crept over him the old insatiable desire to drink and forget. . . . "Another little drink will do me no harm." . . . The old college song went ringing through his head. He removed the cork and sniffed the liquor. He yearned to drink, yet resisted; he filled his glass and held it before the light —raised it to his lips—

The tear-stained face of Marian Haines came suddenly before his vision. He set down the glass, and leaning across the table, his face in his arms, groaned.

"Help me, God!" he prayed fervently. "Help me . . . for mother's sake—and hers!"

An hour passed. He lay silent and motionless; perhaps he slept. When at length he raised his head, and his eyes fell on the flask, they betrayed no interest in the devil that had so nearly mastered him. Quietly he rose, picked up the bottle, and emptied its contents through the open window. This done, he returned to the table and sat, almost as in a trance, till the pale radiance of the coming dawn stole into the room. Then, with a strange light in his hollow eyes, a smile as of some secret joy and lightness in his heart, he undressed and went quietly to bed.

For the first time since his innocent boyhood days, ineffable peace possessed him. But it was no longer the peace of innocence, but that which is granted to the victor in that hardest of all contests, the battle with self. In the happy dreams that visited him, the face of Marian Haines, no longer angry and tear-stained, seemed to smile upon him with roseate promise.

CHAPTER V

THE "Circle N" ranch, owned and operated jointly by Ralph Haines and his sister Marian, was one of the finest of which the valley of Red Sandy could boast. It comprised some ten thousand acres of excellent grazing land, bounded by the purple buttes to the east and west, between which flowed the stream of the Red Sandy at a depth varying from six inches to as many feet. The cattle bearing the Haines' brand numbered two thousand and there were in addition six hundred head of horses and three score or more of mules.

In every sense of the word, the "Circle N" was a model ranch. Haines was no more proud of it than was his charming sister, who was the idol of the eight punchers who rode the range daily under the supervision of Sam Belcher, the foreman. Sam was born on the Rio Grande and what he did not know about ranches, cattle, Mexican raiders and collateral matters wasn't worth talking about. He knew the average cowpuncher as well as his favorite pony knew his oats. He was brave, honest and faithful and his heart was filled with unrelenting hatred for all Mexicans. This was primarily due to the fact that his parents had been killed by greaser bandits and his only sister, whom he cherished, carried captive to their secret haunts in Chihuahua where, after being subjected to atrocious treatment, she succeeded in committing suicide, thereby escaping mental and physical

46

tortures transcending any horror that Dante had conceived as typical of the Inferno.

Ralph Haines had settled in Red Sandy years previously, and to his hard work and unceasing vigilance, the success of the venture was due. He and his sister had inherited the property from their father, a once wealthy stock broker of New York, who had been ruined by the collapse of his scheme to corner Amalgamated Copper. His failure broke Mrs. Haines' heart, and after her death, Marian, her only daughter, who had graduated with honors from Vassar a few months previously, assisted her brother in caring for their father. He languished for a few months and, unable to survive his wife's death, a catastrophe that shocked him far more than the loss of his wealth, he died and was laid to rest beside his wife and ancestors in Greenwood Cemetery.

When the estate was settled, all that was left to the children was a meager thousand or two in currency, some jewelry of like value, several commercial claims of doubtful value, and the ranch near the Rio Grande, which, casual investigation proved, was of such insignificant value as to convince the dead man's creditors that it wasn't worth while to pay any attention to it. So Ralph, bidding farewell to his Yale alumni, and having little more to aid him than a strong vigorous frame, excellent health, two stout hands and the will to dare anything in the struggle for honest existence, hied himself to Red Sandy, leaving Marian with friends pending the completion of his pioneering work on the ranch.

A few months of luxurious idleness at the palatial home of her Vassar chum, Evelyn Roberts, in Riverside Drive, convinced Marian that the hardest task any young woman, or man, for that matter, can undertake, is to live a life of unproductive idleness. Naturally industrous as well as studious, she detested in-activity, and great social functions inspired her with horror. Her beauty and accomplishments had in the old days invited the assiduous attentions of numer-ous young men of excellent families, including a Knickerbocker chap whose ancestors had settled in Manhattan during the Dutch occupation when old Peter Stuyvesant arrogantly stumped along Bowling Green, but when her father's failure was announced, she found herself virtually alone—a sweet rose in an arid desert, the delight of her feminine friends, but ignored by calculating impecunious young spend-thrifts with a keen eye to the business end of a matri-monial alliance.

With each letter from Ralph informing her of his struggles against odds to stock the ranch and place it on a paying basis, her curiosity to see the great South-west grew and her desire to share his toil with him in-creased proportionately. He told her of the troubles he had to contend with in building his "shack," as he termed it, and of the almost insuperable difficul-ties he encountered at the hands of rustlers who ran off his young stock, openly defying the authorities who vainly endeavored to capture or kill them. He described in glowing terms the beauties of Red Sandy, and when the ranch and bunk houses finally were finished and appointed, he hinted that the only bar to his complete happiness was her absence from the little border palace he had builded with such pains-taking care.

"Poor Ralph!" she exclaimed tearfully, when she read this paragraph. "I am coming straight out. I'm ashamed that I should have put it off all these months."

She apprised only Evelyn of her purpose to leave for the Southwest and when the day came sighed contentedly at the discovery that none save Evelyn took the trouble to accompany her to the station. So she made the long and tedious railroad journey alone and in due season reached Butler, where the first to greet her at the station was Ralph. She sobbed happily when she felt his protecting arms about her. What a manly chap he was! Six feet of the finest specimen of strong vigorous manhood she had ever seen!

"Dear boy!" she said, holding him at arm's length admiringly. "How you have grown! A veritable giant of a man!"

"Nonsense, sis," he laughed, leading her to his buggy to which a finely matched team of roans was hitched. "I've been here only a few months, you know. Not much chance to change my physical self in that time, of course!"

"But you have changed wonderfully, Ralph," she persisted as they raced along the dusty road with her baggage strapped on behind. "You are no longer the sallow complexioned boy who left me in New York. My, what a complexion you have! Brown as a berry!" She laughed merrily and he pouted in mock irritation.

"It's the simple life in the glorious open, sis," he responded. "You haven't any conception of the charm and beauty of this wonderful country—the delicious morning air—the wonderful sunsets—"

"And the dust," she interrupted, coughing when a gust of wind blew a cloud of alkaline powder into their faces.

"It's the most healthful dust in the universe!" he returned enthusiastically. "It provides a lining for your lung cells which laughs at microbes. It's a darned sight better than Broadway on a windy day, and there's no Flatiron Building to send your hat whirling skyhigh. But it's not all like this."

"I should hope not!" They were enveloped by another cloud of dust so dense that the heads of the horses were almost invisible. "In comparison with this, I'll take my chances with Broadway any day."

After an hour's drive, which seemed unusually short to Marian despite the dryness of the arid wastes through which they traveled, they reached the southern outskirts of the ranch. The Red Sandy valley opened at this point, and the rough road over which they were speeding was lined with rich green fields in which scattered live stock were browsing. Now and then there could be seen, riding along the lower edges of the giant buttes which rose to right and left, cowboys rounding up the cattle.

"We've got a fine bunch of punchers," Ralph remarked. "They're thoroughbreds every one, and absolutely loyal to me—even if it meant to the death. Only the other day—whoa!"

The horses had shied abruptly, almost overturning the vehicle. The cause of the trouble was seen when from behind a mesquite bush a Mexican stealthily arose. He regarded them menacingly, his ugly features boldly expressing surliness and dislike.

"Pedro!" cried Haines angrily. "What the devil do you mean by frightening my horses? You nearly upset me."

"*Carramba!*" rejoined the greaser with a savage leer. "You bad driver if horses upset you so mooch easy. *Jesu!* How I know dey get skeered when I come?"

Haines' face darkened at the man's insolence. "Get off my ranch, or I'll put you off! I won't have you prowling around here. Understand?"

The man scowled, his hand upon his knife. Haines brought the horses to a halt and tossing the reins to

Marian started to descend, threatening a thrashing. But his sister restrained him.

"No, Ralph," she commanded. "He might kill you."

"No fear of that," he answered. Then turning to Pedro: "You make yourself scarce and stay so, or I'll know the reason why."

Pedro yielded them the road with muttered Spanish imprecations, and as they passed him, he removed his sombrero and bowed mockingly. His ratty eyes devoured Marian, and she drew back, conscious of danger, vague and undefinable. Haines growled impatiently at the impertinence, but the man was soon lost to view in a turn of the road.

"What an evil face!" said Marian, presently. "How did you come to know such a creature?"

"He came to the ranch one day six months ago and demanded employment as puncher. I didn't like his looks, and when he began to threaten, I knocked him down, and Belcher threw him bodily off the ranch."

"What do you suppose he is doing here now?"

"I'm sure I can't figure it out. But there's nothing he can do to worry about. So forget him."

Then he went on to tell her of another adventure he had had with a man known as the "Wolf," who while drunk one day offered his services as range rider.

"I cannot tolerate a drunken man, whether he wears broadcloth or chaps," he explained, "so I declined the Wolf's offer. But he was evidently a gentleman and well educated, so I told him that if he would sober up and pledge himself to quit the booze while in my employ, I would give him a job."

"Of course he agreed?"

"He didn't. He swore he was an American citizen

and enjoyed the inalienable right to drink whenever he pleased without hindrance from any living soul. We quarreled, and when he left he assured me that if we met again, he would demand satisfaction for my uninvited criticism.''

''Have you met him since?''

''No. I'm sorry, too. Although he was aggressive, he did not impress me as being a really bad lot.''

Marion made no comment, but her thoughts kept dwelling on the Wolf, wondering how far he deserved his fierce name—if he were vicious and cowardly like the animals whose cruel deeds in the story books of her childhood caused her many a shudder. Perhaps she would meet him, help him to win back. . . .

''Here we are!'' exclaimed Haines, interrupting her reverie and pointing ahead.

They were approaching the garden spot of the ranch—the place which was to be her home. On either side of the road stretched lusty orchards of young trees, but immediately in front of them stood as pretty a bungalow as one might wish to see, approached by a flower-bordered path which led a rod or two up an incline. On the porch stood wicker chairs, and a cushioned hammock inviting one to rest.

''That's our shack,'' said Haines, assisting her from the vehicle. ''I think you'll like it, once you are used to it and the surroundings.''

''I love it already,'' she replied with enthusiasm. ''How you must have worked to produce all this, you poor boy!''

She walked to the bungalow, finding something beautiful and admirable at every step of the way. When they reached the porch, she paused to admire the splendor of the view that unfolded itself to her rapturous gaze. To right and left, the valley spread like a gigantic oblong emerald, its luster broken at intervals by patches of golden mesquite and sage in which the browsing cattle luxuriated. A mile away rose the Purple Buttes, cutting off the alkali desert, their battlements outlined clearly against the horizon. To the southward, the "Chimneys," a chain of barren hills, reared their grizzly heights.

To the right whence they had come, the road was visible here and there for two miles, its length dying away in the distance like a white ribbon in a fabric of green. Dark clouds lowered upon the sky line, presaging a storm. On the left, the valley dipped downward gently, to rise again a mile away, the ruddy buttes converging into a pass, beyond which lay the desert, hot and uninviting. In this pass she could see several horsemen, who, Haines explained, were his punchers corraling a hundred or more of steers which he proposed to market at Butler during the coming week.

"I'll introduce you to the boys at supper," he went on. "You'll find them a companionable crowd, quaint and interesting. Oh, hello, 'Mandy!"

In the door stood a buxom negress, her broad shining face beaming good nature and hearty welcome. She wore a red bandana handkerchief turbanned neatly about her head, a striped blue gingham dress, and a spotless white apron. She looked the capable housekeeper which later she proved to be.

"This is Aunt 'Mandy Coles, my housekeeper and cook," said Haines. "Aunt 'Mandy, this is my sister, Marian, who will live with us."

"I'm sho' pleased to meet you, Missy Marian," grinned Aunt 'Mandy, bowing with all the grace possible for a woman weighing considerably more than two hundred pounds.

"I'm delighted, I'm sure, Aunt 'Mandy," replied Marian, extending her hand which the negress shook with a warmth and persistency that all but deprived the other woman of breath.

"O' co'se you is, honey!" responded Aunt 'Mandy. "You's gwine to like dis place and me too, Ah reckon. I'se gwine to be yo' servant from dis day on."

"Thank you, Auntie. You won't mind if I call you Auntie, will you?"

"Bress yo' lil heart, chile," shouted Auntie delightedly. "Yo' may call me anything yo' like, so's yo' don't call me nigger, like dat ugly greaser Pedro did who wus yar a while ago."

"Then he was here! What was he after?" said Haines, frowning.

"Nothin', fur as Ah could see," she answered, showing her white teeth angrily. "O'ny nosin' 'round, like he wus plannin' something. Ah don't like dat greaser, and next time he shows his face yar, Ah's gwine to cut his nose off, sho'!"

"Leave him to me, 'Mandy, I'll take care of him," said Haines, leading the way into the house. "Come along, sis, and have a look at things."

Marian followed him into the living room, comfortably though somewhat roughly furnished. There was a large fireplace at one side, a lounge, with pillows, Navajo blanket, and a finely tanned panther skin with the head attached. A heavy rug lay on the floor and easy chairs stood about in profusion. At the wall opposite the fireplace was a large object completely hidden by a tarpaulin. While Marian's attention was engaged by a view from one of the windows. Haines removed the cover and disclosed an upright piano. At sight of the instrument, Marian gasped in astonishment, than ran forward with radiant face and outstretched hands.

"A piano!" she exclaimed. "The very thing I least expected! Oh, you darling thoughtful boy."

She took his face in her hands and kissed him.

"Yo' all is hungry, I 'specs," said Auntie, grinning, "so when yo' all gits ready, we'll jine forces at de table."

The negress vanished, and Haines showed Marian the rest of the house—her bedroom, his own, and a third reserved for possible visitors. There was a large kitchen, clean and neat as a pin, with a store room opening from it, and a rear porch from which Marian could see the bunk house occupied by the men, neatly white-washed. Near it stood a barn, a chicken house, and the corral where lay a half dozen milch cows. Altogether the view was refreshingly fine.

"It is all very beautiful, Ralph," said Marian after she had visited the barn and corral, and made the acquaintance of Rover and Sam, bird and watch dog respectively, as well as of the cows and chickens.

"Yes, I think you will like it, sis," he answered. "It certainly is a change from Manhattan. No fashions, conventionalities, hypocrisies, or veneer, but all that God intended it should be—open, free, hearty."

"Who are your neighbors?"

"There's Colonel Warfield, who lives three miles to the north of us, with his wife and daughter, a girl about your age. They are refined, cultivated people. I spent several evenings with them recently, and enjoyed them very much. Then there is Mrs. Whittaker, a widow, with her son and daughter, who live a couple of miles beyond the Warfields. We'll have a party for them to meet you very soon."

Marian was just about to express her pleasure, but was startled out of speech by the sound of several shots, followed by a shrill whooping. The noise came from the group of men in the valley, who were now skylarking gayly.

"Don't be frightened. It's the boys coming home

for chow. That's one of their regular performances. Here they come now!''

Four punchers dashed behind a grove of trees, yelling and shooting like Indians. They halted at the barn and, catching sight of Haines and Marian standing on the porch, grew mum instantly and slipped silently out of sight within the structure.

''Get ready for supper now, sis,'' said Haines. ''And put on your plainest gown. My punchers are not used to Fifth Avenue fashion displays.''

An hour later Marian was introduced to the men as they filed into the dining room for their supper. Sam Belcher, the foreman, about forty, was reticent and retiring to the point of bashfulness and blushed furiously at Marian's pleasant greeting. Pete Hanscom, a tall young chap, was as shy as a girl at her social début. His swarthy cheeks turned crimson when Marian extended her hand to him, and he seemed ready to bolt in confusion.

Charlie Jones, known as ''Bird's-eye,'' because he had the vision of an eagle and was as constantly alert as that wary bird, was about thirty and had served with the United States Cavalry against Scar Face and his band of Apaches in New Mexico and Arizona.

The fourth man was ''Chaps'' Slicker, whose smile was inexpressibly sad. Marian learned later that his life had been darkened by a great tragedy. Like Belcher's parents, his own had been slain by Mexican bandits, and he still cherished the hope of exacting vengeance upon the brutes who had rendered his life desolate.

They treated Marian with grave courtesy, but their evident liking soon warmed into real friendliness and comradeship when she opened the piano and played a number of popular airs. ''Chaps'' got out his mandolin, as did ''Bird's-eye,'' and serenaded her. Before the party broke up for the night, a fellowship had been established which was destined to endure as long as she remained a part of their little circle.

Marian declared it had been the happiest evening she had ever experienced.

"It'll be a round of pleasure for you, sis," laughed Ralph. "We'll make Red Sandy valley famous as a musical center now that you are here."

The next day and for several weeks thereafter, Marian spent her time exclusively on the ranch, studying the thousand and one details of management which it was imperative she must master if she hoped to be of substantial assistance to her brother. She frequently accompanied Belcher when he searched for mavericks in the dry ravines and caves at the bases of the buttes, and she soon became an expert horsewoman.

"You sure sit your bronco well, Miss Haines," he said admiringly one day. "You remind me of my sister, Jennie—"

He paused and averted his face. Marian's heart went out to him.

"You must learn to forget, Mr. Belcher," she said softly. "However great one's sorrow, time will bring alleviation."

"I can't forget the scoundrel who brought suffering and death to my family," he replied savagely, "and should we ever meet, God help him!"

"Do you know the man, then?"

"Every one in Mexico has heard of him—Cipriano Valdez!"

"Cipriano Valdez!"

The name meant nothing to her, but nevertheless, she could not fail to remember it, for to her intuition it rang uncannily whenever it flashed into her recollection. She thought of Pedro and wondered vaguely if the two had any connection with each other. She wanted to ask Belcher if he knew, but perceiving his preoccupation and emotion, she thought better of it and dismissed the subject from her mind.

Armed with a revolver, and with a rifle strapped to her saddle, Marian frequently accompanied her brother on his trips to the limits of the ranch and beyond. Among her newly acquired accomplishments as range rider, that of exceptionally proficient marksmanship was not the least. Haines had established a shooting range a short distance from the corral, and much of Marian's spare time was devoted to perfecting herself in this essential art of the frontier. Her eye was true, her hands and arms steady, and in every other respect she was an ideal markswoman.

That she had made great progress was demonstrated one day when she scored ten straight bull's-eyes with both revolver and rifle, a record which even Haines found it difficult to equal.

"You're a master hand at the trigger!" he said admiringly. "I hope you may never have occasion to try your skill on a human being, but if you must, shoot to kill! We have no hospitals in this country, you know."

She laughed and observed that he was unduly earnest. "Why this savage warning, Ralph?" she asked. "Has anything happened?"

"Nothing, sis," he replied evasively. "At least, nothing that should worry you."

Marian was not satisfied with the answer, but Haines refused to enlighten her further, if, indeed, he had information of interest. Late that evening, while she was strumming a few random notes on the piano, she observed Belcher, "Chaps" and Ralph as they whispered together animatedly on the porch. Belcher seemed greatly perturbed and his gestures as

Cipriano Valdez . . . was able to equip a mob of malcontents of whom he was the chief . . . destroying and killing under the thin veneer of patriotism.

he talked convinced her that a subject of unusual importance was being discussed. The dogs barked savagely down the road and presently "Bird's-eye," his sweating bronco caked with dust, rode up and dismounted. Marian crept to the door and listened.

"What's up, 'Bird's-eye'?" asked Haines eagerly.

"Valdez is down the valley, boss," replied the puncher.

"Are you sure?"

"Sure as God made little apples," returned the young man. "He has about a dozen riders with him and it looks pretty much like a raid."

"It sure do," assented Belcher moodily.

"They won't attempt a raid to-night," said Haines after a pause. "I'll ride to Purple Canyon and have a talk with Sheriff Thorne to-morrow."

"We'll need a big posse to fight them devils off," urged Belcher, his hand on his revolver. "I hope I'll get a chance at that killer!"

The three went down to the corral, as if to discuss the crisis at length. Marian pondered deeply. The name of Valdez recalled her conversation with Belcher on the range. What did the dread presence of this ruffian mean to the ranchers of Red Sandy valley? When Haines returned to the bungalow an hour later she confronted him resolutely.

"I heard your talk with 'Bird's-eye' and Belcher a while ago, Ralph," she confessed bluntly. "You must tell me all about Valdez. Who and what is he?"

"He's nothing to brag about. Nor to worry about, either. . . ."

"Nonsense, Ralph. Let me share your troubles. We are partners now, aren't we?"

"We are, sis."

"In peace and in war?"

"Quite so, *amigo*."

"Then we share everything, whatever may come!"

"As long as Valdez—blast him—isn't a party to the contract, sis."

"Who is Valdez?"

"About as bad a lot as they make 'em!"

"Tell me what you know of him."

Haines feigned a yawn. "To-morrow. I'm off to bed now. We are safe for to-night, at least."

He left her abruptly, and a few minutes later Auntie joined her on the porch with the announcement that it was eleven o'clock and time for all good little children to be abed.

"Yo's gwine to bed soon, chile?" she asked solicitously. "Gits kinder chilly here o'nights, it sho' do, Missy Marian."

"I'll go to bed soon, Auntie," replied Marian. "Don't wait up for me. Good night."

"Good night, chile."

Marian, troubled and apprehensive, stood for some time, her eyes on the clouds that hurried across the face of the moon, her mind grappling with this new development that threatened. Then, realizing that there was nothing she could do for the time at least, she deliberately threw her fears behind her, like the brave girl she was, retired to her room, and soon fell into a sound sleep.

Next day, at noon, she accompanied Ralph to Purple Canyon. During their ride, he told her the story of Valdez—a dark recital that shocked even her steady nerves.

"What a man!" she commented, when Haines had finished. "A monster in human form!"

Her brother laughed reassuringly, but she could not fail to perceive that he was deeply worried. When they reached Purple Canyon, Haines called upon James Hawthorne, president of the National Bank, who after a brief conference insisted on carrying him and Marian to his home for the night. Here they were accorded a warm welcome by Mrs. Hawthorne and her daughter Rose.

Neither suspected that fate had woven a web in the meshes of which both were to be ensnared with terrifying results.

CHAPTER VI

CIPRIANO VALDEZ, celebrated as the most notorious bandit that Mexico ever had yet produced, was the son of a peon and Yaqui Indian woman. The elder Valdez had mated with the squaw after the fashion of his time and class, and of their marriage no record appears to have been made, nor was its absence a matter of regret or worry to the son of this union when, at the age of sixteen years, he began his career of crime.

Born in the mountains of Sonora, Valdez had from his earliest infancy lived like a rabbit in the open. Miserably neglected by his drunken parents and even when a child obliged to shift for himself or starve, it is not surprising that his predatory habits and sanguinary tastes, which were to be abnormally developed later on, began to germinate within him and to flourish like noxious weeds.

When he was eighteen years old, Valdez seemed a matured man of forty. He was little more than five feet tall, thin, cadaverous and temperamentally as venomous as a snake. From his mother he had inherited vicious traits that found adequate expression in the cruel lines of his face, and in his treatment of such animals as were unfortunate enough to fall into his filthy hands.

He loathed dogs almost as fervently as they hated and avoided him, for in his infancy one day he had been severely bitten by a mongrel cur in retaliation

62

for the cruel amputation of its tail at his hands. By that incomprehensible reversion to type which often occurs in creatures of abnormal tendencies, Valdez lavished his brutal affections upon a panther which he had captured when it was a kitten and trained to decimate every chicken roost within miles of his ancestral cabin. But the animal was shot and killed one night by a peon sheepman, whereupon in great fury, Valdez swore that soon or late he would have that slayer's blood, an oath he kept with fervor some years later.

Valdez was not only an Ishmaelite, but a pervert. Like most of his breed, he was a hypocrite and when threatened by danger his cowardice was pitifully apparent to those who recognized his inherent weaknesses. His braggadocio and strut served in great measure to conceal his delinquencies, but only when the odds were in his favor in personal encounters with his enemies, of whom there were many, did he truly shine. He early won the reputation of being handy with a knife or machete, both of which he could throw with remarkable accuracy of aim. He was, likewise, an excellent marksman with rifle or revolver, his proficiency in this respect dating from the time when, prowling about the camp of some American engineers who were surveying a railroad line in Sonora, he had purloined a rifle and, making his escape, surreptitiously employed the weapon long after its owner had forgotten its loss.

This embryotic bandit was separated from his loot a year later when a band of revolutionists captured him while he was shooting in the hills. To him the event was of extraordinary importance—the supreme tragedy of his youth. After lashing him with rawhide quirts, they appropriated not only the carcass of a fawn he had killed, but his rifle and hard-won ammunition as well. He marked the leader of the band, one Juliano Castro, savagely vowing he would have his life if *Jesu* ever should grant him the privilege of wreaking his vengeance upon him. Four years later, when, while in command of his own band of marauders, Castro fell into his hands, Valdez enjoyed his revenge—the sweeter because it had been nourished so long. That is to say, Valdez with his own hands cut out Castro's tongue, blinded him and literally skinned him alive!

"Carramba!" said Valdez, kicking the battered body of his victim. "You will know how to treat good boys in hell, perhaps! So much for stealing my rifle four years ago! *Jesu!* I have kept my oath!" And with unctuous piety, he crossed himself reverently and mouthed a few prayers to accompany the soul of Castro to that bourne whither so many of his own victims had preceded him in the days of his brief but glorious banditry.

Valdez, like every scoundrel who, with his mercenary cut-throats, inspired terror by the commission of heinous crimes wherever predatory force prevailed in Mexico, piously avowed himself a devout Christian. But his piety was inspired by greed and rapacity rather than by that inner consciousness which distinguishes between right or wrong and which is the fundamental basis of religiosity in humankind. Whenever as a boy he attended mass at the cathedral in the village near which he lived, he eyed the poor box avidly, as well as the gold braided vestments of the celebrant priests, not to speak of the rich altar appointments, the ostensorium concealing the Host, the golden chalices. The spectacle of these to him unattainable riches roused within him a latent instinct for thieving which he found difficult to restrain. While he once or twice rifled the poor box of the few pesos it contained, he dared not steal the golden goblets and altar jewels. He was not assured that he might dispose of them profitably without risk of arrest and imprisonment, if not excommunication.

When his father one day met violent death at the hands of a ruffian in the course of a political discussion in a roadside tavern, Valdez felt relieved. For he had always averred after frequent and painful castigations inflicted upon him by his observing and protesting parent, that the old man would never come to a good end!

So it happened that when his father's murderer was arrested by the rurales and haled to prison, the son sent the man a message of sympathy. The mother of Valdez, relieved of the restraining influence of her man, who had supported her none to well, sank to the lowest depths. One night, in a fit of drunken melancholy, she cut her own throat. When Valdez the next morning stumbled across her body, he calmly lit a cigarette and reported the incident to the Alcalde.

That astute official, who had abundant reasons for believing Valdez capable of any crime, even matricide, held him a prisoner pending an investigation. This resulted in nothing and Valdez was released after a stay of several days in the filthy jail crowded with the riffraff of the countryside, during which interval it had not even occurred to him to inquire as to the disposition made of his mother's body by the authorities.

Cast upon his own resources, Valdez left Sonora where he was too well known, and for two years drifted about Mexico living by his wits. He became enamored of the beautiful daughter of a rich Mexican planter and although she treated him with contempt, he persisted in his attentions despite the fact that she was the fiancée of the son of a banker in Mexico City.

Aided by two other scoundrels one night, he abducted the girl, carrying her off to his haunts in the mountains where he held her for heavy ransom. The money was paid and Valdez and his companions vanished in the silent wastes to the westward where they pursued their banditry with unbridled freedom and fewer chances of interruption. When the señorita told her father the story of her imprisonment, the Mexican offered a reward of twenty thousand pesos for Valdez, dead or alive.

The first mutterings of revolt against the iron rule of President Diaz furnished Valdez with the opportunities he had long sought—to raise and equip a band of rascals who might roam the country at will, looting, destroying and killing under the thin veneer of patriotism. He contrived to capture several wealthy owners of landed property and by threatening them with horrible punishment or death if they refused to respond to the call of the fatherland which demanded the immediate removal of the dictator, he generally got what he wanted in the way of money and munitions of war.

Thus he was able to equip a mob of malcontents of whom he was chief. His supremacy, however, spelt torture, death and devastation wherever he went and presently he was officiallly declared an outlaw, not only by the government he had pretended to oppose, but by the various revolutionary bodies to which he had sworn temporary allegiance.

Harassed by the rurales on one side and by the bona fide, though misguided revolutionists on the other, Valdez ultimately found Mexico too hot for his comfort. He fled precipitately across the border into New Mexico. He made his escape just in time, for had he delayed his departure another hour, he must inevitably have fallen into the trap set for him,

and been shot out of hand. But fortune was with
Valdez, and accompanied by his lieutenant Pedro, a
murderous wretch of his own age, he was compelled,
for the time being at least, to earn an honest liveli-
hood. He obtained employment with a rancher as
cowpuncher and Pedro and he rode the range together.
Both kept their eyes and ears open for possible wind-
falls, the fruits of which they might enjoy without
molestation until the ban against them in Mexico was
removed and they be privileged to return to their beloved but misgoverned country.

The success of Madero's revolution and the flight
of Diaz paved the way for their realization of this
hope. Through influential friends, who, fearing him
as they did the devil, sought by this favor to win his
gratitude and protection, the decree outlawing him
was annulled, and Valdez returned in triumph to his
haunts in Mexico. He now secretly carried into effect
certain plans he had formed in New Mexico, where
he had seen much and learned much, and which knowledge he purposed to put to profitable use. He had
made the discovery that it was comparatively easy
to rustle cattle across the border, an occupation of
great lucrativeness to a resolute man like himself.
He interested a number of choice spirits in the venture and within a few weeks he had established a rendezvous in the hills fifteen miles from the border
where he might corral stolen cattle and hold them in
security until his agents could dispose of them to un-
scrupulous speculators in the states to the southward.

For two years Valdez and Pedro, with their con-
federates, engaged in this perilous traffic with great
success. They had operated with such secretiveness
that they were not even suspected of wrongdoing.
The stolen cattle was re-branded by them with a "V"
on the left hump as soon as the rendezvous in the

Mexican hills was reached, and the live stock was not permitted to appear on the range until the freshness of the brand had vanished. Valdez lived in an adobe house of considerable extent with Señorita Marie Pinosa, a young dancer he had picked up at Juarez, and whom he had promised to marry. She was as jealous as she was pretty, but Valdez knew how to treat jealous women! The hacienda was a charming retreat, and to all appearance Valdez was a prosperous cattle raiser who let it be known through judicious propaganda that having eschewed revolutionary radicalism, politics and war forever, he had settled down to the delights of honest industry.

But Valdez's besetting sin was his inordinate fondness for *vino tinte,* a red wine, to which he added gin in such quantities that a drink or two of the concoction would have quickly put an ordinary drinker under the table. But Valdez, although he frequently drank to excess, rarely displayed signs of intoxication. The invariable effect of his potations was to rouse his bellicose spirit, and when drunk, he was infinitely more dangerous than a scorpion.

He interlarded his language with oaths so horrible that even the most hardened of his hearers were aghast and when his face was turned, they felt obliged to make the sign of the cross to ward off the evil spirits such blasphemies might lure from their haunts. He was extremely violent when in these paroxysms, and heaped abuse and threats of death upon any incurring his ill will.

It is not surprising, therefore, that he was hated by many, if not by all of his followers, whom, despite their protestations of loyalty, fear alone deterred from betraying him into the hands of his enemies—the emissaries of American justice that he had so flagrantly violated.

In the pursuit of his wretched business, Valdez frequently went to El Paso with Pedro, where they represented themselves as peaceable Mexican ranchers, whose speciality was the raising and buying of cattle. They frequented low dives in the Mexican quarter, and one night Valdez met with an adventure that all but ended his career. Lounging at a bar known as the "Buena Vista," there was a half drunken, athletic young American, who, contrary to the rules of discretion, was volubly voicing his contempt for the cowardly bandits who paraded as revolutionists in storm-tossed Mexico.

"They're a rotten bunch of holdup men and assassins," he had said, "and if I were Madero, I'd hunt 'em down and lynch 'em! But what can you do in a country where any scoundrel with a gun can terrorize an entire community, and loot and kill without fear of the law?"

Valdez, who knew English well enough to comprehend the speaker's scorn, grew white at the lips and edged his way through the crowd towards the American. Neither Valdez nor Pedro carried a revolver, but both were armed with knives, and Valdez was resolved to make this American pig, as he said to Pedro, swallow his words.

"Wait!" whispered Pedro, restraining his chief. "We must first find out something about this man. He may be a secret agent of some kind."

They learned that the speaker was widely known as the Wolf and that he had the reputation of being a gun man whom all in the Southwest feared. He was a dangerous chap who would fight man or devil at the drop of a hat.

The inopportune arrival of several cowboys from up country, obliged Valdez to relinquish his design to stab the Wolf in the back as he had hoped to do, undetected. The bandit determined to remember this American rowdy and some day teach him a salutary lesson.

When the Wolf left the den, after having mentioned casually his plan to return to Purple Canyon, Valdez nudged Pedro, winking significantly, and the pair trailed the unsuspecting man into the street.

There were few passersby in the poorly lighted thoroughfare and an opportunity presenting itself, Valdez decided to take advantage of it without loss of time. *Carramba!* he would cut the heart out of this boastful American who dared publicly to asperse the honor of respectable Mexican gentlemen! But Pedro, he decided, must make the overture to the tragedy he longed to stage.

"Stumble against the man and provoke an argument, Pedro," he whispered. "Then I shall step in and between us we will slit his throat, and send his soul to Paradise!"

Pedro did as directed and adroitly succeeded in almost throwing the Wolf off his balance. The Wolf, recovering himself, turned upon the Mexican and cursed him as a clumsy scoundrel.

"D'ye think you own this sidewalk, you greaser?" he asked angrily. "Try it again and as sure as my name's Wolf, I'll beat you to a pulp!"

"*Santisimo!*" responded Pedro, casting an anxious eye at Valdez who was approaching stealthily. "You big American pig! You not know how to fight anybody!"

Before he could draw his knife, the American, his fighting blood roused to action by the insult, seized Pedro by the throat and lifting him bodily from the ground, hurled him a distance of twelve feet. He dropped with a jolt that wrenched every bone in his body, and lay groaning. The Wolf was on the point of running toward the prostrate greaser when he heard some one shout, "Look out for the man with the knife!"

Turning, he beheld Valdez within arm's length, dagger in hand, lunging to stab him in the back. He sprang nimbly aside and as the bandit lurched by, tackled him with the dexterity of the trained football player. Seizing Valdez's arm, he gave it a sudden wrench, dislocating it at the shoulder. The bandit screamed with pain and to silence him, the Wolf struck him on the mouth with his open hand.

"You would have stabbed me in the back, eh?" he growled. "Just like your dirty kind! I'll teach you to attempt the life of an American, you hound!"

He thrust Valdez from him and struck him several times with his fist. The bandit cowered and sought in vain to escape punishment. When the Wolf felt the man growing limp in his grasp, he drew him forward and raising his head, looked down upon his distorted blood-smeared face.

"Don't kill me, señor," whined Valdez. "Have pity!"

The Wolf laughed. "You're not worth killing! What's your name? Tell me the truth, or I'll choke the life out of your body!"

"Cipriano Valdez."

"Good Lord! Not the Valdez of Sonora bandit notoriety?"

Valdez nodded. He instinctively feared this man who had mastered him, and despite himself, dared not lie.

"Who's the fellow lying in the street there?"

"Pedro, my friend."

"Bah!" snapped the Wolf, hurling Valdez from him. "You're too mean for a white man to have dealings with. If you ever cross my path again, you will be sorry. Don't forget," he added significantly, then turned and left him.

"*Jesu!*" muttered Valdez, nursing his arm. "I shall not forget you, American swine that you are!"

He assisted Pedro to the Mexican hostelry where they purposed to spend the night. Pedro was so badly shaken that Valdez found it necessary to send for a physician. For three days they lived in seclusion while they were convalescing, and every hour both renewed their oaths never to rest content until they had exacted a terrible penalty from the human wolf who had manhandled them so effectively.

"*Carramba!*" exclaimed Pedro despairingly. "Where shall we find this man and punish him?"

Valdez ruminated for several minutes and suddenly he beamed with delight.

"I know!" he answered. "He is to be found at Purple Canyon, which is near Red Sandy valley!"

"Sure, I remember the place!" rejoined Pedro thoughtfully. "Many fine cattle there, Valdez."

"You know a rancher there. What is his name?"

"Ralph Haines," replied Pedro, lighing a cigarette. "He has a beautiful sister—the most charming señorita I ever saw!" His dark eyes glittered.

"Beautiful, you say?" mused Valdez darkly. "*Carramba!* I too love beautiful women and Señorita Marie Pinosa begins to weary me! Bah! You say that this man Haines has many fine cattle?"

"Two thousand, maybe, by now."

"*Bueno!* And easy to rush across the border too. I shall kill two birds with one stone! *Dios!* My revenge shall be sweet indeed, once this American pig and the woman are in my hands!"

They returned to the hacienda, completed their plans for raiding the ranches along the Red Sandy, every inch of which territory they knew intimately, and started off on their mission. They were to survey the ground and on a stipulated date meet a dozen of their fellow rustlers at Butler, each of whom was to travel alone so that their mission might not be suspected.

Thus it transpired later, while Pedro sought in vain to kill the Wolf whom he had recognized at the Red Eye saloon, his quarry had unexpectedly encountered and recognized Valdez in the glare of the match as he lit a cigarette on the fringe of the desert on that eventful night.

The fateful hour had struck, but the Wolf, engaged as he was in a mighty struggle with self, was quite unaware that fate had woven another strand of the web in which he lay, bound hand and foot, and from which he had neither the power to escape, nor perhaps, the inclination to do so, even had he known what the future held in store.

CHAPTER VII

FOLLOWING her momentous meeting with Holloway in front of the Red Eye, Marian ran through the shadows with one absorbing desire, to avoid possible contact with her brother until her emotion had been spent. She entered a side street at the end of which stood the Hawthorne home, and walking slowly along in the soft light of the moon, which was just rising above the eastern rim of the desert, sobbingly communed with herself.

She wondered what impulse had prompted her to make what she deemed an absolutely futile appeal to the better nature of this border ruffian known as the Wolf. Now that she had regained her composure, her better judgment warned her that by condescending to speak to a man-killer such as the Wolf, even though her motive had been above criticism, she had descended almost to his level. She shuddered at the conviction that her conduct would inevitably be the subject for adverse gossip.

"What will Ralph say when he hears of it?" she thought. "I was wrong to speak to that man, but under such circumstances, would not every woman have done the same? I wanted him to revoke his threat to kill Ralph, and he laughed at me! No, he did not actually laugh," she reflected, "but he refused to do as I asked. However, at least, I prevented this man from killing himself, and now that I have gone so far, I must go still farther. I must

74

contrive to see the Wolf to-morrow, and then get him to promise not to injure Ralph.''

At the thought of the gossip Marian trembled. How was she to escape the consequences of her indiscretion? It occurred to her to flee to the ranch where she might defy her hostile critics. But there was Ralph, wholly ignorant of the Wolf's threat—he, at least, must be warned of the danger that menaced him. It was her hope that she might communicate the news to him without revealing the entire truth, insofar as she was concerned therein. Her timidity inspired the fear that her motive in addressing the most notorious man in Purple Canyon might be misconstrued, and urged her to maintain silence until ultimate events might render a personal explanation imperative.

"It is perfectly dreadful!'' she mused as she approached the Hawthorne residence, the lights of which were now visible. ''I must learn all I can about this man called the Wolf; but pshaw! why consider him further? I shall think of him no more!''

But she found this resolution obviously impossible, for she was unable to expel Holloway from her mind. Despite her efforts, she visualized him at every step — standing before her, motionless, a whimsical expression in his dark eyes, staring at her wistfully, wonderingly, with sombrero in his hand. She remembered that when she took the automatic from him, she had sensed tears in his eyes and heard a sob, such as escapes strong men in hours of torment. She recalled also the appeal his eyes had expressed, his contrite air, his humility. Was such a man wholly bad? She did not think so, and her hope of impelling him to reconsider his threat revived. She grew almost cheerful.

Approaching the Hawthorne gate and lifting the

latch, Marian drew herself together with an effort. She wondered if Rose Hawthorne, a bachelor maid six years her senior, and indifferently attractive personally, yet of keen penetration, would observe the traces of her emotion. She hoped she would not. She had discarded her powder puff when she left New York, but now she regretted its absence, as any young woman in similar circumstances might well do. She paused for an instant irresolute, then sure of herself, advanced with sprightly steps. A woman's voice hailed her from the porch that framed in the lower story of the dwelling in front.

"Is that you, Marian?"

The speaker was Rose. With a cheery affirmative, the younger woman stepped onto the porch and seated herself in an easy chair, Rose swinging in a nearby hammock. It was not yet ten o'clock and the moon, now at its full, clothed the landscape in veiled silver.

"Did you see the town?" inquired Rose curiously.

"Yes, I did, and it's quite a lively, bustling little place," admitted Marian, glad that her face was hidden in the shadow of a stanchion. "Awfully romantic and all that sort of thing."

"As romantic as Broadway? The Great White Way, I mean, of course."

"Um—quite different, I should say."

"We have a Broadway in Purple Canyon, you know. But the only glow it can boast after nightfall comes from the Red Eye saloon, which, according to the Rev. Mr. Smith, is the canker spot of the town."

"It must be a dreadful place. It is conducted by a woman, I've heard."

"Yes—Faro Jenn—a coarse creature, masculine and terrible. Papa says that steps are being taken to establish a Law and Order League for the sole purpose of closing up her gambling and dance hall, and of driving the women and men who frequent it, out of town.''

''I should not fancy such a spot as helpful, but so long as there are men who support it, how can you suppress it?''

''I can't say as to the proposed methods, but something decisive should be done to rid Purple Canyon of such a plague spot.''

''Perhaps you're right.'' Marian wondered if Rose had knowledge of the Wolf. ''Do you know any of the men who frequent the place, by reputation, I mean?''

''Good Heavens, no!'' exclaimed Rose in horror. ''How should I? Most of the frequenters are criminals, gamblers, drunken cowboys, miners and the like; while the women who make the place their headquarters are unspeakable.''

''But certainly not all who enter the Red Eye belong to that category, I hope. There must be some exceptions, I'm sure.''

''If so, I don't know of them. Quarrels occur nightly, and only a few days ago, a man was shot by a gambler and the players who share their winnings with Faro Jenn, are all sharpers. But it must be said to their credit that when you meet them on the street they invariably treat you with courtesy and respect.''

''Then they are not all wholly debased, Rose,'' said Marian. ''By the way, have you ever heard of a man called the Wolf?''

''The Wolf! Why?''

''Curiosity. I heard my brother speak of him one day—''

''May Heaven preserve you from that man!'' interrupted Rose. ''He is what they call a gun man— with a record as a man-killer. He carries a revolver always ready for use. He is a notorious drunkard, and thoroughly unreliable.''

"Is that all you can say of him?" asked Marian. Oddly enough, she was irritated by this condemnation of the man, of whose existence until an hour previously, she had scant knowledge. "Surely he must have some good qualities."

"If he has, no one has discovered them."

"Tell me all you know of him."

There was little that was informative to Marian in Rose's account of the Wolf, for she knew him only by reputation. She said that the man had appeared at Purple Canyon six months previously in the company of a cowboy known as the Kid, and he made his headquarters at the Red Eye. Never aggressive, he was known to have submitted to certain indignities that most men would have resented vigorously, but only when his honor was impugned or his integrity as a man of veracity assailed, would he be roused to hostile activity.

"He has whipped nearly every braggart in Purple Canyon," went on Rose, her tale comforting Marian unaccountably, "and his bravery has never been questioned. Although he is called the Wolf, he loves dogs and horses and will risk even his own life in their defense. Woe be to him who dares mistreat an animal in his presence!"

"Then he is not wholly lost," said Marian with enthusiasm, for she herself ardently loved animals. "He certainly can't be as bad as he is represented. I fancy he is the victim of habits and tastes which he cannot, or will not, control."

Rose admitted that this deduction might be logical, but her tone implied doubt. According to her simple philosophy, a bad white man, like a bad Indian, was irreclaimable and therefore good only after he had been

safely buried. She related with relish the details of
the card game of the Wolf with Gene, which had
been communicated to her by the wife of a neighbor
whose husband had witnessed the incident.

Marian was horrified when Rose related how the
Wolf, after his discovery that Gene had taken the ace
from the bottom of the deck, had pinned the gambler's
hand to the table with his knife. But a strange happiness soothed her when she learned of the man's
generous distribution of his winnings among the victims of the card sharp.

"As I suspected," she commented dreamily. "He
is a man, after all. A man who will do that sort of
thing isn't to be despised as a being beyond hope of
redemption."

"But who's to reform him?"

"That is as God wills."

A mantel clock in the living room struck eleven.
Marian rose and announced herself ready for bed.
She desired to be alone, so that she might think of
her future course with respect to this ruffian with an
inexplicable love for animals—this detested man-
killer whom she was anxious to forget, but could not.
What magician's spell had he cast upon her? Secretly, the realization that she could not banish him
from her thoughts, afforded her a certain degree of
pleasure, indefinable yet substantial. She realized
that she was playing with fire, but somehow, the possibility that she might be forced to pay the penalty
for her disregard of the conventionalities, did not occasion her discomfort or excite alarm.

"You are strangely thoughtful, Marian," said
Rose, breaking the silence. "Why this preoccupation?"

"Where is Ralph?" replied Marian, woman-like
answering one query with another. "He should have

returned home long ago. What can be detaining him?''

"He must be with father at Sheriff Thorne's office. They're forming a posse to repel Valdez and his band of raiders.''

"I had quite forgotten that.''

Marian was in a quandary. It clearly was her duty to instantly warn her brother of the Wolf's threat, and yet, why should she not wait until morning? Meanwhile, she would outline the form of the confession she was compelled to make regarding her adventure with the Wolf—an action which, she assured herself, would inevitably redound to her disadvantage through exaggeration and endless repetition.

"I shall not wait up for him,'' she yawned. She paused and looked at the full moon, its silvery beams penciling every object that met her gaze, with matchless beauty. "How beautiful is the moon—how restful!''

Rose put her arm about her, laughing softly. "When a girl of your age admires the moon,'' she said, "it means something.''

"Why, what?''

"You silly child! Can't you guess?''

"No.''

"Love!''

Marian sighed. "Nonsense, Rose! It's a fairy tale, beautiful, but insubstantial as air!''

"Beautiful always, but never insubstantial—at the full of the moon.''

"Have you ever been in love, Rose?''

"No,'' sighed the other, "but what on earth has that to do with the thoughts that bestir you?''

"Simply this—I want to know how love affects one in the beginning. Not the puppy love all of us girls have experienced, but the greater love of a strong man for a woman—the attraction of brave hearts and lofty souls towards each other. When this love dawns, how are we poor women to recognize it?''

"Ask the man in the moon! If he can't answer, perhaps you'll find what you seek in the pages of Chambers, London, Norris or Locke."

"Good night, Rose."

"Good night, and happy dreams."

For two hours before her eyes closed in sleep, Marian tossed restlessly, her brain too active to permit her exhausted body to find the rest she so urgently needed. She sought to quiet her nerves by conjuring up scenes of green meadows, counting sheep jumping over hurdles and employing many other mental expedients calculated to invite repose, but centered in each succeeding picture that she called to mind was the image of Jim Holloway, the Wolf! She was at first angered at its persistency, but presently she welcomed rather than repelled its recurrence.

"You are no wolf—Jim!" she whispered dreamily. "You are a man among men!"

Jim's image smiled upon her, as she fancied, and she experienced a great joy suddenly. Even as the Wolf, only a few rods away was struggling in a great spiritual contest for mastery over self, and voicing her name, so did she, when her senses were drifting on the sea of oblivion, murmur his.

"Jim! Jim!"

The image held out its arms to her entreatingly, and sinking into them, she slept.

.   .   .   .   .

Seated in Sheriff Thorne's office, eight men were engaged in animated discussion. Among them were Ralph Haines, Mr. Hawthorne, Belcher, the Sheriff, his deputy and three business men of Purple Canyon. They were discussing the probability of an immediate raid by Valdez, and the best means to be adopted to frustrate the bandit's designs.

"We don't need more'n twenty men fur the posse," said the Sheriff thoughtfully. "I don't reckon Valdez has more'n a dozen greasers with him."

"Twenty men should be sufficient," assented Haines, the others nodding their approval. "What we need are rifles and ammunition—"

"We'll supply all you want," interrupted a business man. "We can outfit a regiment, if necessary."

"Righto!" interposed another. "I've got twenty rounds of ca'tridges for each man in my store."

"So have I," chipped in another.

"I'll see to it that you are paid," said Hawthorne. "The time has come to prevent this and subsequent raids, and they will be, if we go about it vigorously."

"I suggest that Belcher, who knows these greasers better than any of us, give us his advice," said Haines, turning to his foreman. "Have you any plan we might adopt?"

"Wall," drawled Belcher, his brow wrinkled in thought. "Thar's only one thing we must do—kill the bunch if we can't capture 'em!"

"That's the talk!"

"Kill 'em, sure! There's no other way."

Belcher explained that two riders of the Haines' ranch were on the lookout at the lower end of Red Sandy valley with instructions to make for Purple Canyon by the short cut, the instant they had news of value to communicate.

Hawthorne glanced at his watch and observing that it was eleven o'clock, announced that he purposed to turn in. All agreed to meet at the same place at eight o'clock the next morning, or earlier, should circumstances demand it. The Sheriff was urging all to rally early when there came the clatter of hoofs—the sound far away at first, but growing louder momentarily, until the rider halted in front of the building.

"Hello!"

"It's 'Bird's-eye' with news!" said Belcher, opening the door. "Come right in, son. What's doing?"

The puncher entered the office, hat in hand, the others watching him attentively.

"Valdez and his bunch are in the valley making for Sweetwater," he replied, coolly lighting a cigarette.

"How many in the crowd?" asked Haines.

"Fifteen, I reckon."

"If they are aiming for Sweetwater," remarked the Sheriff, "they ain't aimin' a raid to-night."

The Sheriff explained that the "Chimney" in the Sweetwater region would prove an admirable rendezvous for the bandits, because of its caves and screened hollows, which would afford raiders an excellent refuge.

"In some of those spots, one man kin hold off a hundred till hell freezes over," said he, "provided, always, he has ammunition enough."

"Then we must try to head them off," said Haines. "It is certain Valdez cannot reach Sweetwater for six or eight hours, even though he rides all night, which is doubtful.

"Righto!" grunted "Bird's-eye." "They won't do any raidin' this trip, I reckon."

After some discussion, the Sheriff begged that all meet at his office at six o'clock or earlier, if possible, so that no time would be lost in organizing the posse. Haines announced his determination to return to the valley instantly.

"While you gentlemen are forming the posse," he said, "I'll keep an eye on Valdez. We'll meet at Sweetwater. Is that satisfactory?"

The Sheriff expressed his hearty approval of the plan and the men separated for a couple of hours' sleep, all agreeing to meet as arranged. Haines mounted his pony, while Belcher and "Bird's-eye," already in the saddle, were awaiting him in the roadway.

"Then you do not purpose to see your sister before you leave, Mr. Haines?" inquired Hawthorne, as they shook hands. "Perhaps you have a message for her?"

"Say to her that I shall return as soon as we have rid the valley of Valdez and his cutthroats! Meanwhile, Mr. Hawthorne, I am forced to request an extension of your hospitality in her behalf. I will appreciate the courtesy, I assure you."

"My home is open to your sister indefinitely," responded Hawthorne. "But in the event you do not return, which God forbid, what then?"

Haines pondered before he ventured a reply to this significant query. Until now he had not given a thought to the possible dangers that threatened him.

"If I am killed, she will know how to care for herself. As for me—well, *adios!*"

He gave his willing pony the spur and dashed away, the two punchers galloping in his wake. Hawthorne watched them until they were lost to view in a cloud of dust, then returned meditatively to his home, wondering how this unexpected adventure was to end.

When he reached his residence, he found it in darkness. He retired somewhat relieved because he was not obliged to deliver before morning Haines' message to Marian who, he fancied, was sound asleep in her room above. Five minutes later scarcely a living thing in Purple Canyon, except possibly Marian and the Wolf, was awake.

CHAPTER VIII

THE LOVE OF A TIGRESS

AWAKENED by shrill shouts and the neighing of horses beneath his window, Holloway raised his head and listened. Instinctively his hand sought his revolver under his pillow for, still drowsy, he was quite unable to comprehend fully what his sense of hearing sought to communicate to his beclouded understanding.

A pistol shot quickened his faculties to action suddenly as a cold douche might have done. Alert, watchful and keenly eager to ascertain what was transpiring, he sprang from his bed and, revolver in hand, glanced furtively out of the window. He took care not to expose an inch of his body unnecessarily to a possible marksman, until he was absolutely certain that he himself was not the primary cause of the mysterious commotion.

In the open space in front of the stable where Pinto was quartered, a dozen or more horsemen were congregated. All were armed with rifles or sawed-off shotguns, the latter the most deadly weapons known when employed at close range. A half dozen men were saddling recalcitrant ponies, while near them lay their weapons. They were talking and gesticulating excitedly, and it was apparent that an event of supreme importance had occurred to occasion such unwonted activity.

"I don't think they're gunning for me," he thought,

considerably relieved at the discovery. "After what took place last night, I was a trifle uncertain as to what might happen. What the deuce does it mean? Looks like they're aiming to hunt big game. Well, I should worry."

The sun had just risen and its resplendent rays bathed the country with golden splendor, yet with that concentration of energy which, to Holloway's trained perception, betokened another day of stifling heat, to be aggravated to the point of almost physical unendurance by the shimmering reflection of the rays from the superheated sands of the desert that stretched their undulating lengths to the glittering buttes beyond.

Having saddled their mustangs, the men rode away and presently Holloway heard them faintly as they galloped into the main street on a mission of which he hadn't the slightest conception. Convinced that he, at least, was not the cause of the excitement, he laid down his revolver and washed and dressed himself with greatest care. Although his curiosity was keenly alive he in nowise felt it incumbent upon himself to depart from his usual procedure—never to be hasty in meddling with other folks' affairs, when circumstances failed to enforce that course upon him.

Procuring some writing paper and a lead pencil from his suitcase, he seated himself at the table and wrote a letter, to the composition of which he devoted considerable thought. This performed, he scribbled an address on an envelope, inserted the letter, affixed a stamp thereto and inclosed it within a larger envelope upon which he inscribed a name in bold script. He then collected his clothing, books and other effects and packed them away in the suitcase with meticulous precision. This task performed, he put on his sombrero, adjusted his belt and bandoleer, examined his revolver as usual and, sighing, surveyed his surroundings.

"It may be a long time before I return to this joint," he muttered. "I'm not likely to forget my last night here, at all events. The struggle was bitter, but the victory was glorious!" He laughed sadly. "The Wolf has been merged in Jim Holloway for all time, and I will be lost indeed, if my regeneration is insincere!"

Hunger, making itself felt, reminded him that he had not eaten for more than twenty-four hours. He opened the door and carefully scanning the areaway beneath, descended the rickety steps. When he reached the street, he beheld the armed men whose boisterous shouts had awakened him, grouped here and there, engaged in animated discussion. Up and down the street other horsemen cantered, halting at intervals at the Sheriff's office where they received whispered instructions.

"A Sheriff's posse!" he ejaculated, the truth dawning upon him suddenly. "But what the devil is it all about, I wonder!"

"Everybody ready?" shouted a man hoarsely.

"Aye, aye!"

The speaker was Seth Lucas, a merchant of influence in Purple Canyon, who had once served as a Texas Ranger and whose reputation for nerve was generally recognized through the Southwest.

"Ready; mount!" shouted Lucas, nimbly vaulting into the saddle. The others followed and in the next instant the posse was galloping westward.

Holloway watched them until the cavalcade turned into a cross street, but true to form, he made no attempt to learn whither the posse was bound or its purpose in moving out of town. He was, instead, engrossed in the problem of finding his breakfast.

Scarching his pockets, he smiled grimly when he brought forth a silver dollar and a few nickels and dimes.

"Not much coin for a hungry man," he growled, "but it'll have to do until I can raise more. I'm hungry as a wolf—wolf!" he repeated, a sober look on his face. "I should have said Jim Holloway after a football game in the good old days! I must not forget that the era of the Wolf is over and that Jim Holloway's new régime is just beginning! So go to it, Jim, and prove you're no quitter at the reformation game!"

He stood irresolute for a moment and the events of the previous night recurring to his memory, he prayed that he might never again experience the agony he had endured in those hours of torment. Nevertheless, he felt an elation of spirit, because in the battle he had waged with his grosser self, he had conquered the physical tyrant that had hitherto dominated him. He felt reclaimed to a new existence filled with lofty ideals and holy purposes.

Do what he might, he could not forget his encounter with Haines, his pitiable weakness in the hour of danger, his meeting with Marian, her tears, and the wreck of his reputation as a game man in a community in which the reward of cowardice is social ostracism, ignominy and contempt. He upbraided himself bitterly for his crowning act of folly—the threat to kill Haines, a crime he hadn't the remotest idea of perpetrating, even though he had never seen the sister of the man he had sworn to slay.

"Wasn't she great!" he murmured admiringly. "Glorious girl! How her grief affected me. Of course, she believes me to be a brute. God bless her! I wish I were privileged to tell her that but for her tears I might still be the despised Wolf and not Jim

Holloway, reclaimed, repentant and devoted to the highest ideals.''

He marveled at the transformation that had been wrought within him. What agency had caused it? he asked himself again and again. Was it the yellow streak he had always feared was in his blood, and had it come to the surface to exalt and purify rather than to shame and degrade him? Was it the astounding aftermath of his meeting with Marian Haines? If so, he rejoiced that this glorious girl, exquisitely sweet and charming, should have been the instrument by which his regeneration had been effected.

He entered a restaurant frequented by miners and punchers, and after doing justice to a steak, paid his bill, then proceeded thoughtfully to the stable where Pinto was awaiting him. He fed the animal and was refurbishing his saddle trappings when he heard a childish voice behind him.

''Hello, Wolf!''

Holloway turned and beheld Sammie Mason, a boy of five years, a cripple from birth, whom he had often favored with candy and chewing gum. Sammie was the son of Holloway's landlord, and in their hearts an abiding friendship, founded upon the strength of one and the weakness of the other, existed.

''Hello, Sammie!'' echoed Holloway, picking up the child and holding him at arms' length. ''What are you doing up at this early hour, you rascal?''

''You heard about 'em, didn't you?''

''About what, Sammie?''

''They're going to shoot the Mexicans.''

''What Mexicans?''

''Valdez.''

Holloway stared. This was news indeed. So Valdez had begun his devilish work! This accounted for the Sheriff's posse which had just started for Red

Sandy Valley. The mystery of Valdez's presence in the vicinity of Purple Canyon was revealed—he and his men purposed, if they had not already done so, to raid the valley ranches!

The situation had assumed a new and startling phase as far as he was concerned. His blood tingled under the spur of a new emotion. Why shouldn't he be one of the posse, bent on the preservation of law and order and the infliction of summary punishment upon the bandits? Here was a golden opportunity to prove to the world that he was no coward, but a man of courage. If he failed to take advantage of it, he would be a fool indeed.

"Ain't you goin' to join 'em, Wolf?" asked Sammie.

"Perhaps I shall, son," answered Holloway, showing the child the door. "You'd better run home to mamma. Get along now, so Pinto won't kick you."

Sammie's cherubic face clouded and he vehemently voiced his protest against this summary dismissal.

"I wanna ask you somethin'," he said, pausing in the door opening.

"What is it?"

"What's the color of your liver?"

Holloway frowned. Kneeling and placing his hands upon the child's shoulders, he gulped.

"Did any one tell you to ask me that?"

Sammie began to whimper and draw back. "Nobody told me."

"Then why do you ask that question?"

"I heard papa say to mamma that your liver was white, an' when I saw you, I jest wanted to know if it was true. Is everybody's liver white?"

Holloway groaned, his face averted, so that Sammie might not observe the emotion of which he was ashamed, even in the presence of this babbling child.

So then, the punishment he had visited upon himself, had begun! Already they were discussing his degradation in public places, and his shame was being exploited in the presence of children who doubtless would blab it forth to all the world.

He clenched his hands and his face grew white. Ah, that he should have lived to see the day when those who had pinned their faith to him as a man who had never known fear, should speak of his courage in terms of derision and contempt! His liver white! So they spoke of him, and so they would continue to allude to him for all time! The truth was maddening, but he had sown the wind and was destined to reap the whirlwind, with all that this implied —shame, humiliation, disgrace!

"I heard another man say you ain't got no more grit than a rabbit," said Sammie, toying with the butt of Holloway's revolver. "But that ain't so though, 'cause I seen you catch that runaway pony, that girl was riding the other day, didn't you? You couldn't a did that, if you didn't have no grit, could you?"

He patted the boy's head kindly. His eyes were moist and there was a tremor in his voice. The lad clung to him tenaciously.

"What's the matter, Wolf?" he asked. "You ain't sick, are you?"

"I'm all right, Sammie."

"Then you are goin' to join the posse?"

"Yes."

He turned away and saddled Pinto. Left to himself, Sammie began to delve about the place, bent upon exploring the mysteries of this, to him, treasure trove. Holloway was adjusting the bridle when he heard a sound at the door. Turning he was surprised to see Jenn standing in the opening.

"Good morning, Jim," she said affably.

He nodded, then resumed his task.

She watched him in silence as he adjusted the bridle on Pinto, and this accomplished, he confronted her inquiringly.

"This is indeed a surprise," he remarked. "I certainly did not anticipate the pleasure of seeing you here."

"Is it a pleasure? Do you mean what you say?"

The thrust reached home, for he was well aware that her presence disconcerted him. He coughed and stammered a feeble reply.

"You are going somewhere?" she asked, ignoring his confusion.

"It looks like it, doesn't it?" he responded. Somehow, this strenuous woman who professed to love him, rendered him uncomfortable, and he desired to be rid of her as speedily as possible.

"You're not going to join the posse?"

He nodded affirmatively.

"You won't do that!" she went on, turning pale. "Don't do it, Jim. If anything should happen to you, it would break my heart!"

She approached him with outstretched arms, her eyes expressing earnest protest. As he observed her trepidation, he realized that she was a woman whose love might involve him in serious trouble if he failed to deal with her diplomatically, as one must handle high explosives, cautiously, or suffer annihilation.

"It is every man's duty to assist the work in which the posse is engaged," he said firmly. "Why try to change my mind, Jenn? It will be useless—"

"But I don't want you to join, Jim!" she persisted. "Suppose you were to be killed—"

"Killed!" he interrupted. "I hope to God I will be! It is because of that possibility that I am de-

termined to line up with the others against Valdez!
What have I to live for now?"

"Live for!" she echoed despairingly. "Why can't
you live for me, Jim? I love you—!"

"You know what they are saying of me, Jenn," he
returned, ignoring her avowal. "They say I'm a
white livered coward! I showed the yellow streak
last night and naturally I have been branded a quitter! Yet you say you love me! It is impossible!"

She grasped his arm and held him despite his effort
to release himself from her clutch. "It is not impossible, Jim!" she exclaimed passionately. "Let all
the world call you coward, but I, who know better,
will hail you always as a man among men! I know
you are brave, and that under the influence of drink
your real self failed to assert itself. Whatever you
may have done in the past, whatever your life's secret
may be—and I know you have concealed it for years,
I ask you to let me forgive the first and to share the
second with you!"

"Leave me, Jenn! For God's sake, leave me!"

He released himself from her grasp with a rough-
ness he might in other circumstances have regretted,
but stern and effective resistance to her plea was imperative. He was amazed at the vehemence of her
love and puzzled to account for it, inasmuch as he
had afforded her no encouragement, either by word or
deed, to lavish her affection upon him.

"You mustn't talk that way, Jenn," he went on
gently. "I'm unworthy the love of any woman, for
all who know me despise me as a creature beneath contempt."

"But I do not despise you, Jim," she faltered
brokenly. "No matter what you have been, or may
be now, you are worthy of me, and if you will say
the word, I will do all in my power to make you

happy! I know I can do it, for love can perform
wonders for a man who is loved as I love you!"

"God help me!" he responded sorrowfully. "I
can never love you, as a wife should be loved! Were
I to marry you, you would be the most miserable
woman on earth! I can't do it!"

She tried to take his hand again, but he thrust it
behind him beyond her reach. She sighed wearily,
for she felt her hope of happiness in the love of this
man, whom she desired for her mate, dying within
her, just as it had sprung up like a flower in full
bloom to gladden her soul.

"You distrust me, Jim," she answered sadly.
"You think that because I own and conduct the
Red Eye, I must naturally be a woman too low in
the social scale to be your wife."

"Not that, Jenn, but—"

"I know I am not what some prudish cats of women
would have me be," she resumed passionately, "but
I swear to you that I am an honest woman, and true
as steel! Never have I committed an act of which any
pure woman might be ashamed. Never but once has
the tongue of scandal, such as wags at times among
my women in the Red Eye, besmirched me and she
who was guilty of defaming me, had cause to rue it
for the remainder of her days! I was a good and
faithful wife until my husband's gallantries forced
me to divorce him. I repeat, that if you marry me,
I will be your mate in good times or ill! Can't you
see that I love you, and that your coldness will drive
me mad?"

He hung his head, powerless to voice an adequate
reply to this fervent avowal. With that intuitive
comprehension of human tendencies that comes to
strong women in great emergencies, Jenn began to suspect that another woman, perhaps, stood between the

man she loved and herself. Her knowledge of the dominating passions of men like Holloway, rendered it reasonably certain that he loved this woman. She began, therefore, to probe warily for the truth.

"You love some one else, Jim," she said calmly, though her blood was racing in her veins. "Why not admit it?"

He colored and the emotion he manifested told her that her random bolt had found its mark.

"A woman from Red Sandy Valley, perhaps?" she suggested, coldly.

Holloway frowned but made no answer.

"Marian Haines?"

He glared, anger rising up within him. "How dare you mention her name?" he said coldly. "By what right do you question me about her?"

"The right of any woman who loves to know her rival if she has one," she retorted with a laugh that jarred disagreeably.

"Rival!" he echoed vacuously.

"I guessed it, Jim!" she said after a pause. "I knew of your meeting with Miss Haines, and putting two and two together, I could not but feel that her tears had lashed you into loving her!"

"Stop!"

"She not only argued with you, but actually disarmed you—"

He clutched her shoulders with a force that made her wince. She laughed at his vehemence, as she felt her heart harden within her. Her unrequited love was slowly stifling her finer womanly traits, and she began to yield to that grosser self that mastered her at times despite all her resistance.

"Don't be a fool!" she sneered.

"Leave me, I say!"

"You love a woman who no doubt despises you,

and treat with contempt one who honestly loves you!''

He thrust her aside and leading Pinto by the bridle, left the stable, she following him as a faithful dog might have done.

''Well,'' she continued despairingly. ''If you can win her love, go to it! But remember this—you may regret this day and learn to your sorrow that there are women who know how to avenge themselves.''

Her voice broke and she left him abruptly. He watched her until she disappeared in the passage between the two buildings beyond, half expecting she would turn her head for a final glance. But she had given him her parting shot and if she had any such desire, she repressed it successfully until she had passed out of his sight.

''Hey!''

Holloway turned on his heel and perceived Sammie at the door of the stable, eying him curiously.

''What do you want, Sammie?''

''I seed you and her, Wolf.''

''What did you see, Kid?''

''She hugged you!''

''You little rascal!''

He rode into the main street, the child tottering after him with puckered face. Dismounting at Bert Mason's store, he threw the bridle rein over the top of a hitching post and entered the place. Mason lay stretched at full length on a counter, idly smoking a corncob pipe.

''Good morning, Mason,'' said Holloway genially.

''Mornin','' grunted the storekeeper, without as much as a glance at him.

''I want you to do me a favor, Mason.''

''Shoot.''

''I'm going to Red Sandy Valley on an important mission and may never return.''

Mason lifted his head at this. "Goin' to get Haines, I s'pose," he growled knowingly. "I heered about your notice at the Red Eye. You'd better take my tip and lay low on that game, Wolf. The posse ain't goin' to stand any sich nonsense from nobody!"

"That's my business, Mason!" retorted Holloway, frowning. "I presume Haines is able to take care of himself, and as for myself, I'm not asking for any advice of yours."

Mason chuckled. "I guess Haines is able to take keer of hisself, too," he returned significantly, "and as fur my advice—"

"I'm leaving Purple Canyon to-day for keeps," interrupted Holloway. "I have left a letter inclosed in an envelope addressed to you on my table upstairs. I ask you as a favor to mail it if you don't hear from me within four days. I also leave my suitcase in your charge with the request that you express it to the address you will find on the letter, if I fail to communicate with you within the stipulated time. Will you do this for me?"

The storekeeper growled his consent and Holloway left the store without another word. Mounting Pinto, he galloped down the street, gloomy and thoughtful. As he dashed by the Red Eye, a curtain in an upper window stirred slightly, and a woman's face—that of Jenn—appeared. She was bursting with jealous rage and there were traces of tears on her painted cheeks.

"Go your way, Jim," she muttered, "but take it from me that if I can't win you, no other woman shall! May you one day suffer as I do now!"

She clenched her hands until the nails of her carefully manicured fingers pierced her palms. Rage convulsed her and, dizzied by the force of her emotions, she dropped upon the bed. Happily, tears came to her relief and for several minutes she yielded to her bitter grief.

While Holloway was riding on and thinking of Marian, Jenn was formulating plans for revenge. She rose after a time, arrayed herself with care, and leaving the Red Eye, a sinister expression darkening her face, she set forth brazenly on her devil-born, sinister mission.

CHAPTER IX

THE VENGEANCE OF JENN

MARIAN and Rose were breakfasting at eight o'clock when Hawthorne, returning from Sheriff Thorne's office, entered the dining room. He greeted his pretty guest cheerfully and bestowed a perfunctory paternal kiss on his daughter's forehead.

"Been up long, girls?" he inquired, seating himself.

"Only an hour or so," responded Rose, pouring out a cup of coffee. "What got you out so early?"

"The Sheriff's posse, which has just left town."

The girls, who were ignorant of the happenings of the night and early morning, stared at him in surprise.

"By the way, Marian," he went on, "I have a message for you."

"For me?"

"Yes, from your brother."

She turned to him troubled, waiting for him to explain. Why should Ralph send her a message, and what was it? Until now she had believed him asleep in his room upstairs. In anticipation of their meeting, she had prepared with painstaking care the avowal she felt she must make. She asked herself with increasing fear whether Ralph's message might not prove the wretched precursor of intelligence concerning the tragedy she dreaded.

"What has happened to Ralph?" she inquired anxiously. "Is it serious?"

Hawthorne laughed lightly. "Nothing to worry over, I assure you. Your brother left for Red Sandy Valley with Belcher and 'Bird's-Eye' last night in advance of the posse which is to run to earth, capture or kill Valdez and his band of scoundrels! Your brother, on leaving, begged me to ask you to remain here until the trouble has blown over."

"Why no, I could not think of it!"

"I beg of you—"

"No, I could not remain in idleness here while he is risking his life battling with those bandits! I must return to the valley as soon as possible."

"Ridiculous, Marian!" snapped Rose deprecatingly. "What can you do in this emergency? You would only hamper your brother, my dear."

"Rose is right," remarked Hawthorne. "This is men's work and women should remain discreetly in the background until they have finished their task."

"But can't you see—"

"Take my advice," interrupted the banker, "and remain here until the valley has been cleared of this Mexican vermin!"

Marian sighingly resigned herself to the inevitable. "But Ralph had no right to leave without seeing me first. I wanted so much to talk about—"

She paused, the others watching her curiously. She wondered if they had learned of her adventure with the Wolf. If they had, neither manifested any knowledge of it, so that she felt reassured.

"You wished to discuss a subject of importance?" said Hawthorne. "Can I help you in any way? If so, command me."

"No, no!"

"I should be pleased to send my man to the valley with any message you may desire to forward, you know."

Marian replied that she would think the matter over, whereupon Hawthorne, having finished his breakfast, told of the formation of the posse, declaring with emphasis and enthusiasm that the day of Mexican outrages on the border was practically over. He confidently predicted that Valdez would be captured or killed before the expiration of forty-eight hours.

"The United States troops are on the watch," he said. "The recent raids, attended with spoliation of property and murder, have stirred the government to action as nothing heretofore has done. Uncle Sam is aroused and woe be to the scoundrels who dare invade this state, bent on pillage and the sacrifice of American lives! Summary action is imperative and Red Sandy Valley may yet prove the Waterloo of those who recognize no law save their own wills! Doggone their measly hides!"

He pounded the table with his clenched fist, making the dishes rattle. Having finished his exordium which, as far as Rose was concerned, through repetition lacked both originality and interest, he urged Marian to make his home her own and to have faith in the speedy return of her brother, fit as a fiddle!

"These greasers are a cowardly bunch!" he went on didactically. "They invariably refuse to show fight when they are confronted by a superior force. They're yellow, through and through, so you may be sure they'll cut and run when the posse appears. Therefore, I repeat, have no fear on your brother's account."

To Marian's relief, he hied himself off to his room for another brief snooze. Mrs. Hawthorne appearing at this juncture, Marian announced her intention to go riding for an hour. That the town was in the throes of unusual excitement was evidenced by the distant shouting of horsemen who galloped wildly along the streets. Marian saddled her pony, promising to return soon with the latest information and cantered away.

"Something happened to Marian last night, mother," said Rose meditatively. "I'm trying to fathom it, but cannot."

"What do you mean?"

"She acted so queerly when she returned home. I fancied she had been crying."

"That's not strange!" sniffed Mrs. Hawthorne. "Many girls have a habit of doing that."

"And too, she spoke of this man known as the Wolf, admiringly, and seemed profoundly interested in him."

"What do you gather from that?"

"It is possible they met—"

"Nonsense!" interrupted Mrs. Hawthorne. "She hadn't time, and besides, this is her first visit to Purple Canyon. It is impossible that she knows the Wolf. Were that true, her reputation would be shattered."

"That would be a mere trifle to a girl of Marian's temperament. Different minds, opposite viewpoints, you know."

Mrs. Hawthorne shrugged and became engrossed in a copy of an El Paso newspaper. Resolved to make inquiries in certain quarters regarding a matter concerning which she had just enough inkling to whet her desire for more accurate information, Rose sallied forth as eager to get at the facts, as ever a cub reporter on his maiden assignment.

Meanwhile Marian, after a prolonged canter on the Buffalo Wallow Road, returned to town. She enjoyed the refreshing breezes and glorious morning sunshine but she was quite unable to cast off the depression that blanketed her unusually volatile spirits. The

main street was aswarm with horsemen dashing
hither and thither in voluble excitement. All were
heavily armed and eager to join the second contingent
of the posse in process of formation in front of
Sheriff Thorne's office, where she dismounted. With
dignified solemnity, the Sheriff was swearing in as his
special deputies all volunteers who presented themselves, thereby vesting them with all the authority
and police power such a distinction confers.

"Good mornin', Miss Haines," said Thorne, tipping
his sombrero awkwardly as she approached. "Come
out to see the excitement, eh?"

She nodded, a gracious smile on her lips.

"Take it from me, we're going to teach Valdez a
trick or two that may be of value to him, always providing skunks like him can l'arn anything."

"I hope you will make the lesson a good one," she
responded. "If it can be administered without the
sacrifice of lives, so much the better."

"Pshaw! I'm afraid the critters will run without giving us a chance to get at them."

"You believe they will refuse to fight?"

"I sure do, Miss Haines. By the way, have you
seen the Wolf this morning?"

"The Wolf!"

The frigidity of her tone startled him. He became
confused and, coughing violently, averted his face.
She eyed him furtively, her heart beating a wild tat-
too in her bosom, for she was half convinced that he
had knowledge of her adventure with Holloway. If
her supposition was correct, then the affair was the
subject of general gossip. Her doubts urged her to
wrest the truth from him.

"Why do you ask?" she parried.

"Pardon me, I just did it without thinkin'."

"But what prompted your question?" she persisted.

"What can I have in common with that man? What should I know of his movements?"

"Ah, well, what's the use of talkin' ancient history to you now?"

"Ancient history!"

"You see, I came near lettin' the cat out the bag by tellin' you that everybody is talkin' about your pow-wow with the Wolf in front of the Red Eye."

"They're talking about it, you say?"

"Sure they are!"

"And they are condemning me, of course!" Her voice trembled, but she faced the Sheriff smilingly.

"Bless your heart!" exclaimed the official reassuringly. "They're praisin' you sky high!"

She leaned against an awning support breathing heavily. Her pallor alarmed the officer, who approached her with hands extended.

"Are you sick, Miss Haines? Want to go to the drug store yander?"

"No, no!" she replied, her hands upon her throbbing temples. "It is nothing, Mr. Thorne. I'm subject to these attacks. You say they are praising me?"

"They sure are. The only complaint I heard was that you didn't let him finish the job when he tried to kill himself."

"How dare they talk like that! As if I were capable of permitting such a thing."

"You'd'a'been a public benefactor if you had!" he chuckled, "'cause if you had, you'd have saved the people here the trouble of runnin' him out of town, or lynchin' him, which might be a durned sight better, p'raps."

"Is he still in town?" she asked eagerly.

"I hain't heard. Thar come more of the boys. Excuse me, please."

He saluted and left her to join a platoon of horsemen that had just halted in the roadway. Giving his instructions to the riders, the Sheriff mounted and the cavalcade started on its journey to the valley. When the posse disappeared, Marian entered the post office, hoping there might be letters for her from New York. The clerk informed her there was none and turning, she found herself face to face with a huge flashily dressed woman who barred her exit effectually.

"Miss Haines?" asked the newcomer coolly.

Marian nodded. She wondered who this massive creature could be. She studied her brazen face, her eyes red and swollen, her cheeks covered with rouge, her lips painted a fiery red. Marian turned from her in disgust.

"Got me sized up all right, eh?" sneered the stranger. "Would you like to have my photograph?"

"Pardon me, please, I'd like to pass."

"You haven't answered my question yet," returned the other sharply. "I asked you if you were Miss Haines. It's a fair question, I reckon, isn't it?"

"I am Miss Haines. And you—?"

"Mrs. Hemingway."

Marian stared. The name meant nothing to her.

"Of course," went on the woman, "I didn't expect you would recognize me by any name, since this is our introduction. If the title I handed you doesn't suit, suppose I give another?"

"Have you another?" inquired Marian. "Is it customary for women in Purple Canyon to have more than one name?"

"Don't get fresh, kiddo!" rejoined the virago insolently. "I'm not ashamed to let you know that they call me Faro Jenn in this burg!"

"Faro Jenn, keeper of the Red Eye?" She stared at her with mingled wonder and alarm.

"You've got me pat, my lady."

Marian ventured no reply. So this was the woman she knew by report as the keeper of the most notorious resort of the Southwest! A creature whose record was unclean, and a public reproach! What if some one were to see them conversing together—would they not be justified in condemning her out of hand? The prospect of discovery filled her with terror, and she searched wildly for some avenue of escape from the presence of this wanton. In her heart she prayed that the earth might open and swallow her like another Hemithea!

Jenn laughed.

"Guess my introduction didn't make a hit," she said. She read Marian's mind with singular keenness of perception, and she rather enjoyed the effect she had created.

"Let me pass!"

Jenn's manner changed instantly. "You'll stay here until I've finished with you!" she retorted angrily. "You and I are going to have a heart to heart talk, d'ye understand?"

"I refuse to talk to you!"

She sought to pass Jenn, who seized her by the arm with a force that made her wince.

"How dare you touch me!" she exclaimed angrily, seeking to free herself from Jenn's grasp. "Let go, or I shall scream for help!"

Jenn smiled conciliatingly, but she did not release her hold. "Don't be afraid, little one," she said. "Nobody's going to eat you! We're merely going to talk about some one you know—the Wolf!"

"I refuse—"

"It will be for the good of your brother. Let us

sit down on this bench. Don't fly off the handle, for
I aim to do you a service!''

She indicated a bench at one side of the room, and
by mere force of her dominating personality, she
forced Marian forward and both seated themselves.
Marian took care, however, to turn her face from the
street, thereby minimizing her chances of being recognized by chance acquaintances who might be passing
along the thoroughfare. With the exception of the
clerk who was industriously punching mail matter in
the rear, too absorbed in his work to pay them any
attention, they were alone.

An unwonted stillness prevailed. Early as it was,
the heat had suddenly become stifling to Marian, who
fanned herself vigorously with her handkerchief.
Jenn, however, seemed cool as marble.

"What have you to say to me?" Marian inquired
frigidly. "Please be brief, as my time is limited."

"I'll be brief, all right, miss," said Jenn, her white
even teeth showing finely between her parted lips.
"Do you know this man-killer, called the Wolf?"

Marian made no reply.

"Answer me!"

"This man is nothing to me—"

"You had a talk with him in front of the Red Eye
last night!" interrupted Jenn fiercely. "You can't
deny it!"

"What if I did? He announced publicly that he
purposed to kill my brother at sight! He wrote the
threat on a card and it was tacked to the front of the
Red Eye, where I saw it."

"Gave you a shock, didn't it?" chuckled Jenn.

"It alarmed me, and—" She paused, wondering
why she should discuss the topic with this worthless
termagant who watched and played with her as a
cat toys with a mouse.

"Foolish girl! Did you hope to save your brother's life by pleading with the Wolf in public?"

Marian's lips quivered. "I confess I don't know," she admitted, her eyes downcast. "That is why I am searching for him now."

"You're a trifle late—he left town this morning."

Marian sprang up in alarm. "Left town!" she gasped. "Where has he gone?" What if he had ridden away in search of her brother? The possibility that this supposition might be correct, sickened her.

"You know why he left, don't you?" asked Jenn significantly.

"I can only guess!"

"He swore to kill your brother at sight. Since your brother left for the valley last night and the Wolf this morning, several hours later, the inference is plain."

Marian's face blanched at this apparent confirmation of her suspicion.

"You mean—that he intends to kill my brother after all?" she asked tremulously.

"Any fool ought to be able to answer that!"

"He dare not commit this crime! The posse would lynch him if he tried!"

"Nix on the posse stuff!" scoffed Jenn, rejoicing that the seed of distrust she had planted in the girl's soul was bearing fruit. "What does a man like the Wolf care for a posse when he is bent on vengeance? He is absolutely without fear."

"How can I save my brother?"

"You want me to tell you, kiddo?"

"I will tell Sheriff Thorne!" said Marian eagerly. "He will save Ralph!"

"You ninny!" whispered Jenn deprecatingly. "The Sheriff left town a few minutes ago as you know."

Marian clasped her hands sobbingly. "I had forgotten! What shall I do? Please advise me!"

Jenn nodded approvingly. "If I were you, I'd ride to the valley and try to head him off."

"Yes, yes!"

"If I failed in that, and was unable to reach my brother, I would tell Seth Lucas, one of the leaders of the posse, and cause him to hang the Wolf on general principles!"

Marian hid her face in her hands.

"If you don't do as I say," Jenn whispered, "the Wolf will kill your brother without mercy as he has sworn to do!"

"He dare not—he shall not!"

Marian rose, a look of resolution on her face. Jenn had lied with such consummate artistry that the girl was firmly convinced she spoke the truth. She reeled at the thought of Ralph being shot down, unsuspecting of danger; and she upbraided herself bitterly for interfering when the Wolf sought to slay himself. What folly! And now the Wolf, no longer in leash, was on her brother's trail, bent on blood-vengeance!

"It's up to you, girl," said Jenn. "If you don't prevent it, nobody else will.

"I shall ride to the valley!" said Marian, going to the door. "I thank you for the suggestion. Good-by!"

She left the post office hastily, Jenn following her to the door. The girl sprang into the saddle, and applying her quirt with a vigor that surprised her pony, galloped down the street. Jenn signaled to a young Mexican who was smoking a cigarette as he lounged in the shade of the awning. He advanced towards her, she meeting him half way.

"You saw her, Lopez?" she whispered, pointing to Marian, now enveloped in dust.

"*Si, Señora.*"

"She is on her way to the valley to find her brother."

"*Si, Señora.*"

"They must not meet," said Jenn fiercely. "Do you understand?"

"*Si, Señora.*"

"Get in touch with Valdez and Pedro, who are at Sweetwater, and notify them. They will do the rest. You get me?"

"I getta you, *Señora,*" grinned Lopez, holding out a filthy hand, palm upward. "But you must pay good—a hundred pesos!"

"You dirty grafter!" snarled Jenn, thrusting his hand away. "I'm onto your rotten game!"

"No, no! No graft—only pay for what I earn! Valdez no give me not'in' 'cept cuss words—*Carramba!* W'at I do?"

Jenn took a roll of bills from her belt, Lopez eying it avidly. She counted out fifty dollars and grudgingly handed the currency to him.

"If you work this scheme right, I'll give you fifty more!"

"*Gracias!*"

The Mexican mounted his pony and was off like a shot on Marian's trail. Jenn's dark eyes blazed with a light which would have alarmed her intimates had they observed it. Her brain seemed on fire and her temples throbbed, but she was scarcely conscious of physical distress.

"Your punishment has begun, Jim Holloway!" she mused. "The girl you love will be the instrument of your downfall. How sweet is my revenge! When you turned me down you forgot that hell hath no fury like a woman scorned! I told you you would regret it, and since I cannot win you, let the devil care for his own!''

She entered the Red Eye at the moment when Rose Hawthorne emerged from Bert Mason's store, a bundle of purchases in her arms. She plainly was agitated as she ran up the street to the Purple Canyon Bank where her father, seated in his little glass partitioned office, was laboring over a bulky financial report.

''Hello!'' he ejaculated, as she dropped breathlessly into an upholstered chair opposite him. ''What's happened?''

''I knew I was right about Marian, after all!''

''Don't be enigmatical, Rose!''

''Marian Haines made a spectacle of herself in front of the Red Eye last night!''

''Good gracious! How was that?''

With virtuous indignation she retailed the facts of Marian's meeting with the Wolf as supplied to her with characteristic embellishments by Mrs. Mason. Woman-like, Rose did not fail to take advantage of the opportunity to enhance her recital by deft touches of her own, so that when she had finished, the banker was constrained to regard Marian's conduct as rather indiscreet, to say the least.

''I'm sorry,'' he remarked regretfully. ''People are apt to place a wrong construction upon the affair.''

''What shall we say to the neighbors when they hear of this as they are certain to do?''

''We must protect her to the best of our ability. Durn me, I rather admire her for her grit!''

''Why not take her for a visit to Mrs. Smith's at Buffalo Wallow?'' suggested Rose. ''We can remain there for a week or two.''

"Do as you like. Run along, child, for I'm a busy man to-day."

Rose went home, but Marian had not returned. She waited an hour, and wondering what had become of the girl, walked to Mason's store. A young man riding a lame pony dismounted in the street as she approached.

"Why, Harry Anderson!" she said warmly. "Where have you been?"

"Out with the posse," returned Harry, smiling. "My pony went lame and I was forced to return for another mount."

She asked him if he had by any chance met Marian Haines en route. His answer was in the affirmative.

"She's ten miles on her way to the valley by now, I reckon," he said, "and she's lashing her pony like fury every step of the way."

"Did you speak to her?"

"Nope, didn't have time." He leaned towards her and whispered. "But that isn't all, Rose."

She stared at him pop-eyed.

"I met the Wolf two miles ahead of her," he said. "I didn't pay much attention to the matter until I remembered what Sam Smith told me about Miss Haines' argument with the Wolf at the Red Eye last night. Did you hear about that?"

Rose gasped and left him without replying. To her mind, there was only one explanation that would account for Marian's conduct—she loved the Wolf! Had she not left Purple Canyon on his trail? An accident? Oh, no! What was her own duty? She wanted to save Marian from herself, but how was this to be accomplished? She tortured her brain but as she evolved no tangible plan of relief she sighingly relinquished the effort.

It was written that she should not see Marian for

many a day, and that during the interval the tides of the lives of many were to run at the full, a period pregnant with happenings of amazing import to the players in this drama of human temperaments and passion, the scenes of which were hourly unfolding with ever increasing dramatic force.

CHAPTER X

HANK WESTON, DETECTIVE

DELAYED by floods of exceptional severity, the Empire State Express pulled into Grand Central Station two hours late. The city of New York was being drenched by a rain of almost tropical fury, so that the streets contiguous to the great railroad terminal, usually crowded with pedestrians and commuters on their way home in the suburbs, were comparatively deserted.

The taxicab drivers and street car men were extraordinarily busy however, so that Forty-second Street, from Fifth Avenue, the liveliest thoroughfare in the world, as far east as Lexington Avenue, was in a state of congestion unusual even for Manhattan, whose vehicular traffic is not exceeded in proportions by London or Paris, or any other metropolis on the globe.

Among the passengers who left the train and filed slowly through the iron gates into the great, high-ceilinged concourse, was a rather undersized man of about forty years, swarthy, wiry and exceedingly alert of manner. He wore a broad brimmed gray hat, the crown dented after the fashion affected by military men and cowpunchers in the West, and he carried a heavy suitcase of tanned cowhide, the ends and sides of which were badly chafed. From the corner of his firm mouth, jutting out belligerently beneath a draggly sandy mustache, the charred stub of a cheroot protruded.

114

The little man glanced about inquiringly as he made his way with difficulty toward the circular information booth, around which were two score or more men and women. He set down his suitcase and, taking out his metal watch, observed that it was eight o'clock. He drew a match from his vest pocket and lit his cheroot, then flecked some dust from his light gray suit, baggy at the knees, and considerably the worse for the wear.

He scanned the faces of those who hurried past him, as if he expected to meet some belated acquaintance. He surveyed the scene with interest for several minutes, then, apparently having reached the conclusion that his vigil was useless, picked up his suitcase and started briskly up the incline leading to the Forty-second Street exit.

"Guess Peterson didn't git my wire," he mused. "Mought as well go to a hash house an' git some supper, 'cause I sure am hungry as a catamount arter a week's starvation. Hullo! What the deuce—"

The exclamation was due to the fact that a man, who, while closing an obstinate umbrella as he ran, had collided with him, nearly knocking him off his feet. The stranger apologized for his unintentional rudeness.

"Pardon me, sir," he said courteously. "I was hurrying to meet a man from the West and slipped against you. I didn't hurt you, I hope?"

The little man dropped his suitcase and grinned. "Hurt me, eh?" he returned, good naturedly. "You'd have to go some to do that, I reckon. Got a match about ye?"

"Certainly."

The stranger handed him a match and scanned the little man curiously as he relit his cheroot.

"Are you a westerner, sir?" he asked.

"I reckon so, if the Southwest will do as well."

"You're Hank Weston!"

"Gee whiz!" grinned Hank, blowing a series of rings from beneath his mustache. "How d'ye guess it, stranger? Who be you. Peterson?"

"No, I'm Williams, Peterson's chief clerk. He sent me to meet a small man, swarthy, big hat, mustache—"

"You got me pat, Williams! Then Peterson got the wire I sent him at Albany?"

"Yes."

"Wall, here I be. What's the next move in this game?"

"We are to meet Mr. Peterson at the Astor where you will have dinner, after which he is to conduct you to Mr. Holloway's residence."

"Ke-rect!" exclaimed Hank. "Dinner sounds good to me! Do they sarve pork and beans at that boardin' house?"

Williams smiled. "I fancy you can get almost anything in the line of eats you may ask for at the Astor, Mr. Weston. Let's hail a taxi and get a move on."

"You sure don't rile me talkin' that 'ere way."

They passed through the crowded entrance with difficulty and Williams hailed a taxi. Ten minutes later they were at the Astor, the foyer swarming with its cosmopolitan parade of citizens of wealth, nationally famous politicians, and visitors of prominence from all parts of the country. There was present also the contingent of loungers one encounters in the lobbies of celebrated hostelries, all eager to form a part of the brilliant spectacle. A porter seized Hank's suitcase and led him to the desk where he registered in bold uneven script the name, "Hank Weston, El Paso, Tex." When he had finished this somewhat laborious task, Williams introduced him to a tall thin man of some forty years who had meanwhile joined them.

"This is Mr. Peterson," said Williams. "Mr. Peterson, Hank Weston."

"I'm delighted to meet you, Mr. Weston," said Peterson as they shook hands.

"I sure am tickled, as the b'ar said when the jack rabbit ran his way. Got a match?"

The article was supplied and while Hank was lighting the remnant of his cheroot, Peterson said that Mr. Holloway was anxious to see him as soon as possible. He suggested that Hank go to his room for a change of clothing after which they would have dinner in the grill.

"Bein' as how I've got only the clothes I've on my back," replied Hank, "I'll manage to make out with 'em. What are them chaps in swallow tails doing thar? Goin' to a dance?"

"They're hurrying to a banquet to some governor or other in the grand ball room," laughed Peterson. "Don't let the subject of clothes worry you, Mr. Weston."

"Gee whiz! Don't Weston me! My name's Hank!"

"All right, Hank."

"That makes me feel to hum."

The westerner went to his room on the ninth floor, where he washed, shaved and brushed his clothes. A few minutes later, he rejoined Peterson and they adjourned to the grill. The diners were too busy, happily, to pay attention to Hank and while Peterson discussed a porterhouse steak of ample dimensions, Hank enjoyed a double order of Boston baked pork and beans which, to his infinite satisfaction, was included in the menu.

"I sure will recommend this hash house to Bill Haskins when I git back to El Paso," remarked Hank, lighting a fresh cheroot. "This is some eatin' dump, all right!"

Peterson grinned and they left the hotel to enter another taxi. On their way to Riverside Drive in the seventies, where the stately residence of Charles Holloway, multi-millionaire railroad magnate occupied a commanding position overlooking the Hudson, Peterson gave Hank some useful information regarding the man they were to meet.

"Mr. Holloway is a man of many moods, hot-tempered, but kind at heart," said he. "He has many excellent qualities despite his apparent coldness. You've all the facts regarding his son, I presume?"

"Surest thing you know," replied Hank. "Doggone this segar! Got a match?"

"Certainly."

"Let me tell ye somethin'," remarked Hank confidentially, after he had relighted his obstinate cheroot. "Jim Holloway ain't wayward a bit—only wild as a yearlin' colt. His only fault is boozin'. Git him to stop that an' there ain't a finer chap to be found anywhar!"

"I hope you're right, Hank. His mother, poor soul, is worrying herself sick about him. Hello, what's up now?"

The taxi came to a standstill abruptly, a rear tire having blown out with a wheezy report. The chauffeur drew up at the curb with the announcement that he could proceed no further. The rain was still pouring in torrents and Peterson begged the driver to hail the first vehicle that came their way. Traffic was light and, vastly annoyed at the delay, the two men leaned back in their seat to make the best of their situation.

Meanwhile, Charles Holloway, fifty-two years old, slightly bald, tall, thin, but of vigorous physique, was

seated in his study poring over a document which
had been forwarded to him during the afternoon, but
which he had not found time until now to read. The
room was spacious, richly furnished and its tapestries,
of the period of Louis XI, its Oriental rugs, paintings and bric-a-brac, evidenced cultured taste in selec-
tion as well as the possession of unlimited wealth.
That Charles Holloway, celebrated financier and railroad builder, was a brainy man, even his most bitter
enemy, of whom, it must be admitted, he had many,
was willing to concede.

Although a man of genial temperament, Mr. Holloway's smooth shaved face with its prognathous jaw,
seemed perpetually to wear a frown. His dark eyes,
often of so stern an expression that his subordinates
were overawed, beamed with affability when he was
in the company of friends. Possessing all the wealth
that man can crave, with the enormous power that immense capital confers, and moving in high society,
his life nevertheless was embittered by the obsessing
fear that his son, Jim, whom he had not seen for three
years, might in some drunken frenzy commit an act
which would not only disgrace the family name of
which the magnate was justly proud, but break his
mother's heart.

He had watched his son's course vigilantly for
years, and when he returned home one night to find
the boy in a state of bestial intoxication, he sustained
a shock from which he had not recovered for many
a day. While he sought for a reasonable excuse for
his son's weakness, he remembered with sadness that
his own father, a blacksmith, with whom he had swung
a heavy sledge for years, often without wages, had
been a hopeless sot, so that in the little village in In-
diana where the Holloways lived, the name of Jim's
grandfather was publicly proclaimed by temperance

orators as a horrible example of the blighting effects of drink.

When his father died a victim of delirium tremens, leaving his orphaned son penniless, young Holloway was glad to leave his home town to seek his fortune in New York, where, within a few years he had risen from a clerkship in a railroad office to an executive position of power with a transcontinental railroad corporation, advancing by successive stages to the presidency of the greatest institution of its kind in the world.

Resourceful, aggressive, having initiative and faith in himself, Holloway dominated every business affair with which he was identified, so that his wealth, influence and prestige grew by leaps and bounds. He had married at twenty-five, while he was still filling a subordinate position, the daughter of a transportation official, whose name was the open sesame to social circles of prominence. In due course, their union was blessed by the advent of a bouncing boy who was christened James for his grandfather.

When Jim was a lad in knickerbockers, the father observed with alarm that he was inordinately fond of wine which often was served at the family table. He caught Jim rummaging in the pantry one day, only to make the discovery that the boy had been periodically drinking brandy, of which there was an ample store in the house. Holloway caused the liquor to be placed under lock and key, but as Jim grew older, the boy found means somehow to indulge his taste for alcoholic stimulants. Butler after butler was engaged and summarily dismissed when Holloway learned that they had yielded to the boy's entreaties and supplied him with the liquor he craved.

Aside from this weakness, the anxious father rejoiced that Jim was an admirable chap with lofty

ideals, and that properly reared to safe dependable
manhood, his future might be brilliant and filled with
achievement. Brave, truthful and generous to a
fault, Jim early developed those qualities which are
the manifestations of noble natures, and which,
rightly directed, make men great in any field of en-
deavor. The boy was almost fanatical in his love for
the Holloway household pets, of which there were
many in the city and country homes of the magnate.

Jim prized as above rubies a bull dog of ferocious
aspect, yet gentle as a lamb; he idolized a scraggy
Airedale, romped incessantly with a Russian wolf-
hound, and every cat for miles around, whether it had
a pedigree printed in gold letters on a blue satin ribbon, or had been raised in an alley ash barrel, knew
and loved him for his kindnesses. He permitted no
one to punish his pets, he reserving that privilege for
himself alone; and this unaccountable tendency provoked many a quarrel with boys of his own age in the
neighborhood, not to speak of sundry tramps, with
consequent fistic battles from which he usually
emerged the victor, though not without an occasional
black eye or bloody nose, of which punishments he was
extraordinarily proud.

Jim Holloway had two natures, antipodal as the
poles. He was even-tempered and difficult to rouse
to anger, but when he had drunk a surreptitious cock-
tail, he became aggressive, irritable and belligerent.
His father had observed this tendency with solicitude
on several occasions, and he remembered sadly that
his own father had had identically the same charac-
teristics. Meeting an expert alienist one day, he presented Jim's case to that celebrity in the form of a
hypothetical question, taking care to hide his personal feeling in the matter under the guise of interest
in the subject of hereditary influence.

The specialist, without suspecting the identity of the person involved, unhesitatingly asserted that Jim's taste for liquor had been inherited from some bibulous ancestor, and that owing to this fatal circumstance, his cure was extremely difficult, if not impossible. Thus Holloway came to the realization that Jim was not to be rescued except by a miracle, and by what means was this to be accomplished? His own helplessness caused him many a pang, and as the years passed and Jim grew to sturdy manhood, his bitterness increased; and his soul was tormented by cruel and depressing dreams which at times drove him to the verge of despair.

One day, when Jim was in his final year at Harvard, the faculty notified Mr. Holloway that if his son did not mend his ways, they would be compelled to expel him. The father lectured Jim sharply and finally succeeded in awakening him to a full sense of his duties to his family and to himself. When he told Jim that his intemperate habits were slowly breaking his mother's heart, the young man swore that no other spur to his reformation was required. He kept his word, abstained from drink, and graduated with high honors. He wrote a thesis in Spanish which his professor warmly praised for its linguistic purity, and he spoke and wrote French and Italian with equal fluency.

For several months after his graduation, Jim sedulously eschewed the club where he was wont to meet with his alumni to discuss football and kindred college sports, and to make merry with them on special occasions. Fond of pottery, he thought of engaging in that work and to that end went to Japan where he remained for a year dabbling in bekkoware. Thence he went to Italy and Spain and finally to Paris where he interested himself in sculpture. Although he devoted much of his spare time to the Latin Quarter and was recognized as a boulevardier, gay and debonair, he never drank intoxicants. On his return home he told his mother that the craving for liquor that threatened to wreck his life had been eradicated.

Then came the fatal day when, having been severely bruised in a boxing match at the club jinks, a physician prescribed for him a glass of brandy. The liquor, coursing through his veins like fire, awakened the old dormant desire for more, which he had believed extinct. He yielded ingloriously. He went home repeatedly when drunk, to receive the upbraidings of his angered father and the tearful pleas of his mother. He took a bachelor apartment in a hotel downtown, but while he thus escaped the vigilant eyes of his parents, he fully realized his own utter worthlessness, irresponsibility and lack of will power. The knowledge saddened him so that once or twice he meditated suicide.

He believed that a change of locale—a new environment in which he might live, inconspicuously and unknown, offered him a reasonable chance to reform— to cast off this incubus that was shattering his career. So one day he disappeared and his parents did not hear from him for many months. After a prolonged period of suffering, Mrs. Holloway received a letter from him informing her that he was making a man of himself in the great spaces of the Southwest, and that when his reformation was established on an enduring foundation, he would return home to convince the "governor" and herself that he was a son of whom they might well be proud.

Doubting the sincerity of these periodical assurances of ultimate regeneration, Holloway ordered the chief of the detective department of his own railroad in the Southwest to trace his son, if possible. Then to his horror, he learned that Jim had won the reputation of a beast—that he bore the soubriquet of "The Wolf"! How he despised this rowdyish appellation, so characteristic of the brazen West. Hank Weston, one of the most trustworthy operatives of the corporation's intelligence department, had been recommended as the man best qualified to trace the boy without rousing his suspicions that he was being shadowed. He therefore directed that Weston be sent out on Jim's trail and that he remain thereon until further orders.

To the end that his connection with this espionage might not be suspected, or the facts come to the knowledge of certain newspaper editors in New York who were doing their utmost to solve the mystery of Jim Holloway's disappearance, he caused all communications to be addressed to him in care of Peterson's Detective Agency, and reports of Weston's activities were regularly received by him through that channel. Then came the day when Mr. Holloway desired to hear Hank's story at first hand, so he caused him to be sent East. Peterson had telephoned him during the afternoon that, barring accidents, Hank would arrive in New York at eight o'clock or thereabouts that evening. The magnate had ordered Peterson to meet Hank at the station and escort him to the Holloway residence.

Anxious to familiarize himself with the record of the man whose verbal report was to stimulate or shatter his faith in the ultimate regeneration of his son, Mr. Holloway picked up a typewritten report, leaned back in his chair, and read the following concisely written data:

Hank Weston, Detective, W. C. R. R.—About forty years old, born El Paso, Tex. Spent early years on Texas ranch, then served as Texas Ranger, making excellent record for daring and bravery. Made reputation as Indian fighter in campaigns against the Apaches. Clever marksman with rifle and revolver and throws knife unerringly as a Mexican. Kind, genial temperament, but a devil in boots when aroused. Attacked by three Mexican rustlers and killed them all without receiving a scratch. Became a detective in the employ of the W.C.R.R. two years ago and has done highly efficient work ever since. He trailed and killed "Baldy" Simpson, leader of notorious train robber band, arrested four of the gang single handed and brought them twelve miles across the desert to Butler. Was severely wounded in encounter with express thieves led by Jack Stanton, whom he shot dead after fatally wounding two of his men, and later drove the remaining two members of the band to cover. Has made numerous important arrests of mail and freight thieves, frequently bagging criminals with long Eastern crime records. Married and has three children. Character excellent. Doesn't drink, but is fond of cheroots. Quiet and shows excitement only when hungry. As cowboy detective he has no superior. Invariably cool and collected, especially when in danger, gritty, patient and persistent, never giving up once he sets out to do a thing. A good friend, but extremely deadly as an enemy. A devout Methodist, and when at home, teaches a class in Sunday School. Has had little education, but knows more than the average man. Language and mannerisms distinctively Western. Wm. Haskins, Supt. Detectives, Western Consolidated Rail Road.

The financier smiled as he read this naïve document. He made a mental picture of Hank, so that he might test his powers of ratiocination. He was engaged at this task when a noise at the door attracted his attention. Turning, he beheld Thompson, his butler, standing at dignified attention.

"What is it, Thompson?"

"Two gentlemen to see you, sir."

"Send them up."

The butler disappeared, returning almost instantly with the visitors, whom he announced with characteristic dignity.

"Mr. Peterson and Mr. Weston, sir."

"Come in, gentlemen," said Mr. Holloway, surveying Hank with interest. "I'm especially pleased to have a chat with you, Mr. Weston."

They shook hands. In the presence of the famous financier of whom he had heard so much, Hank was plainly ill at ease.

"I'd feel better, Mr. Holloway, if yuh'd call me Hank for short," he said. "It fits me better, ef yuh don't mind."

"All right, Hank," laughed Mr. Holloway, whose fingers were numbed by the heartiness of the westerner's grip. "Be seated, and you, likewise, Mr. Peterson."

The visitors seated themselves in chairs pushed towards them by Thompson, who at a sgnal placed a combination mahogany and glass cigar case and ash receiver between them. The butler produced a box of Havanas and offered the weeds to Hank, who shook his head negatively.

"Ef yuh don't mind, Mr. Holloway," he said, drawing a cheroot from his vest pocket, "I'd ruther smoke this, 'cause I have 'em made specially fur me to hum, yuh know."

"You're at liberty to smoke whatever brand you like best, Hank," laughed the magnate, lighting a Havana. He began to like this diminutive man, every inch of whom radiated energy and good nature. He watched him smilingly as he lit his cheroot and, almost lost to view in the great upholstered easy chair in which he sat, sent clouds of smoke towards the ceiling, in apparent contentment.

"You have a story to tell me about my son?" said Mr. Holloway interrogatively, leaning forward.

"I reckon I hev, sir."

"Is there anything to his discredit—that is, anything of which his mother or I might be ashamed, in the story you are to tell?"

Hank drew his cheroot from his mouth, glanced at the ash, then eyed Mr. Holloway reassuringly.

"Nary a thing!" he replied vehemently. "I swear this by my faith in the resurrection!"

Mr. Holloway beckoned to Thompson who advanced hurriedly.

"Thompson, ask Mrs. Holloway to join me here, as I have important news for her."

"Yes, sir."

The butler vanished like a wisp of smoke and ten seconds later, Mrs. Holloway, charmingly attired, her rich house gown accentuating her matronly beauty, still in evidence despite her forty-eight years, entered the room. The three men rose at her entrance and when her husband introduced Hank with the announcement that he had news of Jim, she shook his hand cordially.

"How good of you to come, Mr. Weston!" she exclaimed warmly. "I'm sure you bring me good tidings of my son!"

"I reckon so, ma'am."

He felt nervous in the presence of this woman, and fervently hoped he might not commit some inexcusable *faux pas* that might shock her or render himself ridiculous.

"You have the floor, Hank," said Mr. Holloway genially.

Mrs. Holloway seated herself near her husband. She smiled wistfully at Hank, and even her stern husband beamed with anticipatory happiness at the thought that now, for the first time in three years, his wife and he were to receive at first hand news of their only son for whose welfare and happiness they unceasingly prayed.

CHAPTER XI

THE TRAIL OF THE WOLF

PAINFULLY aware that all eyes were upon him, Hank wished himself a thousand miles away from this opulent home, as well as from this powerful financier and his demure wife who awaited his revelations with beating hearts. That they wanted to hear the truth he well knew, and, happily, the truth was in the boy's favor, as his investigation of the facts had amply proved. Barring Jim's one besetting vice, there was little of consequence to reproach him with.

"I ain't much at yarnin'," he said apologetically, "so ef ye don't mind I'll tell my story in my own way, an' we'll git along famous."

The financier nodded approvingly while Mrs. Holloway smiled her encouragement. Leaning back in his chair and slyly secreting his half-smoked cheroot in a side pocket of his coat, he closed his eyes meditatively.

"To begin with," drawled Hank, "when I got orders from Bill Haskins, the chief of the Intelligence Department, to trail the Wolf, who wus last heerd from in Death Valley, I cal'lated that as he wus a cowpuncher or desert rat, my best bet would be to be a puncher too. So I togged up as a cowboy, with a big brown sombrero, blue shirt, bandana handkerchief, chaps made of sheepskin, gun and everythin' else that was needful, an' started hotfoot up the road fur the valley. I dropped my real name and floated

129

around among the punchers as the 'Texas Kid,' the
which, I bein' only knee high to a duck, I didn't belie
the title. 'Sides, I wus sartin I couldn't make no
headway no other way.''

"Quite right, Hank," said Mr. Holloway, as the
westerner paused. "I admire your judgment—"

"When I got to Death Valley," interrupted Hank,
ignoring the remark, "I l'arned that the Wolf had
left a trail miles wide and plain as day behind him,
so's a blind Injun could hev followed it. From what
I could hear, Jim had went thar six months before,
some sayin' he had been awhile in Californy whar he
had a rumpus with a Digger Injun, the which he wus
fo'ced to perforate most fatal, arter the savage had
went gunnin' fur his hide.

"So I up and travel to the Siskiyous in Californy
fur to get the facts. I seed the Sheriff who was interested in the killin', not to speak of the Coroner
who buried the Injun carcass. They both assured me
Jim, or rather the Wolf, done the shootin' in self-defense, he bein' badly wounded in the melee fust.
Nobody knowed his name, 'ceptin' he wus called the
Wolf, so when he leaves the hospital, he jest drops
out o' sight, leavin' o'ny his reppytation fur the gos-
sips to talk about. The which, I take it, warn't to his
discredit nohow.''

"I'm so grateful for that!" murmured Mrs. Holloway, smiling wanly.

"When I begin my hike out o' Californy," resumed Hank, "I traces Jim to Frisco, then to the ile
fields near Bakersfield, whar he worked steady like
fur a month or so. He finally gits tired o' the smell
o' the ile, I reckon, and hikes to Death Valley, the
which, believe me, is some hard hole fur any white
man, not even 'ceptin' Jim Holloway, to live in.
Thar he goes cahoots with Sam Bloomer, a desert rat,

on a prospectin' trip, but arter several weeks o' sizzlin' and findin' nothin' wuth talkin' about, Jim makes fur the Rio Grande country to punch cows, the which is as near bein' his native element as water is to a fish.

"I gets next to Bloomer and pumps him regardless. He tells me Jim is the finest chap as ever he see, an' that he never drunk a drop o' anything stronger'n milk while he wus in the valley. Fur sartin, he had a scrap or two, fur he wouldn't be Jim Holloway ef he hadn't, the which mostly wus fo'ced on him 'thout him bein' willin'. Once he whipped three greasers fur sayin' sartin uncivil things 'bout American women, an' ag'in, he belted a loafer on the snoot fur kickin' Bloomer's bull pup, arter bein' warned sufficient. It sure is a fact that Jim didn't live up to his reppytation of Wolf while he wus in the valley, and everybody as I talked to said he wus the finest, manliest, truest, kindest, grittiest and most generous chap as they had seen anywhar this side o' purgatory."

"Poor Jim!" whispered Mrs. Holloway to her husband who glanced at her lovingly. There was an expression of pride on his face; and he began to regard this philosophical little man with kindly affection.

"And after that?" he suggested, relighting his cigar.

"I traced him to a town called Los Vinos, in Sonora, Mexico. He was punchin' cows fur a rancher named Alicante, a rich Mexican. I met him in a dirty inn the fust night I got thar and introduced myself as the 'Texas Kid,' a fellow puncher from the States. Jim was drinkin' consid'able heavy, an' while I wus tryin' to convince him that the average Mexican booze wus real pizen to a white man with a respectable stomach, one of the greasers present up an' says something disrespect'ful o' Jim in particular and Americans several an' collective.

"Jim don't wait to argue the p'int, but lands on the greaser's jaw with his right, like a mule kickin' a bar'el, sendin' him to the mat same's he wus hit by a fallin' house. He is about to cave in the Mexican's slats when I interferes in the interests of peace an' harmony. A mob o' the bandit's friends run up hell bent fur breakfast—excuse me, Mrs. Holloway, my tongue stampedes regardless when I think o' that scrap—but me and Jim stand the bunch off with a brave show o' our gats—"

"Gats?" interrupted Mrs. Holloway eagerly. "What are gats?"

"Jest guns—revolvers," responded Hank politely. "Wall, I tells Jim shootin' would be foolish, seein' as we is surrounded with no chance to make our getaway, 'thout bein' measured fur coffins, the which I didn't hanker fur, on account o' the wife an' kids in Texas. So I tells Jim, who ain't no slouch at slingin' Spanish by the way, to leave the palaverin' to me, an' I talks Mex like I wus a perfessor. Pretty soon I has the bunch on their knees afore me an 'stead o' knifin' us, they hauled us afore the Alcalde who fined Jim fifty pesos fur disorderly conduct, the which I paid instanter to keep him out o' their lousy jail."

"Excellently done, Hank!" interposed Mr. Holloway. "We owe you much for your management of that affair!"

" 'Twan't nothin' wuth talkin' about, I assure yuh, Mr. Holloway. It's part o' the game we play in the Southwest. When I managed to sober Jim up, I induces him to leave Mexico with me, the which country bein' no fit place fur a gent to live in 'thout degrading hisself consid'able an' takin' chances on havin' his throat cut any blessed minute! So we go to El Paso,

aimin' fur the Panhandle whar I hoped to git a job
fur Jim with a teetotaler cowman I knew, beyant the
head of the Clear Fork o' the Brazos. I leaves him
at our boardin' house to report progress at headquarters, an' when I gits back, I find Jim has flew
the coop, 'thout sayin' whar he wus goin' or when
he'd git back, an' believe me, knowin' El Paso as I
do, I wa'n't in no special good humor nuther.

"O' co'se, I starts investigatin' instanter. I have
some consid'able tough time to locate Jim, but arter
an hour's diggin' in the wust Mexican joints I knowed
about, I finally diskiver that he has hit the booze
heavy in Mexican Pete's rum emporium, the which is
o'ny another name fur Hell's ante room. I also
l'arns he has a talkfest with some greaser bandits, an'
when I gits a description o' the chaps he gets mixed
up with, I recognize Valdez, a genuine bandit, and
Pedro, his assistant, two o' the durndest cutthroats
God ever let loose on a unsuspectin' community. Jim
all but kills the skunks in the scrimmage he has with
'em, both bein' manhandled sufficient to lay 'em up
fur a week fur repairs and then some.

"I waits fur Jim to return to the boardin' house,
but he fails to show up. I s'arch most diligent fur a
week and pretty soon, the station agent at Butler
wires me in code that a chap known as the Wolf has
turned up at Purple Canyon, near Buffalo Wallow
mines, and is hittin' it up hard 'cordin' to report,
in Faro Jenn's dance hall. I travels thar instanter,
an' on my way as I is passin' through Red Sandy
Valley, I get wise to the fact that he had trouble with
Ralph Haines, who runs the Circle N Ranch. It
'pears Jim had ast Haines fur a job—"

"Pardon me," interrupted Holloway, "the name
you mention is familiar to me. Is Haines from New
York?"

"That's my understandin', sir. His father was a stockbroker who went broke tryin' to corner copper."

"Ah, my old friend, John P. Haines! I warned him to go slow, but he took the bit between his teeth and was crushed."

"And after Mr. Haines died," supplemented Mrs. Holloway, "his son Ralph went to the Southwest and his sister, Marian, a charming girl, as I remember her, followed later."

"You're right, Mrs. Holloway," assented Hank, who had recovered his cheroot stealthily and relighted it. "She's with him now, an' from what I hear, is the finest gal in the valley."

Proceeding with his narrative, Hank said that Jim had been drinking heavily for two weeks and one day when "he was stewed to the gills," he went to the Circle N Ranch and applied for a job as puncher.

"O' co'se, seein' as how Jim, who calls hisself the Wolf, is in a sorry state of petrifaction from booze, Haines turns him down cold. Jim gits hot under the collar and makes some threatenin' remark to the which Haines pays no attention special. Jim goes back to the Red Eye whar I finds him all lit up, achin' fur a fight, but I take him away an' put him to sleep in his room over Bert Mason's general store."

"Poor, poor Jim!" exclaimed Mrs. Holloway, a sob in her voice.

"The next day we rides to Buffalo Wallow, whar me an' Jim ties up with Bob Watson, a cattle buyer, the which job is fine fur Jim, who knows more'n a minute 'bout cattle than most men do in a month o' Sundays. To keep Jim out'en the gin mills, I induce him to play poker with me so's I kin lose some money to him, the same helpin' him an' givin' me a chanct to swell out my expense account, begging your pardon fur it, Mr. Holloway, the same havin' been orders from headquarters. Jim's high strung as a thoroughbred hoss, an' no matter what I kin do, he refuses loans from me, 'cept on condition he is allowed to chalk it up on the account, the which don't worry me none, seein' as how I didn't aim to dun him fur a settlement.

"You see, when I begins to lose to him at poker, he has enough fur his needs, an' every bum within ten miles shares the benefits thereof regardless. Jim is mighty good that ere way, an' I'm shoutin' the gospel truth when I tell you he'd rather go hungry hisself than see a human derelict suffer for the want o' grub. Like most big hearted men, he didn't seem to know how to protect hisself just right, so incidentally, should he ever play cards with perfessional sharpers, I shows him a few tricks with the pasteboards, an' what he don't know about juggling aces, kings and the rest o' the cyard family, ain't wuth knowing."

"You might have dispensed with that, Hank," said Mr. Holloway. "I'd hate to have Jim develop into a card sharp!"

"Bless your soul, sir!" rejoined Hank with a grim chuckle. "Don't be afeared o' that, 'cause the sight of cyards sure makes him sick! Jim a gambler? Why, 'tain't in him, Mr. Holloway. That wus part o' my game to git him to quit the booze, fur the man who gambles seldom if ever drinks. Them two vices ain't to be found in the same party, an' that's true as Holy Writ!"

There was none to dispute his assertion. Mrs. Holloway, her pale face flushed with excitement, listened to him with rapt attention. Mr. Holloway and Peterson frequently exchanged glances full of meaning, and it was evident that the little sleuth from the Southwest had won their hearty admiration.

"Where did you leave Jim?" inquired the magnate.

"At Purple Canyon," replied Hank. "The day I left him, Jim promised that he wouldn't touch a drop in my absence. That was ten days ago an' I hain't got no reason to believe that he won't keep his word. Thar's my yarn in a nutshell. Any question, folks?"

"Did he ever speak to you of me?" asked Mrs. Holloway, her hand on her heart.

"Several times, ma'am. One night I finds him kissin' your photo, sayin' low like, him not knowin' I kin hear, 'I'll never disgrace you, mother.' I up and ast him if he has a mother, knowin' full well he has, an' a mighty fine one at that, an' he says proudly, 'the best mother in all the world!' When I ast him whar she lived, to git him thinkin' o' home and her, he shuts up like a clam instanter, an' stays mum as a hitchin' post fur a week!"

Mrs. Holloway rose and extended her bejeweled hand to the detective, who blushed furiously as he took it within his own knotty paw. He was afraid to shake it, fearing he might crush the tender fingers that lay confidingly in his palm.

"I thank you so much for what you have done for my boy," she said brokenly. "You will watch and bring him back to me safe and sound?"

"I sure will, if I has to handcuff him!"

"You have—have faith in his ultimate reformation?"

"My faith in salvation ain't no stronger, ma'am!" responded Hank devoutly.

"Thank you. You have given me the greatest happiness I have had in many months."

Mrs. Holloway turned to her husband, who rose to accompany her to her room. She bade Hank and Peterson good night and left the apartment, her husband following. When they were alone, Mrs. Holloway threw herself into her husband's arms.

"There is hope for Jim, don't you think, Charles?"

"Yes, there is hope."

"This little man will bring him back to us?"

"He will, when I give him the word."

"Will it be soon?"

"Yes, I may safely promise that, my dear."

She went to the window and looked out shudderingly, for the storm was raging furiously.

"What a frightful night!" she said, lowering the curtain.

"But you are safe here, my dear."

"I was thinking—thinking of Jim! Where is he to-night?"

"In God's hands," responded he, kissing her. "Good night!"

He left her to rejoin the others, and pacing the length of the room several times, his brow wrinkled in thought, his hands clasped behind him, he seemed oblivious of their presence. Hank relighted his cheroot and calmly smoked, his gaze resting alternately upon the financier and upon the appointments of the room, the richness of which fascinated him. Presently Mr. Holloway halted before him.

"Hank!" he said, "do you believe there is a chance that Jim may be cured of his craving for liquor?"

"I sure do, sir," replied the detective. "I ain't sayin' I'm an expert in them things, but knowin' Jim as I do, I'm sure he'll come out o' this mess all O K!"

"Has he ever had any affair with—with a woman?"

"No, siree! He told me more'n once he hasn't any more use fur a female critter than he has for a last year's autymobile!"

Mr. Holloway smiled. "Perhaps if he were to fall

in love with a good woman, there might be a chance for him," he said meditatively. "Is there such a woman in Purple Canyon?"

"Thar mought be such a woman thar," responded Hank with a dry chuckle, "but to date I ain't seen her, nor Jim either."

"Then, as far as your knowledge goes, he never has met Marian Haines?"

"He sure hadn't up to the time I left him at Purple Canyon."

They continued their discussion in an undertone, a mantel clock tinkling the hour of midnight without being heard by them. At that precise moment there was great activity in the editorial rooms of the *Observer*, downtown. On the desk of Sam Stockton, the news editor, lay a telegram from the *Observer's* correspondent at El Paso, which he was studying with profound interest.

"What the devil does he mean?" growled Stockton irritably. "It's midnight and the first edition dead line twenty minutes off! Jimmy Donlon! Oh, Jimmy!" he roared hoarsely.

A young man of about twenty-five years, tall and sinewy, his sleeves rolled up to his elbows, his abundant black hair much tousled, dashed into the room to halt abruptly before his chief.

"Did you call, sir?" he inquired innocently.

"Did I call! Well, I like that, and I shouting with a piece of one lung gone, too! What are you working on?"

"The storm story, sir. Telephone wires down everywhere—cellars and subways flooded as never before known—electric light plants seriously affected —transportation practically at a standstill—railroad trains stalled—the heaviest storm recorded in thirty years!"

"Durn the rain! Look at this." He handed the telegram to Donlon. "What the deuce do you make of it?"

Donlon scanned the dispatch slowly, Stockton watching him closely for a verification of a certain suspicion that had sprung into his mind.

"This wire," said Donlon thoughtfully, "states that a man known as the Wolf, alias something or other, has publicly posted a notice at Purple Canyon announcing his intention to kill Ralph Haines at sight, and that a Sheriff's posse is now in search of him with the intention of lynching him. That's what I make out of it, sir."

"But the name, you chump!" snapped Stockton. "What the deuce is the name?"

"As far as I can make it out, it begins with Jim. The remaining letters are blurred, but I see l-o-w-a-y. It might be Galloway, Halloway or—"

"Whoopee!" yelled Stockton, "I've got it! The Wolf is Jim Holloway! Sure as shooting, that's it!"

"That's what?" echoed Jimmy, wondering if Stockton had gone suddenly mad.

"This is the biggest beat of the year!" declared Stockton excitedly. "Do you know who the Wolf, the most notorious character of the Southwest, is?"

"Nope."

"He's Jim Holloway, son of Charles Holloway, who dropped out of sight mysteriously three years ago."

"You don't say so!"

"Remember the excitement it caused in social circles and at Jim's club? You ought to know, for you worked on the story long enough."

"I sure do," grinned Jimmy sadly. "You never forgave me for not finding his body in the Jersey marshes where you had buried him—in theory, I mean.''

"Don't get fresh, kid!'' snapped Stockton. ''You rush to Holloway's house on Riverside Drive and if he isn't asleep, tell him you have news of Jim. He'll take you in with both arms, son. Run along now and we'll have a double-headed beat on the front page in the morning—always providing, you don't fall asleep en route.''

"Shall I take a taxi?''

"You might try a hydroplane, my son,'' suggested Stockton with cutting sarcasm as he rushed away to the telegraph room for further details.

"A submarine might be preferable,'' sighed Jimmy, donning his raincoat and leaving the office.

Fifteen minutes later when he alighted from his taxi at Holloway's door, a light in an upper window assured him the financier had not yet retired. He pushed the electric button and a few seconds later, the door was opened by Thompson, who demanded to know his business.

"I'm a reporter for the *Observer* with important news for Mr. Holloway,'' replied Jimmy, grinning.

"Preposterous, sir! It's long after midnight, sir!''

"It's about his son Jim, who disappeared three years ago, you know.''

"Bless my soul!'' ejaculated Thompson. ''Step in, sir, and I'll tell him at once.''

He admitted Donlon into the dimly lighted vestibule, and led him to a long hall at the farther end of which a staircase curved its length majestically to the second story. The butler disappeared, leaving Jimmy to his own reflection. He was calculating the value of an immense Oriental vase six feet high standing in the center of the vestibule, when he saw Thompson on the landing of the stairs beckoning to him.

"He will see you for an instant only," said Thompson as Jimmy bounded up the carpeted steps.

"Righto! Some instants are worth millions, when you know how to utilize them."

Following the butler, Jimmy entered the study where the financier, Hank and Peterson had just concluded their conference. Mr. Halloway stood in front of his desk and greeted Jimmy inquiringly.

"What can I do for you, Mr. Donlon?" he asked after Jimmy had introduced himself.

"A telegram from El Paso that might interest you, Mr. Holloway." He handed a copy of the message to the financier, whose face went white as he read the following:

"El Paso, Tex.—It is reported here that Jim Holloway, son of Charles Holloway, railroad magnate and multi-millionaire, widely known throughout the Southwest as the Wolf, last night posted a notice at the Red Eye saloon in Purple Canyon, threatening to kill Ralph Haines, owner of the Circle N ranch in Red Sandy Valley, at sight. The feud between Haines and the Wolf is of long standing. It is announced that a Sheriff's posse has been formed by Haines' friends and that Holloway will be lynched if captured."

"God!" exclaimed Mr. Holloway, turning to Hank. "This can't be true! What do you think of it, Hank?"

Jimmy watched Hank's face as he read the message, but from the swarthy mask beneath which the detective was wont to hide his real feelings, he gathered little of value to him in his journalistic quest.

"Thar's nothin' in this," laughed Hank, whose heart became a dead weight in his breast. "What's the Wolf got to do with Jim Holloway, anyway?"

"Do you mean to say the man known as the Wolf is not Jim Holloway?" queried Jimmy anxiously.

"That's what I said, didn't I?" snarled Hank, approaching Jimmy menacingly. "You don't go fur to say I'm lyin', eh?"

"Oh, certainly not, sir!" nodded Jimmy, retreating.

"Good night, Mr. Donlon," interposed Mr. Holloway genially. "I think the *Observer* will find it quite expensive, if not libelous, to print this rather unsubstantiated statement, don't you?"

Jimmy rushed back to the *Observer* crestfallen, though not beaten. After a consultation with Stockton, he went to the business office, obtained several hundred dollars expense money and arranged to leave for El Paso by the first train in the morning, his orders being to camp on the trail of the Wolf and never to quit it until his identity as the son of Charles Holloway was established beyond all doubt.

When the three men in the Holloway home were at their parting, Mr. Holloway pressed a roll of bills into Hank's hands.

"Get back to Purple Canyon as speedily as possible, Hank," he said brokenly. "Do what you can to reach Jim and—and save him if possible!"

"I'll do it, Mr. Holloway!" replied Hank, his voice husky with an emotion strange to him. "Good-by, sir."

"Good-by."

Mr. Holloway, who had seemingly aged a year within the last few minutes, seated himself at his desk, heart-broken and despairing. Ah, by what fatality had his son sunk so low! What would that devoted mother, who now, perhaps, was dreaming of her Jim, think when she learned the truth—and he had no reason to doubt the truth of the *Observer's* telegram!

For the first time since his childhood, he gave way utterly to his grief, and leaning upon his desk, his face resting upon his extended arms, he sobbed bitterly, as strong men in crucial hours sometimes do.

CHAPTER XII

THE SCROLLS OF THE GODS

URGING his pony onward at headlong speed, Jim Holloway covered mile after mile on his ride to Red Sandy, on record time. Long before the valley was reached, the mustang found it difficult to maintain the killing pace his rider had set for him, yet true to his nature and training, Pinto sped on willingly.

The sun blazed overhead, but Holloway, immersed in his own dark reflections, seemed indifferent to the terrific heat, which, accentuated as it was by the gyrating alkaline dust, rendered respiration by man and beast difficult, if not painful. Holloway had a duty to perform and he was resolved to allow nothing short of disablement or death to frustrate its accomplishment.

When finally, to his infinite relief, he entered the valley and reached the road leading to the Circle N ranch, several miles beyond which was Sweetwater, where Valdez and his bandits were reported to be in hiding, Pinto was well nigh foundered. The pony came to a halt abruptly and Holloway dismounted so that the broncho might rest. He was aware that Seth Lucas and his men were in the vicinity, possibly at the Circle N ranch unless, perhaps, though he did not deem that likely, they had continued without halting, in pursuit of the raiders.

After a pause of an hour, Pinto had recovered sufficiently to warrant Holloway remounting and proceeding to his destination. He was on the road to the Haines bungalow, for the first time since the day, some months previously, when he had applied to Haines for a job as rider, only to meet with a curt refusal. Holloway remembered the circumstance with the same galling vexation with which one remembers an irremediable act of folly—an imbecility which, in his case, had been fraught with such dire consequences to himself. He hoped to find Lucas at the bungalow; and it was his aim to volunteer his services to him in the campaign against the bandits.

As he had surmised, a dozen men of the posse, fully armed and mounted, were in the road near the bungalow, apparently awaiting orders to proceed. Even as he advanced to meet, as he fancied, the hostile glances of several of the riders as he passed, Lucas appeared on the porch of the bungalow. Holloway dismounted and, leaving Pinto to browse along the grass-edged path, approached the veteran commander who greeted him with a hearty handshake.

"Howdy do, Wolf!" he exclaimed. "You're the very man I wanted to see! Come to join me, I reckon, eh?"

Holloway nodded.

"If you'll let me, Seth," he answered. "I know of no man I'd rather fight under than you."

"You bet I'll let you, Wolf! I'm durned glad of the chance to have you, too. We'll start right now, if you're ready."

"I'm ready."

"Bully! When we join Haines at Sweetwater—"

"Haines!" interrupted Holloway, aghast.

"Sure! He's my lieutenant."

"And I'm to fight with him?"

"Of course, my boy! He's waiting for us somewhere near the 'Chimney,' where Valdez and his bunch are camped. You know Sweetwater by heart, I'm·told."

Holloway did not deny it, for he had traveled through it often in the migratory life he had led for two years on the rim of the desert. The "Chimney" was in the very heart of the Sweetwater country and admirably adapted for defensive purposes, so that a mere handful of men stationed there might hold a regiment of troops at bay for a month unless heavy artillery were employed against them. Even then, he knew their dislodgment could be effected only by the sacrifice of many lives.

But while Holloway knew this, his thoughts were not centered upon the "Chimney." He was confronted by the disconcerting fact that Haines was not only to participate in the campaign against Valdez, but that he held a subordinate command in the very contingent of the posse, which he, Holloway, had avowed his intention to join. What! Fight under Haines? In the light of recent developments he could not consistently subject himself to the commands of the man he had publicly threatened to kill.

"I'm afraid I cannot join you, Seth," he faltered after a pause. "There are vital reasons why I should not do so."

Lucas frowned. "Reasons! I know of only one valid excuse, and knowing you as I do, I'd hate to express it."

"What is it?"

"Fear."

Holloway colored, and a lump rose in his throat.

"That is a false assumption and you know it! There are other reasons."

"What are they?"

"Have you heard of the trouble I had with Haines at the Red Eye last night?"

Lucas whistled softly. "By George!" he exclaimed. "Come to think of it, I heard some of the boys say you threatened to kill Haines, but I was too busy to pay attention to that line of chatter. Come, tell me all that happened."

Holloway reviewed briefly the facts of his altercation with Haines and his subsequent threat. He offered no excuses and finished with the statement that it was impossible for him to meet Haines in the circumstances.

"Moreover," he added mournfully, "I haven't the faintest notion of executing my foolish threat. I am an asinine chump who has been publicly proclaimed a coward, and when Haines hears of my threat, he will be amply justified in blowing my head off!"

Lucas chuckled, though his laughter lacked mirth. "Why did you do it, Wolf?" he asked kindly. "You should have known that such threats are not only foolish but dangerous in this country."

"I knew, but didn't think. I was drunk—"

"That is no justification!" interrupted Lucas sternly. "On the contrary, such a plea might hang you, if—." He paused, then resumed: "Why not renounce your threat before my men in the road yonder," indicating the riders who were regarding them impatiently. "We are all of us apt to make fools of ourselves at times, and though it may be hard to eat crow, you'll find it easy to digest it once you have made up your mind to do so and brave the consequences!"

"It is impossible!" he responded sadly. "In view of what has happened and what may yet happen, it would be tantamount to suicide for me to join the posse. Your men couldn't understand—they would misconstrue my motives, while Haines—"

"Will honor you as I do, Wolf!" interrupted Lucas

with enthusiasm. "I'll have a talk with them and straighten out matters for you."

"I'm afraid I can't, Lucas. I should prefer to work alone against the bandits, with whose methods of operation I am familiar. Let me co-operate with you, without actually being one of you."

"Ridiculous!"

"You will trust me to do what is right, Lucas?" asked Holloway, a far away look in his eyes. "Say you will."

"You bet I will, son! Do your duty as you see it, but I want your promise that you won't do anything rash."

"I promise."

Lucas rejoined his men, who cheered when he gave the order to advance. Holloway stared after them dreamily until the horsemen had passed out of sight behind a clump of trees beyond. He bitterly resented the cruel trick evil fortune had played him. How was it possible for him to associate himself in a campaign against Valdez, with the man he had publicly vowed to kill?

"Better death than that!" he muttered gloomily. "Were I to join the posse and Haines be killed, might not these men who hate me, lodge an accusation of murder against me? I'd much rather quit the country and let matters take their course. My status couldn't be worse in any event."

No, he dared not resort to that subterfuge to escape the duty that devolved upon him. There rose before him the vision of Marian Haines, beautiful and appealing. That she hated him, he was firmly convinced, yet he was unable to banish her from his thoughts. The more he considered her, the weaker his resistance to her recurrence to his shamed memory became, so that his struggles to counteract the power she exerted over him ultimately lost all vitality. The truth had dawned upon him suddenly. With mingled pride and joy, he confessed that he loved her with all his heart.

He realized that the residents of Red Sandy were in grave danger as long as the bandits remained in the valley. He knew it was his duty to save them if possible, even at the cost of his miserable, embittered life. He owed this service to Haines as a sort of penance for the harm he had drunkenly planned to inflict upon him, and to Marian, because she had inspired love in his heart—the first and holiest passion, aside from the affection he bore his mother, that ever had swayed his soul.

But how was his unrequited love to prove a boon to him? He was certain that at their meeting at the Red Eye, when Marian sobbingly pleaded with him to relinquish his evil design, her grief was purely sympathetic, and that at heart she regarded him with scorn, if not hatred. Why had he not given her the assurance of immunity for her brother she had prayed for? He sought to give it, yet the words would not come. What a fool he had been! He had sown the wind and it was inevitable that he must reap the whirlwind, with all the ignominy, sorrow and suffering that retributive justice would heap upon him in the days to come.

Surely, he ruminated, Marian must have left him in the belief that he was a contemptible wretch. He gathered a crumb of comfort from the fact that she had restrained his hand when he was about to yield to an insane impulse to blow out his brains. That she had a heart capable of loving the man who was worthy of her, this spontaneous act clearly indicated. Was it possible for him to win her? It was hardly likely, but nevertheless, he loved her and he was determined to leave no stone unturned to prove his adoration, and, ultimately, to win not only her friendship and respect, but the requital of his affection.

Returning to the road, he whistled to Pinto, mounted and rode away after the posse. Turning to the right, he crossed the ranch property and headed for the buttes which skirted the upper edge of the wild, desolate district known as Sweetwater, so-called because of the numerous sweet springs which abounded among the alkaline deposits in the gullies that scarred its surface like wrinkles on old parchment. There were miniature pools here and there in which the straying cattle from the valley loved to roll, but aside from the patches of vegetation in the vicinity of these tiny bodies of water, the country was a barren waste and a terror to all who dared to venture within its dreary confines.

From the spot where Holloway halted, as far as he could observe, there appeared butte after butte in endless succession, the spaces between broken at intervals by shallow gullies, any of which might serve as a safe hiding place for an enemy. On the crests of many of these buttes, scores of needle points of rock, resembling minarets, reared their tops to from ten to forty feet into the sky. Three miles southward rose the "Chimney," a crater-like depression in an almost inaccessible wall of rock, in the vicinity of which he had reason to believe Valdez and his men had established headquarters until their purpose to raid the valley ranches might be accomplished.

He wondered if Valdez was aware that a Sheriff's posse was on its way to engage him in battle. It was hardly likely, yet he knew Valdez to be one of the most cunning scoundrels on the Mexican border, so that this was not impossible. To a ruffian like Valdez, the realization that he is in peril, however remote, means quick and decisive action. What would his play be? Holloway fancied that the bandit probably would retreat to his haunts in Sonora to await a more favorable opportunity for the consummation of his lawless designs.

Far off to his left, he saw a lone horseman skirting the top of one of the minor buttes that ridged the horizon for miles in that direction. The rider disappeared before Jim was able to determine his nationality by the character of the hat he wore. Inasmuch as the horseman was proceeding towards the "Chimney," it was reasonable to presume that he was one of Valdez's videttes returning from a reconnoitering expedition. That he himself had not been seen he felt certain, but, nevertheless, he dropped out of sight in a gully and proceeded cautiously in the direction of the bandits' rendezvous.

"If I could meet Valdez or Pedro and wipe them out, my cup of happiness would be full," he mused. "I wonder who that chap could have been? I'm not sure, but I'd bet my life it was a greaser!"

The rider he had seen was Lopez, the Mexican tool of Faro Jenn, whose bribe money was securely concealed in his belt. Faithful to his agreement with the dive keeper, he had trailed Marian until she reached the Haines' bungalow, from which point, by a circuitous route he was enabled to avoid contact with the posse, and proceed in safety to the "Chimney." Skirting the crests of the buttes from time to time as he was obliged to do, he finally reached Valdez's hiding place to be greeted with a curt *"Quien es?"* shouted at him by one of the bandit's pickets.

"Lopez!" he answered. He dismounted and approached the guard who eyed him surlily. "I have important news for Valdez! Where is he?"

"With Pedro in the cave there," he said, pointing

behind him with one hand, the other rolling a cigarette with marvelous skill. "Is your news really important, Lopez? Let's hear it, *amigo.*"

"And have Valdez slit my ears?" rejoined Lopez with an oath. "I'm not the fool I look, Pancho."

He left the sentry to enter a small opening in the face of a precipitous wall, passing into a cave some ten feet in diameter and sufficiently high to permit him to walk with ease. Seated on a blanket in the semi-obscurity in which the place was enshrouded, were Valdez and Pedro engaged in an animated discussion with three Mexicans, each as filthy and evil appearing as themselves.

"Who comes?" asked Valdez in Spanish, his hand on the hilt of his dagger. "Ah, Lopez! What news from Purple Canyon?"

Lopez told his story suavely, but he neglected to reveal Jenn's liberality to him. When he spoke of trailing Marian Haines to the bungalow and repeated Jenn's suggestion that it might be wise to capture her, Valdez grew thoughtful.

"Carramba!" he said, stroking the ends of his dainty mustache. "The idea is not bad. In fact, it is an inspiration, as my dear padre was wont to say. Once this woman is in my hands, there's nothing her rich brother wouldn't pay to get her back again!"

Pedro, who had been discussing the possibility of a clash with the posse, and who had a constitutional aversion for adventures which might end disastrously for himself, sensed the design of his chief and readily acquiesced therein.

"It shall be done!" said Valdez. "Why risk life and limb in rustling cattle across the border when we can bag richer and fairer game?"

"Why?" echoed Pedro.

"I shall make this Haines woman my prisoner and

we'll be off before these pigs of Americans learn that I am here in the 'Chimney.' ''

Pancho appeared at the cave opening with the announcement that a horseman had been seen by Ricardo in one of the gullies nearby. Valdez sprang to his feet with alacrity.

"We must look into this!" he said, diving through the opening. "Follow me, *amigos.*"

Led by Pancho, the outlaws trailed single file down the incline to a terrace where Ricardo with several bandits was awaiting the chief. Ricardo repeated his story that he had glimpsed a horseman from his sentry post at the top of the ridge, only a few seconds ago.

"Your glass, Pedro!" snapped Valdez, scowling.

Pedro produced a small telescope and handed it to the bandit. Valdez climbed the sloping side of the cliff to the top, a distance of ten feet, and, screening himself carefully behind a rock, scanned the country beneath him with extreme care. To the east, he saw a man standing on the edge of a gully, his hand screening his eye, evidently on watch. The figure disappeared presently and, turning to the south, Valdez counted some fifteen or twenty horsemen as they crossed a ridge only to disappear in a depression beyond.

"*Carramba!*" he swore angrily. "It is the Sheriff's posse Lopez spoke of! Bah, they might be dangerous but for the advantages the 'Chimney' offers me in the way of defense. They are making a detour so as to get behind and trap me like a rat, but I will fool them!" He spat viciously, then added contemptuously: "The American pigs!"

He turned his glass in the direction where he had last seen the lone white man, but the landscape offered no visible evidences of human life among the occasional tufts of sage and mesquite that fringed the tops of the buttes here and there. He was despairing of seeing the man again when he perceived the tip of the stranger's hat as he lifted his head for another observation. It was apparent that the white man was crawling toward the "Chimney" and Valdez was anxious to learn his identity if possible.

"Pedro!" he called in a subdued shout. "Come up and have a look at this pig of an American scout!"

Pedro rejoined his chief and, taking the telescope, focused the lens upon the spot indicated by Valdez.

"He'll show his face presently. Tell me if you know him."

Pedro had not long to wait. The white man's head rose above the sky line with irritating slowness, but it needed only a glimpse to enable the Mexican to recognize him instantly.

"Haines!" he exclaimed savagely.

"Oh, your *amigo!*" chimed Valdez. "You love him much, eh, Pedro?"

"American dog!" rejoined Pedro fiercely. "The very man I want to meet!"

"Wherefore?"

"That I may kill him!"

Valdez seemed shocked, and he manifested his disapproval of his subordinate's sanguinary avowal by pressing the point of his knife against his throat.

"Say not so, *amigo*," he remarked quietly. "You would not kill the goose that is to lay my golden eggs, would you? Fool! how can I collect rich ransom from a dead man? *Carramba!* Your philosophy smells to heaven!"

Pedro shrunk from his chief with a shudder expressive of fear and hatred.

"I was only joking, Valdez," he faltered.

"I thought so," replied the other, returning his knife to his belt. "*Santisimo!* If you were to kill

Haines, I would surely flay you alive, as I did one other gentleman in my day!''

The two descended the slope and, summoning his men, Valdez explained the situation to them. They consulted earnestly together for a time, and having agreed upon a plan of action, Valdez voiced his final instructions.

''You, Ricardo,'' he said, addressing one of the men, a greaser of the lowest and most cruel type, ''will ride with six men due south through the tunnel-like ravine yonder to the right. You will take care not to show yourselves until you lead the posse by a mile at least—then ride like devils for the border. Understand?''

''*Si, señor.*''

''It is less than six miles to the line. When the posse sights you, they will follow, of course. The Sheriff with the big nose is coming with another bunch of men, but he doesn't count as much as the snap of my finger! When I have finished a certain important task I have in mind, I shall follow you by the Snake Creek route, of which these *Americanos* have little knowledge. We shall meet at the hacienda to-night, if all goes well.''

''To-night, Valdez,'' replied Ricardo, glad to quit the presence of his chief, whose ratty eyes hypnotized him and caused chills to traverse his spine.

''*Adios!*''

The bandits mounted their ponies and descending the terrace, rapidly disappeared in a ravine. Valdez turned to the four men whom he had designated for his special service, and ordered that they hold themselves in readiness for instant departure. He directed Pedro to remain in the ''Chimney'' while he and the men rode away to intercept and capture Marian Haines.

"I understand, Valdez," said Pedro, pleased with this arrangement. "But if you should be prevented from returning to this place—"

"Then we meet at the hacienda," interrupted the bandit. "Your glass once more, *amigo.*"

Valdez climbed the cliff and carefully surveyed the field to the south. Pedro watched him curiously, a smile of satisfaction on his evil face. It had occurred to him that he might yet find a way by which to wreak his long deferred vengeance upon Haines. He hated the rancher with such ferocity that he dared brave even the fury of Valdez to accomplish his vindictive design.

"Not even you, Valdez, shall stand between me and my well earned revenge!" he muttered fiercely. "You talk of flaying me alive, but let me warn you that I know a certain gentleman in El Paso who will pay me well for information regarding you. When the time comes I shall dictate the terms, not you!"

Valdez descended the incline with the agility of a goat. He was visibly excited.

"The hounds have sighted the rabbits!" he exclaimed, vastly pleased. He whistled for Lopez who approached him running. "We will be off in five minutes," he said to Pedro. "Ricardo is leading the posse by a mile!"

"It is a good start, Valdez."

"Lopez," said Valdez, "tell the men to mount. No delays—mind that, *esclavo!*"

Lopez returned to the outlaws and instantly all were in motion. Valdez smiled approvingly as he returned to Pedro the telescope he had borrowed.

"If all goes well, Pedro, I shall return within an hour."

"*Si, señor.*"

"*Adios!*"

The bandit rejoined the others on the terrace, and mounting his broncho, disappeared at the head of his followers in a narrow gully leading to the east. Left to himself, Pedro went to the cave where he had hidden a rifle, of which there were several in the cache, and armed with this weapon, climbed to the lookout on the cliff. Screened by a fringe of shrubbery he surveyed the country in an effort to locate Haines. He waited patiently, and presently saw what he fancied was the shadow of a man outlined against the side of a gully a hundred yards to his right. The umbration vanished, and when it failed to reappear, he was half convinced he had been in error.

"*Carramba!*" he swore angrily. "Where has he gone?"

From the spot where he lay concealed, Pedro was unable to scan as wide a stretch of territory as he desired without exposing himself to the bullets of an adversary. Had Haines seen and recognized him? Pedro was not the creature to give an enemy an advantage if it could be avoided he valued his worthless life too much for that. He decided to leave the butte and to wriggle along one of the ravines so as to get behind Haines, from which point of vantage he might shoot the rancher in the back when the opportunity presented itself.

"It is better to be the hunter than the hunted," he soliloquized as he descended the slope. "If I were as sure of getting the Wolf as I am of bagging you, Haines, my cup of happiness would be full!"

Pedro hummed a Spanish love song as he approached a screened passage in the cliff that led to a gully, by means of which he could flank Haines' position without risk of discovery. He thrust aside the brush that masked the fissure and descended the declivity without mishap.

"*Dios* is good to those who help themselves," he muttered piously. "If I succeed, I will donate a hundred pesos to Father Enrique's poor box at the Cathedral of Los Vinos."

He proceeded on his hands and knees, dragging his rifle after him. None save the All-seeing eye above, observed him. Blind to everything save his desire for revenge he little divined his tragic destiny freshly written in the scrolls of the Gods!

CHAPTER XIII

PEDRO SETTLES HIS SCORE

ON his arrival at the bungalow at daylight, following his conference with Sheriff Thorne at Purple Canyon, Haines had turned in for a couple of hours' rest, leaving Belcher and "Bird's-eye" to shift for themselves. The two punchers were dog-tired themselves and during the brief rest period allotted to them, their stentorian snores made the rafters of the bunk house ring. It was eight o'clock when Aunt 'Mandy roused Haines with the cheerful announcement that "de finest brekfus he ever did eat" was awaiting him.

Rising, Haines dressed and went to the corral where he had installed a large trough filled with running water supplied by means of a pipe line leading from a cold spring on the slope twenty rods from the bunk house. He was sousing himself liberally when Belcher joined him.

"How did you sleep, old man?" he inquired.

"Like a top," yawned the foreman. "Two hours ain't much, though, for a man who needs eight at a stretch, like me."

"You may sleep for a week, once we have driven Valdez and his pirates out of the valley."

"The posse ought to be here any minute now. I reckon you'll be goin' out to the 'Chimney' with 'em when they come?"

"Come to think of it, I should like to look the ground over before they arrive."

Belcher grunted protestingly, a dubious smile on his swarthy face.

159

"I don't favor that, Mr. Haines," he said, his hand on his revolver. "S'pose one of them greasers should pot you when you ain't lookin'?"

"I'll take that chance. You and the boys will await the arrival of the posse. I'll not be gone more than an hour at the most."

"But if you don't return in an hour?"

"Then I'll meet you somewhere on the road."

Belcher seemed ill at ease, and it was plain to Haines that he had something of importance to communicate. He asked him what was on his mind.

"Somethin' that happened at the Red Eye last night," replied the foreman. "It's about the Wolf. You had a run in with him arter we got to Purple Canyon, didn't you?"

"Yes. He wanted to force me to drink with him and I refused."

"Then he drawed his gun, I'm told—"

"But no quicker than I did my own. It was nothing, Belcher. Is that what you wanted to talk to me about? Forget it!"

" 'Tain't that, Mr. Haines," drawled Belcher. "I know you made him weaken, but it's about the notice he posted arter your little affair."

"Notice?"

"Sure. He threatened to kill you on sight."

Haines laughed carelessly. "Why, he wouldn't kill me," he returned, "I won't give him the chance."

"You never can tell about these things, Mr. Haines. The Wolf ain't got no good reputation nohow, so you'd better keep your eyes peeled if you should meet him, 'cause he might do as he says."

"Have no fear on my account. It's dollars to doughnuts he's sleeping off his drunk over Bert Mason's store this blessed minute——"

"Brekfus!" came Aunt 'Mandy's shout from the

bungalow. "It's hot an' ready f' yo', Massa Haines."
"All right, 'Mandy. We're coming."

The two walked to the bungalow and the discussion
of the Wolf was dropped. To the disgust of the diligent housekeeper, Haines bolted his appetizing breakfast with amazing speed, and actually declined her
delicious hot cakes. When she voiced her indignant
protests, he apologized laughingly and five minutes
later, was on his way to the "Chimney." Belcher
and "Bird's-eye" did the chores, while the remaining
punchers rode the range to the southward to prevent
the Haines cattle from browsing in the direction of
Sweetwater where they might run afoul of Valdez and
his raiders, at the risk of being stampeded and lost.

Advised by one of the cowboys that the bandits
had invaded the valley, Aunt 'Mandy became irritable
and pugnacious. She declared that if any of the
greasers dared to interfere with "Missy" Marian, they
would have reason to regret the day "dey wus bo'n!'"

"Ah bet dat oily greaser Pedro is 'mong 'em!" she
asserted, flourishing a huge bread knife in Belcher's
face. "Ef dat low down Mexican trash shows up
hyar, ag'in, I done carve his ugly mug wid dis yar
knife, I shuah will!"

"I don't expect he will show up hereabouts,
'Mandy," said Belcher, prudently retreating. "If he
does, leave him to me, that's all I ask."

Aunt 'Mandy sniffed indignantly.

"I done knowed dat Pedro wusn't no use, nohow!
I told Massa Haines not to trust him no more'n a
rattlesnake, 'cause I done seed him alookin' greedy-
eyed at Missy Marian one day. Good Lawd! if she
come to harm t'rough dat low greaser, Ah hopes de
debbil will burn him up in sizzlin' brimstone!"

She waddled into the kitchen leaving Belcher with
the conviction that Pedro would find the quality

of mercy in Aunt 'Mandy's makeup considerably strained, should chance afford her the opportunity of wreaking vengeance upon him. An hour later, Seth Lucas and his men reached the bungalow. All hands were more than pleased at the prospect of a few minutes' rest. The heat was terrific and there was a regrettable absence of cool breezes. Aunt 'Mandy prepared some sandwiches which the riders ate with the relish characteristic of hungry men in the great open spaces of the Southwest. After Lucas and Belcher had discussed the situation, the latter announced his intention to proceed to Sweetwater with "Bird's-eye" in the hope of meeting Haines whose prolonged absence caused him no inconsiderable anxiety.

"I didn't like the idea of him agoin' alone in the fust place," he growled. "He shouldn't ha' gone, nohow."

"He'll turn up all right, Belcher," rejoined Lucas confidently. "If you can manage it, meet us on the road. When my men are rested up a bit, we'll move."

Belcher hailed "Bird's-eye" and presently the two, after examining their weapons, trotted away. They had scarcely disappeared when Holloway dismounted in front of the bungalow. He was conversing with Lucas when Aunt 'Mandy recognized him.

"Law sakes!" she exclaimed hostilely. "Dar's dat Wolf pussun, fo' shuah! Wha's he doin' hyar, Ah wonder? It ain't fo' no good! Ah wonders ef he ain't in cahoots wid Pedro an' dem other greasers! Ef Ah t'ought so, Ah'd give him a piece of mah mind, Ah would!"

She remained resentfully watchful on the porch until the posse and Holloway had vanished, for she wasn't taking any chances "wid wolves an' sich like animules hangin' 'round."

"Bress mah soul!" she muttered, when she was

alone. "Dese am serious times, wid dem greasers in de valley. Ah hopes nuffin will happen to Massa an' Missy Haines, 'cause ef it do, dis yere chile'll die of a busted heart, sho' nuff!"

The faithful negress was completing her household labors for the day when she heard the clatter of hoofs in the road. Waddling to the door she saw Marian coming up the pathway, a sober look on her drawn face, her riding costume and hat white with dust.

"Fo' de Lawd, Missy Marian!" shouted Aunt 'Mandy, rushing to meet her. "Wha' you come from, chile? Massa Haines done tole me you wus stoppin' wid de Hawthorne folks until dis trouble done be over. Wha' you' mean by runnin' yo' head into de lion's mouth?"

Marian smiled cheerfully. "Don't mind me, Auntie," she said softly, "I'm not going to be injured by any lion—"

Purple lights flashed in her eyes and her strength gave way suddenly. But for the sustaining arms of the negress, she would have fallen headlong.

"Bress mah soul, chile!" exclaimed Aunt 'Mandy, alarmed. "Yo' done tuckered out, yo' is! Yo' ain't sick, am yo', Missy?"

"No; only very tired after my long ride in the sun."

"Well, yo' ain't agoin' to ride no mo', Missy Marian. Yo' get right into de house outen dis b'ilin' sun."

"Where's my brother?" asked Marian, suddenly reminded of her duty. The silence, broken only by the twitter of the birds in the shrubbery, appeared to her to be ill-omened. Deep anxiety oppressed her.

"He done gone to de Sweetwater ahead ob de posse."

"How long since?"

"More'n a hour anyhow, Missy Haines."

Marian gasped painfully. She had been too late!

What was she to do? A thought galvanized her into instant action.

"I must go to him at once!" she said firmly. "Get my revolver, Auntie. I'll have a glass of milk and be off!"

"Lawdy! Yo' ain't goin' to shoot nobody, be yo', Missey?"

"You never can tell in times like these, Auntie. Please hurry!"

"Bress mah soul!"

The horrified negress entered the house to reappear almost instantly with Marian's revolver in one hand and a glass of milk in the other. Marian strapped the weapon about her waist, then drank with relish.

"Ef yo' must shoot somebody, Missy," said Aunt 'Mandy, "be shore it am dat wolf pusson——"

Marian gazed at the negress inquiringly. "The Wolf! Have you seen him?"

"Shore as I have two eyes, Missy Marian! Jest arter de posse left de Wolf hisself done rode away down yander." She waved her hand in the direction of the "Chimney," where a huge dust-cloud lowered on the shimmering horizon.

Marian staggered against the porch railing, her hand pressed to her heart to still its tumultuous beating. Her worst fears had been confirmed—this wretch had started on his mission, and her brother was in peril! She had no time to lose if she hoped to save Ralph's life. A mist blurred her vision and her aching heart grew cold. Ah, how tired she was! She felt herself on the verge of collapse, but terror renewed her strength with marvelous quickness.

"I must follow him!" she said, after a pause. "Good-by, Auntie."

"De Lawd be wid you, chile!"

Marian leaped into the saddle and dashed away at

breakneck speed.   Aunt 'Mandy turned soberly to the
bungalow, grief and terror tugging at her heartstrings.

"Pore Missy! She shore am locoed! Dis yere
place am bewitched, shuah!"

While Marian, spurred on by one dominant desire
—to save her brother—was rushing headlong into the
jaws of the tiger, Haines was cautiously advancing
towards the "Chimney." He was eager to locate the
bandits whose presence somewhere beyond he subtly
sensed, but of whose precise whereabouts he had not
as yet found any trace. On the distant rim of the
horizon he thought he saw a spiral of smoke. His
suspicion that he had stumbled upon the bandits' retreat was verified when he beheld a column of black
vapor ascend lazily from behind a high cliff that
marked the southwestern boundary of the valley.

"Guess I'd better get back while the going's good,"
he said to himself audibly, a habit men readily acquire
on desert wastes. "Hello! What's that?"

The stealthy movement of some living thing on the
cliff riveted his attention suddenly. With the instinct of the born scout, he dropped flat behind a barrier of sand to await developments. After a brief
pause, he removed his hat and peered cautiously over
the top of the mound. Clearly outlined against the
sky he saw the sombreros of two men. That they
were on the lookout he did not doubt. They were
Mexicans, as the character of their hats clearly proved.
He looked again and dropped back with a laugh.

"Pedro!" he exclaimed. "Who is the other? If
birds of a feather flock together, then Pedro's mate
must be Valdez!"

He raised his head again and eyed the Mexicans
curiously.

"By George! They have spotted me with a telescope! Discretion is the better part of valor, so I had better beat it quick!''

He slid down into a gully and crawled backward several rods towards the place where he had left his pony. To his dismay, the animal had disappeared! Here was a pretty pickle! He was three miles from home with deadly enemies within a stone's throw from him, eager, for all he knew, to destroy him. He inspected his revolver with care, for in its chambers, should he be forced to battle for his life, lay his only hope of escape. He realized that his position, now that the bandits had sighted him, was precarious.

"I'll give them a show for their money," he soliloquized grimly. "Still, I can't say I did a wise thing to ride so far alone. Nevertheless, the game was worth the candle, for I know where they are now. What the deuce has become of that bronco?"

He whistled softly several times, hoping to hear the pony's answering neigh, but there was no response. Low as the sounds were, the summer breeze carried them distinctly to the trained ears of Holloway, who was groping along the bed of a gully not fifty feet away. Like Haines, he, too, had glimpsed the two bandits lying on the cliff beyond, but he was confident that neither had observed him.

The Mexicans disappeared suddenly, and he was considering his next step when he heard Haines' whistle. That there was some one almost within arm's length of him was certain, but was it friend or foe? He decided to remove all doubts on that score by crawling into the gully where the whistler lay concealed, prepared to welcome him if a friend, or give him battle should he prove an enemy. He advanced several yards, and looking over the rim of the gully, dropped back in surprise.

A Mexican was moving along at the base of the cliff!

Before he could catch a glimpse of the bandit's face, the man had bounded out of sight in a ravine. That he was one of Valdez's band, Holloway readily surmised. He lifted his head again and waited. The Mexican reappeared presently and Holloway recognized him instantly.

"Pedro!" he muttered. "He's got a rifle and is stalking big game! It's a cinch he's up to some deviltry which it is my duty to prevent if I can."

Resolved to balk Pedro's game whatever it might be, Holloway crept forward on his hands and knees. He had proceeded scarcely twenty yards, when a rifle shot, slightly to his left, boomed suddenly, the detonation startling him as a flash of lightning out of a clear sky might have done. In the belief that Pedro was firing at him, he sprawled upon the ground. He observed a cloud of smoke rising a few yards from him, and he was raising his head for another look, when the rifle thundered again. This was followed almost instantly by another report almost directly behind him.

"A revolver shot—possibly a forty-five," he mused. "Pedro is fighting a duel with some one, with the advantage on his side! I wonder who the other chap is. Hope I'm not in the line of fire."

He reasoned that it was high time for him to get into action against the Mexican. Discovering a break in the hardened sand at the top of the slope on which he lay, he was enabled, without exposing himself, to gain a clear view of the field for a distance of fifty yards on either side. Crouched behind a hillock twenty paces in front of him, he saw Pedro, his eyes glued to the sight of his rifle, the muzzle pointing toward the lower ground that sloped gradually away for a considerable distance beyond.

Before Holloway could determine the object of Pedro's fusillade, the Mexican fired again. At the same instant, a white man rose staggeringly in a shallow ravine below, with arms upraised, only to fall back at full length. Conscious that his bullet had found its mark, Pedro jumped up with a triumphant shout and ran in the direction of Holloway's hiding place with the evident intention of reaching his victim by a circuitous route and of robbing him of such valuables as he possessed. Holloway had not as yet recognized Haines, but it was sufficient for him to know that a Mexican had treacherously shot, if not killed, a white man from ambush, to rouse his fighting blood instantly to vigorous retaliatory action.

"Up with your hands, Pedro!" he shouted, bounding before the astonished bandit. "Make a move and I'll kill you like a rat!"

Pedro paused, a sinister look on his swarthy face.

"*Carramba!*" he swore. "How you get here, Wolf?"

"Drop that rifle! Be quick about it too!"

Pedro smiled cunningly. In his youth, when serving with renegade rurales in Chihuahua, some one had taught him a trick with the rifle that he had employed with success in more than one crisis in the course of his stormy career. This ruse was designed for use in precisely such emergencies as that which confronted him now, when death menaced him.

The maneuver was to permit the barrel of the rifle to slip slowly through his fingers as if he were about to drop it, and then, when it was on a level with his hip, to pull trigger and wing, if he did not kill, his adversary. He had become an adept at this species of murder, and he did not doubt that he would either kill or disable Holloway before he could even suspect the trick. At any rate, he must take a gambler's chance that the Wolf had no knowledge of the artifice, nor if he suspected, frustrate it in time to save himself.

"I savvy, Wolf," grinned Pedro, throwing the rifle forward. "The rifle and all it contains is yours—!"

He fired as he spoke, but quick as he had been, Holloway's revolver was the speedier. Pedro coughed, staggered and fell, an expression of blank amazement in his beady eyes. Holloway had not been deceived in his estimate of the treacherous character of the bandit, the depths of which he had plumbed long since. Therefore, when the greaser brought the muzzle of the weapon forward instead of downward, he instantly divined his deadly purpose. He fired from his hip without taking aim, a feat he had performed at many a rodeo on the frontier with remarkable results. Pedro's bullet passed through his left shirt sleeve, but he remained unscathed.

"You were insane to try that trick on me, Pedro," he said, approaching the prostrate Mexican, whom he still covered with his revolver. "It's old as the hills and I'm surprised that you should try it on an old hand like myself, *amigo.*"

"You got me dat time, Wolf," snarled Pedro resignedly. "But Valdex fix you some time, sure."

Holloway glanced at the cliff, wondering why the fusillade had not drawn the fire of the bandits he believed were quartered in the "Chimney." He examined the greaser, to find that his bullet had passed through Pedro's chest just below the heart, inflicting a wound that must end in death within a few minutes. He thrust his automatic back into its holster and proceeded to make the wounded man as comfortable as circumstances would permit. His duty as a man prompted this course, and neither rancor nor remorse oppressed him.

"Who was the man you shot, and why did you kill him?" asked Holloway, after he had played the Samaritan with beneficial results.

A sudden hemorrhage all but strangled Pedro. The kindness the Wolf had shown him, seemed to accentuate the hatred he bore him for beating him at his own game. He spat at Holloway, who smiled grimly at the savage rage he manifested in the face of approaching death. Pedro realized that his strength was ebbing fast, yet in the dread hour of his passing, the desire to revenge himself upon this man, dominated him.

"*Santa Maria!*" he moaned, "I wish I could killa you like I did Haines." He made a gesture to the right. Holloway looked down at him incredulously.

"Haines! You say it was Haines you shot?"

Pedro nodded, coughed painfully, then closed his eyes wearily. Holloway stood irresolute, his face the color of putty, his brain athrob with the horrible dread the bandit's disclosure had awakened in his mind— a terror as acute as it was indefinable. He ran like an antelope to the spot where Haines lay on his back, his blood-smeared face turned towards the sky. His right hand clutched a revolver, but Holloway ignored the weapon. He knelt by Haines' side to determine the extent of his wound. Haines breathed heavily, and from external appearances, at least, it was apparent to Holloway that he had been seriously wounded.

Holloway had some knowledge of first aid surgery which he had acquired in his travels, and after a careful examination, he reached the gratifying conclusion that Haines had sustained an apparently superficial scalp wound over the right temple. The wound had bled profusely, so that Haines' drab silk shirt had

Pedro has paid in blood the debt he owed to Society . . . His requiem was the yelping of a wolf, and the squawking of birds of prey.

been saturated with the ruddy flow. Holloway folded his coat into a pillow and placed it under Haines' head. The unconscious man breathed more freely, but it was certain, Holloway believed, that he would not revive until his wound was dressed, for which purpose water was an urgent necessity.

But where was he to find water? He had seen none since he left the valley, nor had he observed any signs of it in the dusty beds of the ravines he had traversed. It occurred to him that perhaps Pedro might be able to direct him to some pool beyond the cliff. He tied his handkerchief, which bore his insignia of the Wolf, about Haines' head and ran to Pedro who lay just as Holloway had left him. The dying man's face had assumed that ghastly putty-like pallor that heralded speedy dissolution. Unaware of Holloway's presence, he made the sign of the crucifix and mumbled a prayer.

"Pedro!" said Holloway, kneeling beside the Mexican.

The bandit opened his eyes languidly, then closed them again as if the effort had pained him. Holloway was startled at the alteration that had been wrought in the man in the few minutes he had been away from him—a change which, he knew, portended death within a few minutes.

"Water!" moaned Pedro. "By all the Saints, give me water!"

"Tell me where it is and I shall get it for you!"

"Behind the cliff—plenty there!" He pointed toward the "Chimney."

"But how about Valdez?" inquired Holloway, fearing a trap. "If you lead me into a trap, you don't get any water? Savvy, Pedro?"

"They are gone, I swear it!"

Holloway left him, convinced of his sincerity. He himself was athirst to the degree he had not hitherto

experienced even in Death Valley, where a too long
protracted thirst means a ticket to the Beyond in
short order for the sufferer. He carried Pedro's rifle
with him for use should he be attacked at long range,
and searched the ground for signs of the bandits who
might be lurking in the vicinity.

An object lying in his path attracted his attention,
and stooping, he picked up Pedro's telescope that had
fallen from his pocket unobserved. Holloway thrust
the glass into his hip pocket, and a few minutes later he
skirted the base of the cliff. Finding the opening indicated by Pedro, he passed through the cave and
entered the crater-like depression known as the
"Chimney."

In an open space flanked on the north and west by
dense chaparral thickets, he found the smoldering remains of a fire, and near by lay a battered pannikin.
He picked it up and glanced warily about him for
evidences of human life, but the place seemingly was
deserted. Near the camp site was a pool of water, fed
by a crystal spring. He drank his fill, thanked
Heaven devoutly for the exquisite joy he had experienced, filled the pannikin and returned hurriedly to
Pedro.

"Here's water, *hombre,*" he said, lifting Pedro's
head. "You mustn't drink too much."

The dying bandit drank with the eagerness characteristic of men who are being consumed by fever. He
might have drained the pannikin of the last drop had
not Holloway restrained him.

"That's enough, Pedro."

"*Santisimo!*" whispered the Mexican greedily eye-
ing the receptacle which Holloway had placed on the
ground beside him. "It is the nectar of the Gods!
Gracias! You go to Haines now, Wolf?"

"Yes.

"Haines not dead?" he inquired curiously.

"No."

"Then if this water save his life, he go to Hell with me!" muttered Pedro.

He extended his hand to overturn the pannikin, but Holloway was too quick for him and prevented the wanton wastage of the precious fluid.

"A dirty trick to play on a wounded man," said he reproachfully. "Once a greaser, always one, they say. I didn't believe it until now."

Pedro grinned sheepishly.

"*Jesu!*" he moaned weakly. "You have done for me, Wolf. But when Valdez get Missy Haines, den I laugh at you from my grave! Damn you!"

Holloway, who had turned to rejoin Haines, halted abruptly. "What do you mean by that?" he inquired coldly.

Pedro revealed to him in broken sentences the character of Valdez's mission. Holloway went white with apprehension as he listened.

"And if he should capture her," he asked, "whither will Valdez carry her?"

"To his hacienda at Los Vinos——to make—make her the thing he makes of every woman who falls into his hands! *Santa Maria!*"

Pedro's eyes were rapidly glazing. He clasped his hands and droned a prayer in a voice that was scarcely audible to Holloway who stood over him, staring sternly in the direction where, perhaps, at that very moment, Marian was struggling desperately in the hands of that implacable devil known as Valdez. The dying man now was unconscious of Holloway's presence, for his dark spirit stood at the portals of the hereafter, and blank terror held his shrinking soul in leash.

"Away, you fiends!" muttered Pedro, his face convulsed with terror. "You shall not take my soul! *Jesu,* save me! *Adios—adios!"* He gasped and lay still.

Holloway knelt beside him and listened. Not a tremor was visible—Pedro was dead! A coyote, crouched on a hillock of sand near by, howled mournfully. Holloway shivered. He paused for an instant, hat in hand, then picked up the pannikin and left the body as it lay. The coyote, scenting death, howled again, and trotting in ever-narrowing circles, closed in upon the body. Several specks appeared in the sky and presently a dozen vultures—fierce scavengers of the desert—were circling about overhead, emitting discordant cries.

Pedro had paid in blood the long deferred debt he owed Society at large, and there was none to mourn his memory. His requiem was the yelping of a wolf, and the squawking of birds of prey.

CHAPTER XIV

A STRONG MAN'S AGONY

HAINES' condition had meanwhile changed for the worse. Holloway, worried lest his aid might prove futile, withdrew the shell of the cartridge whose bullet had killed Pedro, thrust it into the pannikin and poured the water drop by drop upon Haines' protruding tongue. He then removed the bandana handkerchief from his head, and soaking the fabric, washed away the extravasated blood about the wound, employing all the skill and tenderness of touch of a professional nurse in the operation.

Despite his efforts to prevent it, the effusion reasserted itself, though in a modified degree, but presently he was permitted to make a more careful examination of the wound. As far as his meager knowledge of surgery went, he was convinced that unless Haines' skull was fractured, the wound itself would prove a trifle. The dressing finished, he retied the handkerchief around Haines' temples. Again he poured some water between Haines' lips, then crouched down beside him. The gnats and flies becoming troublesome, Holloway fended them off with Haines' own handkerchief which he had appropriated for the occasion.

Haines soon began to breathe more regularly and with less effort. In fact, he seemed to be sleeping naturally. Holloway could not understand why he had not regained consciousness inasmuch as fully thirty minutes had elapsed since Pedro's shot had

175

stunned him. A painful nausea seized Holloway suddenly—a frightful retching, the combined effect of the
extraordinary heat that prevailed, lack of nourish-
ment, excitement and, what was more probable, his
voluntary abstention from liquor for a period of ap-
proximately eighteen hours. Even in the paroxysm
that convulsed him it occurred to him that if he only
had a drink of whisky, he would be the happiest man
alive.

The old craving for liquor possessed him to the degree that for the moment, he fancied he would go
mad. The nausea, however, left him as suddenly as
it had manifested itself, but the desire for drink persisted. Picking up the pannikin, he drank freely of
the now lukewarm water it contained. Abominably
brackish and nauseating though the fluid was to his
taste, it had a decidedly beneficial effect, so that he
was soon restored to his normal self.

He could not help thinking of Pedro's startling disclosure regarding Valdez's intention to kidnap Marian
if he had not already accomplished his dastardly design. The prospect of her capture terrified him, and
he shuddered at the awful fate that awaited her
should she fall into the hands of that abominable outlaw. If Pedro spoke the truth, how was he to prevent the abduction? His glance resting upon Haines,
he saw the eyelids tremble and open slightly. He
filled his cupped hand and dashed the water into his
face. Several tense seconds passed, but there was no
immediate indication of reviving consciousness.

Holloway's uneasiness increased momentarily. His
mind was active and as he watched, thoughts of his
own peril in the light of this almost inconceivable fatality, flashed into his mind. Suppose Haines were
to die—was it not inevitable that he would be accused

of his murder? A thousand acts of his pointed conclusively to his guilt—the quarrel in the Red Eye, the death threat, his refusal to join Lucas' posse after he had learned that Haines held a subordinate command in that body! For a moment, consternation seized him, but he assured himself at last that Haines would recover and by his own voluntary statement exonerate him in the face of the most convincing circumstantial evidence that the human brain might conceive·of or set in motion for the undoing of a man innocent of crime!

Marian's peril, which he could not help believing was real, despite his lack of faith in anything Pedro might have said even under oath, weighed heavily upon his heart. Intuition warned him that Pedro had spoken the truth. It was certain that Valdez was not at the "Chimney," for had he been, he must have manifested his presence vigorously during the fusillade. Then he must be elsewhere—perhaps Marian already had fallen into his hands! He hid his face in his palms and groaned.

Thinking again of his own plight, he was conscious that Sweetwater was practically, or soon would be, surrounded by the posse, and that the discovery of Haines, desperately wounded or dead, inevitably must invite a searching inquiry. That he would be suspected as Haines' assailant was a foregone conclusion. How could his innocence be established? Certainly not by the discovery of Pedro's body, or his own unsupported statement testifying to his involuntary connection with the tragedy. Would it not be surmised and accepted as fact, that Pedro, who doubtless was known to have had a grudge against Haines, had been his accessory in the crime, and that the Mexican had been remorselessly killed by the Wolf to forever close the lips of a possible witness against him should be brought to trial as the perpetrator of the crime?

"I'm in a horrible mess!" he said to himself. "I have brought all this upon myself, but no matter what may happen, I shall have the consciousness of my own innocence. My bad luck sure has dealt me a rotten hand!"

It occurred to him suddenly that he still had time to escape, as faith in ultimate rescue comes to a man who is fighting, his back to a wall, against vastly superior odds, despairing, yet not without hope of survival. The impulse that seized him to flee incontinently was a fleeting one, and he dismissed it resolutely from his mind, resolved to accept with stolid equanimity all that the future might hold in store for him.

On turning to Haines again, Holloway observed with profound agitation that he had regained consciousness and was staring at him wonderingly like a man who had just awakened from prolonged sleep. Holloway sat down beside him to await developments. Haines rubbed his eyes as if he could not believe the message they conveyed to his understanding.

"Who are you?" he faltered.

Holloway smiled, but made no reply.

"You are the Wolf!" exclaimed Haines suddenly. "I know you now."

Holloway laughed. He rejoiced that Haines was far from being a dead man. Nothing else, not even insults, mattered now.

"I once was called the Wolf," he replied simply. "But by the way, won't you have some water?"

He offered the pannikin to Haines who spurned it impatiently.

"So it was you who shot me, Wolf?"

Holloway's face colored, but he merely shrugged.

"You don't deny that you shot me, do you?" persisted Haines.

"Do you really believe I shot you?"

Haines groaned. His wound distressed him. He was feverish and irritable, but he would not permit Holloway to touch him.

"In view of what I know, Wolf, it must have been you—"

"If you are convinced of that," interrupted Holloway, extending his automatic, handle outward, to Haines, "then you may revenge yourself by blowing out my brains!"

Haines took the weapon in his weakened grasp and held it waveringly against Holloway's body. The latter smiled grimly, but his lips did not quiver. Immobile as a statue, he awaited Haines' next move.

"Why shouldn't I kill you?" said Haines, after a pause. "You threatened to kill me in a notice you posted at the Red Eye last night, didn't you?"

"Who told you?"

"Belcher."

"I frankly confess I did," replied Holloway, a lump in his throat. "I was a drunken imbecile last night. But when I thought it over, I—I—"

"Go on!"

"Repented!"

Haines dropped the revolver, a scornful smile on his swollen face. "Repented!" he echoed coldly. "I'm afraid that yellow streak you showed at the Red Eye, reasserted itself and—"

"Stop!" interrupted Holloway. "Were that true, you would be a dead man now!"

"Murdered, you mean?"

Holloway shivered at the insult, but nevertheless he showed no resentment. He told Haines how he happened to have started for the "Chimney," of sight-ing Pedro and of all that followed. Haines listened to the recital with languid interest, but his manner evinced lingering distrust of the man who had publicly sworn to kill him at sight.

"You swear you are speaking the truth?" he asked wearily.

"Before God!"

"How came you to change your mind? Was it fear of the consequences?"

"No, no!"

"Then what caused it?"

"Your sister!"

"Marian!"

"She saved me from myself!" answered Holloway. "How she shamed me before that crowd! But for her, God alone knows what I might be now!"

He related in simple language the details of his meeting with Marian, ignoring no circumstance the telling of which might injure him irretrievably in the estimation of this man whose friendship and respect he sought to win. His earnestness, his pitiless arraignment of himself, his candor and convincing truthfulness, impressed Haines. When Holloway had finished he said to himself that here was a man who was not as low as he was reputed to be.

"I rejoice in your regeneration, Wolf, but—but—"

"What do you mean?"

"You must not see or speak to my sister again!"

Holloway recoiled, a frown on his face.

"Not see her again!" he answered protestingly. "You do not know what you are saying, for I love her!"

Haines groaned, then exerting all his strength, lifted himself to a sitting posture. He was weak as an infant from loss of blood and to prevent him from falling backward, Holloway had to support him.

"How dare you love my sister!" he said angrily. "You, who haven't even a name, as far as I am aware!"

Holloway in turn only adjusted Haines' loosened bandage.

"Oh, yes, I have a name of which many a man would be proud," he answered modestly.

"What it is?"

"Jim Holloway."

Amazed, Haines placed his hands on Holloway's shoulder and scanned his face intently.

"Not Jim Holloway, of Harvard?"

"The same."

"Full back of the team six years ago?"

"Righto!" smiled Holloway. "I think I know you now! You were the Yale coach—"

"Quite right," interrupted Haines proudly. "And we beat you ten to two!"

Holloway nodded. "You sure did!" he assented, "but the figures would have been reversed if your bunch of pirates hadn't caved in two of my slats!"

Holloway frowned. The time for reminiscensing was ill-chosen and it was his duty to carry Haines home as speedily as possible.

"There's a heavy weight pressing on my brain!" Haines exclaimed suddenly. "I don't understand—"

"It's the sun," said Holloway solicitously. "I'll carry you to a shady spot where you may rest, while I ride for help."

He observed with increasing anxiety that Haines had grown livid and that he babbled like a child.

"Keep away from my sister, Wolf, or I'll kill you!" he muttered. "I won't stand for a scoundrel like you! Kill me? Bah!" He mumbled some words incoherently. The prescience of evil came to Holloway who trembled at the inexplicable change that had been wrought in the wounded man.

"You're Belcher, aren't you?" asked Haines. "I'm ill and you mustn't let the Wolf get at me! I'm going to the 'Chimney' and will meet you in an hour at the latest. Down with the greasers! No quarter!"

Holloway was genuinely alarmed at this delirium. He sought to quiet Haines, who chattered idiotically for a time, lapsing finally into a stupor resembling death.

"He was wounded more seriously than I thought," Holloway mused sadly. "Fool that I was! I believed him as strong as myself and literally talked him into insensibility! I must obtain help at once or he will die on my hands!"

Wondering how this was to be averted, he turned to behold a spectacle that riveted his gaze instantly. Topping a ridge a half mile to his left, he saw several horsemen, traveling Indian fashion. They were moving away from him rapidly but he observed that there were two riders on one horse—the last of the cavalcade. The pony was cavorting excitedly and it was apparent to Holloway's splendid vision that the riders were engaged in a desperate struggle.

He focused Pedro's telescope upon the horsemen, several of whom had already disappeared in a depression beyond. Fortune favored him, for the broncho carrying the struggling riders pranced in a circle revealing the faces of the riders distinctly. A sort of paralysis seized his limbs so that he staggered, and an agonized cry escaped him.

The riders were Marian and Valdez!

"Merciful Heaven!" he exclaimed. "She is in that man's hands! It is maddening!"

Marian, the prisoner of the most notorious bandit

Mexico had produced! The knowledge infuriated him. How was he to rescue her, single-handed, from that strongly guarded robber chief? At any cost, it had to be done, and it was up to him to find the means to outwit the outlaw and to save the woman he loved from a fate the horror of which he dared not contemplate.

"I shall trail them!" he said grimly. "And if I fail to save her I will deserve to die a coward, despised by all who know me!"

He all but stumbled over the recumbent form of Haines, and his heart sank. Was he to leave Marian's brother to die, alone and helpless? His better nature spurned this as unworthy, yet love spurred him on irresistibly to the rescue of the woman he adored. Strange that with more than a score of American riders somewhere within a circle of three miles from where he stood, not one had appeared on the horizon within the range of his vision! He thought of firing several shots to attract the attention of any white men who might be prowling in the neighborhood. Picking up the automatic revolver which he believed to be his, but which in fact was Haines' weapon, he thrust it in his belt and whistled three or four times sharply.

Came the answering neigh of Pinto and presently he was gratified to see the faithful pony struggle out of a ravine and trot towards him. He vaulted into the saddle and, turning, saw two horsemen a hundred yards to the northward. Here at last was help for Haines! The men at least were white, and Holloway recognized them as cowboys from the valley. He fired twice into the air, and having attracted their attention, pointed to the spot where Haines lay, dying, for all he knew. That curiosity would prompt them to investigate and lead them to Haines, he was certain.

His mind at rest on that score, he galloped towards the south in the bandits' wake.

He rode into the "Chimney" without giving a thought to the possibility that he might be risking his life in the fire of enemies lying in ambush. Reaching the thicket, it occurred to him that if he should be attacked and disabled, Marian would be lost beyond hope! He dismounted and, entering the copse, crawled through to the opposite side, whence he surveyed the valley beneath him with care.

Barring a coyote or two, not a sign of life was visible. Had Valdez and his men passed through the "Chimney," as he believed, and if so, whither had they gone? That they were compelled to ride through the little valley in order to reach the Mexican border without interference, he well knew. Every other avenue of escape, he also was aware, was closed to them by the Sheriff's posse that hemmed in the approaches to and from Red Sandy valley on its eastern boundary. But as far as he could see, nothing stirred. This circumstance caused him intense annoyance.

"Where have the devils disappeared to?" he muttered uneasily. "There must be some hidden road leading out of this place, of which I am ignorant. No matter! Since all roads lead to Rome, so do all in this valley lead to Valdez's hacienda in Sonora! I'll make for that spot without loss of time, and may God protect Marian until I find means to save her!"

He deemed it prudent to make the ride to Sonora along unfrequented paths, for he did not relish the idea of being identified by some chance acquaintance en route. Fortunately for his purpose, the afternoon was well advanced, but to avoid Butler where he was well known as the Wolf, he made a wide detour. Meeting a peon now and then he made cautious inquiries regarding Valdez. The surly replies he received invariably were in the negative. It was dusk when he crossed the border and two hours later, in the silvery light of the full moon, he halted at the store of Sam Jackson, an American merchant in the village of Los Vinos three miles from Valdez's retreat.

Holloway had traded with Jackson often, and the latter knew him as the Wolf, who, he declared to his intimate friends, "was the squarest white man on the border." Jackson greeted him heartily and manifested no surprise when his visitor made several peculiar and, to him, inexplicable purchases. These included among other things some dyes and the complete outfit of a Mexican servant of high degree.

"Goin' to a masquerade ball, Wolf?" he chuckled, placing a bottle and glass before him. "Better have a glass of the real stuff before you start."

"I've given up drink, Jackson."

"The deuce you say! Rather sudden, ain't it?"

"That's as you view it, Sam."

"All right, Wolf. Do as you like!"

Holloway leaned upon the counter and in a whisper asked the storekeeper if he had seen Valdez recently. Jackson replied that the bandit had passed the store less than an hour ago.

"You don't say so!"

"He and his men looked tuckered out like, and judging by their horses, they must have had a rough ride!"

Although Holloway appeared quite unconcerned, his heart was thumping like a trip hammer.

"Did you see a white person—a woman, with them?" he inquired, lighting a cigarette.

"By George! Now you mention it, I believe I did! She was in the saddle while he sat behind her. He hain't been abducting anybody, has he?"

"I have my suspicions, Sam."

"A friend of yours?" asked Jackson curiously.
"Who—Valdez?"

"No! The girl!"

"No," drawled Holloway. "Merely the sister of a friend of mine."

"I see your game, Wolf!" chuckled Jackson, pointing to Holloway's purchases. "You intend to disguise yourself as a greaser and try to rescue her, eh?"

"Right you are, pardner!"

"Can I help you in any way?"

"Yes—by putting me up somewhere for the night."

"Surest thing you know."

He led Holloway to a store room in the rear, filled with bales of goods, boxes and barrels. In one corner, behind a tall screen, was a battered lounge, and near it a small table, on which was a candlestick and a small handglass. The place was admirably adapted for Holloway's scheme, the nature of which the store-keeper shrewdly conjectured.

"There you are. Make yourself at home."

"Thanks, Sam, you're a prince!"

"I'm closing up the shebang soon. You can go to bed when you like, and I'll see you in the morning. Hello! There's somebody!"

Jackson left him and presently Holloway heard him in conversation with the newcomer who appeared to be in a great hurry. They conversed in Spanish, which Holloway spoke like a native Castilian. He went to the door and, hiding behind it, listened. The newcomer's voice had a familiar ring and, catching a glimpse of his face, he recognized Lopez, a greaser whom he once had thrashed severely for insulting a white woman in Purple Canyon.

"I want some camphor," said Lopez surlily. "Quick! I have little time to waste!"

"Is it for Valdez?"

"No—no, a woman!"

"A white woman?" queried Jackson.

"What difference does that make to you?" growled Lopez. "Trot out the camphor and ask no questions."

"Here you are."

Lopez placed the drug in his pocket, tossed a coin upon the counter and wheeled on his heel. He paused for a moment and turning asked Jackson if he knew of a valet who was seeking a position. Jackson scratched his head in perplexity and asked who required such a man.

"Valdez."

"I'll try to find one for him in the morning."

"*Bueno! Adios!*"

Holloway strolled through the store unconcernedly, smoking a cigarette. He stepped out onto the veranda to survey the peaceful scene that lay before him. The houses that lined the village street were for the greater part in darkness, but here and there lights gleamed in latticed windows, despite the soft brilliance of the tropical moon, that illuminated the landscape with noon-day splendor. From a wine shop nearby there floated to him a rich tenor voicing an indescribably sweet Spanish love song to the accompaniment of a mandolin and flute. The harmony was exquisite and it vested the beauty of the night with rare charm and tenderness. A delicious lethargy seized Holloway as he sat entranced; and he felt himself insensibly yielding to that Circe-like spell of the tropics which fascinated and held him in captive chains, a willing and delighted prisoner.

"Guess I'll go to bed," he said with a yawn. He rose, reëntered the store and bidding Jackson goodnight, turned in. He heard faintly the refrain of the love song even as the sound died away sweetly like the soft tones of a soloist in some vast cathedral. He lapsed into slumber peacefully as a child.

.   .   .   .

When Jackson opened the store the next morning, a well-dressed Mexican, young, tall, swarthy, his teeth gleaming like rows of polished ivory between his red lips, a whisp of a mustache showing beneath his nose, saluted him familiarly. Jackson paid little attention to the man who was a stranger to him. He observed that the Mexican's face was disfigured by a livid scar that extended from the right corner of the mouth to the lobe of the ear. The man addressed him in excellent Spanish and inquired if he could direct him to any señor who required the services of an experienced valet or house servant, he cared not which.

"You're the very *hombre* I'm looking for, *amigo*."

And he forthwith told him to apply to Señor Valdez at his hacienda three miles to the southwest, and to say to him that he, Jackson, was glad to recommend him.

"*Gracias, señor*," responded the Mexican graciously. Then in English he said, a twinkle in his dark eyes, "May the saints reward you for your kindness to a stranger, Sam Jackson!"

"Well, I'm hornswoggled!"

Jackson was dumbfounded, for he recognized the Wolf's voice. Holloway laughingly asked if his disguise was perfect.

"I should say it was! You'd fool old Nick himself in them togs, and your Spanish—say, where in tarnation did you get that pronunciation?"

"I studied Spanish at Harvard, and perfected it in Spain and Mexico."

"It's all right, I guess, Wolf, but suppose Valdez gets onto your disguise?"

"Suppose he does—what then?"

"He would snuff out your life as I would a candle!"

"There will be two to play at that game. How does this scar become me?"

"It's the most remarkable change I ever saw in any man! Your own mother wouldn't know you were she to see you now."

"*Bueno!*" responded Holloway. "I'm off, Sam. Good-by!"

Jackson stared after Holloway admiringly as he rode away, but not on Pinto, which animal was resting luxuriously in Jackson's stable to await his master's call when needed.

An hour later, Sanchez de la Guardia, formerly a servant in the employ of the Governor of Durango, became attached to the household of Señor Cipriano Valdez as valet and house servant.

Standing at a window above when the valet approached the hacienda stood a white girl. She observed that he was hideously scarred and turned from him with repugnance. The girl was Marian Haines. Her heart was heavy and she prayed fervently for speedy rescue.

In the newcomer, who sought in vain to attract her attention, she failed to recognize the instrument of her deliverance from bondage. When Holloway entered her prison house in the guise of a body servant, he frankly confessed that only a fool would have embarked in a similar enterprise—a scheme of such daring as no man not totally bereft of sense could conceive with the slightest hope of success.

CHAPTER XV

AN OFFICIAL INQUIRY

EXCITEMENT ran high when the exaggerated news reached Purple Canyon that the Wolf had not only executed his threat to kill Ralph Haines at sight, but had supplemented his murderous act by kidnaping his victim's sister, of whom not a trace could be discovered. The fact that Haines still lived and was quite unlikely to die, did not in public estimation alter one iota the heinousness of the Wolf's crime, and demands for his arrest and punishment were loudly voiced.

That Valdez and his bandits had been expelled from Red Sandy valley without the loss of a single man of Sheriff Thorne's posse was, in the light of the Wolf's crime, a trifling circumstance which interested nobody, and, therefore, excited little comment. When the available facts were revealed, there rose a popular cry for vengeance upon the lawless characters that made Purple Canyon their headquarters to the shame and annoyance of the law-abiding element of the town.

The long advocated organization of a Vigilance Committee to deal summarily with the marauding scoundrels that preyed upon the community, was immediately perfected. The conclusion that the Wolf had slain the Mexican called Pedro, whose body was found near the scene of the alleged attempt upon the life of Ralph Haines, was generally accepted as irrefutable. The popular theory was that the greaser

190

had witnessed the shooting of Haines from ambush, if indeed, he was not actually an accessory, and that to silence the only witness of his crime, the Wolf had remorselessly shot the ruffian to death, thereafter capturing Marian Haines and forcing her to accompany him to parts unknown.

Urged to instant action by the Vigilance Committee, of which Mr. Hawthorne, the banker, was the president and main financial prop, Sheriff Thorne decided that public policy demanded that a reward be offered for the Wolf, dead or alive, preferably the former. Preparatory to taking that step, however, he desired more positive evidence connecting the Wolf with the crime and, incidentally, he was keenly desirous of probing into the fugitive's family history, the details of which were enshrouded in mystery.

To obtain the information he needed, it was necessary for him to hold a court of inquiry at which the testimony of sworn witnesses would be given to the end that all the facts regarding the Wolf's family, as well as his latest offense against the law, might be dragged from obscurity into the effulgent light of day.

It chanced that the publication of the sensational details of Valdez's raid and of the subsequent shooting of Haines in the newspapers at El Paso, had brought Judge Ham A. Hopkins, the southwestern representative of the National Law and Order League, post haste to Purple Canyon. Judge Hopkins was a stern-visaged man of about fifty years, and a staunch supporter of the principles of law and order. The rigid enforcement of the law, he insisted, alone guaranteed the safety and well being of the frontier communities, already too long harassed by the crime waves that had periodically engulfed them for decades past, thereby retarding civic progress.

Of course, Sheriff Thorne was glad to have Judge Hopkins' coöperation and after a protracted conference, it was agreed to hold a sort of ante-mortem inquest over the living remains of poor Haines. The only regret expressed by the eminent jurist was that Haines could not testify, it having been established by competent medical testimony that as a result of the grievous wound he had sustained, his memory had lapsed, perhaps never to return.

The announcement that a public inquiry would be held the next morning, served to attract an immense crowd of curious citizens to Purple Canyon and promptly at the advertised hour, the Sheriff's office was packed with influential residents and others certainly less prominent in the business and social life of the bustling town. The street was thronged with morbid crowds, all eager to witness the culminating scenes of this thrilling drama of human lives, which, through the latest escapade of the Wolf, threatened to become the *cause célèbre* of the great Southwest.

Horsemen, some drunk, some semi-sober, and all whooping excitedly, dashed here and there along the streets, to the imminent peril of the scores of women and children who clung to the fringe of the mob gathered in front of the Sheriff's office, vainly clamoring for admittance to the building so that they might see and hear all that transpired.

In the excitement the unprecedented crush occasioned, it was to be expected that scant notice would be accorded to strangers. Hence it was, that when a weather beaten man of small stature, some forty years of age, who was smoking a cheroot with tranquil enjoyment, dismounted at Bert Mason's store, he attracted no attention whatever from the passersby. He wore the ordinary cowpuncher's costume, with sombrero, bandana, chaps, spurs and the inevitable automatic revolver within easy reach at his side. He tossed the bridle rein over the top of a post and watched the crowd curiously. His cheroot going out as it was wont to do when he was thoughtful, he relit the weed and walked leisurely into Mason's somewhat dingy emporium.

The proprietor, a tall raw-boned man of fifty years, rather unkempt in appearance, but recognized as one of the most substantial citizens of the town, was sweeping up some refuse in the rear of the store when the stranger entered. He finished his task and, perceiving the newcomer, manifested surprise. He threw the broom in a corner and approached with outstretched hand, to welcome his visitor.

"Well, durn me, if it ain't the Texas Kid!" he said genially. "Where you been all this time, pardner?"

"I been away on my annual vacation, Bert," answered the little man, seating himself on a soap box. " 'Pears like they is some excitement yarabouts. What in all-fired nation's goin' on yonder?" He pointed to the surging crowd in the street. "Political meetin' or somethin', eh?"

"It's nothin' like that. Hain't you heard the news?"

"I hain't heard nothin'," responded the other, searching his pockets for a match. "I jest got to town ten minutes ago. Gimme a match, Bert."

"Geewhiz!"

Here was a Heaven-sent opportunity for Mason, a born gossip, to recount events that had stirred the country, far and near, to one who was wholly ignorant of the details. So, like a gourmet mouthing a delicious morsel, Mason related the story of the Mexican raid, enlarging especially upon the Wolf's shocking crime. Of course, as there was none to refute his statements, his imagination had full play, so that his yarn was picturesque and thrilling.

"Well, I declare!" said the stranger when Mason had finished. "That 'ere Wolf must be a devilish wild pusson!"

"He sure is."

"Well, thar ain't a word o' truth in all yuh have said, Bert."

"I hain't vouchin' for its truth, kid. I'm only tellin' yuh what the story is."

"Yuh don't reckon them chumps out thar believe all that rot?"

"They sure do!" said Mason, thumping the counter against which he leaned. "I'm tellin' yuh that if they get the Wolf, old Judge Lynch will be mighty busy!"

The little man relit his cheroot. He smoked reflectively for a moment, then shrugged.

"By the way, Bert," he said carelessly, "I want to have a look at the Wolf's room upstairs. Thar be some things o' mine thar which, seein' as he ain't likely to return instanter, I should like to get my paws on afore Thorne and his bunch get wise to them."

"I'm jiggered, if that don't remind me!" exclaimed Mason. "The Wolf told me when he left here that there was an envelope addressed to me, sayin' as how he wanted me to mail the letter it contained if he failed to show up in a week or so."

"You don't say!"

"It's three days now since he dropped out o' sight, so I guess I had better git the letter—"

"I wouldn't bother about it if I wus yuh, Bert," said the other, restraining him. "I'll attend to it for yuh, if yuh don't mind."

"All right."

"I'm always glad to sarve a friend. Gimme the key."

"Sure thing!"

Mason took the key from a drawer of his desk and handed it to the little man who left the store without a word. Five minutes later he entered the room above. It wore an air of neglect, for it had not been entered since the day Holloway left for Red Sandy valley. The little man raised the window to admit light and air, and the first object that attracted his attention was a large white envelope addressed to Bert Mason, propped carefully against an oil lamp. He picked it up and written in one corner he read the words, "Please mail the inclosed letter if I fail to return to Purple Canyon within five days."

"Bully!" muttered he, tearing off one end of the envelope. "Just in time, too! If they'd got this, the jig would have been up an' the Lord knows what would have happened to that pore mother back yonder in New York!"

He removed the enclosed letter, fully stamped and addressed, and held it up to the light. It bore the address, "Charles Holloway, No. 2650 Riverside Drive, New York." He thrust the missive carefully into the inside pocket of his gayly embroidered vest.

"It's durned lucky I found this!" he thought. "If so be none o' these people know who the Wolf is, the which I don't reckon, I'll see to it they don't get wise to the identification regardless." He relighted his cheroot and fell adreaming. "I'm a constitutin' myself the Wolf's guardeen right now!" he muttered, "an' if anybody disputes my legal rights in the premises as the lawyers say, they is agoin' to run agin a snag!" He paused, then resumed: "Guess I hain't got no time to waste, if I wants to pick up

Jim's trail. Thar's a mystery about the shootin' of
Haines, the which I hev got to fathom instanter! Not
that I believe Jim done it, 'cause I know he didn't,
but—it hain't no use o' speculatin' on the whys
an' wherefores, till I gits the facts an' sift 'em careful.''

He picked up Holloway's suitcase which lay under
the cot, and observing nothing else of value, left the
room, locking the door after him. When he reëntered
Mason's store, he placed the suitcase beneath a counter
with the request that Bert guard it carefully until
he heard from him. To this Mason readily gave his
assent.

"You got the letter, Kid?" he asked curiously.
"Who was it addressed to?"

"To me, Bert," responded the puncher. "By the
way, yuh won't say nothin' 'bout me bein' hyar to-
day, eh?"

"Not if you don't want me to."

"Thanks. See you later. So long!"

The Kid, who, it probably has been surmised, was
Hank Weston, left the store leisurely and mixed with
the crowd of two hundred or more persons massed in
front of Sheriff Thorne's office and contiguous buildings. He found it impossible to reach the entrance.
It occurred to him that he might be more succcessful
if he tried the door in the rear. He had little difficulty in negotiating this spot, but when he reached
the entrance three burly deputies checked his advance.

"Git back, yuh!" snarled one of the trio.
"Whatcha want?"

"I want to git in, o'co'se!"

"But yuh don't git in! Them's orders! See!"

The deputy's autocratic manifestation of authority
was offensive to Hank whose eyes glittered danger-

ously, while his hand rested itchingly on the butt of his automatic.

"I guess yuh is wrong, pardner," he responded quietly. "I'm due to see Sheriff Thorne instanter, so git out'n my way, or I'll pull yore nose an' make a holy spectacle o' yuh! D'ye get me, yuh boob?"

The deputy growled, but after a careful inspection of Hank, he intuitively figured that this little chap was one with whom it was unsafe to trifle. Muttering something about "not knowin' he had business with the Sheriff," he opened the door and permitted Hank to enter.

The interior was packed to the point of suffocation with a motley crowd of spectators and others having more or less pertinent business with the inquiry which had just begun. Directly in front of him, facing the mob that filled the space beyond the railed enclosure, sat Judge Hopkins and Sheriff Thorne with a secretary who was preparing to make notes of the testimony of the witnesses, to satisfy the professional scruples of the eminent jurist who stoutly maintained that the inquiry should be conducted strictly in accordance with the rules of legal procedure.

Seated at a table nearby, making copious notes, was a dapper well-dressed young man, whose face Hank could not see. About him were grouped the witnesses summoned by the Sheriff, among them being Mr. Hawthorne, Dr. J. Sanders, a dissipated surgeon who had treated Haines professionally, Aunt 'Mandy, who, like Niobe, was all tears because of the inexplicable disappearance of her "Missy," Seth Lucas, Sam Belcher and several frequenters of the Red Eye. Conspicuous among the latter, Hank recognized Faro Jenn. She appeared quite unconcerned, but secretly she was ill at ease and heartily wished herself out of the mess into which she had been drawn.

"Order!" shouted the Sheriff sternly. "If you folks don't keep quiet, I'll have to clear the room!"

Except for the occasional shuffling of feet, silence prevailed. Judge Hopkins announced that while the inquiry was a quasi-legal proceeding, he purposed to establish all the facts leading up to the commission of the Wolf's alleged crime and the subsequent kidnaping of Miss Marian Haines.

"The law and society," he resumed oratorically, "demand that this man, known as the Wolf, be brought to justice, if guilty. He doubtless has a name and it is needless to say that the sobriquet of the Wolf is an alias. The law requires the culprit's real name, Mr. Sheriff. Do you know it?"

"I reckon some persons here know it, your honor," answered Thorne amid impressive silence. "The Wolf scribbled a name that looked like Galloway, on the card he wrote, threatenin' to kill Haines."

"Very well, Mr. Sheriff," responded the jurist wisely. "We will determine upon the name after we have heard the preliminary testimony. Call your first witness."

"Coyote Pete! Take the stand!"

Coyote, a cowboy who spent most of his time and all of his money, in carousals and playing poker at the Red Eye, told of the memorable meeting of the Wolf and Haines on the night before the shooting of the latter near the "Chimney" in Red Sandy valley. In cowpuncher style he related all that had happened on that occasion, the crowd listening breathlessly.

"You say that in addition to the term 'the Wolf,' the accused wrote another name on the notice he posted?" inquired the Judge.

"He sure did, Jedge."

"What was it?"

The witness coughed to hide his confusion. "Yuh

see, Jedge," he said apologetically, "I ain't much on handwritin' and readin' them things, but I heard one o' the boys say the name wus Jim Galloway."

"You're sure it was Galloway?"

"Putty sure, Jedge."

"Might it not have been Jim Holloway?"

The dapper young man who was making notes, shot an approving glance at the jurist, who, to restore order, rapped the table several times.

"I ain't a'sayin', Jedge, 'cause I hain't sure o' my ground."

"What became of the death threat written by the Wolf?"

"He tuk it down an' tore it up."

"When was that?"

"Arter his talk with Miss Haines."

The crowd buzzed at this statement, and after a pause, Judge Hopkins asked the witness to relate what he saw.

"It wus like this," faltered Coyote nervously. "Arter the Wolf wrote the notice an' ducked out, one o' the boys read it to the bunch an' then we all rushed outen the Red Eye and tacked it up agin the front of the house aside the door. Jest then Marian Haines came along an' read it herself."

"How do you know the woman was Marian Haines?"

" 'Cause she nacherly said she was Ralph Haines' sister. She wanted us to take her to the Wolf's hangout so's she could beg him to take back what he wrote an' save her brother's life."

"And did you take her to the Wolf's home?"

"No, Jedge, 'cause jest then the Wolf showed up hisself. He wus standin' on the edge of the crowd, alookin' at Miss Haines savage like. Some one yells that the Wolf is in our midst or somethin' to that effect, an' Miss Haines goes to him an' asks him what he has agin her brother sufficient to want to kill him.''

"Did the Wolf make any reply?"

"Not so's anybody could notice it, he didn't, Jedge. He kinder choked like when she says to him tearful, if you've got a sister, I beg you in her name not to shoot my brother.''

"What was his reply?"

" He didn't say nothin', but just looked at her like he wus dreamin'. Then she said, if you've got a mother, I beg you in her name not to carry out your threat. The Wolf pulls his gat and thinkin' he is goin' to pepper us, the crowd scatters fur cover.'' .

"What did Miss Haines do then?" asked the Judge.

"Seein' the Wolf put the gun to his head, she up and takes it from him. The Wolf doesn't make no offer to keep the weapon, and the next minute Miss Haines drops the gun and runs away, cryin' like her heart had gone an' busted.''

"And then?"

"The Wolf picks up the gun. I ducked around the corner of the Red Eye and lookin' keerful like, I see the Wolf take down the notice and tear it up. Then he went up the street an' I never seen him agin.''

Other witnesses testified substantially to the same circumstances. From the comments of Judge Hopkins during the recital of these sensational facts, it was inferred by the audience that in revenge for the humiliation he had suffered at the hands of Miss Haines, the Wolf had conceived the plan to abduct her after shooting her brother and that on the following day, he succeeded in accomplishing his purposes.

Called to the stand, Seth Lucas testified as to the facts of his meeting with the Wolf at the Haines' bungalow on the day of the shooting. His statement that the Wolf, on being informed that Haines was an officer of the posse, declined to serve, caused a commotion among the spectators.

"Order!"

"You say, Mr. Lucas, that he told you he had no intention of executing his threat against Mr. Haines?"

"He did."

"Did his manner impress you as being sincere?"

"He told me he had made a fool of himself while drunk and that he didn't purpose to hurt a hair of Haines' head, or words to that effect. He impressed me as being quite sincere."

"Thank you, Mr. Lucas. You are excused."

Aunt 'Mandy, the next witness called, told of seeing the Wolf at the bungalow, and of his departure for the "Chimney" in the wake of the posse. When the negress gave her account of Marian's arrival at the bungalow and of the girl's resolve to follow the Wolf and save her brother's life, the crowd buzzed excitedly.

"Order!"

The Judge was quite unmindful of the fact that he had no authority to enforce his decrees. Anxious to miss nothing and desirous of facilitating the inquiry, the spectators came to order with commendable alacrity.

"What was your impression of the Wolf when you saw him at the bungalow?" asked the Judge.

"He done make no 'pression on me nohow, Jedge," was the reply. "I done knowed he wusn't no good, an' if he tried to make 'pression on me, I done pull de wool off'n his haid!"

"You don't catch my meaning, Aunt 'Mandy," smiled the jurist, "I mean, when you looked at him did you think that he was meditating a crime?"

"Ah don' know about dat, Jedge. He shore was a bad lookin' critter—jest like a bad man. what ain't got no use livin' nohow, when 'spectable folks is dyin' ebbery minute!"

"That will do, Aunt 'Mandy."

"What Ah wants to know," wailed the negress, "is dis, am you all goin' to bring my Missy back home? I jest kain't live widout her an' ef you all don't do somethin' soon, Ah shore will be locoed!"

Judge Hopkins assured her that every means to that end would be employed by the officers of the law, but Aunt 'Mandy who, evidently, was not satisfied with this promise, shook her head dubiously. Sam Belcher was called to forge the final link in the chain of evidence that seemed to fasten the crime of attempted murder and abduction upon the missing defendant.

"Tell us what you know about this affair, Mr. Belcher."

"When me an' 'Bird's-eye' loped toward the 'Chimney' in search of Mr. Haines," he drawled nervously, "we had consid'able trouble trailin' him fur an hour or two. We came acrost one of Lucas's men who told us that six or eight of Valdez's bandits had been driven south without showing fight. We thought it strange that we didn't strike Haines' trail in a gully somewhere, but when we finds his pony an' no signs o' the boss, we suspicion foul play!"

"What made you suspect that, Mr. Belcher?"

"Wall," drawled the witness, "it didn't look just right to me an' 'Bird's-eye.' We reckoned that if Haines was afoot, we should have got onto his trail long before. We wus thinkin' o' goin' arter the posse and sweep the 'Chimney' foot by foot, when we he'rd rifle firin' ahead of us. Thinkin' Haines might be fightin' with some o' Valdez's bunch, and be in a tight fix, we loped our ponies as fast as the lay o' the land would allow. Pretty soon we he'rd two shots, an' we caught sight o' a man ridin' a pinto. We recognized him instanter, Jedge.''

''Who was that man?''

''The Wolf!''

''You are sure of that?''

''Sure'n Hell!'' replied Belcher. ''Nobody could mistake the Wolf, once you have seen him. He p'inted to'ards the left an' loped along a ravine out o' sight.''

''What did you do then?''

''We crossed a ditch and found Haines lying on his back, bleedin' from a scalp wound. He had a bandana handkerchief tied around his head, and there was an automatic lyin' near him.''

''Was he conscious?''

''No, Jedge. He didn't know nuthin'.''

Sheriff Thorne took an automatic and blood stained crumpled handkerchief from beneath a newspaper lying on the table and showed them to the witness, who examined them critically.

''Were these articles found by you near Mr. Haines?'' asked the Judge.

''Yes, sir.''

''To whom do they belong?''

''The Wolf.''

There rose a loud murmur of voices among the spectators, whereupon the Judge rapped sharply for silence.

''You are sure this revolver belonged to him?''

''Sure'n shootin', Jedge. I seen it one day last summer when the Wolf asked Haines for a job to ride range an' was turned down. He swore angry like that he'd get even with the boss sooner or later for refusin' of him.''

"And this bandana?" asked the jurist. "How do you know it belongs to the Wolf?"

" 'Cause it's got a wolf's head embroidered at one corner thar—" He indicated the tracery in the fabric. The Judge smiled knowingly.

"Did you ever hear the Wolf spoken of as Jim Galloway—or Halloway?"

"I sure didn't."

"That's all, Mr. Belcher, thank you. You may step down. Your next witness, Mr. Sheriff?"

"Faro Jenn!"

All eyes were centered upon the keeper of the Red Eye who rose and seated herself in the witness chair. The spectators craned their necks to obtain a close-up view of the notorious woman. She was agitated and uncomfortable, and to conceal her trepidation, employed her fan vigorously, although the heat afforded her ample excuse for that exercise. When she raised her head, the immobile face of Hank Weston turned sternly towards her, caused her instinctively to lower it again. She wondered where and in what circumstances she had seen that homely countenance.

"You are Mrs. Hemingway, familiarly known as Faro Jenn, keeper of the Red Eye?" asked the Judge.

"Yes."

Hank smiled sarcastically and chewed the stub of his cheroot earnestly. He sought to catch her eye, but she eluded his glance.

"You know the man called the Wolf?"

"I do, sir."

"He frequented your place, did he not?"

"Yes."

"He often drank and played cards there?"

"Yes."

"He got drunk, too, eh?"

"Yes, quite often. I begged him repeatedly to quit

boozing, but all his promises to do so were broken."

"Was he quarrelsome when drunk?"

"He was not only quarrelsome, but dangerous."

"You witnessed the Haines incident testified to here—the gun play, the writing of the threat and the rest?"

"I did, your Honor."

"Do you know Marian Haines?"

"Yes," responded Jenn tremulously. "I saw her the day the Sheriff's posse rode to the valley. We met in the post office and chatted about—about the weather, styles of dress and—and—"

"What?" asked the Judge, observing that she paused.

"The Wolf!"

"What did Miss Haines say to you about him?"

"She told me that he was most revengeful and that she purposed to prevent her brother's murder, if she had to shoot the Wolf with her own hands!"

The crowd hummed like bees again and while the jurist was wielding his gavel, Hank moved forward several inches to assume a position from which he could observe Jenn to better advantage. He conjectured that the woman was lying, but if so, what was her motive? It came to him suddenly that jealousy may have prompted her to attribute false declarations to Marian Haines. Ah, if he could only catch her eyes and hold them for an instant, he felt certain that he would silence her by sheer force of his indomitable will.

"What did Miss Haines do after that?" questioned the Judge, glancing at the dapper young man who sat writing at the table.

"She mounted her pony and rode for the valley."

She raised her head as she spoke and unconsciously her glance rested upon Hank. His steady stare alarmed her. His homely features awoke within her memories of a dark past—pitiless, degrading, terrifying recollections which she had sought in vain to escape. Where had she seen this man with the sinister eyes that seemed to probe her soul? She shuddered, and closing her eyes, leaned back in her chair as if exhausted.

"Are you ill?" asked the Judge solicitously.

Jenn pulled herself together with an effort. "No, it is the heat!" she answered

"Do you know the real name of the Wolf?"

She was about to reply affirmatively when she felt the warning look the little man darted at her. He rejoiced at her hesitation, for by a species of telepathy which he had often employed with success when on the scent, he knew that he had succeeded in warning her that if she possessed the knowledge, she must in no circumstance reveal it. Jenn struggled for a time in mute resistance, but unable to combat the influence of this mysterious man, she yielded.

"I never knew the Wolf by any other name," she answered.

"But you told the Sheriff you knew, didn't you?"

"I thought I knew, but was mistaken."

"Very well, you are excused."

She returned to her chair to await the close of the inquiry. Dr. Sanders was called and explained the mental condition of Haines as a result of the shooting. He declared that the rancher's mind had been wrecked by what he termed a brain lesion occasioned by a gunshot wound on the head. When asked if, in his opinion, Haines' loss of memory would be permanent, he delivered a learned dissertation upon the effects of wounds upon the cranium and brain, as determined by expert alienists, but long before he had finished, the unappreciative audience began to melt away.

"That's all right, Doctor," interrupted the Judge coldly. "What we want to know without oratory is this—will Haines ever regain his memory?"

"There is a chance," he admitted. "A sudden shock might restore his lost faculty. I know of a case recorded in—"

"Thank you, Doctor, but that is all we care to hear on that particular point. Any additional witnesses, Mr. Sheriff?"

"None that I knows on, Jedge," replied that official, who was perspiring freely. "I don't reckon we need any more to make out a legal case agin the Wolf, do we?"

"I think not. There has been enough circumstantial evidence adduced here to convict a dozen men. I venture the opinion that you will be amply justified in filing a formal accusation against the Wolf of attempted murder, as well as of kidnaping. I think the facts justify you in offering a suitable reward for his apprehension, the same to be paid by the county, pending action by the Grand Jury in the premises."

"Correct, Jedge. Everybody out!" roared the Sheriff. "The inquest is ended!"

The crowd rapidly vacated the office and when the Sheriff turned to the door for a whiff of fresh air, he was confronted by Hank who was idly smoking his cheroot. Thorne attempted to step out into the open, but Hank restrained him.

"Yuh know me, Sheriff?" purred the detective, blowing several rings of smoke to the ceiling.

"I reckon I hain't had the pleasure."

"Then yuh've missed somethin' worth while, I'm

atellin' yuh,'' said Hank, displaying a badge pinned
to the inner side of his vest. ''I'm Hank Weston—
jest plain Hank, alias Texas Kid, Broncho Sam,
Slew-em-Hard Bill an'—''

''That's enough Hank! Shake! What kin I do
fur yuh?''

The Sheriff's tone was respectful and his manner
obsequious, for Hank's reputation for indomitable
bravery and swiftness of action as frontier detective
had long since been a household word and a source of
terror to lawbreakers throughout the Southwest.

''I'm goin' to ask a favor of yuh, Sheriff!''

''An' I'm agoin' to grant it in advance, if so be I
kin, Hank.''

''I reckon you kin.''

''Shoot!''

''I want to ask yuh to give up any idee yuh may
entertain of offering a reward fur the Wolf.''

The Sheriff scratched his head in perplexity. ''See
here, Hank, yuh're askin' fur somethin' my duty
forces on me,'' he interposed protestingly. ''I don't
know how I kin do that—''

''I'll show you how, Thorne,'' interrupted Hank.
''The Wolf's my meat an' till I give him up, I won't
stand fur nobody that walks in shoe-leather poachin'
on my preserves! Sure as shootin' if you offer this
reward till you get notice from me, thar'll be a vacancy
in the office of Sheriff in this yere county, an' you'll
be fillin' a neat little two by six hole in the cemetery
out in the desert thar!''

The Sheriff's face blanched, but observing that
Hank tranquilly lit a fresh cheroot, smiled his ac-
quiescence. They conversed in whispers for some
minutes and when they separated, Hank was chuckling
like a man who had heard a new and unusually humorous story. Despite the terrific heat, he shivered when

he thought of the narrow margin by which the dragging into this frightful mess of the proud family name of Holloway, had been averted.

There was one leak, however, he still feared—the dapper city chap who had taken voluminous notes at the inquiry and who had trailed Jenn after she left the building. That he had secured the co-operation of Judge Hopkins through whom he hoped that the name of Holloway would be officially established as that of the Wolf's, Hank was absolutely certain.

The detective chewed the end of his cheroot truculently as he left the Sheriff's office. He vowed that if he failed to stop that leak, before harm was done, he would deliver up his badge of office as an incompetent, and be content to remain the prince of fools for the rest of his days.

CHAPTER XVI

JENN PAYS THE PRICE

SMOKING like a "house afire," as he did whenever he was in a state of unusual mental perturbation, Hank entered the Red Eye, at the bar of which a vociferous crowd had congregated to discuss matters. Seemingly a puncher out for a good time, his entrance attracted no attention and he was permitted to do as he liked.

Hank had a double motive in entering the Red Eye. Primarily, he was resolved to have a heart to heart talk with Mrs. Hemingway, alias Faro Jenn, alias something or other besides; and, secondarily, he sought an interview with that dapper little note-making city chap who had left the Sheriff's office at the close of the inquiry, at Jenn's heels. He was convinced that this was the reporter who had called at the Holloway home in New York on the night he made his report, and who had demanded to know if an El Paso news dispatch to the *New York Observer*, setting forth that Jim Holloway, widely known as the Wolf, was, in fact, the magnate's dissipated son.

"I sure got to dope out some scheme to prevent that dude reporter from sending his yarn to New York and disgracin' Jim's pore mother and father," he soliloquized as he walked, his hands behind his back, his cheroot stabbing the air angrily. "He kinder suspicions that the Wolf is Jim Holloway, but he an' nobody 'cept Jenn in this country is positive sure on that p'int. If he gits hold o' the truth an' wires it to his noospaper, doggone me! the damage sure will be done.''

He gazed at the cheroot reflectively, then addressed the weed as he might a companion in arms: ''Hence and forever, you Satan's weed, it's up to us to find this writin' galoot, an' convince him of the error of his vicious ways, regardless!''

He stepped softly to the rear of the hall to reconnoiter, pausing to inspect some of the lurid prints tacked to the walls on either side—pictures of prize fighters clipped from a sensational yellow police journal; charming actresses of stage and screen cut from the pages of magazines and newspapers, with sundry photographs of men and things of greater or less interest to a casual spectator like himself. He had glimpsed a movement at Jenn's office door which stood slightly ajar, and he heard voices raised in animated conversation. He perceived Jenn and the reporter, but although he could observe them, he took care that they should not see him until his plans were matured. Deeming themselves alone, the two conversed without restraint.

''I'm Jimmy Donlon of the *New York Observer*,'' said the reporter loftily. '''I'm trying to identify this man Wolf, who has flown the coop. I'm convinced he is Jim Holloway, son of Charles Holloway, the—''

''There's nothing to prevent you identifying him as far as I'm aware,'' interrupted Jenn coldly. ''Is that why you have followed me here?''

''I want to talk to you about your testimony at the inquiry.''

''I've nothing to add to it, kid.''

Jimmy smiled genially. He had bumped against similar obstacles before.

"It's frightfully warm," he said.   "May I take off my coat?"

"Sure."

He removed the garment and tossed it carelessly upon the desk before which she had seated herself. Leaning against a corner of the fabric, he lit a cigarette, inhaled the fumes and after emitting a dense volume of smoke, artistically resumed his interrupted task—that of convincing this obstinate woman that the fate of himself, the *Observer* and the entire universe depended upon the celerity with which she revealed all she knew about Jim Holloway, alias the Wolf, and the Lord knew what other et ceteras familiar to the bad lands of the great Southwest.

"Your statement on the witness stand," he began argumentatively, "led me to infer that you know the Wolf's name.   Am I right?"

She regarded him with an amused smile.   "I'm not responsible for what you have inferred."   She became suddenly aggressive.   "As far as I'm concerned," she snapped, "I don't care a whoop in Jericho what you think!"

"Please be reasonable, Mrs. Hemingway.   The Sheriff told me you had all the facts—"

"No more of that talk!" she interrupted angrily. Her face was flushed and she grew belligerent suddenly.   "Get out of my place and be quick about it, or I'll throw you out!"

"Don't be rough on a chap, Mrs. Hemingway."

Donlon realized that he had a tartar on his hands with whom he must needs treat diplomatically or suffer inglorious defeat.

"Will you answer a plain question?" he asked suavely.

"What is it?"

"Isn't it a fact of which you have positive proof, that the Wolf is Jim Holloway? Yes or no!"

She ventured no reply. He was certain that she dared not answer falsely without risk of exposure. He decided to go further in the hope of obtaining her affirmation of the prime fact he sought to establish.

"The Wolf borrowed a hundred dollars of you one night, leaving his gold watch as security for the loan, didn't he?"

"What if he did?"

"Weren't the initials 'J. H.' engraved on the inside of the case?"

"Who told you that?"

"Isn't it a fact?"

"Well, come to think of it—"

She paused, a terrified expression on her face. Turning at a sound behind him, Donlon saw a little cowpuncher standing in the opening, calmly smoking a cheroot. The man smiled blandly as he stepped into the room and closed the door.

"What the devil—"

"Hope I ain't intrudin', son?" interrupted Hank, fingering his cheroot. "Doggone this seegar! It goes out every time I wink! Got a match, young feller?"

Donlon gave Hank a light, but the tender lacked his customary grace. In truth, he was peeved at this unexpected interruption just as he had his cherished prize within his grasp.

"I'm having a confidential chat with this lady, sir," he protested in lordly style. "We are not accustomed to have others break in upon us unannounced, in the country I hail from!"

"The which indicates that yuh be insinuatin' as how I ain't no gentleman, eh?" responded Hank,

purringly. Had Donlon known his man he would
have known that he stood, metaphorically, on perilous
ground, for when Hank Weston purred felinely, the
danger signal for those who knew and understood,
was flying.

"Yuh shore don't think yuh be in New York, son?
This be Purple Canyon, an' we're all gentlemen here!
Lookee here, boy! I've an app'intment with this lady,
so it's time for yuh to vamoose regardless! Git me,
eh?"

Donlon glanced appealingly at Jenn, but she
ignored him. Turning to the little stranger, he concluded that discretion, in this instance at least, was
the better part of valor.

"Oh, very well," he said carelessly, picking up his
coat. "I'll see you later."

He opened the door, Hank following him. "Meet
me at the post office in half an hour," whispered the
detective. "I want to have a talk with yuh, if yuh
don't mind."

"About what?"

"The Wolf."

"Do you know him?"

"He's my pal."

"You don't say!"

"Git along now! Remember the post office in half
an hour."

"I'll be there."

Hank reëntered the office where Jenn, her heart
beating wildly, awaited him apprehensively. He motioned to a chair and she seated herself, he standing
before her, chewing his cheroot, his arms folded, his
eyes searching her face with hostile determination.

"Who are you?" she asked in agitation. "What
do you want here? Have I ever seen you before?"

He puckered his face in a way that aged him some

twenty years, and bent towards her. She gazed at
him in blank terror.

"I know you now—Hank Weston!"

"Uh-huh!"

"What's your game, Hank?" she inquired after a
pause.

"I want to tell yuh a story, if yuh don't mind, about
a man from Frisco, a rich man's son who was shot and
killed in a certain joint in Tombstone one night two
years ago—"

"Stop!" she interrupted desperately. "Why
can't you let me forget the past?"

" 'Cause yuh won't let me, that's why!" he returned grimly. "When this chap—we'll call him
Chester—"

"No, no!"

"Chester Rathom, Bathom or some name like that,
you know. Wall, as I wus sayin', the night he wus
shot, a young woman, middlin' fleshy then, known
as Gertrude Stiles, wus with him—"

A groan escaped her colorless lips. He paused, half
ashamed of himself for baiting this misguided woman,
but necessity knows no law and he proceeded piti-
lessly.

"I gather that yuh recognize the name," he went
on quietly. "Wall, I investigated that case with a
friend o' mine, an' we diskivered that Gertrude had
made her getaway with $15,000 belongin' to Rathom,
an' with the proceeds of the robbery went to El Paso
and later drifted into Purple Canyon whar she opened
the Red Eye gamblin' joint."

"It's a lie!" she exclaimed hotly. "I didn't kill
Rathom! He shot himself, I swear it!"

"I'm not disputin' that p'int with yuh, Jenn. I'm
even kinder disposed like to give yuh the benefit o'
the doubt. But yuh shouldn't have vamoosed with

Rathom's bundle, an' leave his wife an' three kids to the charity o' Rathom's father, who hated the ground they walked on!''

"I didn't know, Hank!"

"I recognized you the minute I see yuh here the fust time three months ago, when I wus tryin' to make a man o' the Wolf. But I wusn't interested no longer in Rathom's wad, and didn't care a tinker's cuss about it or yuh, ontil to-day."

"And now?" she asked hopefully.

"I want yuh to tell me how yuh l'arned the Wolf's real name. Listen! If you lie to me, I'll turn you over to Sheriff Thorne who has a circular in his scrap book offering a reward of two thousand dollars for the arrest of Gertrude Stiles, known to me pussonly under the alias of Mrs. Hemingway et cetry!''

"Have mercy!" she pleaded. "Don't you see how I suffer? I will tell you all, if you will promise to remain silent about that affair!''

"All right.''

With a candor that astounded him, she related the circumstances of her acquaintance with Jim Holloway. She spoke of her love for him, a love that all but drove her mad when, in response to her appeal, he coldly assured her that he could never return her passion.

Falteringly, she alluded to the night when the Wolf had left his watch in her possession as security for a loan—of her discovery of the initials "J. H." engraved thereon—of the Wolf's quarrel with Haines and its sequel—the Wolf's temporary madness when he signed the death threat with his name which he had studiously concealed prior thereto—of her final meeting with him at the stable, and of her interview with Marian, whom she had with Machiavellian subtlety induced to go in pursuit of Jim—in the belief that by doing so she might prevent the crime to the commission of which Holloway had publicly committed himself.

"Anything more?" he asked, chewing his cheroot nervously. He shook with suppressed passion and his voice trembled with an emotion to which hitherto he had been a stranger. He felt like strangling the shrinking Jenn who crouched before him, sorrowful, penitent, appealing.

"Nothing."

"Jenn, yuh shore be a hardened woman! Yuh sent this pore innocent gal into danger by a lyin' trick, didnt' yuh? For two coppers, I'd turn yuh over to Thorne regardless!"

She returned no answer, and he walked to and fro, seeking to regain his composure. "Land sakes!" he exclaimed resignedly. "What's the use? Yuh're as God made yuh, I reckon, an' I hain't got no license to criticize Him!"

"You don't understand the heart of a woman like me, Hank," she said tearfully. "I loved Jim and when I comprehended that Marian Haines was my rival—that he loved her—then hatred filled my soul!"

"You she devil!" he rejoined fiercely. "You sent Miss Haines to a fate wuss'r'n death, if so be she's in the hands of Cipriano Valdez, the most blood-thirsty rascal that ever was spewed out o' the Inferno!"

Jenn wept. She dared not raise her head even in supplication. She felt his burning eyes upon her. A man he might have killed for less, but this abandoned woman—

"Now that I think it over," he went on, "I begin to suspicion the truth—Valdez has kidnapped her, sure as shootin'! Whar's Lopez?" he inquired suddenly.

Abject fear caused Jenn to shiver. What did he suspect? The frightful truth which she had not revealed to him in its entirety? Fearing an indiscreet word might ruin her irretrievably, she remained silent. How those terrible eyes burned—!

"Whar's Lopez? Answer me, Jenn!"

She raised her tear-stained face despairingly. She dared not reveal the truth without a struggle. Woman like, she resorted to evasion.

"How should I know?" she answered, toying with her bracelet. "He left here weeks ago—" She paused, wondering how she could evade those eyes fixed upon her like dark twin stars, seeking to probe the depths of her guilt-laden soul!

"Yuh're hidin' somethin' from me, Jenn! Out with it, or I'll break my word fur the fust time in my life! Come, tell me, quick!"

Bit by bit he drew from her the pitiful confession of her iniquitous conduct—the fruit of her unrequited love and unreasoning jealousy. He turned white at the tale but strangely enough, when his fury had partly expended itself, he pitied this lost woman sincerely.

"Yuh've got a lot to answer fur, Jenn," he said reflectively. "As fur me, I'm through with yuh. *Adios!*"

She hid her face in her hands and he left her. She was not aware that he had gone until she raised her head, only to let it fall again, despairing and hopeless. She rose after a time, still shaken at intervals by the violence of her emotion. She grew calmer presently, and opening her safe, examined its contents with care. She smiled bitterly, swung the door to, turned the combination, sighed and left the room.

There was an expression of unswerving resolution in her eyes when she entered her room above. From the bar beneath, there rose faintly the sounds of tinkling glasses, the oaths of men in angry disputes, of voices raised discordantly in song. Some banjoist

strummed a plantation melody exquisitely sweet, and
though she loved it, the haunting strains now grated
raspingly on her ears. She halted before her dressing
case and, surveying herself in the mirror, smiled wanly
at the reflection of faded loveliness and soul degradation it revealed to her—a woman old and haggard before her time, the shade of her former self. Ah, vanished youth! Farewell forever hope, ambition, peace,
happiness, love—Nirvana beckons now!

She seated herself and wrote her will, by which she
devised all she possessed to her young daughter, Ethel
Hemingway, living in a convent in an eastern city.
She sealed the envelope containing the document and
placed it conspicuously against a pomade jar, so that
it would be discovered by the first comer. The mirth-
ful sounds that drifted to her from beneath impressed
her sadly as the chanting of a requiem in a vaulted
cathedral in happier circumstances, might have done.
She smiled, took a silver mounted revolver from her
bureau, and lay down on the bed.

"I love you, Jim," she muttered resignedly. "Life
without you is more than I can bear. I have sinned
and I am ready to pay the price! Poor, poor Ethel!
May God forgive me!"

She wrapped a Navajo blanket about her to shut out
the sounds of the drunken revelry in the saloon below, then voiced sobbingly a little prayer she used to
speak when a child. A muffled report and she lay
still.

Thus, later in the day, they found her. There was
a smile on her face, for after many trials, she had
found eternal peace.

.   .   .   .

Serenely unconscious of the tragedy that was being
enacted at the Red Eye—that home of the sordid
drama of human lives—Hank Weston was engaged at

the post office in earnest conversation with Jimmy Donlon. Both were smoking and apparently they were on the best of terms. Donlon appeared to be unusually communicative, the little detective listening to him in rapt attention. There was a grin on his homely face, but it was evident from the truculent angle his cheroot had assumed, that he had some highly important mission to fulfill.

"I've discovered just what I was looking for, my genial friend," said Donlon excitedly. "It sure will interest you."

"Mebbe so, mebbe so. What is it?"

"I've had a talk with a tin horn gambler who met the Wolf in California where he shot and killed a Siwash—no, Digger Indian, a couple of years ago. Believe me, that's some story!"

Hank shifted his cheroot, so that it dangled forlornly. "Yuh don't say!" he ejaculated. "That Wolf sure is some bloodthirsty galoot! But yuh can't most always believe a tin horn gambler. Least wise, that's been my experience with the breed in these diggin's."

"But this fellow is on the square! He read the threat written by the Wolf, and he swears it bore the name of Jim Holloway, written in beautifully clear and bold script."

"My goodness!" Hank chewed the end of his cheroot abstractedly—a significant proceeding for those who knew him best. But Donlon, quite unconscious of peril, and thinking only of his journalistic achievement, was all smiles.

"Guess I'll be off for Butler and wire my story," said he, taking a notebook from his pocket. "I've got it all arranged—what the devil!"

The ejaculation, voiced in a tone acutely expressive of amazement and indignation, was provoked by the sudden flashing of Hank's automatic, the muzzle of which, seemingly by accident, was pressed with startling force against his diaphragm. Donlon's brain whirled at this threatening development. He sought to evade the business end of the weapon, but the gun which in his eyes had assumed the proportions of a howitzer, never for an instant severed its perilous contact with his person.

"Yuh've got another guess comin'. It's me who's goin' to censor them notes regardless!"

"But my dear fellow—"

"Hand 'em over an' hesitate not, fur him who hesitates is lost, accordin' to Gospel writ! Come arunnin', son, fur my trigger finger's most remarkably itchy."

Donlon made no further protest, but handed the note book to Hank.

"Good Lord!" he gasped, "they're mostly in shorthand and won't do you any good, for you can't read them."

"Mebbe not," chuckled Hank, thrusting the notebook in his pocket. "But that ain't the p'int at all. Me an' yuh is goin' to enj'y a vacation trip to the country."

"A trip?"

"Fur yore health, son."

"But I won't go on any trip for my health, for I'm sound as a nut! I'm Jimmy Donlon, special representative of the *New York Observer*, and I'm too busy to go junketing just now."

Hank pressed his automatic into Donlon's midriff with a force that made him grunt. He began to think that this little man with the cheroot was a lunatic and that to insure the preservation of the community as well as of himself, he ought to yell for help. He suppressed that desire however, when he glimpsed the sinister glance Hank bestowed upon him.

"Yuh shore do talk a hellava lot, don't yuh?" murmured Hank reprovingly. "But I'm goin' to show yuh that I'll have the last word in this argyfication. If so be yuh hain't aimin' to take a little trip with me regardless, it sure is a sartinty that yuh're goin' to take a ride all by yore lonely in a purty little pine box to that home o' peace behind the schoolhouse yander!"

"Good Lord, man! You—"

"It's up to yuh to choose the route, son, an' choose it quick, 'cause I hain't got no time to lose!"

Donlon yielded to superior force, and when he had announced his willingness to do anything the diminutive detective might demand, Hank pocketed his automatic. His threatening manner changed instantly to one of genial good nature.

"Sometimes even a New York reporter has got good horse sense, an' yuh're it," said he, taking Donlon's arm.

"Who the deuce are you anyhow?" inquired Donlon, wiping the perspiration from his face. He was in a bad humor and his tone clearly expressed resentful hostility.

"Hank Weston."

"That name means nothing in my young life. What's your game?"

"I'll show yuh that in a little while, my boy."

"What's your business?"

"To keep New York reporters from making durned nuisances of theirselves."

Donlon groaned. He remarked petulantly that he hadn't the slightest comprehension, not to say, appreciation, of the comedy Hank was playing. The sleuth abstracted a fresh cheroot from his pocket and lighting it, remarked impressively that the affair in which they were to engage was unadulterated tragedy.

"I'm goin' to tell yuh a yarn, son. Listen, 'cause it'll interest yuh."

In his plain homely way, employing simple language a child might understand, ruggedly eloquent and forceful, he related the story of a young man, the son of wealthy parents, whose dissipation and waywardness all but broke their hearts. This boy, he went on, lived the life of a ruffian under an anonymity, and although he was deemed a lawless character, he was in fact a gentleman with an abiding love for his mother in his heart. One night, this boy, crazed by drink, threatened to kill a man—.

"When this young booze hound wakes up next mornin'," resumed Hank impressively, "he diskivers what a chump he has made of hisself, and he makes up his mind to reform regardless. He clean forgets the threat he has made publicly, an' he don't remember that when he writes the threat he has wrote his real name alongside that of the Wolf by which he is known in the Southwest. Bimeby, a New York noospaper gits onto the facts, an' sends a writing chap down to the bad lands fur to prove that this boy, known as the Wolf, is in fact, the son of the big financial gent, the which, if he did prove it, would sure break that pore mother's heart, the same as I crush this here seegar."

He removed the cheroot which refused to burn, and crumpled it between his fingers, throwing the fragments to the floor. Donlon watched him understandingly, as Hank drew forth another cheroot and lit it.

"I begin to appreciate your interest in this matter, Hank," he said.

"But I hain't finished yet, son," continued Hank. "When I suspicions this reporter's layout, I makes up my mind to play my trump cyards and fo'ce him to quit or make him a fit subject fur an inquest. I'm fo'ced to do it fust, 'cause I promised the Wolf's

mother I would bring her son back to her safe an'
sound, if I has to go through Purgatory to find him,
and second, 'cause I know his pore ole dad is a-eatin'
his heart out fur fear his son will do somethin' real
onery to disgrace the family name. So I argufy the
p'int with yuh, and hev a real entertainin' time—
even usin' a real gun—''

"You win, Hank!'' interrupted Donlon, extending
his hand.

"Thanks, Donlon, I knowed I would.''

They left the post office arm in arm together and ten
minutes later were on their way to Red Sandy valley.
Reaching the Haines' bungalow, Hank questioned
Belcher who had preceded them only a few minutes,
regarding the condition of Haines. He was relieved
to learn that the rancher was convalescent and that his
speedy physical recovery was looked for.

"But his mind's gone,'' added Belcher sadly.
"That wouldn't be so bad, if his sister were here to
attend to him. Durn the Wolf, anyhow!''

"Hold yore hosses, Sam!'' rejoined Hank quietly.
"The Wolf's all right, you bet, an' I don't let nobody abuse him till his guilt is proved regardless!''

In response to Hank's queries, Belcher supplied the
detective with a working plan of the "Chimney,'' and
within an hour, Hank and Donlon dismounted at the
spot where Haines had been found unconscious by
Holloway. Hank inspected the ground critically, the
other watching him curiously.

"The Wolf hunt begins hyar,'' muttered Hank.
"We must find the trail of a hoss with a nicked fore
hoof, off side. That's the kind Holloway's pinto pony
will leave behind him.''

They led their ponies through the "Chimney'' and
scanned the imprint of hoofs in the sand. Hank
grunted with satisfaction.

"Thar it is, sure's my name is Hank Weston!" he said, pointing to the indentation made by a nicked hoof in the caked sand near the spring.

"It points to the southward," added Donlon.

"An' I think I know whar it will lead us, son," remarked Hank, applying a match to his cheroot.

"That's more than I can say, pardner."

"It's goin' to lead us to a hacienda in Sonora, Mex., owned by a certain bandit known as Cipriano Valdez."

"You think Holloway followed him?"

"I'm sartin of it."

"Why?"

"Why?" echoed Hank, vaulting into his saddle. "Jest 'cause Marian Haines was kidnapped by Valdez an' he trailed 'em to rescoo her!"

"I believe you're right, Hank," rejoined Donlon, admiringly. He mounted his pony and they galloped southward. "How long a ride is it to this hacienda?"

"Six hours, I reckon."

When they reached the railroad station at Butler, Hank wrote the following cryptic message and handed it to the telegraph operator with instructions to send it forthwith, collect:

Peterson Detective Agency, New York—Tell party young man is O.K. gone to Mexico on business. Will find him P.D.Q. and assist. Nothing to worry about. Will hear from me in three or four days regardless. All hunky to date. H.W.

They reached the village of Los Vinos in Sonora just as Sam Jackson was closing his store for the night. The storekeeper greeted the detective with warmth and it was evident that they were old friends. Of course, Hank celebrated the meeting by lighting a fresh cheroot, of which he seemed to have an inexhaustible supply, and he alternately puffed and grunted his approval of certain information retailed to him by the merchant in their whispered conference.

"That boy sure is some man, all right, Sam," said Hank after the other had finished. "An' you say he refused to take even a drop o' aquardiente?"

"Not a drop would he drink."

"He's a real Holloway, arter all!"

In the room at the rear of the store, Donlon was preparing to turn in for the night. He was tired as a dog, his joints ached excruciatingly as a result of his long ride, and he yawned fiercely.

"Hank's a devilish fine chap," he muttered, tumbling into his bunk. "That is to say," he added with a grimace. "If you don't stroke his fur the wrong way. Talk about electricity! He's the concentrated essence of it!"

Long after Donlon had begun to snore, Hank sought the rest he needed, but of the lack of which he betrayed no sign. He laughed quietly, for the news of his protégé he had heard was of that character that amply justified the faith he had in Jim Holloway and whom his parents, thanks to himself, would one day be proud to acknowledge as their son before all the world.

CHAPTER XVII

THE SCHOOL OF LOVE

SEÑOR SANCHEZ DE LA GUARDIA, debonair and gay, reduced gentleman of culture and varied accomplishments, now valet to his excellency, Señor Cipriano Valdez, sang blithely as he performed his duties within the living room of the hacienda. The other servants, of whom there were few, wondered what had gone amiss in the fertile brain of their master, that he, of all men, physically as filthy as he was morally a degenerate, should require the services of a body servant. But their wonder lessened when it was whispered that he loved the American señorita whom he had kidnapped to hold for heavy ransom, and that he was determined to wed her anon with or without her consent, which latter contingency to a man like Valdez, was a trifle scarcely worth serious consideration.

"He wishes to appear as a gay caballero in her eyes," whispered the cook, a fat woman of forty, half Spanish, half Yaqui, to the stable man, an evil-faced peon. "So, in order that his courtship may prosper, Señor Valdez has secured a valet who was formerly in the employ of the Governor of Durango, and who is to teach him manners and how to doll up properly for his love making."

"But you can't teach an old dog new tricks," the man replied. "Valdez will be Valdez always, be his clothes of embroidered silks or of leather. *Dios!* As for his temper—"

"The least said the better!" interrupted the cook, making the sign of the cross, shudderingly.

When Señorita Marie Pinosa, the pretty dancer whom Valdez had promised to make his wife and absolute mistress of the hacienda, learned of this gossip, she became furiously jealous and resentful. The conviction seized her that Marian's beauty of face and figure was sufficient to win the admiration of most men including even the bandit himself, who had no aversion for feminine charms. Nevertheless, she convinced herelf that it was the hope of golden ransom rather than love that had prompted him to make the American girl his captive.

The Señorita was loath to confess that the situation, as far as her hopes of becoming Señora Valdez were concerned, had assumed the gravest aspect. She remembered that when Marian, half dead from fright and fatigue, was carried into the hacienda, Valdez had entrusted the girl to a maid servant with the assurance that if the fair prisoner came to harm or made her escape, he would cut off her ears and send them to her sweetheart as reminders of her laxity. The señorita was so agitated, that she forgot to paint herself as was her daily practice before she sallied forth to meet her recreant master.

"Cipriano!" she said, throwing her arms about him. "Who is this white woman—this fair Americano, and what does she here in—my hacienda?"

Valdez swore fiercely and threw her against the wall with such force as to almost deprive her of breath.

"*Carramba!*" he shouted, threatening her with his foot. "If you question me again about her, or as much as mention her name, if you know it, or interfere in any other way with my personal affairs, I will spoil your beauty forever!" He paused, then added malevolently: "Dare to speak to me again until

I order you to do so, and I'll turn you over to my tender-hearted Lopez who loves you much! Understand, *esclavo?*"

While the señorita was nursing her bruises as well as her wrath, and vowing vengeance upon all who stood between her and the realization of her dreams, Marian was kept in solitary confinement in a room immediately beneath the circular red tiles with which the structure was roofed. This apartment was at a corner of the low rectangular building, from one window of which Marian could see the rolling country to the eastward, while from another, facing to the south, she perceived cattle grazing, lazily herded by typically costumed vaqueros. A third window overlooked the patio, with its beautiful garden and small fountain in the center of the enclosure. Here and there, among the shrubbery, she glimpsed statues, stolen, no doubt, by the bandit on his periodical raids on the haciendas of the rich in the neighboring hills.

The quadrilateral was reached by means of doors on all sides; and there were long shallow porches with sharply sloping roofs at each of the four angles. From the weather-beaten, cracked appearance of the adobe, Marian judged that the building was very old. She was privileged to look out of the windows of her room as much as she liked, but when she tried to open the door leading to the wide hall, from which the living room of the lower story was reached, she discovered that it was securely locked. When she protested to the girl who served as her jailor, the latter said in soft musical Spanish, of which Marian knew only a few words, that in no circumstances was the American Señorita to leave her room without the permission of Valdez.

Marian spent the first night of her captivity miserably. She wept much, thought much, and when morning came she had not closed her eyes for an instant in sleep. Hence she had little appetite when a bountiful breakfast consisting of eggs, fruits, frijoles, coffee and muffins, was placed before her by the Mexican maid. She thought of the stories of remarkable prison escapes she had read, and the impulse seized her at times, to overpower this female, assume her garb, and make her escape from the hacienda. But recognizing the futility of such an effort she abandoned the visionary scheme. She ate for she knew she must eat if she hoped to have strength sufficient to meet the ordeals that confronted her—trials, the mere contemplation of which caused her to shiver.

She wondered what had happened in Red Sandy valley after her capture by Valdez and their flight to Mexico. Had the Wolf met and killed her brother as he had threatened to do? The fear that he might have done so, horrified her. If her brother's safety had been threatened by the bandits alone, then there was little cause for anxiety on his account as all of the outlaws who had participated in the raid, with the exception of Pedro, had returned safely to Sonora. She remembered that Valdez had several times cursed bitterly because of the non-appearance of Pedro, but of course, he did not know that his lieutenant had participated in his last raid and would be heard from no more.

Her thoughts reverting to the Wolf, she caught herself struggling with emotions that were diametrically opposed to each other. Sometimes she regarded him with withering contempt and on other occasions, with an indulgence dangerously akin to forgiveness. But why, she could not tell. Why should she not hate him? Yet she could not.

When she was left to herself, for the first time after her entrance into the hacienda, she examined the appointments of her prison house with interest. In one corner was a fine old Spanish canopied bed, with heavy green velvet draperies, deliciously soft and inviting. At another corner was a luxurious lounge with pillows embroidered in all the beautiful tints of the rainbow. In the center stood a round table covered with English and Spanish books, some Mexico City newspapers, an American magazine or two, a heavily shaded lamp and a tray laden with delicious semi-tropical fruits.

Several rustic chairs and rockers stood here and there, while the floor, made of wide rough boards, was almost hidden beneath its covering of rugs and skins. There was a handsomely finished mahogany dresser with a French mirror, at the foot of the bed, and every appurtenance of a fashionable woman's toilette table was in its place.

The walls were papered in gaudy colors while tapestries of medieval design hung between the windows. There were some oil paintings, the largest among these being a portrait of the reigning Pope. Altogether, her room was comfortable enough to suit her taste, but the knowledge that she was a prisoner therein, robbed it of beauty. She was resolved to quit it at the first favorable opportunity.

She was seated at the window facing the east on the first morning of her imprisonment, when she saw a rider approaching the hacienda. There was little about the man as far as she could see that would attract more than passing attention, and yet she felt a thrill when the newcomer, to all appearances a young Mexican of high degree, rode beneath her window to dismount at the main door. He glanced at her, his fingers caressing a dainty mustache, and smiled encouragingly. That he sought to flash a message to her, she did not comprehend. Marian drew back, but when she looked again, the man had disappeared.

Why should this Mexican, who was hideously scarred, look at her? Was he in league with Valdez, or had he a proprietary interest in her? There was a strangely familiar air about this stranger, while his eyes, dark and glittering, reminded her of—pshaw! What was to be gained by reminiscensing again? Still she found it difficult to control herself to the degree that she could dismiss this event as a circumstance too trivial to merit analysis; but ultimately she began to regard it as of wonderful significance to her future and to the hopes she nourished of ultimately regaining her freedom.

When the rider, who was in fact Jim Holloway, was escorted into the presence of Valdez, the bandit was breakfasting on one of the verandas facing the patio. He was alone and comparatively in good humor. Before him was a trellis screened by a heavy growth of vines. Holloway stood with his back to this, for it left his features in semi-obscurity. He calmly awaited the test he knew to be inevitable, with death, perhaps, as his reward should his imposture be discovered.

Under his left arm pit, resting in a holster fastened to his shoulder, hung his automatic, fully charged. The bandoleer he wore swung loosely, and his soft white silk shirt was unfastened so that the weapon was instantly available should the occasion for its hurried use arise. He was resolved to shoot Valdez should he penetrate his disguise, and shoot to kill before he could warn his followers. He had essayed an important rôle, and he was determined to play his part with all the skill he could summon to his aid!

"So you are the valet Jackson has sent me, eh?" said Valdez in Spanish, as he surveyed Holloway from head to foot.

"*Si, señor*," replied Holloway, bowing low, the better to hide his face.

"I've forgotten your name—"

"Señor Sanchez de la Guardia, your excellency." He spoke in easy fluent Spanish, his accent perfect as that of an Andalusian. "The American storekeeper in the village informed me that you required the services of a valet, and being without employment, I beg your excellency to give me a trial."

"*Carramba!*" exclaimed Valdez suspiciously. "Your voice has a most familiar ring! Have we ever met?"

"Not to my knowledge, your excellency," responded Holloway with a laugh. How stupid of him not to have disguised his voice as artistically as he had masked his face! But he would not offend again. "Not unless you visited at the palace of the governor of Durango where I was employed, within the last twelve months."

"I have not had the honor of meeting the governor. What were your duties while in his service?"

"I made life pleasant for his excellency, as I hope to make it delightful for you, señor, should you afford me the opportunity to serve you. I was his valet— I cared for his clothes, chose the garments he should wear on state occasions and was his advisor on matters sartorial. I read poetry to him, beautiful lines culled from the Spanish masterpieces, and in truth, I was his general secretary. Perhaps you—"

"Enough, chatterer!" interrupted Valdez impatiently. He regarded Holloway with increasing suspicion. "You seem rather tall for a Mexican. Come, advance!" he commanded, rising and taking Holloway's arm roughly. "Let me have a look at you!"

Holloway smiled and under the pretense of stroking his mustache, covered his chin with his hand.

"What a devilish scar you have! How did you come by that?"

"It was in his excellency's service," replied Holloway chuckling. "The governor and I were hunting in the mountains one day when we stumbled upon four revolutionists, or rather, they fell upon us, as you may please to view the incident, your excellency."

"Bandits, you mean?"

"Perhaps. Be that as it may, the governor and I gave battle and I am happy to assure your excellency that I killed three of the men and captured the fourth, but not until he had paid his respects to me with his machete." He fingered the scar tenderly. Valdez regarded him with a stare in which incredulity struggled with admiration for mastery.

"You're the very man I need, Sanchez!" he said, slapping Holloway on the shoulder. "Let us drink in celebration of our acquaintance. What you did for the governor of Durango, you may have occasion to do for me. Lopez!" he roared suddenly.

Lopez, who evidently had been awaiting the summons, bounded through a doorway. He cast a sharp glance at Holloway who took care to turn his face. He was determined to minimize his chances of being recognized by this surly ruffian, until he had firmly entrenched himself in the hacienda.

"Some wine, Lopez," commanded the chief.

The wine was brought and served. Valdez held his glass aloft, while Holloway, his back to the trellis and his face in the shadow of the vines, held his crystal on a level with his nose. He felt Lopez's hostile glance fixed upon him in a steady stare. Indeed, to Lopez this tall Mexican did not ring true. A cruel smile wreathed his thin lips.

"I require the aid of a trained valet," said Valdez

after a pause. "I have important business on hand. I will not deny it—I am in love!"

"In love!" echoed Holloway. Lopez turned to Valdez in amazement. Holloway took advantage of the opportunity to empty his glass among the vines and replace it on the table.

"I am wooing a young woman who, I have reason to believe, does not love me. But with your assistance, Sanchez, I hope to bring her to my feet! What say you? Are you versed in the art of prospering the love of men—like me, for instance?"

"Your excellency," returned Holloway, bowing, "I am a past master in the art of serving both Cupid and my employer! Come, say the word—one hundred pesos a month and found, and I shall be your mentor in the game of love as well as your valet. Is it a bargain?"

Valdez grinned, then swallowed his wine. *"Santisimo!"* he said, "your services come high, but if I win through your efforts, I will cheerfully double your pay. That is right, eh, Lopez?"

"It is not becoming for me to doubt your wisdom, señor," growled Lopez resignedly.

"Then consider yourself engaged, Sanchez. What is the first step in the game of love we are about to play?"

"Tell me something regarding the woman you love. Is she Spanish or Mexican?"

"Neither! She is an American, beautiful, proud and rebellious."

"Is she aware that you have honored her with your love?"

"Not yet, but I shall tell her soon. When I do so, I must be properly garbed. You must advise me on that point, Sanchez."

"I will make it my duty, your excellency."

Valdez dismissed Lopez, and rising, led Holloway into a large room, filled with the rich proceeds of his numerous and sanguinary raids on abodes of wealth. Valdez opened the door of a closet, revealing various Mexican costumes of fine texture and beauty of design. He tossed several of these upon a table, and, playing his rôle admirably, Holloway proceeded to examine them critically as became a skilled valet.

"Your excellency!" he exclaimed, after he had completed his inspection. "These are not fit habiliments for a man of your wealth and social importance! See! this coat is almost threadbare—this bandoleer is frightfully frayed, while the lace actually is motheaten! This shirt—well, it lacks ruffles and a button or two—but it may do in a pinch!"

"But I have no other," growled Valdez peevishly. "What have I employed you for, *esclavo?* It is for you to remedy the faults you have discovered."

"And it shall be done, your excellency!" responded Holloway with enthusiasm. "Leave the matter to me, for though I affirm it myself, there isn't a handier man with the needle in all Mexico than your humble servant. But first, permit me to offer an important suggestion?"

"What is it?"

"In the game of love, your excellency, wherein a rebellious maid is concerned, he who hopes to woo successfully—" he leaned over and whispered in Valdez's ear— "positively must bathe more than once every six months!"

"*Carramba!*" growled Valdez angrily, "are you jesting with me?"

"Far from it, señor. I am most serious. First, you must bathe and shave daily. You positively have a musty, horsey smell! How can you woo a delicately nurtured woman and hope to win her love when you emit the sickening odor of stinkweed? It's against nature, and in such circumstances, even Cupid takes wing and leaves you desolate."

"Perhaps you are right, Sanchez," muttered Valdez resignedly. "But had any one other than you spoken to me as you did, I would have killed him! I shall place myself under your orders at once. If I win, I'll reward you richly. If I lose, I'll skin you as I would a cat!"

"If I lose," repeated Holloway enigmatically, "I shall deserve that or a worse fate!"

Holloway kept Valdez under his thumb rigidly for the next thirty-six hours, grooming and coddling him as he might an unruly boy. The task was exceedingly repugnant to him and at times he felt like throttling the wretch, whose blasphemies shocked him. At the close of the first period of his novitiate in the school of love, Valdez scowlingly acknowledged that he had bathed and shaved more in that brief interval than he had in any three years of his turbulent career.

Holloway taught the bandit how to wear his fine raiment, though behind the rascal's back he smiled at the grotesque figure he presented—that of a vulture parading in the gaudy feathers of a bird of Paradise. The valet urged his master to refrain as much as possible from the use of that perfervid language which he was accustomed to employ when in the company of his intimates, as being *de trop* in the presence of the woman whose love he hoped to win. Valdez grinned and scowled by turns as the valet preached, he finding this tuition not much to his taste; but he ended invariably by complying with all of the valet's commands, however disagreeable he found them at times.

On the evening of the second day, Valdez announced his intention to visit Marian the next morning, to impress upon her the urgency of accepting him as her

husband. Valdez was determined to possess her with
or without her consent. He was eager to hasten the
nuptials, for once they were legally wedded in the
Cathedral at Los Vinos, he could afford to laugh at
the American pigs, who, doubtless, were scouring the
border for traces of the missing girl. His fear was
that they might make an international matter of the
abduction, in which event the marriage should not
be unduly delayed.

"No matter what they may do, I am safe," laughed
Valdez over his wine. "If the Americans crowd me
too closely, I will make my plea to the President in
Mexico City. Then will follow diplomatic notes,
threats of embargoes, intervention, reprisals and much
else, until both sides finally drop the incident without action being taken. Bah! the American pigs are
fools! Though we kill, rob and plunder hundreds of
them, they fear to intervene in our internal affairs,
for they know that with our system of guerilla war-
fare they never can subdue or control us without the
expenditure of millions of capital and the sacrifice of
thousands of lives!"

"But Uncle Sam is a patient old chap," said Holloway, flecking a grain of dust from Valdez's waistcoat. "He has a mighty kick in him when he gets
started, as history proves. It might be best for us
Mexicans to let the sleeping lion lie lest we awake him
and he swallow us whole."

"That is a problem for the diplomatists to solve,
Sanchez! Let us concern ourselves with our game of
love."

"*Si, señor.*"

Valdez left the hacienda to oversee the branding of
some cattle which his rustlers had brought in during the night, and this being Holloway's first opportunity to examine the building and its appointments,

he began his quest with extreme caution. He was aware that Lopez was watching him, and it was only when that worthy was away on some mission for the master bandit, that he felt himself free and unhampered. Strolling into the patio, he was delighted to see Marian seated at her window above. She glanced at him with mingled curiosity and wistfulness.

Placing his finger to his lips to enjoin silence, he drew a note he had prepared in anticipation of just the opportunity that now presented itself. She nodded, indicating that she understood. He moved slowly towards her window, eying each bush narrowly for possible witnesses, but saw nothing to excite alarm. Picking up a pebble, he attached the note thereto and tossed it through Marian's window. Humming a song he walked to the fountain, drew a small volume from his coat pocket and sat down, apparently to read, but actually to await the signal he knew she would flash to him.

Amazed at this unexpected development, Marian picked up the note, untied the string and with quickened pulse read the following:

Miss Haines:—Have courage—do not despair. I shall somehow find means to effect your rescue and return you safely to your brother and friends. Be wary and give no one cause to suspect that you know me. I shall contrive to see you to-night. Let me know by any means at your command, that you understand and will co-operate with me. Destroy this at once. Leave the rest to me.

Jim Holloway, alias the Wolf.

She raised her eyes in joyous thanksgiving. God had not deserted her! He had answered her prayers and Jim Holloway—that man among men—was to be her deliverer! Ah, how her trust in him flamed in her bosom! She kissed the note, then thrust it into her bodice, determined after she had memorized the message to destroy it as Holloway had commanded. She went to the window, nodded to Holloway who rose instantly and sauntered away, his face bent over the pages of his book. Presently he disappeared into the room allotted to him by Valdez, and Marian sat down to think.

She was wondering what steps Jim would take to drag her from the jaws of the lion, when the sound of a footstep startled her. Rising, she turned and beheld Señorita Marie Pinosa, charmingly arrayed in a rich Spanish dancing costume, deliciously soft and colorful. Marian was fearful lest the señorita, whom she now saw for the first time, had observed the incident of the note and would reveal her secret. The señorita smiled affably, but her eyes, brilliant as stars, flashed jealousy and hatred.

"*Buenos dias, señorita,*" she said softly. Marian nodded without venturing a reply. The señorita laughed to show her pearly teeth, then addressed her in strongly accented English. "You do not speak the Spaneesh?" she asked, fanning herself vigorously.

Marian replied in the negative. She wondered how her visitor had gained access to the room without a tell-tale sound. Had she seen her receive and read Jim's note? If so, what did she intend to do? She sensed danger, and her anxiety increased momentarily, not because of fear for herself, but for Jim who was gallantly risking his life in her service.

"How luckee for you, señorita," exclaimed the girl. "I speakee English ver' well. I· dance many mont's in London. Oh, we can talk mooch togedder."

"Who are you?"

"I am Señorita Maria Pinosa, the—the, what

you call eet? Ah, yes, the fiancée of Señor Valdez.''
She paused, frowning, then resumed coldly, ''Dat ees,
if you don' try to cut me out wiz heem—''

''Have no fear of that, señorita,'' said Marian
earnestly. ''I am not your rival in his affections.''

''How do I know?'' rejoined the señorita eagerly.
''If you try eet, I cut your heart out wiz dis—''
She drew a jeweled dagger from her coiffure and
brandished it before Marian threateningly.

''Foolish woman!'' said Marian. ''You are welcome to Valdez, for I hate him with all my heart!
He has brought me here against my will, and if there
is any law in Mexico, he shall be punished!''

The señorita seemed vastly pleased at this out-
burst. She concealed the dagger in her abundant
hair with the assurance that inasmuch as Marian now
had a friend in the hacienda, her escape should not be
delayed an instant.

''What do you mean?'' gasped Marian in alarm.

The señorita thrust the pebble Holloway had
thrown into the window, forward with her slippered
foot. Marian's heart sank and she turned away to
hide her agitation. How much had the señorita seen?

''Some one t'row you dees stone wiz a note which
lies on your heart now, señorita?'' The señorita
paused, then resumed, ''Who write you dat lettair?
Was eet Valdez?''

''No, no!''

''You no lie, señorita?''

''No!''

''From a servant, p'raps?''

''Yes.''

''You make me almos' happy like a bird!'' said the
señorita. ''Ah, you wanna leave dees hacienda, eh?''

Marian wondered how far she might trust this flip-
pant young woman. Could she take her into her con-

fidence without endangering Holloway? No, she
dared not risk that step until she had consulted with
Jim. She decided to be non-committal, trusting to
good luck to win the señorita's half-promised co-operation in their plan to escape.

"*Señorita,*" said Marian, taking her hand, "I am in
peril. I need a friend. May I count on your aid?"

"*Si, señorita!* I help you, if I can." She went
to the window and looked out. It was growing dark
and storm clouds lowered on the western sky line.
"Ah! Valdez comes! I mus' leave you now! If Valdez find me weez you, he keel me! I help you to-night
—to-morrow, mebbe! *Adios!*"

She opened the door silently and disappeared.
Marian felt that she could trust this woman implicitly.
She drew Jim's note from her bosom, memorized it,
then tore it into fragments. Finding a tiny hole in
the floor at one corner she dropped the bits of paper
therein. At least as far as the note was concerned,
Jim would not be betrayed! With two staunch
friends in Valdez's household, how could her escape
be frustrated?

When she thought of Jim, a wonderful, exhilarating
sense of security and contentment possessed her.
That he, of all men, should be her deliverer, filled her
with joy. Was it possible that this man, who did not
fear to risk his life in her service, was the reckless
abandoned man-killing scoundrel he was reputed to
be in every evil haunt along the border? Jim Holloway a wolf? She vowed never to couple the odious
appellation with his name again.

She sat at the window and watched the storm clouds,
rent at intervals by lightning flashes, scudding across
the sky. Fear had vanished and exultation filled her
heart.

. . . .

Riding to Los Vinos on business for Valdez, Holloway dismounted at Jackson's store. He was whispering some message to the storekeeper, when a Mexican vaquero of small stature, who was smoking a cheroot, approached them. Holloway had not observed him and he was urging Jackson to obtain the services of a half dozen reliable riders who were to meet him at the hacienda at midnight, when the Mexican addressed him.

"Want some hands, *señor?*" he asked, in faulty, though intelligible Spanish. "If you don't mind, I'm open to an engagement."

Holloway stared. The Mexican's voice had a familiar drawl that reminded him of a pal he had lost sight of long since. He stooped, studied the little Mexican's face for several seconds, then with a shout of joy, picked him up bodily and held him aloft at arm's length.

"Oh, you Kid!" he shouted. "If it isn't my pal, I'm a goat! I'm going to spank you!"

Suiting the action to the word, he lay the little Mexican across his knee, but before he could administer the threatened punishment, Hank, for it was he, had with the dexterity of an eel, squirmed out of his hands.

"Not by a dinged sight will you spank me, Jim," he drawled, picking up his cheroot he had lost in the scuffle. "Nobody 'cept my good mother—God bless her!—has spanked me yit, an' even yuh ain't agoin' to apply no layin' o' hands on me! Jim, howdy? Shake!"

Holloway shook Hank's hand until he winced, telling him the while over and over again that the sight of him was good for sore eyes. Neither observed the stealthy entrance of a Mexican who eyed them curiously as they skylarked in the exuberance of their camaraderie. It was Lopez. He smiled malignantly at Holloway, who, turning on his heel, confronted him. He instantly divined that his secret had been discovered.

"As I suspected! You are the Wolf, after all!" said Lopez sarcastically. "So Sanchez de la Guardia, one time valet in the employ of his excellency the Governor of Durango, is a myth! This will be glorious news for Valdez!"

So eager was Lopez to play cat and mouse with Holloway's fears that he failed to see Hank, who, like Holloway, had recognized him the instant he spoke. Hank was determined to stop another possible leak, and to that end he sprang toward the door, preventing Lopez's escape in that direction. Then he crept towards the Mexican cat-like, his automatic in his hand. Holloway, who divined Hank's purpose, smiled affably at the Mexican.

"You have wonderful eyes and ears, Lopez!" he said carelessly. "You won't give me away to Valdez, will you?"

Lopez chuckled spitefully. "You didn't deceive me, Wolf," he replied. "Valdez will punish you finely when I tell him who you are, and believe me he is a very devil when it comes to punishing traitors—"

Hank's automatic collided with Lopez's temple with force sufficient to crack his skull, and he fell to the floor as if he had been stricken down by lightning. Donlon, who appeared at this juncture, assisted Hank in binding the unconscious Mexican's hands and feet. A gag was thrust into his mouth and limp as a rag, he was dragged into the stable in the rear and tossed into a corner, inert as a dead man.

"What are you going to do with him, Kid?" asked Holloway curiously.

"Dunno yit, Jim," replied Hank, chewing his cheroot contemplatively. "Leastwise, he won't tell nobody his trouble until we git Marian Haines out'n Valdez's hands."

Hank introduced Donlon to Holloway and after some discussion they adjourned to the storeroom.

"You'n me is goin' to have a powwow, son," said Hank, lighting a fresh cheroot.

"Go to it, Kid."

They talked in whispers for many minutes and it was nearly dusk when Holloway, after repainting the scar on his cheek, and otherwise perfecting his disguise which had, so to speak, become slightly shop worn, rode back to the hacienda. His heart was light, for Hank and Donlon had agreed to contribute their aid in the rescue of Marian within the next twenty-four hours. All had sworn to win or die in the attempt.

CHAPTER XVIII

MARIAN DECLARES HER FAITH

IT was eight o'clock when Valdez sent for Sanchez with the request that he sup with him. Holloway found the bandit seated at a table with a man servant hovering about him. He observed with anxiety that the outlaw had been drinking heavily. The rogue was irritable, ugly and threatening.

"Sanchez," he remarked angrily, "you don't drink enough to please me. Isn't my liquor good enough for you, who once was employed by the Governor of Durango?"

Holloway laughingly assured Valdez that the fame of his liquor had reached even the precincts of the governor's palace at the capital, but that his official duties forbade his indulgence in intoxicants until His Excellency's magnificent purpose had been achieved.

"Be it so, Sanchez," grunted Valdez, appeased. "You are a valuable fellow and if all goes to my liking, I shall reward you well."

While the bandit was helping himself liberally to the liquor, Holloway's half-formed purpose to rescue Marian that night if possible, matured. The hacienda seemed to be deserted, but he knew that somewhere in the vicinity, Ricardo, with several armed men, was on guard. It was necessary for the success of his project that Valdez be helplessly intoxicated and to that end he encouraged him to drink by refilling his half-emptied glass whenever the opportunity presented itself.

"Where's that scoundrel Lopez?" hiccoughed Valdez. "He had an important matter to execute for me at Los Vinos and now he fails to appear. I'll cut his nose off when he returns!"

"It is the love moon that shines brightly in the sky," sighed Holloway, pouring wine into Valdez's glass. "Perhaps Lopez has a fair maid somewhere to whom he is paying his vows. You know the saying, 'as the master doeth, so doth the slave.' "

"*Carramba!*" growled Valdez pettishly. "I'll teach him to go awooing while I have need for him!" He raised his glass. "A toast!" he said tipsily. "A toast to my lady love."

"Well spoken, Excellency! To my lady love!"

Valdez drained his goblet, but he failed to see Holloway toss the contents of his glass beneath the table, to follow the others he had poured there. The odor of wine nauseated him. Remembering his oath to abstain from drink, Holloway thanked Heaven that his craving for intoxicants no longer existed to torment him.

Valdez yawned and stretched his arms across the table.

"I am dog tired and would rest an hour," he muttered with an oath. "Wake me, Sanchez, when the clock strikes nine, for then I shall speak to the woman I love—this dainty American girl whose beauty has bewitched me."

He murmured some meaningless words, grinned horribly and, resting his head upon his arms, fell to snoring. Holloway stood over him, his fists clenched, hatred and contempt on his face.

"You hound!" he exclaimed. "For a centavo, I would strangle you as you lie!" He leant over the drunken man and grasping him roughly by the hair, lifted his head to let it fall again with a thump. Valdez was in a stupor and helpless as an infant.

"I predict you will not go awooing to-night, your Excellency," remarked Holloway coldly. "If I dared, I might serve as your substitute. Why shouldn't I? I shall try it on my own account! *Adios*, Valdez!"

Leaving Valdez where he lay, he ascended the creaking staircase to the hall upon which, he was aware, the room occupied by Marian opened. That he should find the maid on watch near the door, did not surprise him. He accosted her courteously in Spanish, but her response was cold and listless. The place was dimly lighted by means of a lamp fastened to the wall. Through the window streamed the light of the waning moon which had just risen.

"All alone, señorita?" said Holloway genially. "Why are you not enjoying yourself in the patio? The night still is early—"

"But not for me, Sanchez," interrupted the girl sighingly. "Valdez has ordered me to guard this American woman whom he hopes to make his bride as I've heard, and here I must remain until he gives me leave to quit my post."

"Then you may go now, for he has ordered me to take your place."

She looked surprised and, though willing to go, was restrained by fear of her stern master of whose cruelty she had heard much. She rose and went longingly to a window. At that instant a man's voice, singing a rugged song and accompanied by a softly strummed mandolin, rose to them from the patio. The girl clasped her hands longingly.

"It is Ricardo singing to his lady love," whispered Holloway.

"Ricardo!"

"He is singing to you! Will you ignore the call of love? Shame on you, girl! Return in one hour! But stay, my girl, give me the key."

She handed him the key and tiptoed cautiously down the stairs. He went to Marian's door and rapped softly. There came to him almost instantly Marian's response.

"Who is there?" she asked.

Placing his lips to the keyhole, he whispered his name. At her request, he unlocked the door, and entered the room, closing and relocking it after him.

"Miss Haines," whispered Holloway, "please pardon me for forcing myself upon you, but it is imperative that you listen to me if you hope to make your escape from this place."

"I have nothing to pardon," she rejoined gratefully. "If you only knew how happy your note made me! Now that I have the opportunity to do so, will you forgive me for my conduct at the Red Eye that terrible night?"

"You cannot perhaps realize the great service you did me on that occasion," he answered soberly. "But for you I might not have regained mastery over self. I have learned that life is indeed worth living when women like you exist to inspire faith, hope and love in mankind."

"Love!" she murmured, "let us not talk of that now. We must plan our escape."

"Yes, but tell me how you came to be captured by Valdez."

She told him all that had happened after she left the bungalow in search of her brother Ralph. She had searched diligently here and there near the "Chimney" without success, when from a ravine there sprang five Mexicans led by Valdez. Before she could draw her revolver, Lopez, who had crept behind her, had seized and disarmed her. She fought desperately, but the bandits merely laughed at her helplessness and distress.

"The scoundrels!" muttered Holloway, wrathfully. "How I wish I had been there to aid you! I would have made them pay dearly for their outrageous conduct."

"Perhaps it is just as well you were not there," she sighed. "They might have killed you, and—and—"

"And what, Miss Haines?"

"Who would protect me now?"

"True, I hadn't thought of that. Please continue."

"After I had been made prisoner, Valdez and the others held a whispered consultation in Spanish. Valdez offered to assist me to mount his pony. Resistance being useless, I complied and when I was in the saddle, he sprang up behind me. Ugh!" She shuddered at the recollection. "He placed his arms about me, talking incessantly. Fortunately, however, he spoke in Spanish and I understood little of what he said. I gathered that the bandits were to flee to Mexico, and that they were more than anxious to elude the Sheriff's posse, which I prayed, might intercept us."

"Poor girl! It must have been a horrible experience."

"I shall never forget it," she responded. "My only desire throughout the ordeal was to escape at any cost. I tried several times to leap from the broncho, but Valdez restrained me with brute force. Overcome finally by the horror of it all, I must have fainted, or rather, lapsed into a comatose state, which lasted for several hours. My recollection of that long ride which was to end where and how, I neither knew nor cared, so dejected was I, is quite hazy. I only know it was almost dark when we reached a village near this place where we stopped to water our horses."

"It was Los Vinos, three miles from this hacienda," remarked Holloway. "Many white men live there.

Did you make any attempt on your arrival to attract attention and obtain help.''

''I was too utterly worn out for that,'' she replied. ''Once it occurred to me to cry out for help while we were riding by a cathedral, but I was unable to utter a sound. We did not spend much time in Los Vinos, and in half an hour or so, we drew up here. Valdez carried me up to this room and after placing me in the custody of the Mexican girl who serves as my jailor, he left me to my own reflections. And here I am, Jim—pardon me, Mr. Holloway.''

He leaned over and took her hand. ''Call me Jim,'' he urged softly. ''I never knew the name sounded so well, until you voiced it just now.''

''Very well—Jim.''

He asked her, after a pause, why she had left Purple Canyon that morning to court the danger that threatened all in Red Sandy valley. She colored and for some seconds made no answer.

''It was on your account, Jim,'' she said, her face downcast.

''Mine?''

''I suspected that your notice—''

''Stop!'' he commanded indignantly. ''Surely you did not believe that I purposed to carry out my threat —that I was capable of injuring your brother, after our meeting at the Red Eye?''

''I wasn't sure,'' she answered apologetically. ''You hadn't given me your word that you would relinquish your design, so when I met Faro Jenn the next morning, I—'' She halted doubtingly, he staring at her amazed.

''You met Jenn!'' he gasped. ''You talked to that creature! Tell me all that was said.''

Little by little he drew the story from her. He was horrified at Jenn's vengeance, and he wondered

how any woman with a heart could knowingly send
another to possible death or to a fate infinitely worse.
That she should have sought revenge upon him, did
not surprise him, but for her to cast Marian into the
clutches of a man like Valdez was beyond belief.   He
marveled that Jenn had not alluded to her meeting
with him in Mason's stable.   He realized that it was
his duty in the circumstances to reveal the truth to
Marian, but he was reluctant to make the avowal.

"I owe you an explanation regarding this unhappy
woman," he began uneasily.   "You will forgive me
if what I am about to say displeases you, Miss
Haines?"

She looked at him reprovingly.   "You call me Miss
Haines," she said, smiling gently, "while I call you
Jim.   It is unfair, now that we have come to an un-
derstanding."

"You are right, Marian," he rejoined.

Then without equivocation and a frankness that
merited her forgiveness, he told her of Jenn's plea to
him to marry her, of his curt refusal and of their final
meeting at Mason's stable just before he rode for the
valley on the trail of the posse.   Marian listened to
him with emotions of doubt, respect and admiration.
She doubted because her unsophisticated nature could
not comprehend non-resistance on the part of a man
to a woman who hurled herself at his head; she respected him for his candor and admired him for his
manliness in voluntarily revealing his secret to her.
Neither was aware of Jenn's unhappy fate, for Hank,
who had revealed much to Holloway at their meeting in Los Vinos, had not been apprised of it before
he and Donlon had left Purple Canyon on their quest.

"But you do not love this woman, do you?" she
asked, after he had finished.   "Surely you cannot return the love—"

"No, decidedly no!" he interrupted warmly.

"Then let us talk of other things," she said. "Tell me of yourself and your career." She paused an instant, then asked: "Are you by any chance related to the Holloways of New York—Charles Holloway, the railroad president?"

"He is my father."

"Your father!" she echoed, amazed. "I know your mother well."

"Ah, little mother! I owe her reparation for the sighs my insane conduct has wrung from her—the tears she has shed on my account!" He rose and walked to and fro, she watching him anxiously. "But the debt shall be paid, and if I fail to bring happiness to her, I will be undeserving of forgiveness!"

Returning to Marian he related briefly the somewhat sordid story of his career in the West. He dwelt upon his adventures after leaving Purple Canyon not, as she believed, to do her brother an injury, but to ask his pardon. Marian listened with eagerness to his graphic account of Haines' duel with Pedro and of its tragic ending for the Mexican assassin. When he told of finding her brother wounded and unconscious, she wept softly.

"Poor Ralph!" she murmured. "May God speed his recovery!"

"He is doing as well as can be expected."

"What do you mean?"

"Physically he is all right, but mentally—"

"Mentally?" she repeated. "Please tell me all."

"His memory is gone!"

She sobbed and hid her face in her hands. Leaning over her soothingly he related to the minutest detail the incidents of the inquiry held by Sheriff Thorne at Purple Canyon, the particulars of which had been divulged to him by Hank at Los Vinos. Her agitation soon subsided, however, and when he had finished she smiled at him cheerfully.

"Your innocence will be established when we return to the valley," she said, "I am sure of it, Jim."

"I don't doubt it, Marian. Your brother will exonerate me, once his memory returns. Let us pray that it will be speedily restored."

He glanced at his watch with a start. Rising, he assisted her to her feet. He fancied her fingers pressed his lingeringly and the thought that this wonderful girl might after all be won, thrilled him. Yet he dared not voice the avowal he longed to make.

"I must leave you now," he said. "Valdez gave me an hour and I have overstepped my leave thirty minutes. Listen to me, Marian—I have arranged with Hank for your rescue at noon to-morrow when Valdez is to inspect the stolen cattle that came to-night."

He was telling her to be prepared for instant departure, when a muffled scream from below interrupted him. He ran to the door and opened it a few inches. Angry shouts, mutterings, and the sound of footsteps of running men, ascended to them.

"Something dreadful must have happened," said Marian, clinging to him.

"I must go," he replied. "I shall contrive to keep you informed of all that happens. Meanwhile, have faith!"

"I have faith, Jim—faith in you."

She leant towards him as she spoke, and her head rested for a moment upon his breast. He caught the perfume of her hair, and before he was conscious of it, he had pressed his lips to the lustrous strands. She raised her face and smiled at him understandingly, longingly. He repressed an overwhelming desire to kiss her on the lips—to draw her to him and whisper in her ears the secret of his abiding love.

"I hope to rejoin you soon," he said, stepping into the hall. "Retain this key and admit none but me. I shall manage to quiet the fears of the girl on guard when she demands its return."

He left her, she relocking the door after him. She stood for some moments in a listening attitude. Her thoughts were centered upon him and upon certain words he had spoken—words that filled her with inexpressible happiness.

"He loves me!" she thought. "I read it in his eyes! To-morrow I shall be free and he may lead me where he will, for I love him—my Jim!"

Unmindful of the mysterious clamor beneath, she sat at the window, her hands clasped, her face radiant with a new joy. She thought of the days to come—days filled with the golden promises of happiness for the man she loved and for herself. Her faith in him was supreme, and on that faith she was content to stake her future and all it held forth to her trustful understanding.

CHAPTER XIX

A TRAGEDY AND A SURPRISE

PAUSING at the door for an interval after it had been relocked by Marian, Holloway turned the knob to find the barrier secure against all but forcible intrusion. His face was grimly set and could Valdez have seen it then, he might have had reason to ponder before he leapt, now that the fortunes of the woman he sought to degrade were under the guardianship of a resolute man who feared neither Valdez nor his master—the devil.

"Be the results what they may," he muttered, "if Valdez attempts to enter this room to-night, I'll kill him!"

The commotion below increasing, he went to the stairway and was about to descend, when his progress was checked by the maid who stared at him in speechless horror.

"What has happened, girl?"

"The Señorita!" moaned she, wringing her hands.

"What of her?"

"Valdez has killed her!"

"Killed her!"

"With a single stab of his knife to the heart! Oh, how horrible! It may be my turn next." She squatted down on the floor, clasped her knees and rocked herself in an agony of fear.

Holloway leaped down the stairs and entered the living room where Valdez sat moodily at the table, with Ricardo and several of the hacienda guards who surveyed their chief with horrified eyes. The bandit lurched drunkenly to his feet and seizing a bottle filled a glass to the brim.

"Here's to a happy journey to Paradise for *Señorita* Marie Pinosa!" he shouted, laughingly.

Holloway, making sure that his automatic was in a position where he could reach it without fumbling, entered the room. At Valdez's feet sprawled the figure of the señorita in a pool of blood. A dagger had been plunged into her breast, and the weapon still remained in the wound. He was accustomed to scenes of horror, but the wanton murder of this beautiful woman shocked and enraged him so that he was tempted to destroy this pitiless monster as one might crush a viper beneath one's heel. But he thought of Marian, and her perilous situation rendered him prudent.

"What has happened, your Excellency?" he asked, pointing to the señorita's body.

"It is nothing, Sanchez," replied the Mexican with an oath. "This woman was a vampire and I killed her!"

"A vampire?"

"I was awakened to find her kneeling beside me, her lips glued to my hand! Oh, I know these vampires well, I assure you! I had been dreaming of bats and when I awoke, I saw her shake her wings and laugh at me! Slowly she changed her personality, I watching her the while. Then I snatched the dagger she wore in her hair and struck hard and deep!"

Surely this sodden wretch was a madman, thought Holloway. Ricardo whispered to the other men, two of whom picked up the señorita's body and carried it out of sight into an adjoining apartment. Valdez laughed and drank again.

"Ricardo!" he shouted raucously.

"I am here, señor," responded that worthy.

"Has Lopez returned?"

"No, señor."

"Treacherous dog! He is making love to some kitchen maid! He shall pay dearly for keeping me waiting! Sanchez!"

"Excellency!" answered Holloway, advancing to the table.

"How do I look?"

"As usual, señor."

"Am I fit to play the rôle of bridegroom?"

"Bridegroom!"

"*Carramba!* You are dense indeed, Sanchez. Haven't you heard that I am to wed to-night?"

Deadly fear gripped Holloway's heartstrings. "You are not serious, *señor?*" he asked hoarsely.

"Most serious, Sanchez! Father Enrique awaits us at the Cathedral at Los Vinos even now, for it was all arranged by Lopez this afternoon." A clock in an adjoining room struck ten. "See!" continued he, "It is ten o'clock and the ceremony is set for eleven! Ricardo!"

"*Si, señor.*"

"Are the horses ready?"

"*Si, señor.*"

"Then I'll have a chat with my bride and we'll be off! *Pronto!*"

Holloway could not believe his ears. What had occasioned this sudden change of plan? How was he to frustrate the devilish design of the bandit to marry Marian by force? What now of the scheme he had arranged with Hank for Marian's rescue? How was he to communicate with his friends in Los Vinos in time to prevent the immolation of Marian on the altar of lascivity builded by Valdez? He protested in vain, urging that a midnight marriage must inevitably redound to his patron's disadvantage when the news was divulged. To all his pleadings, the Mexican turned a deaf ear.

"Enough, Sanchez!" he retorted angrily. "I am responsible for my own acts and accountable to none. Be in readiness to follow me, for you're to be my groomsman!"

"It is for you to command and me to obey, your Excellency!"

Holloway bowed in patient submission to his whim, as Valdez believed, but he sought thereby to conceal the grain of satisfaction that this unexpected order had provoked. At least he would be by Marian's side to shield her from danger and he would trust to luck to point out a way of ultimate escape from the net of circumstances in which he and Marian were entangled. He vowed grimly that if a thousand devils of Valdez's breed stood between Marian and her safety, he would kill them all.

"Go, Sanchez, fetch my bride," said Valdez, rising. "Break the news to her gently, for the girl may not relish the prospect of wedding me without first experiencing the delights of courtship! I leave that to your superior generalship in affairs of love."

"Trust me, Excellency."

"But I warn you, that if she comes unwillingly I shall punish you!" resumed Valdez, a ferocious grin on his face. Holloway was about to turn when the bandit drew a revolver from beneath his velvet waistcoat and held it waveringly against his body.

"It is thus I punish traitors!" he snarled, his finger on the trigger.

Holloway's face paled, his eyes fastened upon the madman's swollen countenance with an air of confidence he was far from feeling. He was in the power of this sanguinary wretch, who, if he but pressed his finger a hair's breadth, would send him to follow the señorita across the Styx. There was little for him to do other than to show unconcern and, accordingly, he laughed as if he heartily appreciated the bandit's humorous whim.

"Excellency," he said significantly, "they who deceive you deserve any fate! If I have betrayed you, blow out my brains!"

Valdez hesitated. Holloway was on the point of dealing him a right upper cut on the jaw, when, with a cackle, the bandit tossed the weapon upon the table. He motioned to Holloway to leave him and turning on his heel, Jim ascended the stairs to the hall above. The Mexican girl sat at the window, her face hidden in her hands, vainly seeking to shut out the scene of horror of which she had been the involuntary witness. He paid her scant attention, and halting at Marian's door rapped the panel softly.

"Who is there?" came Marian's voice.

"It is I, Sanchez de la Guardia, on a special mission for his excellency, *Señor* Valdez."

He delivered this announcement in a high pitched tone, so that it could be plainly heard by any spy of Valdez's who might be lurking on the stairs, eager to report to his chief how his messenger was acquitting himself. He fancied he heard Valdez chuckle, then followed a whispered consultation. That Valdez had trailed him he was certain. The door opened at this juncture and he entered the room, closing it behind him with care. He took Marian's hand; she was trembling.

"What has happened, Jim?"

"You will be free or I a dead man to-night!" he whispered. "Be brave and all will be well."

Briefly he acquainted her with the unexpected development that threatened to disrupt the plans he had made to insure her escape. Marian sighed apprehensively but with him by her side, she experienced no fear.

"Have you a weapon, Marian?"

"I have a dagger," she replied.

"Take it with you and should you be compelled to use it, strike with all your strength! Listen!"

He instructed her as to her duties in the premises; adding that he would guard her as far as the Cathedral, when he would slip away for a few moments to summon his friends to their aid. He spoke admiringly of his little friend and in simple terms expressed confidence in his resourceful comradeship.

"You must trust to me," he said, when he had finished.

"I do trust in you, Jim!"

"Brave girl!"

"May God help us both!"

She sighed and tidied her hair a bit, praying earnestly meanwhile for strength that she might pass unscathed through the coming ordeal. She felt that with Jim on the watch, her safety was assured. Placing the dagger in her corsage she donned her hat and announced herself ready for the journey.

"You will be brave, Marian?"

"Yes, Jim."

He opened the door and she followed him in silence to the room below, where Valdez and Ricardo awaited them. The bandit stood hat in hand, and advancing towards her, bowed gallantly. Playing her rôle, she inclined her head slightly and waited patiently for him to speak.

"Welcome, Miss Haines," he said thickly. "I trust my friend Sanchez has removed any scruples you may have entertained regarding our prospective marriage?"

"He has, *señor*," she replied. "I await your commands."

"Bravely spoken, *señorita!* Let us seal the bargain with a kiss!"

He advanced towards her, she shrinking from him. She was wondering how she might escape the loathsome embrace she dreaded, when Holloway stepped between them.

"Not so fast, your Excellency!" he said coldly. "You would undo the good work I have done in your behalf. When your nuptials have been celebrated, *señor,* you may kiss her; and I need not assure you that it will be the sweeter for the delay!"

The bandit snarled in disappointment and his hand instinctively sought the revolver. Holloway glared at him so menacingly that he paused in bewilderment. He scowled, but presently the fit of passion that swayed him died away and he laughed.

"You may be right, Sanchez," he assented, leering at Marian. "Let us be off, Ricardo! It grows late and Father Enrique is likely to be angry with us."

They left the house, Holloway walking beside Marian in the footsteps of Valdez and Ricardo. In the foreground they found awaiting them, not the four riders Holloway had counted upon, but a dozen or more! Valdez held out his hand, palm upward, to assist Marian to mount, and with a repugnance she could scarcely repress, she placed her foot in his palm and sprang into the saddle. Valdez and Holloway leaped upon their ponies, and at the bandit's command the cavalcade started off at a gallop.

With Valdez at her left, and Holloway on her right, Marian rode in silence until the outskirts of Los Vinos were reached. The streets were deserted, though here and there lights gleamed in the barred windows of the houses as they passed. At intervals scared faces showed; those of men and women who often had been awakened at night by similar bands, when foul murder was done, and all human rights and privileges violated! No sooner had the band ridden by than the lights were extinguished and the village was silent as death, except for the clatter of hoofs, that sounded like the ringing of the tocsin to frightened ears!

The front of the Cathedral was in darkness, but in the rear, a light showed, as the troop trotted within the sacred grounds. The moonlight touched the bell tower with a silver sheen, and to Marian the night was one of the most calmly beautiful she had ever known. Valdez had already dismounted when Holloway leaned towards her.

"I must leave you now, Marian," he whispered. "I shall rejoin you in a few moments."

"God speed you!" she sighed bravely.

"Do all in your power to delay the ceremony. Faint if need be—do anything to kill time until I return, if by chance my absence should be unduly prolonged. Be brave!"

He sprang from his horse and throwing the reins over a branch as the other riders had done, he vanished in the darkness. Two minutes later, he rapped on the door of the storeroom where Hank and Donlon were domiciled.

"Who's thar?" cried Hank sleepily, awakened by the noise, slight though it was.

"Jim!"

Hank opened the door and Holloway hurriedly told him all that had happened. Hank listened in such visible perturbation of mind that he forgot to light a fresh cheroot.

"You say there be fifteen greasers in the bunch?"

Holloway nodded.

"Well, I've got three American punchers in the

stable guardin' Lopez, with Donlon here.   That makes
five and if one American hain't as good as three
greasers, then it's time we wus agoin' to the boneyard,
regardless!''

"We'll beat 'em, old chap!" responded Holloway.
"I'm off now! See you later."

He ran down the street like a deer and soon reached
the church where Valdez was treating Father Enrique
to a volley of picturesque Spanish oaths.   The padre
was shocked and his lips moved in prayer.

"What's the matter, Excellency?" asked Holloway
curiously.

"*Carramba!*" swore Valdez.   "I am a bridegroom
without a bride!"

"I do not understand, *señor!*"

Valdez swore again and again, the padre lifting his
hands supplicatingly at this wanton profanation of
his house of worship.

Marian had disappeared!

CHAPTER XX

THE BELL CLAPPER

BITTERLY disheartened, Marian watched Holloway with moist eyes until he disappeared in the shrubbery beyond. She felt herself at the brink of hysteria, but escorted by Valdez and Ricardo, neither of whom had observed the absence of Sanchez, she entered the church with fortitude. Once or twice she faltered, but when Valdez attempted to take her arm and assist her, she shrunk from him in horror and bounded through the doorway. The bandit laughed significantly, but followed her without protest.

They were welcomed at the portal by Father Enrique who had been chosen, or rather commanded, by Valdez to perform the nuptials, he receiving them with that obsequiousness of manner habitual with all who knew and had reason to fear the bandit. He led them into a small room where Marian, wearied unto death, her feet like clay, dropped despairingly into a chair. She prayed with all her heart that Holloway's return would not long be deferred, in which event, she felt she must kill herself or go mad.

Valdez discussed the formalities of the wedding ceremony dictatorially with the priest, who nodded frowningly at intervals. A gush of cool air swept over Marian and on turning to ascertain its source, she saw a door, slightly ajar, which opened on a narrow stairway leading upward. It flashed to her mind that if Holloway and his friends failed to come to her aid she would flee whithersoever the stairs might lead her, trusting to Providence to reach some hiding place.

She was about to rise when Valdez for the first time observed Holloway's absence. The bandit stormed, raged and cursed bitterly. The padre sought to calm him, but Valdez, who was now feeling the ennervating effects of the mixed wines he had drunk, was in a murderous humor and refused to be appeased by the honeyed phrases of the priest.

"I'll teach this valet to leave me without permission!" he fumed. "I'll strangle him once he falls into my hands! Come, Ricardo, we will search for him outside!"

They left the room hastily, the padre following them, leaving Marian alone. A prey to sickening terror, not so much on her own account as on Holloway's, she sprang through the doorway and found herself in Cimmerian darkness. She ascended the winding stairs with all the speed of which her limbs were capable, some forty steps or more, then paused to regain her breath. She fancied some one was following her, and pressing her hand to her heart to still its tumultuous beatings, ran on again, emerging finally upon a platform, the extent of which she could not divine.

Exhausted by her violent exertions, she crouched upon the floor to restore her overtaxed energies. Far above she saw a moonbeam, which, passing through some open frame work or lattice, cast a faint ghostly light upon the void. Although she was totally ignorant of the plan of the sacred structure, she was certain that she stood beneath the belfry and that if she sought diligently, she would discover the door leading thereto and find sanctuary among the bells where, she earnestly hoped, none but Holloway would be able to follow her.

She began to grope hesitatingly through the gloom when the soft plaintive notes of an organ, intoning some exquisite melody, quaint and hauntingly beautiful, broke the silence. She paused, wondering what this portended. It was, doubtless, some assistant priest who was manipulating the keys to assure himself that his instrument was in readiness for the service that was to be performed. The notes reëchoing sweetly through the nave, died away suddenly, to be succeeded by the angry shouts of several men. Marian shuddered, then ran on with bursting heart, she knew not whither nor cared. Her sole desire was to widen the distance separating her from Valdez to the furthermost limits possible.

The pursuit had begun!

Without knowing what lay before her, or into what pitfall she might stumble, the frightened girl sped on through the gloom. Aside from the abject terror that oppressed her, one all-absorbing desire spurred her onward—to elude the clutches of the monster who was seeking to make her his wife.

But whither could she flee? She was appalled at the thought that in seeking refuge, she might run directly into the arms of Valdez or one of his devils prowling in the darkness. She advanced hesitatingly with extended arms, praying that she might find some opening in the walls and hide therein like a snail in its shell. Gradually, as her eyes became accustomed to the gloom, she beheld objects more distinctly, and presently she discerned at her right hand an aperture which yawned a ghostly welcome.

Gasping painfully, she darted into what proved to be a doorway, to fall against the lower step of a circular stairs. She ran up these falteringly until she reached a landing, whence it led her upward to another and then a third, from which she passed onto a platform some six feet wide, protected by a heavy railing. Approaching this cautiously she looked downward—far, far down, to the stone floor of the nave, fully one hundred feet beneath. It seemed to her as if she were searching the depths of a well, and seized by a vertigo, she covered her eyes and shrank back shudderingly against the wall.

Lights flickered here and there beneath her and the shouts of men echoed and reëchoed in the distance with weird effect. To her distorted fancy, the pursuers seemed to be at her very heels. The clamor served to renew her efforts to find refuge as speedily as possible. Above her, the openings in the belfry tower admitted sufficient light to enable her to discern the outlines of three bells that swung from a massive platform, some fifteen feet, as she judged, above her head. This staging was reached by means of a vertical ladder fastened to the opposite wall, and to attain this ladder she must cross the yawning abyss on her hands and knees! She shuddered at the terrifying prospect and shrank back. She must think. A false step now meant ruin to her hopes if not death!

Near her gaped the mouth of a gigantic bell, the huge clapper of which she might grasp by standing upright and extending her hand. Beneath yawned that frightful chasm into which she dared not look lest she lose her balance and fall to instant death. The support on which she crouched was scarcely two feet wide, and at her slightest movement it vibrated with terrifying effect upon her nerves. She realized that there was no other course for her to pursue. Bolstering up her waning courage with an effort, she crawled forward on her hands and knees, inch by inch. A portion of the lace of her skirt was wrenched away by a sliver, but she was too agitated to observe this. The staging swayed and creaked dismally as she advanced, but presently, to her great relief, she clutched the lower rung of the vertical ladder. She drew herself upward with a sigh of satisfaction. From the depths below rose the muffled shouts of her pursuers, and once she fancied she heard her name. That Valdez and Ricardo were at her heels she did not doubt; and her conviction that this was a certainty prompted her to continue on her course without cessation until her strength gave way or her progress was barred by the rafters of the belfry tower above.

She climbed the ladder, unaware that her hands had been painfully lacerated by the splinters of the plank and that they left their imprint in blood upon every rung she grasped. How she reached the upper platform, directly beneath the domed roof of the belfry, she never knew, but she remembered that several times in her ascent, she nearly lost her grip and all but fell backward into space. She finally reached the dust-laden floor, her heart filled with gratitude to God that she had been privileged to make her perilous ascent without accident.

She sprawled upon the platform panting violently as she had seen a fox gasp when cornered by hounds after a long chase. She was reasonably certain that the only means of reaching the platform upon which she lay was afforded by the vertical ladder she had ascended. She drew her dagger, sharp as a needle, and holding it firmly within her bleeding fingers, vowed with all her heart that she would defend herself against her pursuers to the bitter end.

Meanwhile, in the nave, while Valdez and Ricardo were conducting a quest in the garden of the Cathedral, Holloway had begun his search. Failing to find traces of her, the two bandits returned to the church, determined to punish her severely for the trouble she had occasioned them. When told by Father Enrique that the door of the crypt was unfastened, they hastened below, but after a brief examination of the damp musty smelling place every nook of which they fancied harbored a ghost, they returned to the room above just as Holloway opened the door leading to the upper regions of the edifice, and, closing it carefully after him, ascended the stairs.

"*Carramba!*" shouted Valdez in amazement. "Wasn't that Sanchez?"

"I think so," replied Ricardo, who was heartily sick of the whole business and wished Valdez and his lady love to the devil.

"Then we must nab him! There is something wrong—*Santisimo!*"

Standing at the door they beheld Lopez. He was panting like an exhausted hound. He held one hand to his heart and motioned to Valdez with the other. The bandit approached him threateningly.

"So you have returned, you dog!" snarled he savagely. "I'm almost tempted to carve my name on your ribs—"

"I come to save you, *señor,*" gasped Lopez, breaking in upon Valdez's speech. "Sanchez is a traitor who has betrayed you!"

"A traitor!"

"He is no Mexican, but—but—"

"Proceed, *esclavo!*"

"The Wolf!"

"The Wolf!" repeated the bandit, amazed. "You say he is the Wolf, and not a valet?"

"*Si, señor.*"

Lopez told his story briefly, the bandit listening to his recital with increasing rage. He had two objects in life now—to recapture Marian and to make the Wolf his prisoner so that he might enjoy adequate revenge! *Dios!* what a vengeance would be his once this detested American was a prisoner in his hands!

"He has gone after her to some hiding place above," he shouted, opening the door of the stairway. "Follow me!"

He led the way up the stairs, the flickering lantern he carried providing sufficient light to enable them to see their way without difficulty. By this time, however, Holloway had reached the second stairway, and pausing only to shout Marian's name he proceeded upward until he found himself on the precise spot where she had paused in perplexity, undecided which way to turn. Lighting a match, of which he carried an ample supply, he searched the floor as a scout scans a trail in the desert. His persistency was rewarded, for in the accumulated dust of years that encrusted the rough flooring, he discovered the imprints of Marian's shoes! He lit another match and by its feeble illumination followed the trail unerringly to the second stairs, which he negotiated as nimbly as a bloodhound on the scent.

When he reached the plank that spanned the abyss beneath the bells, he beheld a shred of white lace clinging to a splinter. How had it come there, he wondered? Had Marian crossed this fragile plank, or had she—? He dared not think further, for the mere supposition that she might have fallen or thrown herself to death, tortured him almost to madness. His heart throbbed painfully and to relieve the tension, he made a funnel of his hands and cried out her name.

"Marian! Marian!"

With his cupped hand at his ear, he listened for an answering cry, but except for the patter of footsteps on the stairs below, he heard nothing. He shouted again and his heart leapt when the answer came, sweetly soft, from he knew not where.

"Jim!   Jim!"

"Where are you, Marian?"

"Here, above the bells!"

"Are you safe, sweetheart?"

"Yes."

She leaned over the platform and waved to him. The vertical ladder, bathed in the moonlight, stood out in bold relief. He stepped upon the staging, determined to rejoin her without loss of time, for his pursuers, he knew, were ascending the stairs only a few feet behind him.

"Be careful, Jim!" urged Marian earnestly. "The crossing is dangerous and were the plank to fall—"

"Don't worry on my account, Marian," he responded. "I'll be with you in another minute!"

The plank buckled and swayed dangerously under his weight, for Holloway tipped the scales at fully one hundred and ninety pounds. Marian watched his progress with a wildly beating heart, her hands clenched in an agony of apprehension. He crept along the plank spider-like, nimbly as iron workers glide across narrow steel beams at dizzy heights. He reached the ladder in safety and had risen to grasp the rungs when a voice which he recognized as Valdez's, startled him.

"There he is!   Shoot him!"

Holloway drew his automatic and turned. Sensing his danger, Marian closed her eyes and prayed. Holloway's figure was as clearly outlined in the moonlight as if he were a statue sculptured in white marble. A shot rang out and a bullet slivered the rung an inch above his head. Taking a long chance, he fired directly at the vivid flash of the barking revolver in the gloom beyond. He fanned the weapon until five shots had sounded and turning, swung himself rapidly up the ladder beyond the pale radiance of the moonbeams. He heard a groan, followed by a heavy fall. One of his pursuers, at least, had been wounded, if not killed.

Ascending the ladder, Holloway sprang upon the platform beside Marian. She knelt, her hands clasped in gratitude. He placed his arms about her and drew her to him, she yielding to his embrace with joyous sobs.

"You—you aren't hurt, Jim?"

"Not a bit, sweetheart."

"That shot? You are sure the bullet missed you?"

"By a mile, my dear."

He kissed her again reassuringly. Yielding to hysteria, occasioned by the nervous strain to which she had been subjected, she laughed and wept by turns. Then her mood changed, and lying down, she peered cautiously over the edge of the platform.

"What if they should try to climb the ladder, Jim?"

"We'll give them a big reception if they try it, dear!"

Automatic in hand, he lay down beside her to listen. She placed her arm over him protectingly, gloriously elated at the miraculous coming of her great champion to guard and protect her. She watched him in silence as he scanned the gloomy depths.

"What are they doing?"

"Sshh!" He drew her back from the edge. "They are on the plank!" he whispered excitedly. "Fools! The staging cannot possibly sustain their combined weight!"

"Who are on the plank?"

"Valdez and Ricardo!"

"And if they should make the crossing?"

"I'll kill them both!"

Holloway's surmise that his bullets had not been wholly wasted, was correct. At his first fire, one of his three pursuers crumpled to the floor with a cough. It was Lopez! Before Valdez could find tongue to inquire who had been hurt, the outlaw was dead! Eager to resume the pursuit, Valdez paid scant attention to his ill-fated follower, whose body lay in a huddle at his feet.

"*Carramba!*" swore Valdez furiously. "They shall not escape my vengeance! They have climbed the ladder yonder! After them, Ricardo!"

Ricardo grunted his disapproval of what he believed to be a suicidal course, seeing that Holloway was armed, but Valdez urged him on with bitter curses. Ricardo stepped upon the plank with his chief close at his heels, his hand on his shoulder to steady himself as they crossed the abyss. The plank bent horribly under the strain and as they advanced, Valdez was seized with the gripping fear that he might after all have offended the Virgin to his own undoing. But his absorbing desire for vengeance urged him on, be the cost what it may.

"Forward, Ricardo!" he growled. "Only a step further, and we have them at our mercy!"

They had spanned one-half of the abyss when the plank, buckling to the breaking point, emitted a crunching, crackling sound that should have warned them of their peril, but it served only to impel them on at increased speed. Valdez nearly lost his footing, and to steady himself, clutched the clapper of the giant bell above him. The trend of his weight being downward as a result of this effort, the plank snapped like a rotten cord beneath their feet.

"*Dios!*" exclaimed Valdez in terror. "We are lost!"

Sensing his peril, Ricardo turned instinctively to

seize Valdez, but he was too late. With the report
of a pistol shot, the plank, until then held together
by trembling slivers, parted. Uttering a cry of agony,
his hands grappling space, Ricardo shot downward
like a plummet, the ends of the severed plank following him. Valdez, too frightened even to whimper,
clung despairingly to the clapper. He scarcely had
time to realize his danger when there rose to him from
the depths the crash of falling timber and the thud
of Ricardo's body as it crashed down upon the floor, a
shapeless mass.

"What has happened, Jim?" whispered Marian,
peering over the platform.

"Back!" commanded Holloway, seizing her arm.
"They have fallen to death!"

"How dreadful!"

"It is God's vengeance, sweetheart!"

"Listen!"

An agonized cry, like the whimper of an animal in
distress, ascended to them. Looking down, his ears
strained to catch every sound, Holloway caught the
grind of grating metal, and the bell moved slightly.
He comprehended the truth instantly and could
Marian have seen his face, its pallor would have
frightened her. He groaned.

"What is it, Jim?" she asked wonderingly.

He leaned over the edge to listen, without replying.
The bell emitted a deep throated moan like that of a
gong sounding faintly in the distance. Turning to
Marian, he drew her to him.

"It is Valdez—" he faltered.

"What of him?"

"He is swinging at the end of the bell clapper!"

Horror stricken, she covered her face with her
hands. "Poor creature!" she moaned in pure sympathy. "What will be his fate?"

"He will swing until his strength is exhausted and then—!"

A horrible gurgling cry interrupted him. Marian clung wildly to Holloway, her fingers in her ears to shut out the sounds of the terrible tragedy that was approaching its climax almost within reach of their hands and which they were powerless to prevent. What was to be their own fate? They were in the hands of Providence.

. . . .

Although he realized to the full the seriousness of his position, Valdez was not devoid of hope; and he battled bravely to sustain himself until the help he hoped for should come and he be rescued. When the crash came, he had narrowly escaped falling with Ricardo, and he all but lost his grip upon the clapper just above the bulb. He managed by a great muscular effort to retain his clutch and, bringing the oscillation of his body to a halt, to raise himself upward so that he might seat himself upon the knob and by crossing his legs, sustain himself.

"Help!" he shouted despairingly, pulling himself upward inch by inch with laborious effort. "For the love of God, help!"

He repeated his cry several times, only to discover that violent vocal exercise weakened him, and breathing like a man exhausted after a long run, he desisted. He was dangling within the encircling bell which had a height of some five feet as he judged. In settling himself firmly upon his bulbous perch, his feet struck the rim of the bell, the response being a deep vibration of sound that wrenched his tympanums so painfully that he nearly lost his grip. As the minutes sped, he retained his hold upon the clapper with increasing difficulty. He held his crossed legs rigid, but exert himself as he might, he slipped downward bit by bit, so that he was again and again compelled to pull himself up in order to secure anew his precarious seat upon the knob of iron that now was the only barrier between his sinful soul and the gates of Hell!

Valdez had been, in his day, a man of exceptional strength and powers of endurance. He was accustomed to outdoor life, and at rural sports, of which he was inordinately fond, he seldom had met his master. He had enormous iron-like biceps so that his muscular strength had enabled him often to throw a bull by the horns, a feat not accomplished by dexterity alone. But in recent years, his dissipations had played havoc with his muscles, robbing them of their vitality; and in time they had become flabby. Still, his despair, desperation and the will to survive even though the odds against him were insuperable, renewed his strength for the time being, so that he retained his hazardous seat with comparative ease. That his patron saint, whose name in his terror he could not remember, would not desert him in his hour of trial, he did not doubt, and he clung to the clapper buoyed by the hope of ultimate rescue.

He had twisted his limbs about his scant perch for the twentieth time when his mind began to wander, giving birth to strange and horrible phantasms in his disordered brain. Directly in front of him he saw the outlines of a human face delicately traced in silver on a black background. He closed his eyes to shut out the spectacle which fascinated and terrified him by turns. When he opened them again, there were two faces where one had been before! Wondering what satanic alchemy had accomplished this marvel, he closed and opened them again and again without experiencing relief.

Thrills shot along his spine and he blasphemed horribly, when he recognized one of the faces as that of the bandit who had deprived him of the gun he had stolen when a boy, and whom he later had killed with revolting brutality. The other was that of Señorita Marie Pinosa whom he had so cruelly slain less than two hours before. Both faces grinned at him abominably. He closed his eyes to shut out the sight!

"*Dios!*" he moaned in agony. "Leave me, or you will drive me mad!"

But the figments of his disordered imagination refused to quit him. On the contrary, whenever he opened his eyes, their number seemed to increase! Instead of two, there were now six—a dozen visages staring at and mocking him! They circled about him ceaselessly, above his head, by his side and beneath him as far as his vision went. Each time when he slipped along the clapper which now because of his sweating hands had become dangerously lubricated, he fancied they danced in unison, and when with infinite labor he drew himself painfully back upon his perch again, they laughed at his distress!

Turn where he would, the ghastly faces, with their hideous leers, sneering lips and mocking glances, appeared! To make sure that he was not dreaming, he counted them audibly one by one—a dozen or more —many of them women, all of whom owed their untimely fate to him! The more they mocked and derided him, the more he reviled them with bitter curses!

Valdez had been clinging to the clapper only two minutes at the most, yet each second had been to him an æon in its duration. As one who is drowning is privileged to review the course of his career even to the most trivial detail within the few seconds that intervene between consciousness and annihilation, so did Valdez's thoughts revert to the days of his innocent childhood in his mother's hovel in the mountains of Sonora.

With wonderful clearness of vision he saw the little garden with its hyacinths, roses and lilies which she had cultivated with loving care. He remembered how, one day, when he had plucked an unusually beautiful rose, she had punished him severely. He had revenged himself by twisting the neck of her pet peacock, and he recalled with keen delight the horror that darkened her face when his atrocity was discovered, and he held blameless because of his physical weakness which rendered the commission of such a crime by a child impossible!

He reviewed the events of his young manhood days, distinguished by offenses too numerous to mention, and then his maturer years, filled with ribald orgies and crimes against God and man, in the perpetration of which he gloried as achievements that were distinctly worth while. He saw again the pretty young women he had abducted and held for ransom only to violate and cast off as one throws a faded rose into the gutter when its beauty has vanished.

He thought of the raids in which he had engaged during the last three or four years—expeditions that had netted him much valuable loot, no inconsiderable portion of which, in money and jewels, was secreted in a hiding place known only to himself, in the hacienda. When he reviewed his experiences with that hated American called the Wolf, who had not only grossly betrayed but brought him to the deplorable pass in which he found himself, he lamented bitterly that his patron saint had not afforded him the opportunity of liquidating in blood the debt of hatred he owed the Wolf and which he would continue to owe until the gates of the Inferno had closed upon him forever!

And now he was to be punished for his manifold offenses, as Providence ultimately punishes all who treat with contempt the precepts of God's laws, and who spurn truth, wisdom and all those sacred obligations honest men owe society at large. He could not comprehend the obvious truth that he who transgresses the law, human or divine, must pay the inexorable penalty. He had defied Nature's decrees with impunity, and the result was apparent in his rapidly waning strength of muscles which refused longer to sustain the weight of his body.

He felt his vigor ooze from him with every breath he drew, and each time when he renewed the clutch of his crossed legs upon his little perch, acute pains shot along his arms and spine, causing him exquisite agony. His hands, cramped by the force of the grip he was obliged to exert to maintain his hold upon the clapper, became numbed and icy cold so that he had almost lost his sense of touch. When he relaxed his fingers slightly to restore the waning circulation of blood, it seemed as though he were holding them in the blue flame of a brazier. A sort of paralysis caused his muscles to relax further, filling him with horror. He could not repress the desire to shriek aloud, but from his parched throat there issued only hoarse sounds, weak as an infant's cries. He felt a ponderous weight on his breast, which was crushing him with a slowness devilish in its fatal purpose.

His mind began to wander as his power of resistance to the inevitable lessened. A choking sensation in his throat seemed to be strangling him, and he fancied he felt the dainty fingers of the señorita tearing out his eyes. He was so terrified that he lost control of his faculties, and his muscles relaxing, he slipped, but instinctively pulled himself upward to regain the inches he had lost. Hideous phantoms danced about and beckoned to him, their ceaseless gyrations nauseating him. Presently, he made the terrifying discovery that his legs were dangling in space, and he was powerless to draw himself upward sufficiently to enable him to sit astride the bulb of the clapper. *Dios!* it was the end. Though his hands slipped little by little, his love of life kept hope alive, and under its mighty stimulus his stiffened fingers held on he knew not how.

Beautifully tinted lights flashed before his vision and he began to admire the rainbow hues that darted hither and thither with lightning speed, each pointing the way, as he fancied, to safety! He sought to raise his dangling limbs, but they had become enormous weights that dragged him irresistibly downward. He struggled madly to rid himself of his burden, thereby causing the clapper to sway from side to side. As this oscillation increased, his clutch relaxed in like proportion, so that his wrists came for the first time in contact with the iron bulb. He maintained his slipping hold waveringly, alternately praying and blaspheming. Again he cried out for help, but the effort served only to weaken him further. Fiendish hands plucked at his fingers to tear them loose and hurl him into the abyss that yawned, and which was to swallow him up unshriven, accursed of God and men!

Then a strange thing happened. The clapper, eaten by the rust of the years, broke from its fastenings with a twang that sounded like the snap of demon jaws, and descended into space with terrific velocity. Valdez still clung to the bulb, seemingly holding the iron clapper aloft with his extended arms. Both shot down—down—ever down!

CHAPTER XXI

THE AMBUSH

HUSTLING out the three American punchers whom he had picked up the Lord knows where, Hank Weston, with Jimmy Donlon as his chief aide, left Jackson's store and, concealing their ponies in a grove of trees near by, so that they might be ready for instant service, proceeded to the church. Hank counseled the men to move with caution and thereby prevent Valdez's friends and adherents from hurrying to the scene to handicap them in the perilous game they were playing.

"How's that greaser Lopez?" asked Hank of one of the men.

"He's tied hand and foot in the stable," was the reply. "If he gets loose, I'm a Dutchman!"

"Bully! From what Holloway tells me, there be some fifteen greasers in Valdez's outfit, all of 'em armed fit for the Watsons. We jest got to git 'round 'em somehow an' put 'em out of business. Hullo! What's up?"

From the rear of the church as they approached, appeared several men swearing volubly, and presently the riders stationed here and there, after receiving whispered instructions, galloped down the road in the direction of the hacienda. The others searched noisily in the shrubbery, but, convinced that their quarry had successfully eluded them, they reëntered the Cathedral, from which their muffled imprecations floated discordantly to the ears of the watchers.

"Somethin' wrong, boys," said Hank, chewing his cheroot. "I hope they ain't got Jim Holloway in a corner where he can't help hisself. 'Pears like Miss Haines has given 'em the slip somehow."

"Guess I'd better creep up to the church and have a look," said Donlon excitedly.

"An' have 'em plunk you like a rabbit! Not much, Jimmy. When we move, we go in a body with our artillery bristlin' like a hedge o' bayonets. Come along, boys, you kin hide in that clump o' bushes near the door thar, while I take a peek at what's goin' on inside. When I whistle, come a-runnin'."

"Righto!"

The quintette crept towards the bushes and hid behind them without fear of discovery. Hank entered the church guardedly with his automatic on the level of his hip, and he was approaching the entrance to the nave when he heard the reports of a revolver above followed by the resounding crash of rent timber, and the thud as of a sack of grain falling from a great height.

"What in thunder's that?" he exclaimed, mystified. "The old shack ain't fallin' to pieces, I hope."

He heard the cries of Father Enrique and his assistants who, attracted by the uproar, had entered the nave by another door and by the glare of a lantern which one of them carried, found the fragments of a plank as well as the crushed body of Ricardo. They looked upwards in alarm, then crossed themselves and discussed the mysterious tragedy which, they feared, would forever blacken the fair name of their beloved Cathedral.

"It is the plank the workman placed in the belfry to-day to repair the clapper of the great bell," Hank heard one of the priests say. "This man, whom I recognize as Ricardo, evidently was trying to cross upon it in pursuit of the maid and fell to his death."

"*Pax domini!*" exclaimed Father Enrique, mystified. "What does it all mean? Why all this shooting above?"

"It must be that they traced the American girl to the belfry," suggested an assistant. "*Santa Maria!* This is a horrible night! Hark! Don't you hear a cry?"

They listened shudderingly, their hands to their ears, and all caught distinctly the hoarse shout of a man in distress.

"It seems like the wail of a lost spirit!" said the padre, shuddering. "Wasn't that the bell which sounded faintly just now? *Dios!* Away with you!"

A haunting noise in the belfry caused them to scatter in abject fear. They had proceeded only three or four steps when a human body hurtling through the air, struck the stone floor with terrific force. It fell beside the body of Ricardo, and with it came the clapper. The horrified priests returned and one of them held the lantern aloft so that they might see the creature that had fallen to a horrible death at their very feet. The padre, a crucifix in his hand, stooped over the body, then turned to his companions, his thin face ashen.

"It is Valdez!" he cried. "God has punished him —his blasphemies have brought him to death as he deserved! Lift up his body."

The priests hastened to do as they had been bid. Puzzled, Hank advanced to reconnoiter.

"Valdez dead, eh?" he muttered. "I wonder did Jim kill him arter all? If so, he an' Miss Haines must be up thar somewhar." He glanced upward, seeking to pierce the gloom, and fancied he heard a distant shout.

"Help!"

Hank whistled and Father Enrique with his assistants appeared in the door opening beyond.

"Here, *padres!*" he said, approaching them. "Thar's somebody in the belfry whar them dead men came from. How do I git up thar?"

The priests, too dazed to wonder where this little apparition, holding a revolver in his hand, had sprung from, showed him the entrance to the stairs leading to the bell tower. He ran to the door and whistled softly. Donlon and the three punchers appeared immediately. He ordered one of them to fetch a lariat and rejoin him in the belfry without delay. The puncher disappeared and led by Hank, Jimmy and the others ascended the stairs. When they reached the floor above, they heard Holloway's hail.

"Hello!" he shouted. "Is that you, Kid?"

"Betcher life!" yelled Hank. "Whar be yuh?"

Holloway cupped his hands and explained the precarious situation in which Marian and he were placed.

"How's Miss Haines?" asked Hank.

"Safe and anxious to get to mother earth again. Have you a rope?"

"Not yit, but Bill's due now with a lariat."

Bill ran up the stairs with a seventy-five foot rawhide and following Holloway's instruction they went to the platform, twelve feet above which Holloway and Marian lay. Although the moon no longer illumined the belfry, it was still light enough to enable Hank to cast an end of the lariat to Holloway who fastened it to a rafter. After Marian had descended he followed. In their excitement none beheld the body of Lopez stretched at full length against the wall.

"And where's Valdez?" they asked in unison.

"He's deader'n a mackerel!"

The party descended to the ground floor where they were met by Father Enrique, who held his hands aloft over Marian as he spoke his benediction.

"You have had a wonderful escape, my lady," he said in excellent English. "God has punished that man"—he pointed to the spot where the two bandits, now covered with blankets, lay cold in death—"as He will punish all who break His solemn commandments. Amen!"

They left the church and advanced to the clump of trees where the bronchos were hidden. Among them was Holloway's pinto. The pony neighed and Holloway fairly hugged him, the animal playfully nibbling his shoulder.

"Good old boy!" said Holloway. "We'll be off for home in a jiffy, Pinto!"

From far away came the faint clatter of galloping horses. The moon had disappeared in a bank of clouds so that it was difficult to see clearly for any considerable distance. A Spanish oath reached them distinctly as the riders halted at the church.

"It's Valdez's men returning," said Hank. "Everybody mount!"

All except Marian, who was already in the saddle, leapt onto their ponies and as they debouched into the road, a hail reached them.

"*Quien es?*" shouted the leader of the riders, some twelve in number. "Halt or we fire!"

"Move along real smart, boys," commanded Hank in an undertone. "We'll take care of the rear while you, Jim, and Miss Haines ride on ahead. Don't shoot, boys, until you have to. Giddap!"

They advanced at a gallop and instantly several shots were fired by the Mexicans. Luckily, the whistling bullets went wild. Hank turned and fired.

One of the Mexicans fell from his saddle, bringing the others to a halt. They consulted for a moment, then resumed the pursuit.

"As long as they don't get too close, it don't matter," said Hank quietly. "What's the matter, Donlon?"

"One of those Mexican bullets clipped a piece off the little finger of my left hand," responded the reporter cheerfully. "It's only a flea bite."

"You'll be able to write a good story about this trip, just the same, eh, son?"

"Oh, boy! Wait until I get the chance! I'll make the wires hot between El Paso and New York!"

"Remember, Jimmy, I'm the official censor of this here party."

"I won't forget it, Hank."

Galloping side by side for several miles in the van, Holloway and Marian were too engrossed in their own thoughts for conversation. They remembered shudderingly the events of the last few hours—happenings neither was apt to forget as long as life endured.

Marian pondered over the bitter experiences she had known during the last three days, from the hour when she fell into Valdez's hands. But for the appearance of Holloway to dissipate the gloom of her prison house, threatened as she was with a fate worse than death, she might have yielded to despair and lost her reason. But now, after all their bitter trials, they were riding homeward side by side, with the future, filled with splendid promises, beckoning to them. She was serenely happy, but terribly fatigued. She longed to close her eyes in sleep.

"How do you feel, Marian?" asked Holloway, when they halted to water their ponies at a stream. "You must be very tired after all you've suffered, poor girl."

"I am quite fagged," she sighed, though her tone was cheerful. "How far have we ridden?"

"About five miles. We shall cross the border in another hour at the latest. Then for Red Sandy valley where you may rest to your heart's content."

"And you?" she asked wistfully.

He chuckled.

"I shall exculpate myself and return home."

"Exculpate yourself?" she repeated. "I do not understand."

He told her of the outrageous charges made against him at the inquiry in Sheriff Thorne's office, which fact he had not disclosed to her in their conference at the hacienda. Marian smiled, but her expression, could he have studied her face in the gloom, would have impressed him as being soberly thoughtful.

"The abduction charge is absurd, and I shall disprove that," she said. "But how can you establish your innocence of the accusation that you shot Ralph?"

"That doesn't worry me much," he replied. "The Kid forced a confession from Lopez in Donlon's presence which proves that Pedro had a strong motive for attempting to kill your brother. And then, perhaps, Ralph may recover his memory and a word from him will exonerate me."

"I hope he may recover. And after your return from the East—"

"I shall come back—for you, if you will consent to—"

The arrival of the other riders interrupted him. Hank announced that the Mexicans had separated, one-half of their party continuing the pursuit, the others having ridden off at a tangent, evidently with the view of heading them off somewhere beyond.

"We have to make a consid'able detour arter we

reach Los Vinos pass in the hills just ahead," he said. "These greasers know of a short cut an' they're likely to try to head us off. I hain't afearin' them any, but I don't like the idea of too much shootin' with Miss Haines in the party."

"Don't mind me," interposed Marian. "I'll take my chances with the rest of you."

"All right; we'll push ahead fur the line. Once we cross that, we're safe. I reckon we don't stand much chance o' being hurt in any ambush, seein' as how it's 'most dark as a pocket."

They rode on in silence, Hank leading the pace. He knew every foot of the country they were traversing and he recalled suddenly that it was at this very place where, a year previously, he had ridden down three Mexican raiders and, after depriving them of their loot, returned home with them as his prisoners. Two miles beyond he knew there was a dangerously narrow valley which offered a well armed entrenched party excellent opportunities for doing effective work. He hoped that they might pass through the valley before the Mexicans who, he was certain, were heading therefor, would reach it.

They were cantering into the opening of the pass when a rifle cracked a hundred yards ahead of them. Then another and a third spat venomously. Shouting to all to follow him, Hank gave his pony the spur and dashed forward at breakneck speed. Behind him rode Donlon, and after him Holloway, side by side with Marian whose winded pony was laboring in great distress. The three cowpunchers brought up the rear.

When they reached the ambush, the location of which was clearly revealed by the rifle flashes, they returned the fire and the weapons of the Mexicans in front of and behind them sputtered incessantly.

Hank heard the zipp of a bullet as it passed by his head while another pierced the crown of his sombrero. He smiled grimly, wondering if all of his party had been as fortunate.

They passed through the ambush within a few seconds and drew up a half mile beyond to discuss their situation. Listening intently, they heard nothing to indicate that the pursuit was still in progress and Hank was certain that the Mexicans had abandoned the chase. All breathed freely again, for the line was less than a mile away and beyond it lay safety. Hank, after counting heads, congratulated himself that they had passed through the gun fire without a casualty.

"Anybody hit?" he inquired anxiously. "How about you, Donlon?"

"Only the clip on my little finger," answered he lightly.

"And you, Jim?"

"A bullet grazed me, but did little harm," he replied in a voice that trembled slightly.

In the excitement of their miraculous escape, none observed that he clung to the pommel of the saddle, and that his teeth were firmly set. Even as he spoke he smothered a groan.

"Bully for you, Jim! How about you, Miss Haines?"

"I am uninjured."

"Same here," chimed in the three punchers.

"We sure are a lucky bunch! Let's git on out of this durned country!"

They crossed the line presently and headed for Butler where they arrived just as the eastern sky line showed the first rosy glimmer of the approaching dawn. Soon after they had left the scene of the ambush behind them, Marian had observed that Holloway was strangely reticent, or if he spoke at all, he addressed her falteringly in monosyllables. She wondered what had occasioned this change, and turning to him as they approached the station, observed with alarm that his head drooped and that he swayed in the saddle like one overcome by sleep.

"What's the matter, Jim?" she asked, taking his hand in which the bridle rein hung limp. "Are you hurt?"

He pulled himself together with an effort, and his voice had a faraway sound when he answered her.

"It's nothing, Marian," he gasped. "I'm all right."

He swayed again and she placed her arm about him to steady him. She uttered a terrified cry for her fingers were covered with blood! Jim had been severely wounded and like the big man he was had minimized his hurt as a thing too trivial to mention! And he had ridden all these cruel miles in silence, facing death perhaps, resolved that their progress should not be halted on his account and that she be returned safely home!

"You are wounded!" she moaned. "And you did not let me know. I shall never, never forgive you, Jim!"

"It's all right, Marian," he muttered, leaning towards her. "It's only a scratch, so pay no attention to me."

They walked their ponies to the station platform where Hank and the others were awaiting them. Marian, her arm about Holloway to prevent him falling, signaled to Hank for assistance.

"What's up?" asked Hank anxiously.

Before Marian could reply, Holloway slid inertly

from his saddle into Hank's arms. He was unconscious when they carried him into the deserted waiting room. Marian hung over him sobbingly.

"Jim! Jim!" she moaned. "Dear God, do not take him from me!"

Hank turned away, the stub of his cheroot drooping disconsolately out of the corner of his mouth. Donlon gulped while the punchers, their eyes misting suddenly, averted their faces in sympathy.

"Dr. Clark lives a few rods down the track," whispered Hank to Donlon. "Hustle him out of his bed, son."

Donlon darted away on his errand. Marian turned back Holloway's coat and found it saturated with blood. She could not determine the location or seriousness of his wound, but she rejoiced that he breathed. She felt that while he lived, there was hope of recovery and her brave heart refused to yield to despair.

"He will live!" she said, caressing him. "I know it in my heart!"

Nearly ten minutes elapsed before Dr. Clark, a man of sixty years, gray, hollow-eyed, and yawning prodigiously, arrived. Holloway had fainted from loss of blood and the physican feared that it would be a difficult matter to revive him for an hour at least. Aided by Donlon who had gained some knowledge of surgery while serving on the hospital and police assignments when a cub reporter, the physician extracted the bullet.

"Serious though not necessarily fatal," explained Dr. Clark when he had finished dressing the wound. "He was shot in the side under the right arm, but the bullet being deflected by a rib and turning downward lodged in the abdominal wall. How he rode all those miles with that wound is a mystery. I may safely predict that with good nursing, and barring unforeseen complications he will recover within three weeks."

"He shall have the good nursing, all right," said Marian, wonderfully relieved by the statement. "Can he be removed to Red Sandy valley in his present condition?"

"I should not advise that course until he becomes stronger—say in about a week."

"We can't keep him here," grunted Hank, chewing his cheroot.

"That reminds me!" said Dr. Clark, returning his instruments to his hand-bag. "There is an old-fashioned army ambulance at Tyler's livery barn down the street. It's the very vehicle you need, but you must drive slowly so as to jar him as little as possible."

"We'll attend to that, doc," said Hank.

"Then I wish you a safe and speedy journey to the valley," said the physician. "By the way, who is this young man?"

"Jim Holloway."

"Any relation to Charles Holloway, President of the Western Continental Railroad?"

"His son."

There was nothing else to do but tell the physician how Holloway had received his wound and how, in order that there might be no delay in rushing Miss Haines out of danger across the border, he had studiously concealed the fact that he was desperately hurt.

"A chip of the old block, all right," commented the physician, glancing admiringly at Holloway. "Good morning and good luck. I'll drive up to the ranch to-morrow and look him over."

Dr. Clark left and, running to the livery barn, Donlon secured the ambulance, together with a team of horses, and drove back to the station. Holloway, who breathed much easier, was still unconscious when they lay him tenderly on a stretcher and swung it in place in the vehicle. Marian sat at one side with Donlon at the other, while Hank drove the horses. Anxious to render all the assistance in their power, the punchers trailed along in the rear, leading Pinto and the other ponies.

Three hours later, the party reached the bungalow. Holloway was put abed in the spare room opening on the rear porch, by Hank and Donlon. When he had been tenderly tucked away, Marian entered and, taking her stand by his bedside, began her devoted ministrations. Aunt 'Mandy, too profoundly astonished at the turn events had taken, to talk, prepared some gruel for her two patients—Holloway and "Massa" Haines.

"De Lawd am in dis," she muttered piously, "so 'tain't nothin' fo' dis chile to argufy about, I reckon."

Marian fanned her patient incessantly, for the heat was intense, and presently he opened his eyes and glanced inquiringly at her. She leaned over and kissed him lingeringly on the lips.

"Jim, Jim!" she said softly. "Thank God, you will live!"

He smiled wanly and when she raised his nerveless hands she realized how terribly weak he was.

"Marian," he whispered happily. "My Marian—sweetheart!"

He closed his eyes and fell asleep. Hour after hour passed, but Marian remained at her post determined to maintain her vigil until the period of danger that menaced the life of the man she loved, had run its destined course.

CHAPTER XXII

THE END OF THE TRAIL

THREE weeks passed—days fraught alternately with anxiety, hope and joy for Marian when, at last, Holloway was pronounced out of danger. He had tossed in delirium for ten days, and while the devoted girl rejoiced that in his ravings he spoke only the names of his mother and herself, she was at times in despair when Dr. Clark shook his head gravely, and whispered that the crisis had not been passed. But the dreaded peril sped at length and when Holloway, wan-faced and weak as an infant, was convalescent, she traveled the sunny road of happiness with joyous song on her lips.

Another source of worry to Marian throughout that trying period was her brother Ralph, who, although he had quite recovered from his wound, had lost all recollection of events antedating the day of his duel with Pedro. He could not remember how he was shot or who inflicted the wound, nor had he any recollection of Holloway or of anything that had transpired near the "Chimney" on that fateful day a month ago.

He did not even recognize Marian, but at times he stared at her wistfully. Frequently, when she addressed him, he would turn from her to resume his incessant whittling of mesquite branches at the door of the bunk house where he chose to live in care of Belcher and the punchers, rather than accept the hospitality of Marian, whom he regarded as a well-meaning stranger, but with whom he had little in common.

Hank Weston remained at the bungalow, bunking with the punchers, swapping stories with them and smoking his inevitable cheroots of which he carried a seemingly endless supply, in his traveling bags. When Holloway was convalescent, he had a confidential chat with Jimmy Donlon, who had moped unceasingly because he dared not send a dispatch to the *Observer* until the outcome of Holloway's illness was finally determined. He wondered what they thought of him at the office, inasmuch as they hadn't heard from him since he left New York on his mission—to locate Holloway and wire the mystifying details of the dual life he had led while under the dominance of a vice he seemed utterly unable to control.

"Guess you'd better send that dispatch to yore newspaper, Jimmy," said Hank, searching his pocket fruitlessly. "Got a match, son?"

Donlon smiled and handed the little detective the desired lucifer. "I have it all written, Hank," he said, displaying a pad of manuscript. "Want to hear some of it?"

"Sure," responded Hank, lighting his cheroot. "O'co'se yuh know as I'm the censor an' court o' final appeal?"

"What you say goes, if I bust the *Observer* and myself in the bargain."

Jimmy read aloud an unusually well written story recounting in graphic style the adventures of Jim Holloway, the celebrated Harvard football player, only son of Charles Holloway, multi-millionaire railway magnate of Riverside Drive, following his disappearance from New York three years previously. The yarn was quite up to date and Hank smiled approvingly at the lack therein of any reference to Jim's nickname of the Wolf.

Its tenor led one to the conclusion that Holloway had been discovered to be a hale, gritty, splendid chip of the old block, who, by his thrilling achievements had not only honored his family, himself and society at large, but had rendered a valuable service to the Southwest by saving the honor and life of one of the most respected young women of the Southwest (a former New York society girl, by the way) after she had been abducted by Cipriano Valdez, the most notorious bandit Mexico had ever produced.

"That's the stuff, Jimmy!" said Hank admiringly, chewing the end of his cheroot. "That'll be good news to his mother when she reads it in yore noos-paper."

"I'll amplify the Mexican incident to Holloway's credit, you may be sure. I'm off to Butler now so I can file this yarn for to-morrow's issue."

"Go to it, son."

There was a great commotion in the *Observer* office when Jimmy's dispatch arrived. It was displayed under a bold four column head on the front page and made the subject of a pithy editorial in which the *Observer* prided itself upon having located a young man of wealth and mystery whose strange disappearance had been the subject of considerable gossip. Only the merest reference was made to the boyish escapades that distinguished Holloway's college career, but stress was laid on the fact that, according to reliable reports, "Jim Holloway had proved himself to be one of the strongest and manliest characters of the great Southwest, and that he was a source of pride not only to his parents, but to his friends and fellow citizens as well."

The editorial stated further that Holloway's bravery

in trailing the notorious Mexican bandit to his lair whither he had carried a young American woman as his captive was wonderful, and that he was the means of bringing the outlaw to death in a Cathedral at Los Vinos in the most dramatic circumstances imaginable. This exploit had made him a national character of whom, doubtless, even the President and Congress would in due season take notice.

When Mr. Holloway saw the glowing headlines as he sat down at his breakfast table that morning, he ordered the butler to have Mrs. Holloway join him instantly. His eyes were fastened upon Donlon's brilliant article, although some of the facts were not unknown to him.

"What has happened, Charles?" asked Mrs. Holloway anxiously as she approached him. "Are you ill?"

He rose and embraced her. "Ill, my dear?" he repeated with the heartiest laugh she had heard in many a day. "If all news I receive makes me as ill as I am at this moment, then I shall have little to complain of hereafter!"

He waved the newspaper before her and asked her to guess what it contained. She glanced at him wonderingly.

"It can't be—about Jim?" she asked eagerly.

He nodded emphatically.

And they read both the article and editorial together, the staid butler watching them and listening with all his might, so that he would not miss a single word of the tidings that had brought such joy. When they had finished, Mrs. Holloway fell into her husband's arms with a glad cry. Thompson gulped and left the room to conceal his own agitation.

"Bless my soul!" he exclaimed. "This is the hap-

Haines heard the story of his loss of memory. . . . He gazed at Marion
thoughtfully.

piest day of my life, now that I see them happy, God bless them!''

"I want to see Jim," said Mrs. Holloway. "The poor boy must need my help! Why in the world did they not notify us days ago that he was wounded?"

"I knew it all the time, my dear."

"And you didn't tell me! Why, Charles—"

"Hank wired me the morning they reached Butler on their way from Sonora," responded the magnate contritely. "I knew he was in danger, but I did not desire that you should be needlessly tortured, so I kept the news from you. Almost every day for three weeks I have received a confidential message sent by Hank, keeping me fully informed as to Jim's condition. And here is his latest telegram announcing that all danger is passed."

"Thank God!"

"Shall we be off for Red Sandy valley to-day, my dear?" asked Holloway. "I think I need a brief vacation. Besides, I have some important business in that desert country."

"It will do both of us great good."

And so, in due course, they reached the bungalow in Red Sandy valley. When Mrs. Holloway saw Jim sitting in an easy chair on the porch, his face pale and haggard, but the old humorous twinkle in his eyes, she sank to her knees by his side and hid her face on his breast. Tears blinded him as he hugged and kissed her.

"Little mother!" he said softly.

"Jimmy, my boy!" she sobbed. "How happy I am to see you after all these years, and to hold you in my arms."

"You're wrong, mother dear," he laughed, "it's I

who am holding the sweetest and best mother a boy ever was blessed with. This is the most delightful moment of my life. If ever I give you the slightest cause to worry about me again, mother, may I be—''

"That will do, Jim," she said, her fingers on his lips. "You need say nothing more."

"And why not, *ma mère?*"

"Because you should not emphasize what is obviously true."

"We'll let it go at that, mother," laughed Jim.

It was Mr. Holloway's inning next. When he clasped his son's hand, he stooped over and kissed his forehead.

"I'm proud of you, Jim," he said huskily. "You have proved yourself a man, and a good one, worthy of the Holloway blood."

"You'd have done the same had you been in my place, dad," rejoined Jim, smiling happily. "Besides, I had an object, you know."

"An object?"

"Yes—the dearest, sweetest girl in all the world— Marian Haines. There she comes now! If you don't agree with me, dad, you're the most hardened old money fiend in the universe!"

Jim introduced his parents to Marian, who blushed at his praises of her. He took her hand and drew her to him. Mrs. Holloway kissed and thanked her warmly for her self-sacrificing services in behalf of her son.

"And Marian has every nurse in the wide world beaten to a frazzle, mother," Jim added admiringly.

"You are a most ridiculous person, Jim Holloway!" returned Marian with a severity palpably unreal.

"As long as you continue to love me, sweetheart, I'll be content to have you call me a doggone galoot, as the Kid says!"

"You mean Hank Weston?" asked Mr. Holloway, glancing at his wife.

Jim looked up in surprise. "Who's Hank Weston, dad?" he asked, nonplussed. "I never heard of him."

And so Hank, who appeared on the scene at this juncture with Donlon, was a witness to his own exposure, as it were, but in this instance when Mr. Holloway shook his hands in his frank and hearty way, Hank was too agitated even to chew his cheroot which drooped despondently as he voiced his solemn protest against being lionized.

"I was only obeyin' orders, Jim," he said apologetically, when the story was told.

"Durn you, Hank," responded Jim heartily, "if I wasn't as weak as a kitten, I'd spank you good for playing a double part with me! But you did me a good turn and, believe me, I'm your friend and debtor for life!"

They were holding a merry conference when Belcher appeared and calling Hank aside, whispered that Haines had sustained a serious fall from Pinto while chasing a steer, and was lying unconscious in the bunk house. Hank looked at the others and placed his fingers to his lips.

"Mum's the word, until we know the wust," he said quietly.

They went to the bunk house where "Bird's-eye" was fanning the injured man with his sombrero. Hank examined Haines, who was breathing easily like a man sound asleep. As far as he could observe, aside from an abrasion of the scalp near the scar of the bullet wound, there was no visible sign of any serious injury.

"Just stunned like, I reckon," he said thoughtfully. "No bones broke as I can see. Souse a little water in his face an' revive him."

Belcher brought some water in a jug and dampened Haines' temples. He opened his eyes slowly and looked about him with a bewildered air.

"Hello, Belcher!" he said, sitting up. "What's happened? Have we licked those bandits?"

"Wall, I'm plumb gafoozled!" muttered Hank, amazed. "If he hain't got his reason back, I'm a dodgasted sinner! Do you know me, Mr. Haines?"

Haines rose to his feet, and held out his hand. "I haven't that pleasure, sir," he answered.

After Hank had introduced himself, Haines expressed his pleasure at meeting him. He looked about with a puzzled expression. "I seem to have been dreaming," he resumed, vigorously rubbing his head. "I remember I had been shot and Jim Holloway was attending me. Where is he? By the way, where is Marian?"

Marian, who had sensed something unusual when she saw Belcher whisper to Hank, followed them at her leisure. She entered the bunk house and advanced wonderingly towards the group.

"What has happened?" she asked anxiously.

"That's what I want to know, Marian," replied Haines, puzzled. "I found myself lying here and the last thing I remember is that I lay wounded near the 'Chimney' talking to Holloway. Where is he? I want to thank him for saving my life after that dirty Mexican, Pedro, shot me—"

"Thank Heaven, you are yourself again, Ralph!" interrupted Marian, throwing her arms about him. "Oh, how happy I am!"

"Myself again? Explain!"

When Haines heard the story of his adventure and of his temporary loss of memory, he gazed at Marian thoughtfully.

"I thought I had slipped a cog somewhere," he

said. "I seem to have just awakened from a long sleep."

"No wonder," remarked Marian happily. "You were out of your mind for twenty-six days, Ralph."

"Great Cæsar!" he exclaimed. "What a fortunate accident!"

Marian dragged him off to meet the Holloways, who congratulated him heartily upon the miraculous restoration of his memory. He renewed his acquaintance with Jim, so inauspiciously begun, and they discussed their affairs for an hour or more. Naturally Jim told him of his love for Marian, whereupon Haines expressed his hearty approval.

"She couldn't find a better man, old chap!" he said, as they shook hands. "And, I may add incidentally, you couldn't find a finer girl in the world!"

"Amen to that, old man," sighed Jim; and he fell to napping so that he might dream of the wondrous prize he had won.

Ill news travels fast, so it was not surprising that a grossly exaggerated story of Faro Jenn's suicide should have reached the bungalow. There were vague rumors that the Wolf had been the cause and Hank determined that the reports should not reach the Holloways to embitter Mrs. Holloway's newly-founded happiness or retard Jim's recovery. But the convalescent heard Aunt 'Mandy discussing the suicide with Belcher one day and although he experienced a shock, its effects were quite harmless.

"I'm sorry it ended as it did," he said to Hank. "Jenn had many good qualities, and might have made an excellent friend in other circumstances. But to love her—it was impossible!"

"A Wolf can't mate with no wildcat, Jim," commented Hank philosophically. "It's agin nature." And so the matter was dropped.

The death of Jenn caused little commotion in Purple Canyon except among the members of the newly organized Vigilance Committee, who were actually put out of business thereby! The passing of its mistress was responsible for the closing of the Red Eye, and the dispersion of its habitués so that Purple Canyon lost its pep with the consequent loss of trade. In order to do something worth while, the Vigilance Committee, having no criminals longer to deal with, was transformed into a Board of Trade with eminently satisfying prospects.

The only cloud that threatened the happiness prevailing among all hands at the bungalow, was the unexpected appearance one morning of Sheriff Thorne, Seth Lucas, and three or four men who had served on the posse. It chanced that Hank was enjoying a cheroot on the veranda, while Jim sprawled in his easy chair. He was still weak, but growing stronger every hour. The Holloways and Marian had ridden up the valley on a sightseeing expedition, so that with the exception of the convalescent, the detective and Aunt 'Mandy who was in the kitchen humming the chorus of a plantation ditty, there was none to greet the visiting delegation.

"I reckon thar'll be trouble 'round hyar soon," muttered Hank, chewing his cheroot with unusual vigor.

"What's up, Hank?" asked Jim, curiously surveying the oncoming party.

"Nothin' that'll interest yuh, son. Jest yuh let me do the talkin' and don't butt in."

With the Sheriff in the van, the visitors approached the veranda. Lucas seemed nervous and ill at ease. The others, with the exception of the Sheriff, lagged with a hesitation that clearly indicated their disapproval of the business that had brought them to the valley.

"Hello, Hank!" said the Sheriff pleasantly. "How be you?"

Hank nodded, then relighted his cheroot.

"On'y tol'able fair, Sheriff. How be yuh?" he responded coolly.

"Bully!" returned the official, turning to Jim. "Howdy, Wolf?" he asked carelessly.

Hank rose and faced the Sheriff with that peculiar smile which invariably presaged trouble for somebody.

"Yo're mistaken in the party, Sheriff," he drawled, puffing a cloud of smoke towards Thorne who drew back chokingly. "Thar hain't no wolf in these parts. Let me introduce Jim Holloway to you. Mr. Thorne, Mr. Holloway of New York. Mr. Holloway, Sheriff Thorne of Purple Canyon. Shake hands, both o' yuh!"

Thorne shook Holloway's hand with perceptibly bad grace, but Jim smiled ingratiatingly.

"Come to have a look at the valley, Sheriff?" asked Jim curiously.

"Naw! I've come for you!"

"For me?"

"I've got a warrant for your arrest on a charge of shootin' with intent to kill, one Ralph Haines—"

"But I deny that, Sheriff," interrupted a voice. All turned and recognized Haines. "I was shot by Pedro, one of Valdez's bandits, and Jim Holloway is innocent!"

"That's the gospel truth!" interjected Hank.

"But this man is well known as the Wolf!" cried Thorne. "Thar's a warrant out fur his arrest—"

He paused to regain his breath, for Hank had all but strangled him with a well directed cloud of smoke.

"Yuh got another guess comin', Thorne," said Hank coldly. "I'm tellin' yuh that the Wolf left these parts a month ago never to return. Savvy me, old timer?"

"I reckon I do, Hank," admitted the Sheriff resignedly.

There came to them the sound of laughter and in the distance they beheld the picnic party returning. Hank was twirling his automatic with the dexterity of a veteran, and although it seemed merely accidental, the Sheriff observed with uneasiness that the muzzle was centered upon his belt line.

"I'm goin' to introduce you to Charles Holloway, president of the biggest railroad system in the world," went on Hank calmly. "I think you an' your friends thar, aim to injuce him to build a branch line from Butler to Purple Canyon, an' you've come to talk to him about it. I reckon that's true, eh, Sheriff?"

The automatic almost slipped from Hank's fingers, but when he recovered it with a twist of the wrist, the business end of the weapon was pressed against Thorne's stomach. By an accidental lurch, Hank held it firmly in position, despite Thorne's effort to wiggle away from it.

"Yuh hain't answered yet, Sheriff."

"I reckon you're right, Hank," responded Thorne, a sickly smile on his face. He glanced at his companions, who nodded their approval of the sentiment.

Hence it came to pass, according to report, that a delegation of prominent citizens, headed by Sheriff Thorne, rode to Red Sandy valley to urge upon Charles Holloway the necessity of constructing a branch line from Butler to Purple Canyon, which dream ultimately was realized and made the occasion for a grand jollification by the residents of that enterprising town. Thus is the wild Southwest gradually receding under the civilizing influences of men like Hank Weston. More than one salutary reform in that vast section has been effected by the persuasive use of a revolver and the occasional employment of hemp at stringing bees.

The proposed extension of the railroad was made the subject of a stirring story by Donlon, who left for the East the next day after assuring Jim and Hank that he was proud to be numbered among their friends. Their vacation over, the Holloways planned to return home as speedily as possible, and it was agreed that Jim and Marian were to accompany them. Finding Jim in conversation with his parents on the afternoon of their last day in the valley, Hank handed him an envelope addressed to Charles Holloway.

"I found it in yore room," he said, lighting a fresh cheroot. "Thought as yuh mought want to give it to sumbody—" He nodded towards Holloway *père*.

"By Jove!" exclaimed Jim, opening the envelope. "I had forgotten all about this. Here's something for you, dad."

Mr. Holloway read the letter written by Jim after his night of agony, with profound interest, Mrs. Holloway leaning over his shoulder:

"Dear Dad and Mother: I have found myself after many years, but not until I passed through the fiery crucible that is the lot of those who violate nature's laws. It was a woman who helped me to make the discovery that no man may sink so low as to utterly destroy hope and the will to conquer self. I have conquered, because I have found love—and love is powerful enough to master all the evil forces of which mankind has knowledge. When I have proved this beyond doubt, I shall return to you and beg your blessing. Believe me, love, sincerity and firmness of purpose are henceforth the guiding stars in the life of your once foolish, but regenerated son,

"JIM."

Mr. Holloway placed his hand upon his son's shoulder, while Jim put an arm about his mother. Thus they stood for several seconds, the picture of supreme happiness.

"We do believe in you heartily, Jim," said his father. "And we thank God that we are privileged to have faith in your sincerity and firmness."

Mrs. Holloway smiled happily and Jim was compelled to stoop so that she might kiss him.

"Jim, my boy!" she said, "you have made me the happiest mother in the world."

"I'm happy because you're happy, mother," he responded, kissing her.

All rose with the dawn to enjoy breakfast prepared by Aunt 'Mandy, who, realizing that she was to lose her mistress for a time, was inconsolable.

"Ah knowed dat big young man was bound to make trouble in dis yere place sometime," she confided to Hank. "He jest like a wolf—agrabbin' de best and sweetest missy a pore nigger like me could wish fo', an' carryin' her off to de Lawd knows whar! Ef he don't make her happy, Ah will git his scalp shua' some day!"

"But yuh got to scalp me fust," rejoined Hank, lighting his third cheroot of the morning. "He needs his now that he's goin' fur to git married, an' I don't need what ha'r I got left, I reckon, seein' as how I been married a consid'able time."

While Hank, the punchers and Haines assisted the Holloways with their belongings to their automobile, which had been shipped from New York for their convenience, Jim and Marian stood on the veranda taking a final look at the place where they had found their happiness. He drew her to him.

"A penny for your thoughts, sweetheart," he said, observing her pensive air.

"I am thinking," she mused, nestling closer to him, "I am thinking of—"

"The night we met at the Red Eye?" he asked with a laugh.

"Don't, Jim! Why speak of that which both of us should be glad to forget?"

"Not speak of it, Marian!" he rejoined earnestly. "Why, that meeting was the making of me. But for it where would I be now? It was your appeal in behalf of my little mother awaiting us yonder, that led me to the Road of Regeneration to which I had been blinded for so many years. But for your tears, I would still be the same old wastrel of the desert, a mere human wreck instead of standing here by your side holding that little hand which is to lead me further along the royal highway of happiness."

She hid her beaming face on his broad shoulder.

Their lips met in a lingering kiss and presently they walked hand in hand down the path to where the automobile was awaiting them, their hearts filled with love and contentment.

THE END

PETER B. KYNE'S NOVELS

THE PRIDE OF PALOMAR

When two strong men clash and the under-dog has Irish blood in his veins—there's a tale that Kyne can tell! And "the girl" is also very much in evidence.

KINDRED OF THE DUST

Donald McKay, son of Hector McKay, millionaire lumber king, falls in love with "Nan of the Sawdust Pile," a charming girl who has been ostracized by her townsfolk.

THE VALLEY OF THE GIANTS

The fight of the Cardigans, father and son, to hold the Valley of the Giants against treachery. The reader finishes with a sense of having lived with big men and women in a big country.

CAPPY RICKS

The story of old Cappy Ricks and of Matt Peasley, the boy he tried to break because he knew the acid test was good for his soul.

WEBSTER: MAN'S MAN

In a little Jim Crow Republic in Central America, a man and a woman, hailing from the "States," met up with a revolution and for a while adventures and excitement came so thick and fast that their love affair had to wait for a lull in the game.

CAPTAIN SCRAGGS

This sea yarn recounts the adventures of three rapscallion sea-faring men—a Captain Scraggs, owner of the green vegetable freighter Maggie, Gibney the mate and McGuffney the engineer.

THE LONG CHANCE

A story fresh from the heart of the West, of San Pasqual, a sun-baked desert town, of Harley P. Hennage, the best gambler, the best and worst man of San Pasqual and of lovely Donna.

GROSSET & DUNLAP,   PUBLISHERS,   NEW YORK